THERE GOES THE GALAXY, BOOK 2

by JENN THORSON

Waterhouse Press

PITTSBURGH, PENNSYLVANIA

Published by Waterhouse Press. Pittsburgh, Pennsylvania, U.S.A.

ISBN: 978-0-9838045-3-6

Cover Art by Dave White

Printed in the United States of America

FOR ALAN
Paar too, cosmic fellow.

Other Books by Jenn Thorson

THERE GOES THE GALAXY (*TGTG*, Book One)

Science is always wrong. It never solves a problem
without creating ten more.
—GEORGE BERNARD SHAW (1856—1950)

Just because something doesn't exist,
doesn't mean it's not being employed regularly.
—CAPT. ROLLIAM TSMORLOOD

Any amusing deaths lately?
—MAURICE BOWRA (1898—1971)

ACKNOWLEDGMENTS

It has been a supernova two years since *There Goes the Galaxy* was released. I launched it into the universe with the hope it might bring a smile to one or two lifeforms out there. In response, I've discovered an amazing bunch of people whose support has meant the world. Thanks to all who have read the book, reviewed it, foisted it on friends and relatives and stopped people in the street shouting, "Here, read this, total stranger!" Thank you to the book clubs that have invited me to join them and the people who have poked me with sticks to ensure a book two. (A puncture wound is a badge of honor, donchaknow.)

Thanks to my buddy and editor Scarlett Townsend, for her keen brain and eyeballs. When not editing, she keeps them in a container on her coffeetable. It's a conversation piece.

Thank you to Dave White for yet another cosmic cover and for inspiring Bertram's dive into daring intergalactic cuisine. Thanks to Claire Pitt, because of whom a few laughs transformed into the perfect subplot. Thanks to Michael Whiteman-Jones for lending his noggin to my character Pate Maesyn's. Huge appreciation to all of my beta readers, who helped me reduce pre-publication neuroses. And, lastly, thanks to my two furry in-house editors, who feel a certain amount of cat butt is critical to the creative process. I'm not sure that I agree. But hey—we'll run with it.

1

The hull of the Interplanetary Cruise Vessel groaned a song of last days, a lot like the Titanic did, just as the music score went weepy. Its mournful cry bounced along beams and pitched through pipes, only to bump into its human audience and fall flat on deaf ears.

Well, not *quite* deaf, if you take the glass-half-full view of things. The crew was still largely conscious and their eardrums hadn't burst—two strong points for the upbeat side. But with life support down and the remaining oxygen low, even the fullest glass would be vapor soon.

It's an unpopular but well-known fact that astrophysics trumps optimism in these cases through a clever Universal grandfather clause.

Bertram Ludlow and Rozz Mercer were in no shape to quibble.

CLANG!

Bertram found himself wishing, not for the first time, that they'd never taken over the creaking, crumbling craft. They'd launched themselves from imminent danger on the planet Skorbig, only to be trapped in the more drawn-out perils of free space.

Irony loves a big entrance, Bertram thought.

True, the spacecraft's nav system had always been fluky, and the ship's interface was as intuitive as your standard in-home nuclear reactor kit. Then there was Rozz's knowledge of space travel, the finest education you could stuff into an infopill. She'd embraced this science like she'd teethed on the rings of Ragul-Sfera. Unfortunately, she'd never digested anything about the more fiddly bits of intergalactic piloting. Like maintenance. Or achieving that special lack of "boom" we all enjoy so much on landing.

When irony really rolled up its sleeves and got down to work, they found out the ship's utilities had been cancelled. And why not? The ship's real owner, Rolliam Tsmorlood, had served his death sentence on Altair-5, paying the ultimate price for his colorful criminal past. What he couldn't pay were the Uninet and vis-u bills. And since the former was their one chance to download landing instructions, and the latter, the only way to call for help, their options burnt away like the fuel supply.

So for six months now, it had been just the two of them: Rozz and Bertram, Bertram and Rozz. Initially, mutual attraction was fanned by fear, despair and (as Bertram watched an empty one float by) more than a few bottles of Carsoolian pod liquor they found in the storeroom. But with isolation came the irritation that eventually tests even the most compatible couples...

When trapped in a cramped ICV without operational propulsion capabilities, doubly so.

Yes, all too soon, daily life smothered under the weight of futility, depression and a recurring argument about which single album they would have brought along with them if they'd known they'd be stranded in space.

Their relationship lost its grip well before the shipboard gravity field did.

BONG!

So now Bertram and Rozz bobbed around the main cabin like stray balloons. They were losing bone mass, deteriorating with every tick of the Universal clock. The good news was they'd run out of oxygen, lose consciousness and their blood would boil long before their bones would shatter.

It was about damn time something worked in their favor, Bertram thought.

CLANG!

Through space-sticky eyes, Bertram struggled to catch one final glimpse of his cosmic companion in the darkness. "Goodbye ... Rozz," he said. "It was nice ... almost saving ... the Earth ... with you."

"So long. ... Bertram," he barely heard her say. "I did ... kinda really ... love you." Her voice held a tired smile, a flash of the Rozz he knew from their Earth days, when things were simple and the oxygen was plenty.

"Me ... too ..." said Bertram and meant it.

"But honestly ..." she continued, "Jumpin' Jimmy Jive's ... *Swingin' on ... Saturn's ... Ring*s? Your one ... album ... forever?"

Bertram felt his blood pressure rise, or maybe it was the first signs of boil. This should have been a poignant last moment, but Rozz just had to ruin it with her disrespect for one of the 1940s most underappreciated swing albums. "Oh yeah? ..." Bertram choked out. "Well ... no one's even heard ... of the band ... Angela's Shark."

But Rozz had passed out—a slippery way to win an argument, he thought. Yet there was no sense wasting more valuable oxygen running down a willfully obscure, pseudo-artistic glam band that probably had a shelf-life only slightly longer than Bertram and Rozz currently did.

Bertram lost consciousness as step one to prove it.

"Yo, Bael, the pan-ICV seal's a lock. We got air and tempgrav's a go. Bring 'er in!"

"Bring 'er in!" relayed a voice.

"Bringin' 'er in," affirmed a third.

Not what you'd expect from guides to any sort of Afterlife, thought Bertram.

Even to his own mind, this observation felt distant. As if most of him—the limbs and heart and talking bits—were dead and dumped down a long, narrow well, while his ears and more enterprising parts of brain were topside and taking care of business. The world thumped and clomped around him.

"A Protostar 340-K, huh, Piel?" mused a gruff female voice, presumably Bael. "I didn't know any of these deathtraps even existed anymore. Weren't they recalled, like, a bazillion years ago?"

Piel let out a snorting laugh. "I remember when *ICV and Pilot* reviewed 'em, back before you were even incubated. Called 'em 'the worst off-planet vehicle since invention of the wind-powered space probe.'"

Bael gave a humored sniff. "There go my dreams for hot market demand. Maybe we can spin it. Resell as a 'curiosity.'"

"Kid, no one has ever been that curious."

"So standard rip-n-strip?"

"And here I thought you didn't pay attention." The man's voice was proud. "Rip 'em and strip 'em!" Piel shouted. And power tools ground to life, vibrating Bertram's ears, proactive brain bits and everything else in range.

This is not Death, thought Bertram. *This is the Greater Communicating Universe at its most GCUy.*

They were hardly revved up before another voice, gravelly with age, rattled over the sound. "Hey, what's this? Hold it, hold it, hold it!" And the power tools rumbled to a stop. The floor still buzzed lightly, or perhaps that was just the feeling creeping back into Bertram's limbs. "What's wrong with you froobs? You didn't notice we got ourselves two Clingers over here?"

"Two Clingers!" yelled a voice that echoed down a hall.

"Clingers," relayed a distant voice. "Two."

"Well, what do you know?" Piel sounded amazed. "Good eye, Stak. And I thought the only life left on this ship was the Kreblat barnacles on the hull."

"Few minutes more and you'd've been right," assessed the old man. "You know who this Clinger is, don't you?"

Something nudged Bertram's shoulder, possibly the toe of a boot. "It's that Berglat Largo guy."

"Who?" asked Piel.

"Sure," the aged being continued. The voice was very close now and the lifeform's breath stank like old, wet salad. "Take away the face bristles, cut the mane back and no question, it's him."

Bertram knew space changed a person; he hadn't thought it was that much.

"Who in the GCU," began Piel, "is Berglat Largo?"

"He means Bertram Ludlow," said Bael in a dismissive tone. "And he's only the star of one of the most popular Uninet series of all time. C'mon, Piel, even you must have heard of *There Goes the Galaxy?*"

"Hey, I'm running a business. Do I have time to sit around watching the Uninet?"

"Keeping up on current events is a part of being well-rounded," sniffed the old man. "Gives you depth of character."

Someone lifted Bertram's head. He could just about feel it. And seconds later a flood of oxygen filled his lungs. The lungs, not terribly hopeful about anything lately, were surprised at this turn of events.

"The first season of *There Goes the Galaxy* just ended," explained Bael. "See, they took a guy from the planet Tryfe who didn't even realize there was other life in space, and then they tossed him into the Greater Communicating Universe to save his planet from this mysterious threat."

Yes, Bertram knew all about that. Even his still-foggy mind was able to conjure enough flashbacks of his quest to fill a standard-sized novel.

"It was a stellar finale," Bael went on. "You should have seen it. I hear they're using a different Tryfling with an entirely new challenge this coming season."

"So you know what this means, don't you?" mused Stak. "This means this isn't just any Protostar 340-K. This is Captain What's-His-Name's—"

"Rolliam Tsmorlood," input Bael.

"—Rolliam Tsmorlood's Protostar 340-K. This isn't just one of the absolute worst ships ever made in the Greater Communicating Universe. This is a pivotal entertainment prop once owned by a historic Underworld figure who's likely at the bottom of a tarpit by now."

"Or digested by some carnivorous Altairan daisy," Bael suggested. "I hear they're fierce."

"So you're saying on auction we could rack up some pretty hefty yoonies with this?" Surprise and hope filled Piel's words.

"It's why it pays to give a little attention to the universe around you," rasped the elder.

"I guess there's only one thing left to do, then … Bring in the dollies!"

"Bring in the dollies!" someone called down the hall.

"Dollies, bringin' 'em in!"

Here Bertram summoned just enough energy to open his eyes, and what he saw crouched before him was a snouted, pink lifeform in a bright orange jumpsuit. The being had curved tusks that projected out from a bristled face. Bristled hair rolled down the man's head and neck in a jet-black mane that perched between two alert, pointed ears. In response, the being offered him a broad, welcoming smile. "Hey, good afternoon, Mr. Ludlow! Glad to see you with us. I'm Piel Liddlebigg, Three Liddlebiggs' salvage. And we're here to save your life."

2

Justice.

The word crept into Rolliam Tsmorlood's brain like an intracranial borebeast, silent and single-minded. It slipped slyly between thoughts on Karnaxian philosophy, memories of star systems he may or may not have visited and an annoying internal monologue on mathgar kidney he couldn't seem to shake.

Justice. Clearly it meant something, but these days it was hard to recall what that might be. He recalled recalling once, but that vanished as quickly as it came.

Besides, it wasn't like he could concentrate on it—not with the ceiling shaking like this.

Ancient sands sifted down onto the cavern floor and filtered into the sun-fried tangle of Rollie's white-blond hair. The humming sound from above was too heavy to be the rampaging tread of a ravenous worgsloot, too even to be from a feisty acidic steam blast and too sustained to be two hungry daisies locked in a wrestling match over the latest unsuspecting tidbit.

It was the perfect sound, however, for—

No, but that was impossible. It couldn't be. There was simply no reason for it, no blasted reason at all, unless—

Rollie leapt up from the woven mat on the floor of his makeshift living room, scattering the bones and stones and twine that, if things went as planned, would become a handy anti-daisy, long-range, projectile-based deterrent system, and he cupped a hand to one wickedly sunburned ear.

Yes, yes, he could hear it now, and it had to be either a ship landing on the surface of Altair-5 or a very detailed hallucination of one. From the sounds of it, it was a Quasar 920-XE Deluxe Model short-range runabout with roto-rocket boosters, upper lower lomb casings and—was it? yes, quite possibly!—titanium retractable cup holders.

He dashed to the wooden elevator to greet this sight, to see what poor slaggard had been exiled to Altair-5 this time and how long the newbie would last against the local attractions. Then he remembered: supplies. He couldn't just go up there like this was some normal, livable planet, could he? He had to prepare, suit up, arm. What had he been thinking?

(*Justice.*)

"Too much," was the answer. He was thinking far too much at once, and it was getting in the fragging way again.

But, after all, that was the tricky bit with systemic hypermotocerebrostasia. Under normal circumstances, it could be well-regulated with prescribed medications. In a non-medically-approved way—which was the way Rollie much preferred—the condition was eased with a nice Carsoolian pod liquor or twelve, followed by a Feegar high-impact bourbon and a Zlorgon chaser.

He'd heard a cudgel worked well, too, but that was less easily self-applied.

Without this regular health regimen, Rollie's brain processed the world around him far too fast, and that brain had been without proper treatment for six months to date. Six months, it turned out, was exactly how long it took to work through all of the indigenous leaves, berries, roots and flowers on Altair-5 and ferment each of them into something that was not only instantly, unhelpfully poisonous, but also didn't have that nice bouquet the Unimags were always so flared about.

Most of the time, Rollie could make a rough kind of sense of all the information coming at him, filter it down to a handful of more pressing matters—

(*Justice.*)

—And relegate the rest into pushy background noise. But actual focus, well, that was so very much six months ago.

So he dashed from the elevator platform, ducked a stalactite and grabbed up his Hand-Woven Acid Deflector. Handle hooked over an arm, he moved to the console table he'd built from scraps of wood and the carapace of the thousand-toothed meng that had gotten over-aggressive on his last surface expedition. On the tabletop were dozens of gadgets and concoctions (patents not yet applied for) designed to ease life on Altair-5. There was the Spew Mobility Containment Spray, Thousand-Toothed Meng Repellant and something that looked a bit like an upholstery stapler, but he couldn't remember what that was supposed to do anymore.

He snatched up these and stuffed a number of them into a satchel he'd made from the emptied skull of a trajectadon that once filed a complaint with him over a property line dispute.

He scanned the other objects on the table and seized a dagger he'd carved from the tusk of a gliding empt, a chem-gun he'd pulled together from stuff he found lying around and the tiny shovel the Hyphiz Deltan RegForce had given him back when they'd dumped him on Altair; the lawmen had told him that digging out the tarpits could be an engaging hobby. Given the size of the shovel—and the size of the tarpits—this was clearly the kind of joke you got from people who didn't believe in taking their sense of humor out for exercise often.

It had, however, helped him unearth his current subterranean abode.

He hung a few of his most popular necessities on a utility belt that he'd made months ago from his left sleeve. He also grabbed a hat he'd formed from some large acid-resistant leaves. Altair-5 had proven to be a poor climate for the fair Hyphizite complexion. As it stood, it was unlikely his skin and hair would ever recover.

Secure in his preparations, Rollie now leapt back onto the elevator platform and seized the ropes attached to the pulley in the ceiling. With three great heaves, he reached the surface hatch and released it.

In poured the sickly light of the GCU's version of Hell.

As Rordon Moonwax set down the Quasar 920-XE Deluxe Model short-range runabout on the surface of Altair-5, his heart thundered and his nerves went electric. This planet had loomed large over his youth; it was a strategic threat, a well-woven lie and a frightful fascination that had never quite faded. Altair-5 was the bedtime story he'd begged to hear. It was the nightmare he woke from, sweating.

Now he was all grown up. And Rordon Moonwax— scientist, adventurer and spirited Uninet personality—was coming to kick fear's ass.

Yes, he'd already proven that Zarquon-12's "Feggy, the Three-horned Gobgrinder" was a fable born of powerful imagination and weak eyesight. Rordon had shown viewers across the universe that Calderia's Razor-Toothed Stangwhistle was actually a hermit with the GCU's most chronic snoring problem. Rordon had sniffed out the Pungent Purkbeast of Pow-4 and aired the truth about its sulfur spring origins.

Slipping into his acid-resistant outerwear, he flipped on his pocket vis-u and turned it to his camera-ready face. "I'm Rordon Moonwax, and you're watching *Myth and Myth-Taken*. I am just about to step onto Altair-5, the planet that spawned a million screams from progeny around the GCU. Join me today as we explore the truth of this strange world and boldly probe into the birth canal of terror." He settled the handheld vis-u into his stabilizing harness, turned on his landscape lighting vest, flipped on his infrared video, powered up the chemical emissions sensors, initiated the Magnetic Field Assessment BlippyLights™ and secured his XJ-33 handlaser for personal safety.

He took two deep breaths, clicked his safety helmet into place, made sure his protective suit was tight at the neck and lowered the ramp from his ICV, leaving the remote right by its side for easy access.

"At this moment I am standing on the surface of Altair-5," said Rordon in hushed tones, poised at the base of the ramp. "You are witnessing a landmark moment for intergalactic exploration and dramatic Uninet programming. Few sentient lifeforms have set foot on this planet and survived ... Or have they?" He raised his trademark Quizzical Eyebrow™, which had been surgically enhanced for additional ironic emphasis. The left half reached clear to his hairline when properly employed.

It was very big with viewer focus groups.

"For centuries," he continued, "GCU law enforcement agencies have used Altair-5 as a place to exile and ultimately eliminate the cosmos' worst criminals. Yet the most memorable horrors of this maligned land are not the galaxy's irredeemable sociopaths, unrepentant murderers and relentless sales associates on commission. In the tales of our youth, Altair-5 is a world where the rain cuts through flesh and bone. Where the very land groans and rages. Where the lakes bubble black and thick, and its monstrous residents have been hideously molded by cruel evolutionary hands."

He checked the heat detector. While Altair-5's baseline atmosphere ran hotter than some planets, panning the area revealed no movement, no lifeforms giving off heat. Everything looked clear to the horizon.

"And yet, I see I am alone here. A lone figure in the vast, lonely landscape of isolation. Far from help or other sentient lifeforms or beings to aid me if I needed help or aid or companionship in this deserted wasteland of desolation. A single, solitary intrepid—"

"Fraggin' Altairan rain," grumbled a nearby voice. "Color me not surprised..."

Rordon Moonwax whirled to face the sound and found his XJ-33 trembling trepidly, the in- having shaken off somewhere in transit.

Before him was a tall, lean, sun-scalded lifeform. The figure stood in the sizzling drizzle, struggling with a long, hook-handled implement. Then POP! The thing opened up into a leafy canopy that he swung up over his head. "You law?"

Rordon blinked. The guy's complexion was as red as the throat of a crimson-gulleted squink. Hair the general color and consistency of sun-bleached straw poked from under a wide-brimmed hat made of leaves. He was clad in black from shoulder to boot, with the exception of a single sleeve that had been turned into a makeshift weaponry holster. The bare arm was all sinew and scars, and it clutched a bucket made of some large, unfortunate creature's skull. Rordon shifted uncomfortably in his boots. This could be none other than Rolliam Tsmorlood, infamous Underworld Society member, supporting actor in *There Goes the Galaxy*, Altair-5 exile and, by all accounts, dead.

"Law," repeated Tsmorlood. "RegForce? Peace Guard? Constabulary? RightGuide? Klinker? StunnaGunna? Gray Gang? Cop?" He tried each of these in a number of popular GCU languages, as if Rordon might not use Translachew™ brand translational products like everyone else in the cosmos.

By now the reporter had recovered from the shock. "Er, Rordon Moonwax," he said, lowering his weapon. He considered extending his hand in greeting but decided against it. The man's bright orange eyes looked too wild, quick and calculating to make Rordon feel sure of the result. "I'm with Uninet channel Sciencey-9, host of *Myth and Myth-Taken*. And I already know who you are, Captain Tsmor—"

Tsmorlood had walked away, admiring Moonwax's ship with a thoughtful twirl of the leaf canopy. "Hm. Quasar 920-XE Deluxe?"

"Yes, it is. Um, Captain Tsmorlood, I was wondering if—"

"Roto-rocket boosters?" the man asked.

"Of course," Moonwax said, holstering his weapon. Roto-rocket boosters were a staple on these kinds of missions. Everyone knew that. "Um, since I have you here, I was thinking, our viewers would be fascinated to hear how you—"

CLICK! The leaf canopy collapsed, and Rolliam Tsmorlood ducked under the ship's ramp. A voice echoed from beneath. "Upper lower lomb casings?"

"Yes, I suppose so," Moonwax called. "I never checked. Look, I would love to intervie—"

Tsmorlood peered around the other side of the ramp. "Titanium retractable cupholders?"

"No." Moonwax steamed an exasperated sigh onto his visor. "We do have budgets."

"Pity," Tsmorlood said. And he touched the ship in a way Rordon Moonwax thought merited buying it a tank of fuel first.

"Captain Tsmorlood," he began, injecting patience back into his voice, "if you could just stop for a moment." The man did stop, and he tilted his head in a stance that seemed attentive. "I'd love to ask you some questions about your time here on Altair-5. I don't know if you've ever seen our program, but what we do is—"

He wasn't listening. At least, not to Rordon. The man frowned, his eyes distant, angular features set in concern, as if hearing out some worrisome inner directives.

Rordon tried again. "What we do is—"

"Shhp." Tsmorlood raised a cracked and peeling hand. "Spew's coming."

"Spew?"

But now Moonwax did notice a certain rushing, an almost musical sound coming from somewhere in the vicinity. He scanned the area with his tech but picked up nothing on any of the systems. It sounded like buckets of crystals showering heavily onto a tinkling, glass surface, and it seemed to be growing louder. Growing … *growing* … Now it was a relentless shriek from all directions, like some out-of-control, high-speed hovercraft you could not see. In a moment, Rordon Moonwax was off balance and tumbling through the air, as Rolliam Tsmorlood knocked him to the ground. Yellow steam blasted up from the place he'd stood seconds before, and in it was a burst of tiny armored insects. They surged toward the men with a predatory drive.

Rordon Moonwax scrambled backwards on palms and feet, but the insects closed the gap, screaming toward him, wings buzzing, pincers twitching. He screamed, too, less in solidarity and more in a good ol' primal freaking out.

Rolliam Tsmorlood pulled a gourd-like canister from his homemade utility belt, held it aloft, pressed its trigger, and Moonwax was enveloped in a cloud of fine mist. Droplets crystallized on his protective helmet and dried firmly on his jumpsuit. Crystals crackled across his vis-u and hardened onto his landscape lighting vest. Crystals blocked his infrared video and encrusted the chemical emissions sensors. Crystals refracted and reflected the Magnetic Field Assessment BlippyLights™ in a way that seemed far too festive for the occasion.

The insects showered to the ground in a crunchy sugar coating.

It took a moment for Rordon's breath to return. "What was—?"

"Dunno their name," the convict said, smashing the offenders with a grinding stomp of his boot. "RegForce didn't leave infopills on the local wildlife, did they? So I just call 'em—"

"Spew," supplied Rordon.

"Good as any." Rolliam Tsmorlood turned to face the ship. "So," he said, clapping long-fingered hands together. "About that lift."

Rordon's eyebrow did its duty at the sudden shift in discussion. "Um…"

"Didn't we talk about a lift? I could have sworn we did." At first, Rordon thought the man was being coy, but his tone held genuine surprise.

"Um, no," Rordon said.

Frowning, Tsmorlood tapped at a spot in the center of his forehead—once, twice, a third time—like he was trying to bump a loose connection into place. "Didn't we discuss how, what with all your pretty equipment covered in Spew Mobility Containment Spray and you unable to continue your filming, you'd have to return to your channel ops and you'd give me a lift off this monstrosity of an orb?" His eyes met Rordon's with a very direct, very disbelieving gaze.

Rordon found himself, possibly for the first time ever, without words. He shook his head.

"Hmp. Worrisome." Tsmorlood withdrew a second gadget from the belt at his waist.

It took a moment before Rordon realized it was a gun, one made of found objects collected into an uneasy unity of purpose. Rordon wasn't sure if the thing were functional or simply theoretical, since it was becoming increasingly clear the guy was a few degrees short of a full-orbit. But the man aimed it with assurance, as if it worked.

"In that case, here's how the discussion goes," he said. "I tell you you're going to give me a lift off this planet, and you're going to say, 'Stellar, Rollie, where to?' Then we go into the ship and take a short, merry trip to anywhere that is not, in fact, here."

But Rordon—who had boldly faced lifeforms more unnerving than this, even if they hadn't been real—pulled his XJ-33 and aimed.

"Interesting," he said over the handlaser. He wished his vis-u were still recording; it would have looked so good in post-production. "See, I was thinking it would go more like this: you *ask* me for a lift, and I say 'Ah, but you're a notorious criminal serving time on this planet, and it's not my fault you haven't been eaten away by spew, acid rain or a giant carnivorous fern. So as a law-abiding citizen of the GCU working to enlighten and protect the good people of this galaxy, I cannot in good conscience—"

"Daisy," said Tsmorlood, interrupting his speech.

It would have been such a stellar soundbyte, too. Rordon felt himself practically spit the word out: "What?!"

Rolliam Tsmorlood looked up, his keen, amber eyes wide. "Giant carnivorous *daisy*," the man hissed.

Rordon rolled his own eyes. "Look, fern, daisy, does it really matt—"

But the man pushed back his leaf hat and shot in rapid succession over Rordon's shoulder. "Giant carnivorous daisy *behind—*"

Rollie had wanted the ship, wanted it like he wanted a bath, and Carsoolian pod liquor, and a trip to the Simmiparlors on Vos Laegos, and to go outside without protective gear and—

(*Justice.*)

—A hearty meal and a day without spew. But he hadn't wanted it this way. His handmade gun barely dented the thirty-foot-tall flowering carnivore; truly, it was the wrong tool for the job.

The only up side to the whole ugly thing was that the reporter probably never even knew what hit him. Altairan daisies believe in chewing each bite one hundred times before swallowing, true. But that first bite, that one's the real slaggard.

3

"You are a cosmic person ... No one in the universe has the precise molecular configuration of your physical being ... Interstellar elements have been assembled into the wondrous organic machine that is You."

Bertram Ludlow opened his eyes to find himself embedded in a cloud. Squishy walls cradled his head, caressed his cheeks and pinned his arms neatly to his sides. A comforter—one so soft ermine would have developed self-esteem issues over the quality—was tucked up to his chin. Above, a small ring of sky drew his bleary gaze. It shifted through a palette of delicate pastels. Every now and then, a shower of stars, rainbows or shimmering bubbles cascaded across the view.

From the evidence at hand, Bertram Ludlow had been kidnapped by unicorns.

The voice went on, "You matter because you occupy space and possess mass ... No one can take your place, not even a high-quality clone ... You are a cosmic per—"

Bertram couldn't stand it anymore; he tried to sit, but it was a challenge. It was a simple case of Man Versus Mattress, one designed with containment as much as comfort in mind. He railed and flailed against the nest of nefarious fluff, but the more he moved, the more the cushions sucked him in.

It was possible he was being digested alive. But in a happy way.

"Our guest is awake," announced the voice, pausing in its admiration of All Things Bertram Ludlow. "Our guest is awake."

Something rustled, and a figure appeared in the circle of light. "Why, hello, Mr. Ludlow! How are you feeling today?" It was a sweet face, covered in gentle white feathers, with a mouth and nose Bertram could only describe as a bill. Feathery hairs formed a soft halo around her head. She wore a pale blue uniform with an emblem.

Bertram fixed on it. "Beddsyde Manor Wellness Center," he read.

"That's right, Mr. Ludlow." Though the bill was unyielding, her eyes held a smile. "I'm Wellness Worker Goslyn. I'm here to care for you on your journey toward recovery."

"Um, thanks! So how did I—?" But memories of orange jumpsuits and grinning tusked faces flashed in his mind; they felt both very long ago and like yesterday. "How long have I been here?"

"Several days," she said.

"And Rozz?" He was afraid for the answer.

"Miss Mercer is in the room next door," said Goslyn. "I'm pleased to say, she's recovering very nicely."

Bertram nodded. The simple movement buried him deeper in the cloud. "And that voice?"

In the background, someone was still detailing the various ways Bertram Ludlow metaphysically rocked.

"Oh, that's our In-room Personal Affirmation System. Designed specifically to encourage patients toward good health through positivity and self-value."

"Awesome," said Bertram, "can we turn it off?"

"Whatever you wish, Mr. Ludlow. We aim to make your stay comfortable." With a click of a switch he could not see, the voice was gone. "Your arrival, Mr. Ludlow, has been the talk of the Manor. But I assure you, we value your privacy and will do our utmost to ensure your stay is pleasant. Now," Goslyn said, "if you feel up for it, I have a nice hoverchair waiting to take you to our Invigoration Station."

"That's not mass transit, is it?" The words were out of his mouth before he even knew he'd said them. He'd taken GCU public transportation before, and he was pretty sure he didn't have the energy—or the balance—required for it.

But the lady laughed gently. "Oh, that's very funny, Mr. Ludlow. But no, there's no travel involved. The Invigoration Station is the first stop on every patient's personalized journey to happy healthfulness. Wellness Worker Millard, your assistance, please?"

Bertram was surprised to learn there had been someone else beyond the circle of sky. But a second billed face appeared and with expert heaving, Workers Goslyn and Millard extracted Bertram from the bed. Soon he was neatly harnessed into a throne-like chair.

"To VigStat, please, Bob," Goslyn announced, "Floor Three."

"My pleasure!" chirped the chair. "Floor Three, VigStat!" And Bob glided Bertram from the room.

In a sunny hallway, Bertram and Bob joined Rozz, who was, quite coincidentally, sweeping off to VigStat herself. Much had improved since Bertram last saw her. Her cheeks had a fresh pink glow that matched her hair (or, at least, the half that hadn't grown out), and her dark eyes were bright and alert.

"Bertram!" she greeted. "Hey, they said you were up! Will you get a load of this place? It's like a palace!"

"Or a Trapper Keeper," Bertram said.

Rozz's hoverchair explained, "Beddsyde Manor is Daglann-Da's premiere location for medical treatment, recovery and personal aesthetic revision. We have a tradition of unmatched wellness services dating back four hundred Universal years, when our founder Velnus Beddsyde started out with a jar of Velgarian Woundswiggers and a dream. Since then, we have been host to some of the GCU's most illustrious lifeforms."

They had arrived at a pair of golden doors, noble gates that swung wide.

"Floor Three, VigStat," requested Bob, gliding into the elevator.

"You got it!" said the elevator. "Good morning, Miss Mercer and Mr. Ludlow."

"Er, morning," said Bertram. Back in Pittsburgh, his home furnishings weren't quite so chatty. Just as well, too. He had mostly build-it-yourself stuff and didn't know any Swedish.

The doors swished shut.

"Feeling improved?" asked the elevator.

"Um, yeah. Thank you," Bertram said. And something compelled him to add, "How's your day going?"

"Ups and downs: you know. Miss Mercer, are you well today?"

Rozz said, "Well, it'd be great if you guys could do something about this head hobble." She touched the stylish Klinko Cranial Boundary Determinator, an unwelcome and thankfully inactive souvenir of her previous life as barista slave labor.

"That should be no problem for our experts," said the elevator, swinging its doors wide to emphasize the point. "Here we are! Floor Two."

Bob, however, did not move. "There seems to be some confusion," the chair said. "I asked for Floor Three, VigStat."

"Oh. Pardon me," said the elevator, burnishing a little at the doors as they closed. The elevator jarred upward.

"Nice weather we're having, isn't it?" said the elevator. There was an awkward silence. The elevator seemed used to it. It went on in a confiding tone, "Make sure you visit the grounds while you're here. Our Rejuvenation Gardens earned a five Golden Leaf rating by *GalactiGardener Monthly* ... Ah! Here we are: Floor Four." The doors whooshed apart.

"Not to nitpick," Bob began, "but do you need me to contact maintenance for you and file a request?"

"I'm sure I have no idea what you're talking about," snapped the elevator.

"Skip it." Bob glided into the hall, a hollow hydraulics sound expressing what was left unsaid. "We'll take the stairs."

"Suit yourself," said the elevator. And with a punctuating thump of its doors, the lift left.

Rozz and Bertram exchanged glances. Funny, the things you took for granted back on Earth, Bertram thought. Like never having to mediate between your small appliances.

The stairwell door opened with gusto, but at least it wasn't big on conversation. Bob paused to let a Wellness Worker carrying a tower of folded linens go ahead of them. The guy nodded thanks, and Bertram could hear some faint, upbeat alien tune move along with him.

"Hey, that's cool. Surgically-installed music system?" Bertram asked him, pointing at where the guy's ear might have been under his feathers.

"No, they're called Dumbbell Nebula," the guy shouted cheerfully. "Have a healthy day!" And he took off down the stairs.

Bertram was considering how, at over six months of popularity, Dumbbell Nebula might just be the longest-running GCU band of all time, when his attention was drawn to something even more shocking than intergalactic pop culture longevity.

Because it was at the very spot where half of the stairs to Floor Three should have been, they weren't. And in their absence pooled a field of swirling, hazy energy.

Bob stopped short. "What in the GCU is that?"

"You mean that's not the usual around here?" Bertram's eyes flew to the guy with the linens, who was heading right toward it. "Dude! Wait!"

But the guy was on a mission and humming a little tune.

"Hey, mister!" screamed Rozz, whose slim figure had always been an effective disguise for her power as The Human Megaphone. "STOOOOPPPPPP!"

That got through, all right. And it was one step from that mysterious roiling, boiling mass that the Luckiest Wellness Worker on the Planet turned and peered at them around his armful of fresh laundry. "Oh, I'm sorry. You guys want something?" he yelled conversationally. "Look, I'll have to send another Worker to assist you, okay? I'm supposed to bring this stuff to Floor Three right away. You know, *She* asked for them." He gave a conspiratorial wink, like they had any idea who "She" was, then noticed their pointing fingers and panicked faces. His downy brow furrowed. "What?"

He followed the fingers to see, but this simple movement jarred a towel from the top of the stack. It tumbled forward. He reached out to catch it and the whole stack wobbled.

Now *he* wobbled.

In what Rozz would cite later as one of the GCU's finest examples of human/furniture teamwork, Bob rushed forward as Bertram reached out for the teetering Wellness Worker. Straining against the chair's safety harness, the Earthman stretched for desperate, flailing hands.

He came away with feathers.

A crepe-soled shoe dipped into the roiling pool before them. The stairwell lit up in a blinding blip of blue.

Silence.

Bertram blinked spots away from his eyes, struggling to see beyond them. But he didn't need to see, did he? He knew.

The Unluckiest Wellness Worker on the Planet and nine pastel blue towels (bath size) were gone.

Bertram looked down and noticed a single white feather still hung on the breeze. It swirled high for a fleeting moment. Then it spiraled back down into the space that wasn't.

Another bolt of blue and it was gone, too.

Rozz's eyes looked glassy, and her hands seemed permanently affixed to the spot over her nose and mouth. She swore under her breath behind them.

"Maybe, um ... maybe he just dropped through to the other side," suggested Bertram numbly.

"Oh yeah?" Rozz's hands sunk to her lap. "The other side of what, Bertram?" Her eyes were still riveted to the field. "The other side of *what?*"

Bertram wished he hadn't said it.

By now, Bob was backing up, beeping, and hitting his integrated communications system. "Um, Maintenance? We're going to need to cordon off the staircase between floors Three and Four right away."

"What about Two and Three?" murmured Rozz.

"Yes, check between Two and Three, too," Bob relayed to Maintenance. "No, don't touch anything. There seems to be some sort of matter demolecularization phenomena camped out on the landing...No, I don't think a mop will help."

They were gliding into the fourth floor hall now and Rozz gave a backward glance at the door. "What about the guests booked on Three? Do you think they got all ..." She searched for the right word. "... blued to bits, too?"

"Fragged," said Bertram. He had never seen a full-fragging in person before, but he had a powerful feeling that's what this was.

"I am so sorry for the inconvenience," Bob told them. "We'll get this sorted out right away." Bob could have been talking about lost hotel reservations and not the total vaporization of a living, breathing lifeform. "In the meantime, I sense your heart rate is up, Mr. Ludlow; perhaps you would both like to recuperate from your adventure in the Pastime Pavilion on our ground level. I assume our ground level still exists?" This last comment was apparently addressed to Maintenance, who affirmed that it was.

It didn't take long before the Pastime Pavilion had become a key gathering place for many Beddsyde Manor guests. Bertram noted the facility's gaming stations, holobooths and mini-infopill chat areas, but the real attraction was one of four giant holovisions; it was tuned to the *Heavy Meddler* Uninet channel.

Bertram recognized the reporter's determined, chiseled face. "This is Zaph Chantseree, and I'm here in the Sargos System, on the border of the GCU's Quadrant Three. If you look out our starboard hatch window, you can see the Coalition of Planets' safety vehicles, guarding the mysterious field that appeared here just hours ago."

The camera focused in on a strikingly familiar swirling energy field, only of a much larger scale, blanketing that part of space.

"Reports from viewers all along the border indicate that this same wall of energy may be encapsulating the entire quadrant, sealing it in."

"Like a giant T'murp-ItWare™ container, Zaph?" suggested Qwerty Zaqwer from the newsroom.

"In some ways, very much like a giant T'murp-ItWare container," agreed Zaph. And the details of T'murp-ItWare, made by DiversiDine Entertainment Systems and Aeroponics, scrolled across the bottom of the screen for viewer purchasing convenience.

"It's different in one important way, however," continued Zaph. "Moments ago, a RightGuide patrol made the first attempt to penetrate this mystery field. That ship and all of its crew were instantly disintegrated on contact."

"And that would be something our viewers shouldn't expect to experience with a set of T'murp-ItWare, right, Zaph?"

"That's correct, Qwerty," said Zaph. And the words: "DOES NOT MAKE YOU DISINTEGRATE" also scrolled across the bottom ticker.

"So far, contact with anyone in the Quad Three has been unsuccessful. Scientists theorize that transmissions may be unable to penetrate the shield or that the response itself is blocked. Quad Three, as you know, is home to many of the GCU's top businesses. For one, Rumoolita is located there, home to infopill innovator Spectra Pollux. So if you're a member of Spectra's CapClub waiting for your infopill of the day, you'll probably find this news particularly hard to swallow." Chantseree flashed his whitest smile.

"I hear the GCU's mass transit is down, too. Is that right, Zaph?" asked Qwerty.

"You heard correctly," said Zaph. "With the main hub on Mig Verlig trapped behind the Quad Three field, most Farthest Reaches Cosmos Corral flights have been cancelled. So for viewers who take the Secondary Corral to work, it might be a cosmic time to call in health impaired."

Zaph and Qwerty shared a laugh.

"I'll update you as things unfold."

"Thanks, Zaph," Qwerty said and turned to the camera. "Increasing reports indicate the troubles facing Quad Three are not an isolated problem. We are being told the same type of field has been found at pinpoint locations in Quadrants One, Two and Four. Eye-witnesses say the mysterious shields are wrapped around the third planets of a number of solar systems, as well as the third floors of many prominent corporations, hotels and medical facilities."

A murmur of wry knowledge swept across the Beddsyde Manor pavilion. Bob promised to apologize to the elevator later; the hoverchair had not guessed what it was going through.

"Manufacturers of popular products like Third Rock Sun Salve™ and Triopticon's Favorite Eyedrops™," Qwerty continued, "report their production lines have bafflingly ground to a halt due to technical errors. Even trilogy installments of favorite holofilms have vanished from Uninet channels."

"Shit: third planets?" Rozz mused, her expression grave. "Where does that leave Tryfe—er, Earth?"

Bertram hated to even think about it. "Darkness, mass panic and no *Return of the King?*"

"Plus side, no *Star Wars: Episode Three*," said Rozz.

She had a point.

"Viewers report Uninet applications won't recognize the number three in any calculations," Qwerty Zaqwer went on. "This has put the bite on Pi and rendered most Uninet functionality useless. Many businesses are sending all but key personnel home until they can find the cause of this strange phenomen—"

The screen went black, and for a moment Bertram thought the strange phenomen had hit the *Heavy Meddler*, too.

Then a message appeared in the center of their holoscreen in yellow lettering.

People of the GCU:
I have your number.

Bertram's head swiveled to the three neglected holovisions in the room, which had been playing GCU kids programs, financial reports and Beddsyde Manor promos respectively. These, too, had been transformed to black backgrounds with yellow lettering.

Guests whipped out pocket Uninet devices, mini-holoapps and vis-u watches. From what Bertram could see, they all said the same thing.

Then everywhere, the words wiped away and were replaced with a second message:

**If you ever want to see Three whole again,
each participating world in the GCU
will deposit the equivalent of 500 million yoonies
in small, non-traceable currency
to Chee's Crater on Central Midblig.**

You have one Universal Week to comply, starting...

The words faded away.

Now.

The word grew, filling the screen until it was so large, it vanished.

**Fail to meet my demands
and your number's up
for good.
Then I choose
a new one.**

The black screen hung with a deadly finality, while the room exploded with discussion.

"Is this a joke?" someone cried. "It has to be a joke."

"Five hundred million yoonies, from every world," someone else said. "A Universal week won't be enough!"

And blip, blip, blip, blip! The holovisions and pocket Uninets, holoapps and vis-u watches all around the room returned to their programming as if nothing had ever happened.

In the *Heavy Meddler* newsroom, Qwerty Zaqwer sat in stunned silence. Then she realized she was on camera again, and threw on a smile. "Um, so there you have it! It appears the widespread mystery fields and Uninet errors we have witnessed today are not due to an accident or a natural anomaly. The number three has been stolen and is being held for ransom. Who is responsible for this fallacious felony against figures? How do we find this dastardly digitnapper? Stay tuned right here to the *Heavy Meddler* for the total story as it happens."

As the channel moved to commercial break for Popeelie-made BlackHole Bags™, the Beddsyde Manor guests traded concerns about their sequel royalties, intergalactic stock market resilience and third planet vacation homes.

Looking around, Bertram had a feeling he should be really impressed by the company he was keeping, if he'd actually known many GCU celebs. The name of one he did recognize—Stella Cygnus—had come up a few times. The famed dancer was apparently trapped on Beddsyde Manor's third floor, suffering from a case of something called crudfoot.

Bob said, "My systems indicate you may be growing tired, Mr. Ludlow. It's best not to overexert yourself so soon after your rescue. Would you care to return to your room and rest?"

Nearly dying in space ... Watching other people get disintegrated ... It did take a toll. "Thanks," he said, strangely moved by the suggestion. Back on Earth, Bertram never found his furniture terribly protective of him.

"My pleasure," said Bob. "And I'll see what I can find out for you about Tryfe. I have connections."

"Really?"

"Yes, I charge up next to a Uninet console."

4

"Aw, get that outta here, pal. This is an establishment for fine libations. It ain't the Shop-O-Drome."

On the planet Sarulia, in the cultural district of Gwash, the bartender was a four-armed fellow with a centralized scowl. "I don't even know what *this*," the man motioned to the technologies sprawled across the bartop, "is."

"Don't you?" Frowning, Rollie Tsmorlood turned over one of the items with concentrated deliberation, then brightened. "Cosmic! Neither do I."

He wasn't sure if he'd forgotten or if he never knew, but this consensus of opinion took off some of the pressure. "So what'll you trade me for it? Carsoolian pod liquor? Sarulian stout? I'm certain your joy of discovery will far outweigh any monetary considerations."

Okay, so he'd just rummaged around Moonwax's ship and grabbed whatever looked salable. It wasn't like the man would miss it.

But the bartender's hands slapped down hard on the counter. "We accept good, old-fashioned yoonies here, mister. Or local currency, if you got it. But we haven't done trade for drinks, and we ain't starting a tradition now. What makes you think for one moment I'd be interested in this junk?"

"There's always a 'bar' in 'barter,'" Rollie suggested. It had taken all of his focus just to come up with that, but the bartender didn't appreciate the effort.

The handlaser he drew from under the bar implied it, anyway. "Launch. You're ruining the ambiance for the paying customers. Not to mention the air quality."

Underestimation: it was like a lit match to Rollie's mood. It took all of his willpower not to reach for the chem-gun on his own belt and give the fellow just a sample of who he was dealing with. He felt his fingers actually brush the piece, before he recalled some vague sense that he'd chosen this city specifically because he didn't want any trouble.

Gwash was full of artsy-craftsy types, hardly a draw for the Underworld. And that was perfect. The longer everyone thought he was pushing up the daisies in a very real way, the better. He wanted some time to get a few drinks in his system, straighten his brain, stop twitching at every noise and come up with a decent plan for (*justice*) his new life.

But with no currency on hand and all his yoonie cards cancelled, his options weren't exactly plentiful. Sure, the pre-Altair Rollie might have just swept into the nearest establishment and made it a self-serve. But that sort of behavior tended to draw attention. It tended to get on the Uninet news. He had to approach this calmly, subtly.

He had to come up with something less natural to his disposition than shooting the guy.

"Is there a …" Rollie searched for the word. Parts of his brain were getting in the way again with rapid-fire visions of places he'd been, print he'd read and past Underworld jobs he'd done. Other parts were still thinking about ravenous flowers, the Simmiparlors, a bowl of homemade flash stew, (*justice*) and how the bartender was staring at him in a concerned and suspicious manner. He finally discovered the word standing in this crowd of thought. "Pawnshop!" he shouted. "There a pawnshop round here, then?"

"I have no idea." The bartender adjusted the laser in his grip. "Now blast. Before I do."

And there was that underestimation again. Rollie took a deep breath and counted to three slowly in his native tongue, went on to six since the temptation lingered, then channeled his energies to sounder action. He gathered his wares into the homemade bucket.

By now, the bartender had lowered his weapon and turned to the nearest customer. "I tell ya, lady: big city like this, we get all kinds in here. Some days it seems half of 'em are off their orbit."

"I know for a fact that one is," answered the woman in a bright, melodic voice. "Completely zonked. No hope at all, I'm afraid."

"Tried to barter with you, too, huh?"

"I'm just familiar with the gentleman's...body of work."

The woman's words fell into step with Rollie's thoughts of pawnshops and Altair and the effervescent buzz of a good handlaser, and they butted them all aside. He realized he did know that crisp, fluty voice. He knew that northern Hyphiz Epsilonian accent. As he popped the last item into the bucket, he turned for the visual. Yes, frag it all, there was the tilt of the head. The curve of the neck. The sweep of the sleek, midnight blue hair that just brushed her chin. And the skin that was so white, it reminded him of a Deltan winter moon. He had come to an artsy-craftsy place, and here was the lady of artsy-craftsy herself. He should have known.

Or perhaps he had. He knew so many things he wasn't telling himself lately.

He removed his leaf hat in a reflex gesture. "Meena?" It wasn't like he hadn't thought of Meena Tsoogarkken over the past six months. But then, he'd thought of so many things recently, often in groups of ten.

Meena swiveled to him on her barstool, guarded gladness on her face. "My stars, I scarcely would believe it: Rollie Tsmor—"

He shushed her over the "-lood" and scanned the room for signs of listening ears. There was no dearth of ears here: big ones, little ones, ones with points—even antennae, if you wanted to get technical. Fortunately, most of the patrons seemed fixated on their drinks, the holovision or the general regrets associated with both.

An amused little smile had crept over Meena's lips. "Trying to keep a low profile again, are we? Still on someone's Naughty List? Well, what else should I expect? I'd heard they dropped you off on Altair-5."

"True enough." He commandeered the stool next to hers.

"No one survives Altair-5."

He smiled. "How do you know I have?"

"Evidence suggests it." She looked him up, down and wrinkled her nose. "Mostly."

"A drink would help me know for sure."

At this, she rapped the counter in front of the bartender. "One Zlorgon Sub-Atomic Headbanger, two shots of Feegar High Impact Bourbon and I shall have a Sunspot Sparkler." This, Rollie remembered. It was a drink from her home planet, a bubbly concoction that elegant Hyphiz Epsilonian women enjoyed in the company of other elegant Epsilonian women to show how elegantly Epsilonian they were at elegant events. Her order placed, she took a moment to study Rollie's face. "I must say, you've looked far better and not smelled worse."

"Could be the death." He shrugged. "Time'll tell."

She nodded and tucked a lock of hair behind her ear. "I imagine you're wondering what I'm doing here," she said.

In the herd of different thoughts thundering around his brain, wondering what Meena Tsoogarkken was doing in the artiest section on Sarulia hadn't actually been one of them. Yet, he hated to disappoint. "I'll make time for it later," he promised.

"Well, it turns out," she pressed on unfazed, "that Gwash has become quite the unexpected cultural hotspot for…"

Rollie's breath caught. A too-familiar tinkling had risen from somewhere near the end of the bar and, for a moment, Rolliam Tsmorlood froze in horror. It was unmistakable, that maniacal, musical hissing that for six long months had signaled a salivating swarm of inbound suffering. Rollie rose from his seat, every muscle in his frame braced for battle.

"Rollie, what is it?"

"Spew." It came out more air than word, as he listened for the coming onslaught like so many times before.

"Spew? You've had nothing to drink yet."

But there was no time to explain. His hand flew to his makeshift holster, fingers searching frantically for that spare gourd of immobilizer. He scanned the area, poised to pull Meena to safety and—

The bartender finished pouring the crushed ice into the bin.

With the illusion broken, better sense re-emerged. Son of a Keeltsar, this was *not* Altair-5. This was the Sneezing Snoogle Pub in Gwash. He had to get a grip. He had to find focus. Rollie mopped his brow with a cocktail napkin and wondered if he'd ever get his spacelegs again. "Sorry." He dropped back into his seat. "It's confusing."

"What is?" A shadow of concern had crossed Meena's bright moon face.

"What isn't?" he replied.

Just in time, the bartender set four glasses onto the bartop between them, and Meena guided three to Rollie. He reached for the tall thin glass first, the one with a fine fog hovering over its surface. The Zlorgon Sub-Atomic Headbanger was a stellar drink, but it was also very versatile. Not only could you get a decent buzz simply by touching the moisture on the glass, a medium-sized bottle could fuel your ICV for at least an hour. He'd heard it was also excellent for removing the finish from most painted surfaces, but to his mind, that was just a blasted waste of good Zlorgi. After a long draught, he pressed the cold glass to his forehead, soaking in what he could. "There may be life yet," he sighed, shifting a curious gaze to Meena. "What brings you here?"

"Oh." She had to pause and regroup. "Well, Gwash has become quite the cultural hotspot for—Oh, blast!" She'd caught the time on the clocks over the bar. There was one marked "Local" and one "Universal Standard." She took a hurried sip of her Sparkler and gathered her bag. "I've got to get back. I'm exhibiting, you know. The gallery. It's a very important show for me. I would stay but—the show—it's so very important and—" She turned to Rollie, kneading her small white hands. "Are you going to be quite all right?"

He had finished the Zlorgon HB and was knocking back one of the Feegar bourbons. The Feegars were a species of power- and flesh-hungry bullies with, as far as Rollie was concerned, no redeeming qualities whatsoever *except* they made an inspired bourbon. He often wondered how any people who'd gladly bite your face off by way of hellos could create a beverage of such patience and perfection.

And it wasn't like he could just forget about his time in the Feegar Rebellion, either. He didn't even have to close his eyes to picture the Klimfals' fuzzy heads teetering on pikes, smell the stench of blood and decay and hear their child-like screams echo across the fields as his troop struggled to get there in time. Yes, enjoying the drink now would have been absolute hypocrisy, *if* every purchase of Feegar bourbon didn't go straight into the Klimfal Restitution Fund, per a Coalition of Planets court order.

Funny how these things worked out.

"Rollie?" came Meena's voice.

Now his mind went to the war camp iso pit, those days sealed in darkness and musty rot, relentless interrogation and torture the only time he saw light, since the Feegars believed any proper torture merited a really good look-see and—

"Rollie." The word was firm and accompanied by a vague sense of pain. Meena was pinching his arm, possibly with more energy than the situation required.

"Yes? Hi," he said, finding himself present again. He realized she had slipped a hand around his waist. He was disappointed to see her come away with the remote to Rordon Moonwax's ship.

"Rollie, I want you to drink that—" she indicated the last bourbon, "—and wait here for me. Understand? I hate to leave you like this, but I really do have to go." She hopped off the bar stool, flowing garments tumbling down around her feet. "I've got a very important potential buyer coming to the show that I can't afford to miss. But I'll be back." She pressed something into his palm. He opened his hand and found a yoonie card. "There's not much on that, but enough to order another drink or twenty. So please just stay here. You will stay here, won't you?"

Her expression was so concerned. It had been many Universal years since Meena Tsoogarkken had sent any sort of concern Rollie's direction. Well, except for that once, after the termination of their second life-merger, when she'd caught him in a rough patch lurking around one of her art shows. That was the time she'd explained the hazy line between caring and stalking. And now that he thought about it, the concern had been more toward him than for him. He nodded.

"Cosmic," she said. "I'll be back soon." And she hastened away in a swirl of fabric.

The moment she was gone, Rollie wasn't entirely certain Meena had been there at all. The only trace of their interaction was the Sunspot Sparkler sitting half-consumed on the bar. He finished it off, ridiculous thing that it was, then ordered a glass of Carsoolian pod liquor. Halfway through that, he was pretty convinced the encounter with his Epsilonian ex had been real. An Ottoframan Smorg wine later, he had a firmer bead on life. But the Jarendi Jolt Juice really brought home how poor his critical thinking had become. He examined the technologies tucked into the trajectadon skull on the bar. *I tried to barter for drinks?* Even now, the bartender was giving the skull the stink-eye. The skull returned the honors.

Rollie left it between them. He cleared his throat and turned his attention, such as it was, to the pub's holovision.

The *Heavy Meddler* news was on, and it sounded like they were saying the number three was missing.

"Number three what?" Rollie asked the bartender. "Coalition of Planets ambassadors ranked by height? Entropy Burger franchises by revenue?"

The bartender stared at him with new disbelief, which was really impressive given the disbelief he'd already shared. "No, the number three. The number three."

Rollie blinked, eyed his remaining Jolt Juice and blinked again.

"The thing before four and after two. The number three's gone. That's why our pricing's changed. It froze the whole system." The man indicated an electronic menu board on the wall. It was updated with cocktail napkins stuck where, presumably, the threes had been. The guy had handwritten fives in its place, taking a chance at profits where he could. "We're lucky our registers still run. I hear over on Gloftu there's a three percent 'Entering the Atmosphere' tax and it's gummed up the works."

"Number three's vanished as far as Gloftu?" Rollie had once looted a freighter outside of Gloftu.

The bartender folded one set of arms. "Mister, the problem's everywhere. Quad Three's blanketed by an unidentified defense shield. Anyone who tries to get in gets fragged. Same with some third planets, third floors … Not to mention Uninetworked systems. Even the new Translachew gum won't recognize three in any language. Where've you been? It's all anyone's been talking about."

"I've been … off-grid." Rollie knocked back the last of the Jolt Juice and clunked the glass to the counter. "But wait: systems, databases *and* force field interference? This can hardly be an accident."

Over a Sarulian Stout, the bartender filled him in on the part about the ransom.

If possible, it made even less sense to Rollie than before the drink. "Then who do they think done it?" he asked. "Underworld Society?"

While the level of drama was about right for an Underworld-sponsored gig, it was so self-defeating, so against Underworld Principles, that no one Rollie knew would have touched the idea with a thirty-krom mootaab poker. If the Intergalactic Underworld was about anything, it was loyal, insular self-preservation for all. Anyone Rollie could think of who had a fraction of the resources needed to pull off a job of this scale, well, they'd be facing the same problems everyone else had. Shutting down a quarter of the blasted crime operations wasn't exactly good for camaraderie. Plus, once things got back to normal, you'd have a large, victimized chunk of the GCU's most talented criminals who'd be seriously flared-off. At the very least, it wasn't bright.

At the mention of the Underworld, a horned lifeform at the end of the bar piped up. "That's what I thought at first. But this morning, the *Heavy Meddler* said the Mathematicians for the Protection of Prime Numbers took credit." The MPPN *were* single-minded about promoting the unique properties of non-dividing digits. But would they really go to these lengths just to earn Three some respect?

"That's not what I heard," said a female being with tall hair. "It's that fringe anarcho-military group, the Chaos Coalition." They were big into chaos dynamics, but this seemed unusually hands-on for their tastes. Largely, those fellahs just went about places in heavy gear, waiting around for unexpected things to probably not happen.

"No, you're both wrong," rasped an elderly Triopticon on the left. "Zaph Chantseree was just investigating the Null Set—you know, those semi-nihilists who believe nothing exists, including numbers? Their leader said the loss of Three is the first proof, if proof existed, that the illusion of the universe is systematically breaking down. But," here he raised a knowing finger, "he also said that they would have gladly stolen the number three, if they believed in that kind of stuff. That's as good as a confession to my ears!"

"Aren't they the ones that think life is really a figment of the imagination of a giant, transdimensional cephalopod named Gerry?" asked the horned man.

"That's them," the Triopticon wheezed.

Rollie sighed. In practical terms, it didn't matter whether he blamed the anarchists or Gerry's mates. His safehouse was on Ejellan, a planet in, yes, Quad Three, holding his emergency stash of fenceable goods, clothes, weapons, alternate IDs and a particular pet project he'd been looking forward to. The whole thing was highly inconvenient and blasted infuriating. For the love of Karnax, he'd just gotten off of Altair-5. He was only now properly medicated and down to a mere two or three thoughts at once. Was there no—

Justice.

The memory flooded back like bright light after days in the Feegar iso tank, and he squinted at the pure truth of it. Justice. It was all so obvious.

He leapt from the barstool and signaled the bartender. "There's an art gallery round here, yeah?"

The bartender hooked two thumbs leftward. "Next door."

Rollie nodded and started off. There was no time to waste.

"Um, mister. Your...skull?" The bartender pointed.

Rollie followed the man's digits to his makeshift bucket on the bar. "Oh. Thanks." He snatched it up, swiveled on the tarry sole of his heavy-treaded boot and stalked out the door.

Memory, he thought, *welcome fraggin' back, mate.*

The ForthEye Art Gallery was surprisingly large. Or maybe it just looked bigger for its total lack of art.

What it contained, as far as Rollie could see, was white floors, a white ceiling, white walls and forty lifeforms wandering around looking really pleased with themselves. Also a table of nibbly things. Small metal plaques dotted the walls. Stone pedestals stood like steadfast soldiers. And in between, glass cases sat, tall, polished and empty as a *GCU's Top Million* pop song.

Rollie paused, scanning the room for the petite lady with the glossy blue-black cap of hair. Nearby, a voice said, "You seem quite taken with this piece." It was a multi-limbed lifeform in rich, fluid robes. His art must have been selling well. The cost in sleeves alone had to set him back a pretty yoonie.

"Piece?" Rollie re-evaluated the nothing he'd noticed before and found his perceptions were at least scoring higher for consistency.

"Yes," pressed the being. "I saw you examine it. I'd love to hear your take."

"I beg to differ." Was that Meena over there by the snack table? No. That was a guy actually wearing a blue-black cap of hair.

Interesting.

"Oh, but everyone brings something different to a piece," the artist was saying. "I find it fascinating to hear the interpretations. So don't hold back. I'm open to all ideas." The being gestured, drawing Rollie's attention to a plaque mounted next to a platform by their feet. It read: *Portrait of a Magkrom at Rest.* "What do you think?"

"I've seen nothing like it," Rollie told him sincerely. "Meena Tsoogarkken. Is she here?"

"Meena Tsoo—" And then the solicitous tone went flat. "Oh. The Visualist. I should have known." The tone suggested being a Visualist ranked only slightly higher than the crumbs below the snack table. "The next room. Through there." Five arms in five sleeves pointed to a doorway, hard to see for all the white and the nothing.

Rollie nodded thanks and shot through the crowd.

Here were items that at least resembled something Rollie would call art. One wall featured paintings done in the ancient Robonesque style, where well-fed, long-exiled mythic figures posed, while robots flitted about them in rocket packs, pointing out the symbolic elements. In the center of the room, a statue evolved, feature by feature, into a new lifeform. And there on the left was a collection of sculptures made of layers of paper, collaged over bent wire frameworks and smeared with drips of paint. The materials were distinctly backspace. The muddy colors were instantly depressing. And that was where Meena Tsoogarkken stood, talking to a wormlike being who looked exactly the same in the back as the front, except the front was the part wearing the blazer.

The art lover was saying, "The compelling element of your work, Ms. Tsoogarkken, is its unabashed embrace of the archaic. And while that past is seized with force and gusto, it isn't romanticized. It wears its lack of hope like a comfortable set of astrotogs."

Meena beamed, her hands fluttering in that way they did when she couldn't quite express her excitement, so she jiggled it out through the fingertips. "Oh, Mr. Spacecaps, you have no idea how delighted I am to encounter someone who truly gets—"

"Where's the ship remote?" asked Rollie, stepping between Meena and the Someone Who Truly Gets. "I'm going to Diwaal-1."

A handkerchief went from the guest's pocket to his nose in half a second.

"Rollie," Meena's gaze could have flash-frozen a bucket of water. "This is Mr. Spacecaps. A very nice man who happens to appreciate my art. I believe I asked you to wait next door?"

Rollie was scouring the area for her bag, which always seemed to get tucked somewhere outside standard spacetime dynamics during these shows. "Tell me where it is. I'll fetch it myself."

"I'm terribly sorry, Mr. Spacecaps. Some of our performance artists have an inconvenient sense of timing." She shooed Rollie and led Mr. Spacecaps to a second work. "Now I think you'll like this piece," she went on. "It's called *Total Annihilation of Life, with Cuddly Snoogles*. For me, this was a seminal work as it represents the beginning of my Optimistic Period and—"

Rollie caught her gaze through what presumably was a pair of romping snoogles, pre-annihilation, though like everything else, it mostly looked like crumpled wire fencing wrapped in pasted paper and slopped in paint.

In a low voice, he said, "Give me the fragging remote, Meena."

Meena turned her back on him, drawing her client's attention to a third work. "Or perhaps this is more to your taste, Mr. Spacecaps. I call it *Death Duel: A Dance of Two Galaxies*."

Rollie squinted and tilted his head at the collection of assorted lumpy objects jimmied together. "Looks like that time we had on Caligula-19."

"Oh, for the love of Hyphiz!" She whirled on him. "Why exactly do you need to go to Diwaal?"

"Well, I've remembered, haven't I?" The very thought of it, after all this time, was pure elation.

Her gray eyes narrowed. "Remembered what?"

"See, that's the thing: I can't believe I forgot." He was unable to control his smile now. The relief just seemed to radiate. "I knew, oh, I *knew*. In the beginning, it was all I thought about. But then there was Spew. And daisies. And trajectadon turf wars. And the fragging rain. And nothing came in order anymore. They were just images, weren't they? Sense and reflex and images, coming faster and faster. And in all of this, one word stood out. One word remained to remind me to remember to not forget. But it's okay now. It's all okay. I know where the path leads. So that's why I need the remote."

Meena didn't look as happy about his good news as he'd expected. A single line creased her smooth forehead, and her voice held what, absurdly, sounded like pity. "Oh, Rollie…"

"This seems to be a bad time," said Mr. Spacecaps glancing from Meena to Rollie and back again.

"Oh no, but it's a stellar time," Meena assured him. "Really!"

"Look, Ms. Tsoogarkken," said the lifeform, "I'm headed out of town shortly anyway; several of my branches have been hit hard by the Number Three Virus, and I need to see what can be done. So why don't you and I meet after this ransom thing is over? Say, here, next Moonsday, sixteenth hour Sarulian time? But I'll vis-u to confirm." He handed her his contact chip and she, hers.

"Perfect!" She turned the chip over in her hands like a child with a bright new toy. "Twinkly! I look forward to it!"

"No more than I." The man nodded and, with a last worried glance at Rollie, oozed off.

She waited until the client was out of view. Then: "All right," she said, "let's go. I'll grab my bag."

"What? Go where?"

But she was already gliding to the back of the gallery. "Diwaal, of course." She ducked through a door. "If we leave now, we'll be back long before my meeting." The room, Rollie saw, was filled with a distinctly non-white clutter of wrapped art, coats and equipment. It might very well have been a parallel universe, but one where cleaning professionals and personal organizers didn't exist.

Rollie forced himself to focus. "There is no fraggin' 'we,' Meena. I just need the flamin' remote."

She emerged, bag slung over a shoulder. "You, Captain Tsmorlood, are in no shape to fly."

"Frag that. I'm doing much better now."

"Yes, I know," she said. "And that's the scary bit. But I also know you. Once you get an idea, there's no dissuading you, short of full-sedation. And I don't happen to own a laser with a stun setting on it."

"Neither do I, at the moment. Or I assure you, *na tseenee*, we would not even be having this conversation."

"So there's nothing else for it." She looked like she'd won something. "You can tell me all about Diwaal on the way."

They were almost to the exit.

"You realize, I could just *take* the remote," he said darkly.

"You could," she said. "And I could tell the Hyphiz Deltan RegForce that you're actually alive."

He stopped in the doorway and stared at her. "You wouldn't."

"Keep moving, Rollie," she sang, looping an arm through his and guiding him onto the street. "Time waits for no interstellar lifeform, you know. The sooner we go, the sooner we're back. One, two!"

5

"Now, I want you to keep calm, Mr. Ludlow, and try not to worry yourself unduly," began Bertram's hoverchair. Wirelessly, it lowered the volume of the in-room holovision and turned up some soothing ambient music. "After all, your job is to recover, and worry can sometimes prolong illness if—"

Bertram knew soft-pedaling when he heard it. "What are you driving at, Bob? Spill it."

"It's about Tryfe," said Bob. "I talked to the Uninet console, who got it from a feed, who heard it from a newswire it's known for years and—"

"Tryfe has the Number Three Virus, doesn't it?" Bertram said. "It's trapped in the field."

There was a pause. A reluctant whir. "It looks that way," admitted the chair.

Bertram nodded. He'd been braced for it. So far today, he'd watched nearly ten solid hours of *Heavy Meddler* programming; it was disheartening and repetitive—and that was just the commercial breaks. In the actual news, he saw lifeforms desperate to reconnect with trapped loved ones. There were whole blocks of yoonie card holders struggling to draw on suddenly invalid accounts. And kachunkettball hall of famers were wiped from history simply for the number they wore—

not for illegal betting or a few tiny murders or anything. There were experts debating every aspect of the crime, addresses that vanished from fast food delivery databases, and Non-Organic Simulants discussing the importance of practicing safe downloads for overall health.

"I sense your blood pressure has elevated," said Bob. "Would you like me to summon a Wellness Worker?"

"No," Bertram said quickly, "I'm good." Goslyn checked in every ten minutes as it was. She poked. She prodded. She buffed. She trimmed. She even drycleaned him, so now he had this awkward new insight into life from a suit's perspective. He hadn't been fussed over this much since he was ten and Aunt Sylvia took an unnatural dislike to his cowlick.

"Then perhaps now is a good time for us to go over tomorrow's schedule," suggested Bob. "First, you'll have breakfast in our dining room, with your choice of garbel of k'ned or stiltflibber with looba berries. I hear Chef does an inspired garbel; he once made it for the king of Zarquon-4."

Bertram's most lavish dining usually had the words "Filet O'" in it. So this was exciting.

"Then you have physical therapy with Worker Wadelle, lunch out on the Vigor Veranda and, for afternoon, there's a total cellular massage. You're going to love that. Guests say it relaxes you on an almost atomic level."

Bertram wasn't sure what relaxed atoms meant to the integrity of his body as a whole. But he figured these guys were the experts. "Sounds great!"

"After that, we go to the Invigoration Station—that's been temporarily set-up on Floor Five—where you can have your choice of a Marglenian Mite bath for the ultimate in exfoliation or a genetic makeover to tackle those stubborn areas where heredity failed you. Then there's dinner, followed by some self-guided holostory interplay, a warm glass of mootaab milk and then bed. Now, would you like to hear your messages?"

"I have messages?" He couldn't imagine who it would be.

"One is from the *Heavy Meddler*. They'd like to interview you about your rescue. What should I tell them?"

Bertram didn't know which was funnier, that his chair kept his calendar or that the *Heavy Meddler* wanted an interview. "Seriously?"

"I think you don't realize how popular *There Goes the Galaxy* is right now," said Bob. "You're a celebrity, Mr. Ludlow. A name. That's why you were brought to us."

"A name, huh?" It was hard to picture. Bertram Ludlow: Earth guy, grad student and connoisseur of the ramen noodle... a name. He recalled his last time on the *Heavy Meddler*—under a different name, yes—but it wasn't exactly in Bertram's comfort zone.

An uneasy thought crossed his mind. "They won't expect me to sing, will they?"

"They didn't mention it, sir," said Bob. "But they did say they'll pay one thousand yoonies for an exclusive."

An exclusive. With Bertram Ludlow, a name. For one thousand yoonies.

He'd sing for that. "You know, after a total cellular massage, I always like to sit down with a few reporters and shoot the breeze," Bertram told the chair.

"Will you be requiring firearms?" Bob asked. "I can make some comms."

Hoverchairs had no sarcasm chip. "I don't think that will be necessary. Um, any other messages?"

"Why, yes. *BiPedal Fashionista* would like to do a feature on your favorite brand of interstellar footwear."

Bertram's eyes flew to the closet, the current location of the Popeelie sandals he'd picked up back in his intergalactic fugitive days. "And would *BiPedal Fashionista* happen to want... oh... an exclusive on that?"

"Five hundred yoonies, they said. Is that adequate?"

Bertram said it probably was. An idea had come to him, and it couldn't hurt to see just how far this celebrity thing would go.

"You've also gotten a request from *Backspace Backpacker* eager to discuss what camping's like on Tryfe. And *Eye on Daglann-Da* wants to know how you're enjoying this planet. They'd like a quote for their tourism infopills."

"Tell them yes," said Bertram. "Tell all of them yes. I can meet with them as soon as possible."

Bob sounded surprised. "Very good, sir."

"But let them know I have a fee. I'll go five hundred yoonies a piece, but see what they offer first."

"I will do that." The chair made a note of it. "Oh, and there's one other message. It's from a Dootett woman. A Xylith Duonogganon? She said she was a friend of yours."

"Xylith." The effect was electric. This lady had been indispensable to Bertram on his campaign to save Tryfe. (Er, Earth.) Unfortunately, they'd lost touch in the mayhem. Now it appeared she'd found her way off Skorbig after all. It was terrific news and one less blot on Bertram's somewhat guilty conscience.

"Mr. Ludlow," began Bob, "your pulse rate has elevated rather wildly all of a sudden. Would you like me to summon—"

"No, I wouldn't," Bertram said. "What did Xylith say?"

"That she'd been worried about you, heard you had been found and wanted to see how you were."

Bertram smiled. "Did she leave a number?"

"You mean a vis-u link, sir?" asked Bob.

"Sure. A vis-u link."

"No, Mr. Ludlow. Regrettably, the message center didn't capture one. As you know, a number of our systems right now are…"

Bertram knew. But now he also knew that Xylith Duonogganon was out there, safe, sound and wanting to chat.

6

"I don't like it." Meena squinted at Rollie from the pilot's chair of her Astrocrat. "The effect is distinctly unnerving. You're only semi-present. It's like it wants me to forget about you, but then you move and the whole pattern goes zonky again."

Rollie smoothed the shirt of his new urban camouflage. "I think it's stellar. Automatically matches any surroundings. Offers the element of surprise," he said with a wink.

"It offers vertigo and nausea. Nothing more."

He stretched out in the copilot's chair and clunked his boots onto the dashboard, one by one. "Your artist's eye is hypersensitive," he said. "What does your artist's nose say?"

"It's for it. It's voted twice, once for each nostril."

"Well, that's something, then."

And it was true; without their short stop at a Sarulian military surplus, the trip to Diwaal-1 would have been entirely too long to spend in a confined space with the man. Thankfully, a shower and the new clothes had changed much for the better. She noticed his hair was still wet and sticking up like it had been hacked off by a robogardener. But Meena had given up long ago trying to improve Rollie's sense of style. This was the same man who normally wore black everyday, not for some existential statement but because "it hides blood so nice."

"So tell me about this epiphany of yours that's dragging us to Diwaal," she said, checking her coordinates once more. "I'm not going to end up in confinement, am I?"

Rollie was examining a camouflaged boot, tilting it to catch the effect. "No, you'll like this. This is about justice. Very noble."

"You mean revenge."

"I meant what I said." He shot her a solar glare. "Justice: since I never should've set foot on Altair-5. But instead, I was targeted, blackmailed, lied to, set up, abandoned and left for dead. And while I was pretty scorched over that initially, I came to realize: that's business, innit? I got no expectations for trust in business."

"It's good to take these things in stride," she agreed.

"I mean, I won't lie." He withdrew a knife and applied it to the bit of Altairan dirt still under his fingernail. "Not blanking my archive and setting every fraggin' law enforcement group in the GCU on my tail was something of an inconvenience…"

"I do so hate it when that happens," said Meena.

"…But everyone knows business lifeforms are a bunch of ignoble slaggards. Believe otherwise and you got only yourself to blame when they frag you sideways. I can accept my part of the responsibility now."

"So glad you've found such clarity." Meena double-checked the propulsion gauge.

"The Underworld Society, however," he continued, "now that's supposed to have higher standards. We've Guiding Principles, haven't we? It's crime with style, dignity, finesse… It's like art." Meena had heard parts of this speech before. It was one of his favorites. "We join because we choose to stand for something. And we don't sell out our own. That's Principle Number Two."

"What's Number One?"

He paused thoughtfully, dagger in mid-air. "No giant robot spiders."

She nodded. "Standards are so important."

"Yeah, well," he grumbled, "since Zenith Skytreg's taken over as Official Leader of the Intergalactic Underworld, he's changed all that."

"I see him on Uninet programs quite often," she said. "Commercials, too."

"Not surprised. He's so long and deep into it with business, he practically owes it progeny support." He gave a bitter laugh. "And that's not counting what happened on Skorbig. Now that, that's gone personal, that has. Oh, yes," Rollie said, "justice will be—"

"I thought Zenith Skytreg lived on Vos Laegos." It was never easy to keep up with all the Underworld figures Rollie used to talk about, but Skytreg had been popular for some time, and the *Heavy Meddler* simply adored him. They even toured his crime compound as a special feature once.

"Yes, Meena, Skytreg lives on Vos Laegos." His tone was impatient.

"Then what's on Diwaal-1?"

"Second First City's on Diwaal-1. That is where we'll find Rentar Proximetra. And she," he said, "is where justice begins."

7

It was one helluva start, Bertram Ludlow thought, as he happily hovered away. He had his first interview under his belt (or, rather, his drawstring waistband) and he didn't even have to sing.

Who would have guessed it: that all the time he was stranded in space, he'd been a Name, a Personality—a role model, even—for the GCU's most alienated aliens? And the *Heavy Meddler* viewers, they couldn't get enough.

Oh, they asked about his life as a fugitive, his dramatic rescue and his current recovery. They wanted to know how he felt about the Three Virus, his final pick for the kachunkettball playoffs and all about his love life. ("Ah, a Tryfeman never tells.")

They were fascinated by his species, his face—even the color of his hair. ("I call it Woodland Brown.") People asked his opinion, and they actually seemed interested in the answers. He couldn't recall that happening before. It was good for the soul.

Even better, if he kept very quiet and very still, he swore he could almost hear that little plastic card with the thousand yoonies on it, just sliding around in Bob's built-in drawer. There was something infinitely satisfying about securing a piece of the GCU economy for himself. And best of all, this was only the beginning.

Because, while he wouldn't—couldn't—say it aloud, a wonderful, crazy idea had crept into his mind and camped there.

What if he could earn enough money from his newfound celebrity to buy back the Earth? For the right price, surely even Eudicot T'murp might be tempted to sell. He could snap up the planet and give it back to his people. Of course, there was that little thing about them possibly all being dead or disintegrated behind the Number Three Virus shield. But hey: if not, this would be the gift that kept on giving.

Bob was whisking him off to physical therapy, wrapped in these dreams of independence and interstellar real estate, when he spied Rozz hovering the other way.

Her face lit up. "Bertram Ludlow, just the guy I wanted to see! Got a second?"

Bob pulled to the side and paused.

"Hey, you look great," Bertram told her. "It's been, what, a day? And I see your tiara's been -ectomied. You doing okay?"

The Klinko Boundary Determinator was gone and the holes where it had been hooked to her skull were completely filled in. A hand went to her head. "Oh, that, yeah. Easy procedure, apparently, when you're not trying to pry it off with a table knife. Who knew?"

"I like the hair." he said. It was short and back to a single, uniform shade of shocking pink. It seemed even brighter than before.

She shrugged. "Genetic alteration. They say I'll never have to deal with my roots again. And speaking of roots," she leaned in and lowered her voice, "did you know Tryfe's been hit by the Number Three Virus?"

Bertram patted Bob's armrest. "A little Barcalounger told me," he said.

"Yeah, well, now all these media creeps are contacting *my* chair, trying to set up interviews to exploit the whole 'she comes from Tryfe' angle. Are they driving you nuts, too?"

"Uh," Bertram fiddled with his pajama sleeve. "Oh. Well, you know... I just..."

Her large, brown eyes grew narrow, suspicious ... then cold and hard. It was like a Bizarro World Bambi finding his mom dead and going into Vendetta mode. "Wait. You're not seriously *talking* to them, are you?"

"Not serious at all. I try to keep it light and entertaining," he said with a grin. "It's daytime Uninet."

Her mouth dropped open. "You really are taking these interviews."

"Interview. I had one interview so far," he said. "Because, y'know, the rest of them are later." At the abject horror on her face, he added, "Hey, they're paying me, aren't they? If there's one thing I've learned from my alien abduction experience, it's that you don't get far in space without a few yoonies in your pocket."

"Oh my God. You are so feeding into this, Bertram. You are a part of the heinous intergalactic media machine. You suck." She was laughing, but over a generous layer of Not.

"It's the GCU, Rozz. Even if things'll be okay back home, living permanently on Tryfe is not an option. Not for me, anyway, not after what I've seen. And celebrity isn't going to last forever. I bet our Popularity Curves are in a downward arc as we speak."

"Let 'em," she said. "Let 'em drop right down off their stupid Y axes. You cannot graph integrity." There was a whir as her hoverchair started up again. "Okay, you *can*. But it'd be completely subjective, with totally arbitrary assignations and..." Her face went as pink as her hair. "Screw it. I gotta go. I have a cellular massage. Which I *need* now." She gave him a pointed look as her chair pulled away.

"Sure," called Bertram, "go ahead and judge me. You can always fall back on your LibLounge barista skills, right? Or maybe teach intergalactic piloting? As long as no one ever expects to land."

"Low blow, Bertram," she called back. "Low friggin' blow."

8

Meena had been to Diwaal twice now and each time, the streets of Second First City made her feel claustrophobic. She thought it had something to do with the architecture, a grid of long, tedious metal facades, like Cosmos Corral cars stretching on forever.

Second First City was known as an incubator for some of the GCU's biggest trends. Its boutiques, galleries, restaurants, channels and official tat manufacturers popped in and out of relevance instantly, like charms on a bracelet or drawers in a dresser. It was virtually impossible to keep up with it all. The cosmic little bogbaby grooming bar of this morning might be the too-twinkly zakari adoption center of this afternoon. And the streets were organized by themes. Right now, the Number Three Virus was front and center, with shops devoted to anti-disintegration gear, Number Three translational supplements (in liquid, powder *and* pill form) and souvenir shops selling shirts reading things like, "I Have Your Number" available in ten designer colors and an assortment of tasteful ransom fonts. Then there was—

"Psst! Wanna buy a pocket Uninet?" The salesman held up the tiny tech with a flourish. "This special edition runs nothing but Number Three Virus news, so you won't miss a thing. It's got an app that shows you how much ransom money's in Chee's Crater in real-time. It also shows you how much Universal time is left until the ransom's due. See here? Three Universal days. Now that's accuracy! It *also*, also tells ya which planets have turned in their ransom—like Ottofram and Golgi Beta—and which ones are still in-process, like...No, don't go, lady. Look, I'll do you a practically backspace price on it. Wait!"

Meena and Rollie pressed further into the city.

They hadn't gotten far before a failed theater production, examining the ransom from the perspective of a kidnapped number three, barreled out of its slot. Meena stopped just short of it becoming a hit-and-run show.

"Watch where you fraggin' drive that thing, mate," Rollie shouted, as the play bounced over the curb and jounced into the street. He gave them a Deltan gesture Meena had used once or twice herself until she found out what it actually meant.

By the time they turned back, the show had already been replaced by a cube-shaped unit selling virus-themed holowatches with the Threes stylishly removed.

"Sell it while ya can, mates," muttered Rollie, as customers flooded into the holowatch shop. "It'll all be over in three days."

"A perfect example of why I never cared for this place," said Meena. "Do you know, the front room artists from my ForthEye show started out here?"

Rollie motioned her down a side street. "Is business not good for you, then? You did seem a tad...desperate...back at the gallery."

"Well, sales have been somewhat challenging, yes," she admitted, following him past another strip of silver cubes, this one devoted to music artists. She had to raise her voice over the samples piped into the street, vying for attention. "But look at the competition!"

Rollie gave a short laugh. "Looking at it was the issue."

"Cloaking is 'in,' Rollie, for better or worse."

He scanned the block carefully. "So it was all cloaked, was it?"

"Not all. Yes, some of it uses invisibility plates to deflect the image. But some of it works a bit like your camo and mimics its background." Glancing up, she caught his expression. "You look relieved."

"Everyone staring at a room full of nothing? Not the best welcome for a teetering sense of reality." He paused, eyeing the street. "Why would anyone want a whole blasted show of art we're not supposed to see?" He started counting the cubes, beginning from the end of the block.

"We have the technology, Rollie. Art must change with the times, must it not? Personally, it's not a medium that speaks to me."

"If it spoke, I wouldn't have near tripped over it." He pointed at a cube three doors down, muttered "Eleven," and drew his pointing finger in an invisible line across the street.

She trailed him as he walked into the road. "Unseen art's scorching hot with collectors these days," she went on. "Not to mention the blackmarket. Given your profession, I would think you'd be a little more knowledgeable about these things. If you're still in the profession, that is."

"I been dead for the past six months," he reminded her. "You tend to lose track of Underworld trends."

Watching for local traffic, which mainly consisted of cube-swapping, he crouched down and brushed some dirt from a sewer cover. Meena was surprised to see writing emerge—not your standard city labeling but symbols stamped faintly, fascinatingly, into the disc.

It reminded her of writing she'd seen on ancient Hyphizite tombs, but the style was not familiar.

"What does it say?" Meena asked, drawing closer. "Translachew isn't working for me. It keeps giving me suggestions, all of them drivel."

"Well, the Underworld's a bit like your competition, Meena," Rollie said, offering her that slow, knowing smile she always found vaguely irritating. "If it does its job, you'll never see it. But make no mistake, it's there all along."

And with that, he pried up the manhole cover.

✧

"So the head of the Quad Two Underworld works out of a sewer," Meena said, climbing down the ladder rungs. "It's just endless glamor with you people, isn't it?"

Initially, she had debated joining Rollie on this leg of the journey. But since half the establishments on the street began to change to new vendor cubes, Meena chose stench and grime over being run flat by a passé music trend.

It was only when she reached the bottom of the shaft that she realized this was not a sewer at all, but a very old, very musty hovercraft park. Some crafts were still there, hatch windows crusted with time and slime and churned dust, their lines speaking of eras long past. Many were stripped of their little glories: shining trim and status symbols long-forgotten. Even more were burnt out, charred shells that told a tale of loss and rage and change.

Here, something shuffled in the corners and crackled in shadow. Meena caught a glimpse of it, many legs and green eyes glowing in the dim. Possibly a skaggett, one of those urban crustaceans that clattered around in the dark, damp corners of the GCU's cities. They could get big, but this seemed too big. Her head turned, as she swore an antenna twitched in the heavy, stirred air.

Meena realized their path had been steadily descending as the hovercraft garage eroded onto an ancient cobble street. Facades of home-units stood in dark crumbling brick.

Looking more closely, the architecture revealed the faces of the past—early holograph technology, it seemed—used to tattoo a lost world. Here, unblinking alien eyes floated over arched windows. Patterns of perfect triangles adorned eaves. Eggmen with smooth faces alternately smiled or shrieked from ledges. Bards and flute players posed for eternity.

The images flickered and buzzed, their projectors still soldiering on. Music wafted, coming from somewhere she could not say.

"The Gropkor tribe," said Rollie before Meena could ask. "Built the First City hundreds of U-years ago. Called it Groppenkrol, then."

"Ah, I remember now." Excitement stirred at the memory. Meena's hand reached out to stroke a beast of light that could not be touched. For a moment, she held the light in her hand. "The Gropkors did everything in symbols, didn't they? Their art, architecture, even their language: it was metaphor, imagery, stories, aphorisms, all tied together."

"Yep, long on the details, they were. Lots of fiddly bits, symbolizing this or that. They got so absorbed in making meaning, they didn't realize they were being invaded by the Vidiaks, who had a schedule to keep. Vidiaks slaughtered 'em. And they built Second First City on Groppenkrol."

"So all this time, this," she gestured wide, "has been running? All on its own? Or—" She drew in a short, quick breath. "That's right. Someone," she said, "is still here." In all her fascination, she'd almost forgotten why they'd come. She eyed a symbol of a sun overlapping a moon, as it wavered in holographic instability over an eave.

"Oh yes," agreed Rollie, "someone's here all right."

And as they stepped through an archway into a town square, the music grew. The throb of rhythm, the lilt of an orchestra unseen. And finally, Meena saw who was there.

At first, Meena wasn't sure the figure wasn't a holograph herself, the woman's hairless head shining in the limited light, her broad face, pointed nose and chin so much like the round expressive masks in the architecture. She sat in a gazebo bent over a series of computer terminals and staring at a screen with a satellite image on it. It looked like Diwaal-3; Meena had noticed it on the way here, one more poor little planet trapped in the viral field.

Then the figure turned and rose, quickly tucking some remote into her jacket and exchanging it for the most ornate and beautiful gun Meena had ever seen. It seemed a long moment that the weapon was fixed on them, but she followed

Rollie's lead and stood still and silent, while Rentar Proximetra squinted in the half-light.

Finally, the woman said, "A planet at the furthest point from its sun cries lost, but soon finds itself where it began."

"That's right, Rentar," said Rollie, stepping forward, "I'm back."

Proximetra smiled and holstered the gun. She reached out and clasped his hands.

"This is a friend of mine," Rollie said, "Meena Tsoogarkken."

Meena offered a standard Epsilonian greeting, and the woman nodded coolly.

"So how've ya been?" Rollie asked.

"Warm are the solar days, for those who feel its light but don't meet its gaze."

"Yeah, well, that's bureaucracy for you." Rollie directed Meena to a wrought iron chair and pulled up a second one for himself. "Which leads me to why I came. We need to talk, you and me. About Zenith Skytreg."

At the mention of Skytreg's name, a twitch of a wince crossed Proximetra's face. She replaced it with neutral interest, but not quite quickly enough.

Rollie caught it, too, and laughed. "I see I'm not the only one who isn't a fan."

"As progeny young, we built our worlds brick by brick," she said. "Brick by brick, they tumble down."

"So how's Skytreg been knocking your bricks off?"

Meena was starting to feel like she would have understood this conversation a little better over another Sunspot Sparkler.

Proximetra pushed a button on one of the consoles before her, and from the screen sprang the holographic head of Zenith Skytreg, his silvery swoop of hair particularly coiffed.

"Are you looking for an exciting new career? Are you quick with your hands, limber with a lie or accurate with any of today's popular handlasers? Do you have a ruthless sense of self-preservation and think items come in two types: Yours and Not Yours Yet? Then the Intergalactic Underworld Society wants you. Hi." He smiled. "I'm Zenith Skytreg, Official Leader of the Intergalactic Underworld four times running. Take our Underworld Uninet Membership Course for just five hundred yoonies a class and you can specialize in areas like pickpocketing ... piracy ... hacking ... protection services ... visu scams ... mob boss management ... and so much more."

Rentar Proximetra hit a button, and the image cut away, but Rollie had already stood up, face hot. "He's selling Underworld membership as a fraggin' correspondence course?!"

"Another brick tumbles," said Proximetra, her thin lips a serious line.

"Clearly, I've come just in time." He sat back down again hard, pulling in his chair with a metallic screech. "I've come because I want to bring Zenith Skytreg before the Underworld Tribunal. Since you're second in command, I thought you could help make that happen."

Proximetra fixed him with a long, hard look.

Rollie leaned forward. "Aw, come on, Rentar. You know as well as I do he's fragged at least seven of the Underworld's Guiding Principles. Good crime used to be a craft we learned at the knee of a mastermind—knees optional o' course. It's not something you just pick up by filling out a form on a Uninet site. We used to support each other. A lifeform's word mattered, and you could trust your mates to hold their tongues when the law came calling. Want to know how I ended up nabbed by the Hyphiz Deltan RegForce and dumped on Altair-5? Skytreg pointed me out to them in the fraggin' crowd."

Proximetra's ice blue eyes grew wide.

"Oh, yes. First our illustrious leader gleefully regaled me with how he'd borrowed and apparently improved on my military record from the Feegar Rebellion. Then he dropped the law on me. Fine sense of solidarity, that is! Not to mention, a direct violation of Underworld Principles Two, Four, Seven, Twelve and Nineteen. I'm willing to press the charges. I'm willing to stand up and witness."

Meena knew Rollie had hit trouble with the man back on Skorbig, but she hadn't realized it was quite this dramatic.

Proximetra tapped her chin thoughtfully. "Many planets orbit the one who shines. The pull is strong, and their faces half-dark."

"You think I won't be able to get an honest Tribunal? You think too many members are still launched about him and we won't have the votes?"

She shrugged.

"Well, that's all very nice, innit? I expected more from you, Rentar. We didn't look round the Feegar Rebellion and say, 'What a bunch of nasty slaggards. Better give this one a miss,' did we? No. We stood for what we believed in and battled it out. That's what I want to do now."

He waited. And for a long moment, Rentar Proximetra stared out over the commons of the lost city of Groppenkrol, as if trying to draw answers from its flickering ancient walls. Then she slid open a file drawer. She ruffled around in it. And she pulled out a thin polymer sheet.

She held it up to her face, and a pinpoint beam scanned her pale blue eyes. She pushed the sheet across the desk to Rollie.

Meena could just read the top of it: "Intergalactic Underworld Leader Tribunal Request: Short Form."

Proximetra had included her retinal scan as the Underworld Manager of Quad Two.

Rollie picked it up, checked it and nodded. "So, I'll need two more sig scans, then: Meep-Meep's and Flutterbitt's. Because I s'pose right now Jym Ragobar in Quad Three is ... uh ..."

"Behind the moon," she said. "Behind the clouds."

Rollie nodded again and rose. He rolled the polymer sheet up and tucked it into an inside pocket of his camo coat. "Well, ransom willing, in a few Universal days we should have Jym back again. Thanks, Rentar," he said. "It's a good thing you've done. Next time we meet, it'll be at the Trib Court, and our friend Zenith Skytreg will be guest of honor."

"The bricks are being stacked," she said. "The mortar is all we need."

✧

"I must say, that was a unique way to spend an afternoon," Meena said, as her ICV hit the skies and its aft was finally to Diwaal. "And so we look down and we say, 'Good-bye, Second First City.' And, 'Hello, Gwash!'"

Rollie looked up from the Tribunal Petition he was rereading. "We don't absolutely need to say, 'Hello, Gwash,' do we?" he asked. "I mean, not this very minute?"

Meena frowned. "Why wouldn't we want to say, 'Hello, Gwash' right this very minute? What else would we possibly want to say hell—Oh no." She gave him her firmest, most determined expression. "No."

"I think, 'Hello, Dodaeba,' has a friendly sort of sound to it, don't you?"

"Do you? Because I think it sounds decidedly unfriendly and like it won't get me back to Gwash on time. Isn't that in Quad Four?"

"Only just over the border. Technically, it's practically almost sort of on the way to Gwash."

"Ah, but can't you hear it? Dodaeba's saying, 'Meena, you're bound to be delayed here. You'll never make your appointment. Skip me and ignore the zonky Deltan man for one time in your life.'"

"You've misunderstood its accent. I believe the words were 'easily make your appointment'…"

"Using what astrophysics?"

"…Not to mention the sense of fulfillment you'll feel. See, you'll be there on Gwash, as Mr. Whatsisname tosses yoonie cards at you and hauls away that thing with the exploding snoogles, and you'll be thinking, 'This is nice. But it's just so much more cosmic knowing I also helped Rollie by going to Dodaeba.'"

"And let me guess: an Underworld manager you need to meet just happens to be Dodaebian born and bred. Would I be right?"

"Meep-Meep," he said. "Jor-Jan Chatta-Chu-Bular Meep-Meep."

"My stars, is that a name or some kind of mating call?"

"I was aiming for a name, but I could be persuaded. What did you have in mind?" He smiled.

Meena's grasp tightened on the propulsion lever. "We are not getting together again."

"Of course not," he said. "That would be disastrous."

"I mean it, Rollie." She shot him a look, her darkest. "It's never happening."

"And I agreed. I know, because I heard me."

Meena turned to enter coordinates into the system. "That's right. So just put it out of your mind."

"I will. I'm erratic and impossible to deal with."

"Exactly."

"Unstable and not at all appropriate for an Epsilonian lady such as yourself."

"Precisely."

"Those were the coordinates for Dodaeba, weren't they?"

"If you're going to keep talking, I shall be forced to push you out the airlock. You realize that?"

"Yes. Thank you."

9

"Just show it to me one more time," said Bertram. "Once more. Please?"

They were in Beddsyde Manor's Catharsis Courtyard. The creatures in the pond hummed at the precise frequency to promote relaxation in many sentient species. Yet Bertram was way too wired to chill-out to some singing space frogs.

"Very well, Mr. Ludlow," said Bob reluctantly. "Once more." From the chair's base popped a drawer brimming with cash. "Would you care to count it again, as well?"

"Nah," said Bertram, not because he didn't want to count it again, but because he hadn't really counted it the first time. He had no idea how to calculate half the currency there, but he just loved looking at it all in a pile like that.

It was the ransom note for the Number Three Virus, actually, that had given him the idea. It had reminded him how easily yoonie cards could be cancelled or traced, but that cash was always in style. The past three days, he'd earned a serious deck of yoonie cards from interviews, remote celebrity appearances and souvenir retinal scans. (He was really cleaning up on the retinal scans. It seemed half of Beddsyde Manor's visitors and staff were raging *There Goes the Galaxy* fans.) He exchanged it all for some tokens from Hyphiz Delta, cubes from Calderia and some things that looked a little like carved tongue depressors courtesy of Marcus-4. There were small plastic chips. There were papery shapes. Bertram Ludlow was diversified. He was prepared.

It was hard to believe how quickly he had gone from being a sorry sack of bones, hand-delivered to Death's doorstep, to a living, breathing and increasingly solvent Uninet star. Even the largest financial crisis the GCU had ever seen hadn't put a damper on his earnings.

"So how much you think is in there?" Bertram asked. "Enough for a nice dinner?" He knew it was more than that; he was trying to play it cool.

"Due to its variety, I am unable to estimate based on weight. But given your agreed upon tallies per interview, sir, I would suggest it's a good deal more than a dinner," said Bob.

"Okay, then a portable Uninet? A hovercraft? An ICV? Two ICVs? How about a planet? Maybe a habitable blue-and-white little bugger in an up-and-coming neighborhood?" This was the first time he'd even hinted at his plan aloud.

"I'm afraid a habitable planet is well out of your current price range," Bob responded. "They tend to range in the billions."

Bertram whistled. "That's a lot of retinal scans."

"You may, however, be able to purchase a star on its way out," suggested Bob. "A small obscure moon perhaps. Or a gently-worn meteor. Would you like me to put you in touch with a real estate agent who could more realistically set your absurdly-elevated expectations?"

"No. No real estate agents," Bertram said quickly and sighed. He'd had such dreams for his home planet, too. But disappointment washed over him now like water over that fat mythic statue that was sweating into the courtyard fountain.

"Then it's about time for your next interview," Bob said, closing the drawer.

"And what's this one again?"

"It's with the *Dogstar* teen Uninet channel. They want to present you with their 'Snargiest Backspace Lifeform in a

Uninet Series' award and discuss what single music selection you would have brought with you if you knew you'd be stranded in space."

"Ah, that's right! Controversial topics! Excellent!" He liked to think he was doing the GCU a service, giving them a break from all the news about what was broken, who was disintegrated and why the Shop-O-Drome was out of Smorgs.

"Very good, sir. Just remember, after the interview, you still have physical therapy," the chair continued, gliding Bertram into the hall. "I hear your improvements are right on target. The effects of dehydration are almost gone, your bones are nearly refortified and your muscle tone has improved. I hear we've even almost kicked that nasty case of dandruff. Yes," continued Bob, "I'd say you should be discharged in another couple of days. That must be pleasing to you."

"Er, yeah," Bertram said. "Pleasing."

He thought he could slip it by, but Bob was made of swifter stuff. "Genuine pleasure, Mr. Ludlow, usually triggers the sensors more. Are there concerns about your leave here? Is there something I can do?"

"No," Bertram said, "I just thought I'd have raised a lot more money before Tryfe gets free tomorrow. That's all."

"To buy the planet?"

Bertram shrugged. "Instead, it looks like I'll be using some of the money to hire a ship, head home and survey the damage. A lot can change in six months, and I have this rotten feeling I won't like what I find."

"Seems to me, Mr. Ludlow, you've taken on a great deal of responsibility for one lifeform."

"There are no do-overs in saving Life as We Know It, Bob."

Bob turned the corner. "What if you didn't have to worry about Tryfe?"

Bertram laughed. "It's a hard habit to break. You guys offer therapy for that?"

"I meant: what if Tryfe were safe and everything were fine?"

"You mean if I knew my parents and brother weren't dead or diseased or mutated or enslaved by our alien landlords and stuff?" He shifted in his seat. "I mean, let's be clear here. I don't need to, y'know, see or actually talk with them or anything." It was a sure way to ruin months of fond, idealized absence. "I'd just need to know they're okay."

"Yes," said Bob, "How would you occupy yourself then?"

Bertram couldn't say the thought hadn't crossed his mind once or twice. In between the stunning, running and laser fire, anyway. "Well, this is space; how many Earth people get a chance for space travel? So I'd love to visit some big natural wonders. Nebula. Quasars. Ice planets. Stuff like that."

"A stellar choice," said Bob.

"But I'd also want to see all the GCU's cheesiest alien tourist crap. I mean, I got just a glimpse of Vos Laegos, so I know what you guys are capable of. I want to see giant monuments created by kooks. I want to buy kitschy t-shirts with stupid sayings that completely embarrass the lifeforms I'm with. And eat weird stuff that'll probably make me yak just because it's not compatible with my pathetically-unevolved digestive system."

There was a pause, a whir. "The joys of taste sensors are not personally known to me, and I'm unfamiliar with this 'yakking,'" Bob began, "but I do acknowledge the spirit of what you say."

Bertram could see the cheerful sign for the visitors' area up ahead. Engineered rainbows and sunbeams marked the spot; it was subtle.

"I hope you'll get the opportunity to follow your dreams sometime," said Bob.

"Thanks." Something about talking to Bob had made Bertram feel a little better about the Armageddony fun he'd be facing soon. Yes, someday, he might actually get that intergalactic vacation he knew was out there waiting for him. It made thoughts of his impending trip to Earth, in all its dusty, disease-clotted, mutated, scavenging-on-motorcycles, shackle-bound possibilities seem slightly less daunting. "You're a credit to your manufacturer, Bob, and a great listener, too."

"Very kind of you, Mr. Ludlow," Bob said. "But it's nothing, really. In my previous upholstery, I used to be a psychiatric sofa."

10

"... Now in this footage, you can clearly see the ransom last night as it was picked up from Chee's Crater," Qwerty Zaqwer said from Meena's in-ship holovision.

On screen, the enormous pile of currency seemed to jut into the room, then grew blurry and vanished.

"Technical experts from the Coalition of Planets believe that beaming technology was used to remove the cash."

"Beaming technology?" Rollie leaned forward on the sofa and squinted in close to the projected image as it was replayed. "There is no fraggin' beaming technology in the GCU."

"Currently," continued Zaqwer, "there is no known beaming technology in the GCU, though groups like the TeleportThis! Research and Development Team, the Beam 'Em Back Alive Project and the No Atom Left Behind initiative have reported minor progress in the teleportation field.

"The Coalition of Planets is organizing an expert Teleportation Task Force to work with the task forces currently tasked in the investigation. Together, they will form a multidisciplinary, pan-jurisdictional Mega Task Force to examine this new development in the Numeroterrorism case. The number three is still missing at this time. No further communication has been heard from the digitnappers."

"Of course not," said Meena. "At five hundred million yoonies per world? They're too busy counting it all." She took a last sip of her Sargos spore tea. It was wonderful stuff; it almost made the *Heavy Meddler* feel soothing.

"In other news, a Quasar 920-XE Deluxe Model short-range runabout was found abandoned on Sarulia near Gwash today. It's registered to *Myth and Myth-Taken* presenter Rordon Moonwax. Moonwax was reported missing a Universal week ago, after leaving the Sciencey-9 station for an investigative event. Moonwax, true to his independent, close-to-the-astrotogs filming style, never revealed to colleagues where his latest episode would take him. So far, a search of Gwash has turned up no sign of the Uninet host. Authorities are examining Moonwax's ship, files and last week's Uninet tabloids for leads."

A Quasar short-range runabout near Gwash.

Meena's mind flew to a certain ship remote, still in her bag, and she turned her gaze to her ex. Rollie didn't look suspicious, *precisely*. But he cleared his throat, rose and turned off the holovision with a slight stretchy yawn. This man was not tired. This man was Hyphiz Deltan. The average Deltan slept less than three hours any given night (Rollie was more like forty-five minutes), and this one had done so already, dead to the world and on the lounge floor because cushions, he felt, were "excessive."

"Right," he said now, clapping his hands together with bright enthusiasm. "Should be coming on Dodaeba. Best see to the pre-landing procedures." And he vanished into the cockpit.

"Don't you touch anything in there," Meena called. "I will come take charge of the ship in one moment. I just need to…" She peered around the corner to make sure he was truly in the control room, and she drew her bag from the under-seat storage. "…To put away the tea things first." She dug around in the satchel, unearthing small tubes of paint, her portavis-u, a few brushes, an old decorative bit of metal she'd liked, her deck of yoonie cards, her holographic portfolio, some infopill catalogs of her work, an unopened packet of tea spores and …

ah! Here it was. She turned the remote over and ran a finger across the name on its face. It was imprinted in silver letters: Quasar.

"Hm." They would talk about this, but now was not the time. Now they had to meet the GCU's third most powerful criminal in the Intergalactic Underworld as part of a subversive game of honor, betrayal and...

I wonder how Meep-Meep's office is set for art, Meena thought. She stuffed the remote into the bag, tucked away the satchel and remembered, only at the last moment, to grab the tea things.

"This won't take long," Rollie said, as the ICV swept in over Dodaeba's browned fields. "Should be simple. Dash-and-flash. Nothing to hold us back."

The open grasslands transformed to a patchwork grid of thickly-parked ICVs. Which led to clots of disembarking lifeforms. Which led to one impossibly long line, trailing from the ICV lot to Meep-Meep's factory and wrapping around its walls.

"Nothing to hold us back, eh?" said Meena. She felt oddly vindicated, considering she was the one who'd agreed to come here. Even with a few wrinkles, vindication wore so nicely.

"What the frag's going on today? You'd think Dumbbell Nebula was playing." Rollie had unfastened his harness, leapt out of the copilot's seat and darted into the main cabin in half a second. She could see him reflected in one of the cockpit mirrors, peering out the various hatch windows. "Is that a portable food preparation unit? Are those beverage dispensing droids? I don't get it. Normally, the place is deader than the sands of Natta Ree N'tay. Today, people are camped out like it's a flamin' interstellar parade."

But parades had a way of clearing eventually, whereas Meena spent twenty Universal minutes looking for a free spot to land. It was ten more before they were walking the distance to the factory grounds.

"Er, pardon me. Hello?" Meena flagged down a small group of beings dressed in Gapoochi emblems from the tops of their stylishly-helmeted heads to their curly-toed leviboots. Each guided an empty hoverdolly. "Could you tell us what the occasion is?"

"The release of the newest knockoff Gapoochi designs, of course," answered one man who wore a striking Gapoochi jacket with the word "Spacecadet" emblazoned all over its surface. It was cut in a military style. Holographic badges and medals swung pertly on the front, and holographic epaulettes perched on the shoulders. "It's unveiling any moment."

Rollie raised an eyebrow. "You do know 'knockoff' means fake, right?" he asked. "Forged? Counterfeit? Off-the-back of an ICV?"

"Sir, I am the head of the Quad Two Gapoochi Collector's Society. I think I know where True Gapoochi comes from," the man snapped, trying to size up Rollie's decidedly non-Gapoochi camo and conveying his disdain with a flick of the eye. "We've simply had an uncomfortable lull in our collecting since Gapoochi-3 got hit by that disgusting virus."

"It's been awful," chimed in a woman in a bright Gapoochi scarf, waders and a hat shaped like a capsule. "Gapoochi doesn't export, you know. So all that supernova design has been trapped in there, completely out of reach."

"My hands were shaking by day two," admitted another in the group. "And since the virus is still in place with no end in sight, well, *something* has to fill the void. This isn't True Gapoochi, but it feels so right."

Meena turned to see if Rollie had caught all this, but discovered he'd lost interest and was already halfway across the lot.

Meanwhile, the president of the collector's club had latched on to her arm. "The Collector's Society, of course, does not recognize these knockoff pieces as True Gapoochi," the man assured her, and the group nodded. "But they really are the finest fakes in the GCU. Did you know Meep-Meep uses real Non-Organic Simulant artisans to stitch all the detailing by hand? Some of them add their own creative twists to each piece. We're thinking of including a separate section in our collector's guide for quality knockoffs."

Ahead, Rollie waited in a restless sort of way. "Meena," he called, "remember, you're the one who has to get back."

"Oh, I'm afraid he's quite right. Cosmic chatting with you," she told them, magic words that released the grip on her arm. As she hastened to catch up, the whole thing reminded her of cocktail parties, back when she and Rollie were life-merged; he was so skilled at extracting her from awkward company. It was the benefit of not caring who you offended. Also, being very armed.

Rollie grinned like he recalled it, too. "Make friends did you?"

"I am in the wrong industry," she told him. "I could be universally cherished for the artistic way I embroider blackmarket hover apparel."

"Well, I wouldn't start designing your leviboot line quite yet. Something is definitely up." They moved around the side of the building and through a factory door marked, "Administration."

Inside, the office was utilitarian and uninspired, and the vis-u buzzed like a swarm of dandle gnats.

"Meep-Meep's office. No, we're not taking advanced orders, thank you … Meep-Meep's office. Yes, we still have fake Gapoochi. But you'll have to come down … Meep-Meep's office. Please hold … Thank you. Please hold … Hold please." There were three holographic heads jutting from the device now, frozen in the queue while the receptionist's eyes—all six of them, like shiny red beads—shifted to the in-person guests. They took an extra second to focus on Rollie. "May I help you?"

Rollie propped an elbow on the desk and leaned. "Dax Q. Phlyjollee, here to see Meep-Meep." Meena couldn't believe he was still using that alias after all these years. She'd expected its goodwill would have worn thin long ago.

The receptionist flicked the holoheads out of the way to check a sub-screen in the system. She had one of those stellar vis-u/Uninet combo techs Meena wanted. They were such a time-saver; the woman barely glanced at it before saying, "I don't see an appointment here."

"Then your vision's perfect," said Rollie, "as I made none. But Meep-Meep will take my meeting. We go way back."

"Mr. Phlyjollee..." Her tone was strained. The vis-u buzzed. "Meep-Meep is leaving shortly on an urgent matter and has asked not to be disturbed. Things are a little busy for us as you can see. Now I can schedule you for—"

"Oh, I'd comm Meep-Meep, if I was you." Rollie's voice had gone cold, smooth and quiet, like the air before an oncoming storm. The receptionist sensed it brewing, too. "I leave, and it gets back that you turned me away? And trust me, it will ..." He smiled and drummed his fingers on her desk slowly: rat-a-tat...rat-a-tat. "...The heads on your screen won't be the only ones rolling."

Meena watched the receptionist's face shift from empowered control to wavering uncertainty, as the woman weighed her options. Go against her Underworld boss' orders, or turn away an important (and somewhat unsettling) crime contact?

It was but a moment before she reached for the comm button.

It was less than that, before she said, "Please go in."

Jor-Jan Chatta-Chu-Bular Meep-Meep: the lifeform behind the desk reminded Meena of clay that had been drawn into long, rounded tubes, molded together and baked to a golden brown. Its face consisted of a fleshy beaklike nose underneath two alert black eyes. There was no mouth. There were no genitals. She could say this with relative certainty because Meep-Meep was also completely nude.

It was a look.

Behind the Underworld Manager stood two very large fellows with their more conventional features worked into uniform scowls. Meena wondered if there'd been an interview process for scowl effectiveness, with these two ranking highest in both ferocity and symmetry.

"Meep-Meep," greeted Rollie, with barely a glance at the bodyguards. "Good to see ya, mate. This is Meena Tsoogarkken, friend of mine. How's life treatin' ya?"

"Unexpectedly busy. I imagine you've noticed business is booming." The voice was high and buzzy, but it didn't seem to come from the beaklike face. "With Gapoochi-3 behind the viral field, the strangest thing has happened, Rollie. People are knowingly adding my Gapoochi fakes to their collections. They just can't get enough."

"Yeah, it's a mob scene out there."

"Before this, I would ship the merchandise to Shop-o-Dromes and Underworld bazaars across the GCU. I would invite select buyers to secret sales rooms for clandestine points-of-purchase. Now customers are coming here in droves for limited editions and outlet shopping. No mystery, no pretense. I consider myself a visionary of market change, but this ... I never saw this coming."

Meena smiled and said, "Well, I do hear your blackmarket boot crafters are rather talented with a quality knockoff."

"True. But after a lifetime of using my products to undermine mainstream business and maintain a certain mystique, now we *are* the business. I find it all ... unsettling. Profitable, but unsettling."

Rollie and Meena acknowledged that they could see the philosophical conflict.

"So please—sit. What can I do for you?" Meep-Meep asked.

Meena sat. Rollie stood, surveying the manager over folded arms. "You're not at all surprised to see me, then?"

"Should I be?" Meep-Meep gestured to a boot-shaped candydish levitating a few inches over the desk.

Meena took a candy, just to be polite, but Rollie ignored it. He said, "It's fairly common knowledge I was sent to Altair-5. It's also common knowledge that is usually a one-way trip."

Meep-Meep waved a hand. "Ah, but what is 'usually' to a clever member of the Underworld? Tell me what brings you both here." Meep-Meep peered over the desk to Rollie's feet. "I can set you up with a very stylish pair of collectible leviboots."

"Er, not my thing, thanks. I'm here because of this." Rollie drew the rolled polymer sheet from his coat and dropped it into the center of Meep-Meep's desk.

The Underworld manager picked it up. "Request for Underworld Tribunal for... Zenith Skytreg?"

Rollie gave a slow nod. "That's right. And Proximetra's with me."

The eyes narrowed. "On what grounds?"

"On grounds that Skytreg's made a mockery of the Underworld's Guiding Principles and over-extended the power of the OLIU."

"And you have evidence of this?"

"His whole blasted career is evidence," said Rollie. "But if you want specifics, I can give 'em to you. Personal ones, at that. I got a list."

Meep-Meep listened intently as Rollie explained the scene leading up to his stay on Altair-5.

Meep-Meep stroked the area alongside the beak but didn't initially respond.

"You ran against the man for OLIU," Rollie continued. "Surely that means you were able to see some flaws in his leadership style."

"I see room for improvement, yes. But I would not underestimate his popularity."

Rollie gave a sniffing laugh. "Same song as Proximetra, eh? 'Skytreg's gone popular again.' Well, I say, 'Big flaming deal.' If you and Rentar hadn't split the vote, this whole thing would have been a non-issue." Rollie pushed the document toward Meep-Meep.

Meep-Meep sighed, grabbed a candy from the candydish and popped it around the back of its head. A fleeting aroma of spicy sweetness stirred in the air.

"Well?" asked Rollie.

"Understand, if I sign this document, it doesn't mean I agree that Skytreg should be deposed," began Meep-Meep.

At this, Meena noticed a vein throb at Rollie's sunburnt temple. "Doesn't mean you agree—"

"It means," continued Meep-Meep, "I agree to a Tribunal, where a fair and balanced assessment of your charges can be examined. Nothing more, nothing less."

Rollie clenched and unclenched his hands. "Sounds like someone else is walking the blasted political fault line these days, now doesn't it?"

The manager grabbed up the document and held it aloft. "I *could* take a side and not sign. In Skytreg's hands, the Underworld has become more lucrative than ever. Perhaps we really have been clinging to outdated Principles. Perhaps, I venture to say, this shift in focus is long overdue."

"Or perhaps you're talking out of the back of your neck," Rollie snapped, and then twitched slightly at his unfortunate choice of words. He went on quickly, "You said it yourself: you don't even know what to do with the fanclub you got."

"Consider this a gentle reminder that while temper may guide you, Rollie, temperance assures a longer, happier life. In fact," Meep-Meep leaned forward, "I urge you to start embracing it now or your crusade will stop, rather abruptly, here."

Rollie's jaw was set in that defiant way Meena recognized from past domestic discussions. Like the tighter he fixed it, the less likely he'd say something that would become problematic later. Which, in this case, was quite true.

He sized up Meep-Meep. He sized up the poised bodyguards.

Finally, he made a low rumbling noise. It brought words along with it for the ride, though reluctant ones. "You're right, of course," he mumbled. "Carry on."

Meep-Meep gave a slight, satisfied bow of the head. The manager held the item to those sharp black eyes, and in a moment, the scan was complete. The Quad Four leader returned the document to Rollie's outstretched hand. "Was that all you required?"

Rollie didn't answer. He rolled up the petition and returned it to its pocket. "Thanks, Meep-Meep. Guess we'd best launch; the lady has an appointment I promised we'd keep."

Meep-Meep might have smiled. "If you change your mind about the boots—" The Manger drew a token from a holder on the desk and held it out. It was good for twenty percent off one pair of handcrafted knockoff Gapoochis.

Rollie made a short noise that might have been a laugh. "Er, generous, but—"

"And here's mine," said Meena, taking the token and tucking an infopill exhibition of her work into Meep-Meep's palm. "In case you're ever in the market for a little fine art. The style is appropriate for home or office. Conversation pieces that never cease to arouse the imagination. I do custom work, as well."

Meep-Meep blinked at the capsule.

"Er," Rollie's face was redder than usual, "sorry 'bout that, Meep-Meep. I'd no idea she was armed." He pressed a hand to her back and was now ushering her quickly to the door.

"Cosmic to finally meet you!" Meena called with backwards wave. "Hope you feel better soon about your skyrocketing sales. Buzz me if you need anything!"

"'Buzz me if you need anything,'" Rollie muttered, as he connected the fuel hose to Meena's ICV and hit the seal lever. "It's the blasted Manager of the Quad Four Underworld, the being was one step from dusting me for insubordination, and there's you: 'Buzz me if you need anything.' You're lucky you didn't get yourself fragged, you are."

"I don't know what came over me," Meena said, fanning her face with a hand. They'd stopped off at a conveniently-located fueling moon on the way back to Gwash, and she entered her payment information into the system. This was the second yoonie card she'd tried, the first one having been rejected for its excess of threes. "There was just this strong feeling Meep-Meep had an eye for sculpture."

"Which reminds me, Meena…"

"Yes?"

"I, um, I want to thank you for your help with this." Rollie patted the coat pocket containing the signed petition. "And what you did for me back at the Sneezing Snoogle. I'm not sure how I'd have managed it otherwise. It's meant a lot."

"Oh." Meena hadn't seen this coming. His expression was unguarded and his bright amber gaze looked sincere. It was a bit unnerving, actually. Rollie was not what you'd call the sentimental type. His last anniversary gift to her was a thigh-holster-style handlaser, beautifully-engraved with the phrase, "Plant your feet." "Well, you're quite welcome. I—"

He nodded and mumbled something about whether she'd changed the fluid in her vo weavers recently, then disappeared to the front of the ship.

She took a seat by the pump and put her yoonie cards away, chuckling to herself how the day had been just filled with little surprises. Even the fueling station was more luxurious than most. Normally, you were lucky if it had a snack dispensing robot and a few Uni-mags chained to the pump. But this one had a waiting room filled with comfortable chairs, and the built-in holovision looked new.

Of course, it was tuned to the *Heavy Meddler*. Until the number three was recovered, she imagined that's all anyone cared about. What a relief it would be when this ransom nonsense was over, and the GCU could get back to normal. On the screen, a man with big, silvery hair was being led away in Klinko restraints. It occurred to her that he was a very familiar man and that was a very familiar Vos Laegos landmark behind him.

She stood suddenly, her card case clattering to the ground. "Rollie, come here!"

A voice rumbled from somewhere near the front of the craft. "Do you never maintain this thing? You got Kreblat barnacles crusted in your fraggin' scurb retractors."

"Look now, lecture later," she told him. "Zenith Skytreg has been arrested."

Rollie became fleet-footed. "What?!"

Meena turned up the volume.

"—Is the scene right now outside Zenith Skytreg's Private Collection Room at Underworld Society Headquarters in Vos Laegos City." On screen, a *Heavy Meddler* reporter stood before a sea of assorted currency. It rose as high as the ceiling in some spots and had surged into the hall like a spent tidal wave. "The money you see here was discovered just Universal hours ago when a Vos Laegos Historical Society guide accessed the room for one of its rare, behind-the-scenes Underworld tours. With me now are eyewitnesses to the event."

The reporter turned to someone off-screen. "Tell our audience what you saw."

The camera swung to three piles of souvenir hats, shirts and gift shop bags that happened to have some lifeforms inside.

One piped up, "We was just about finished with this special tour we was on, when our guide opened the Private Collections Room using his badge? But there was this rumbling like a mountain had shifted back there, and we thought we was having an earthquake. And the door had hardly but opened when this rush of things come at us and we was up to our necks in money! Well, I dug out and I said to Ertl here, I said, 'Ertl, why, this is just like hitting it big on the Cherchinga machines down at the Crater Club!' Only there, you get to keep what you win when you leave, and that money probably ain't stolen."

The reporter looked right into the camera. "You heard it right, folks: stolen! That is the suspicion on the lips of everyone with lips here in Vos Laegos City. Authorities believe this currency is a match for the ransom funds that were mysteriously drawn from Chee's Crater last night. Zenith Skytreg, owner of the Underworld compound, has been taken into custody for questioning on the matter, while Vos Laegos City RightGuides analyze the crime scene. Is Zenith Skytreg responsible for the single largest crime in GCU history? Have law enforcement finally nabbed the evil mastermind behind the chaos? Where is the Number Three and why hasn't it been returned? Stay tuned to the *Heavy Meddler*. We'll have the latest."

As they cut to a commercial break for TwinklyTech, Rollie sank down onto the fueling center sofa. "Unbe-fragging-lievable! Two sig-scans away from Underworld Tribunal and Zenith-blasted-Skytreg is Klinkoed for numbernapping."

Meena frowned. "But I thought you'd be delighted. Isn't this what you wanted? If it's true, Zenith Skytreg will be the most widely-loathed lifeform in GCU history. And he can't lead the Underworld from confinement, can he?"

Rollie shot her a flaming glare. "Of course not. If he's charged and found guilty. But that's the problem, innit? Skytreg's not guilty."

"Um...what?"

Rollie's knee was jouncing with energy, like preparing for lift-off itself. "Skytreg didn't take the number three. Sure, as crimes go, it's big...the biggest. But it's not fraggin' Skytreg."

"Are you sober again?" She touched his forehead to see if it was cool. He swatted her away. She said, "The money was found in the man's home. He's leader of the universe's biggest criminal society. And you said it yourself: this is the biggest crime the GCU has ever seen. How isn't it Skytreg?"

"It's not the Underworld. It's not Skytreg. And it's a feeling." The fuel pump buzzed and Rollie leapt up to unhook the hose.

"A feeling? Pardon my skepticism, Captain Tsmorlood, but not long ago, your feelings were somewhat on the ... shall we say?...rickety side. You couldn't keep track of time. You didn't even remember who you'd wanted revenge on—"

"Justice."

"Justice," sighed Meena, closing the fuel entry valve. "And might I remind you, the relative coherence you're enjoying this moment is chemically-controlled?"

"Sure. Blame the medical condition." Rollie rolled the hose and hung it up at the station. "Just because I don't have my spacelegs every single minute, doesn't mean I'm not right about this." He gave one last look around the area to make sure they hadn't left anything and said, "And what's Ludlow doing on the *Heavy Meddler*?"

Meena turned and noticed that the commercials were over and that Tryfling fellow from *There Goes the Galaxy* was being interviewed again. "Oh," she said. "A salvage crew found his ship last U-week, floating in free space. Your friend Mr. Ludlow was very lucky. They'd latched onto the ship for the scrap but ended up saving him and that Tryfe woman just in time."

Rollie folded his arms and looked to the sky for support. "And this is the first I'm hearing of it?"

"Well, I thought you knew," she said. "It was all over the news."

She wasn't sure, but his eyes seemed to turn a deeper orange. "You do realize that Ludlow didn't just have any ship, Meena. That's my ship."

She blinked. "The Protostar?"

"One of the finest, rarest ships ever made."

"That awful Protostar? It was impossibly uncomfortable. There was no food processing unit. No hot water. You didn't even have a proper bed, just one of those slabs of rock you Deltans like so much."

"I keep telling you; it's great for the posture. But that's not the point. What kind of sick person would knowingly dismantle a Protostar for scrap?" He exhaled and shook his head. "Where is Ludlow now?"

"That big celebrity hospital on Daglann-Da. I can't think of the name of it. My Maternal Archetype went there once for a total derma upgrade. Though, she still claims it was because she'd had a fall. 'A fall of your jawline, perhaps,' I told her. But you know how she is."

Rollie was already thumping up the ramp and into the ship.

Of course, now Meena knew where this was headed. Fortunately, Daglann-Da was right near Sarulia. If they were swift, she could still be ready to meet Mr. Spacecaps with a tick of time to spare.

"I have an inspiration," she said, joining Rollie in the Astrocrat, as he was headed for the cockpit. "What say we pop by Daglann-Da, and you can ask Mr. Ludlow about your ship?"

This was bound to happen regardless, but she liked the feel of having some control in the matter. She pressed the ramp retraction button. "I know how it is with you and that Protostar. And besides, you'll need it especially now, won't you?"

"Why 'especially?'" He closed the hatch and checked the seal.

"Well, because of the Gwash lawpeople. They've taken your stolen Quasar runabout for evidence in ..." She pressed a thoughtful finger to her lips. "What was it again? A Uninet presenter's disappearance? Rordon Moonwax, I think his name is."

Rollie's expression teetered in a pleasing balance between annoyance and amusement.

She smiled and patted his arm. "Perhaps you'd like to discuss that on the way to Daglann-Da. You know, just to pass the time."

11

"Skytreg's in the ZapTrap, M.C. Blyte. Is there anything else you need?" asked Middly.

MesoCommander Waranda Blyte of the Vos Laegos City RightGuides examined the prisoner through the two-way mirror. There was simply nothing like seeing the Underworld's favorite son clamped into a ZapTrap™ to power up a good mood. The electrified cylinder was designed to restrict the funny business of their more unruly guests, and Zenith Skytreg would get no special treatment here. "How's he been?"

"Compliant," said R.G. Middly. "To the point of downright chipper. If I didn't know better, MesoCommander, I'd say he was loving this."

"Then he hasn't heard the angry mob outside calling for his head."

"Oh, they're not all angry, ma'am." He referenced the electronic clipboard in his hand. "An independent survey shows some are also sad, perplexed, ambivalent and thirty-one percent of them believe this is a spin-off of that *There Goes the Galaxy* show Skytreg was in." Middly was a stickler for details.

"Diverse emotions aside," Blyte continued firmly, "here are the rules. As long as Zenith Skytreg is with us, he's either in his cube or the ZapTrap, understand? These native Vos Laegons are tricky, Middly. They might look pretty and pearly on the outside, but underestimate them and your dream date's a jaws-and-claws nightmare in half a second. I assume you have the vocal projection diffuser on there, too?"

"Yes, ma'am."

"Good. Because that singing of theirs can turn even the toughest Guide into a drooling sack of sorry. Remember that. It'll keep you safe."

She looked in on Skytreg who did appear rather comfy and snug in his confined space. "Sometimes I wonder who bribed evolution to stack the deck for these people."

"Um, begging your pardon, ma'am…" The kid's saucer eyes scanned her face attentively, but his ears were down in submission. "Aren't you native Vos Laegon?"

"Yes," she said.

"No," she said.

"Well…" she said, "it's complicated."

Those big, sad eyes were still staring, taking it all in.

She sighed. "My Paternal Archetype volunteered for an interspecies gene splicing trial. Needed the cash. I'm the results." He preferred the cash. She didn't blame him. How could she? The results simply didn't live up to the hype.

Blyte enjoyed none of the bells and whistles of native Vos Laegon defense, a fraction of the pheromone magnetism and a jumble of interspecies phenotypes that were, in her opinion, to questionable aesthetic success. Yet she had one hundred percent of the identity issues.

On the plus side, she could read people better than most, and her inner rage channeled nicely into the law enforcement profession.

Normally, she wouldn't even talk about her background. And if anyone else had asked the same question, Waranda Blyte probably would have lasered their lips shut.

Thing was, she happened to like Middly. The kid was so earnest, eager and hard-working, if you sniffed him you could probably still smell the New.

She didn't sniff; she'd have had to write herself up and she hated reports. "Any comms from the Coalition of Planets yet?" she asked.

"Three," said Middly. "One politely requesting we turn over the cash evidence. One politely requesting we turn over Skytreg. And one gently threatening to slam us with a Jurisdictional Override from the GCU's Most Elevated Court, if we refuse the first two."

"Excellent. We're at sixty-six percent fake courtesy. We still have time," she said. "Have you gotten to sit in on an interrogation yet, Middly?" she asked him.

"No, ma'am, not yet."

"Like to?"

"Really? Cosmic!" His face lit up, and his whole body shook with excitement. These Alpuckite cadets were always so enthusiastic. She just hoped he wouldn't urinate on the floor, like that last one did.

Fortunately, Middly just gave his throat a quick clear and tried to reset his features into something more Academy.

"Follow me. And say nothing unless I cue you," she said, and they ventured through the door to the confession room.

"Ah, MesoCommander…" Zenith Skytreg squinted to read her nametag, "Blyte, is it? So nice to finally see someone of rank. I thought perhaps you weren't taking my confinement seriously."

"That's funny," said Blyte. "I heard the same thing about you." She sat down at a little table in front of the ZapTrap and Middly grabbed the seat next to hers.

"I suppose you're here to wring a confession out of me," said the man in the clear tube.

"Why? Do you have something you'd like to share?"

"Well, stealing the number three for ransom … It really is masterful. Elegant. Devious. And so multi-faceted." Zenith Skytreg unleashed a perfect white smile. "How it pains me to admit it's not my plan."

"So, you're saying you have no idea how the GCU's ransom money got into your facilities?"

"I am," said Skytreg.

She nodded. "You're saying you have no clue how piles of cash ended up in your compound, in a room with restricted access?"

"I did."

"You're saying how, Universal hours after the deadline at Chee's Crater, witnesses discovered the ransom money just kicking around in your personal collection room, and it had absolutely nothing to do with you?"

"Precisely so. You are as eloquent as you are intelligent, M.C. Blyte. I couldn't make it more clear." Skytreg flashed another charming smile.

She drew on her inheritance from the Vos Laegon gene bank to return the gesture. And for a moment, it was a smile showdown, grin to grin. But she had surprise on her side. "So you're saying you don't have very good control over your employees."

His grin faltered first. "Excuse me?"

"Well," she began, "if only a few people had access to that room beyond you, and this all happened on your watch, obviously your reported skills as this dynamic, fearsome Underworld Leader are, well, somewhat exaggerated. That's all." She shrugged and typed something into her handheld device. "No problem."

She gave it a long pause while she typed in her notes. Or in this case, her grocery list. She needed to remember to pick up SnoogleNums at the local Shop-O-Drome, if they weren't completely out. It was remarkable how something so small could eat three times its weight in food pellets. And don't even get her started on its output container.

She could feel Skytreg's icy, deep-set eyes settle on her. She heard Middly shift in his chair.

Finally, she snapped the handheld shut. "I admit, I am a little disappointed," she continued and slipped the gadget into her jacket pocket. "I'd been really looking forward to meeting you. I'd heard you were the real deal. Old time Underworld, controlling everything with a double reinforced titanium hand

and all that. I guess that's why they say, 'The stars at a distance shine, but up close they … something-something.'" She turned an inquiring gaze on R.G. Middly.

"'Too close and they burn,'" supplied Middly.

"Ah, that's right! Thanks, Middly. That would have been bothering me all day."

Middly looked like he wasn't sure whether to be really launched at giving his commander the answer she needed, or they were playing GoodGuide/BadGuide and no one had bothered to tell him. So he just nodded.

"You know how when you can't remember something, it just nags at you? And then in the middle of the night, you wake up and—"

By now, she wasn't sure if Skytreg were more irritated at being undermined or being ignored. Either way, it had the desired effect. "So my having been voted Official Leader of the Intergalactic Underworld four times running is a fluke? Being named *CrimeDaily*'s 'Single Best Thing That's Happened to the Underworld Since Reasonable Doubt' is an empty gesture to you? Saving the Klimfal race from extinction through my leadership in the Feegar Rebellion, that's an accident, too, I suppose?"

"It is impressive," Blyte admitted. "But now I'm very puzzled."

He looked intrigued. "Oh?"

"Either you are the glorious Underworld leader in complete control of everything across the GCU …" She leaned in. "… Or the people you work with can sneak things in under your nose. Tell me: which is it?"

Skytreg was quiet a moment. "M.C. Blyte …" He shook his head as much as the ZapTrap allowed. "Succumbing to childish games … I had really enjoyed our little discussion until now. I'd had real hopes we could be friends."

"Have I fallen out of favor already?" she asked, giving a click of the tongue. "Oh, and I'd thought it would last until, at least, we got into the good stuff. Tell me, where were you when Chee's Crater was emptied?"

His broad jaw jutted with confidence. "I was in my Underworld Headquarters, with a few friends."

"And none of you heard a thousand toks of currency making its way into your home?"

"I have a comfortable-sized abode, M.C. Blyte. My Private Collection Room is on a separate wing from my living facilities."

"So if we contact your friends, they'll say the same thing? That you were with them and nobody heard a thing?"

"Of course they will. And I have a question for you, M.C. Blyte." He leaned as close to the ZapTrap wall as possible without touching it. His breath steamed a shape onto the clear surface. "How do you even know this is the same money? Currency is currency. And if I recall correctly from the ransom message, that currency wasn't supposed to be marked."

"Well, that's true, yes, Mr. Skytreg. But here's the quirk," said Blyte. "Discovered along with the currency was a holographic message from the president of Zarquon-5 directly to the numeroterrorists. Let's see if I recall it properly. I believe it said, 'Here is our money. Please, please, please, pretty please return the number three to us soon. Our third moon was a real hit with the newly life-merged tourist set. We'd kinda like to get it back. Hugs and kisses, The President.'" She turned to Middly. "It was something like that. Wasn't it something like that?"

"I believe it was something like that, yes," agreed Middly.

"But because it was such a big, greedy pile of money," continued Blyte, "it seems the kidnapper never noticed the message before somehow it showed up at your house. Then there's the question of your comms."

Skytreg frowned. "My comms?"

"Immediately after the ransom message went out, you vis-ued Jymkrax Ragobar, once at his Quad Three headquarters and once at his ship. I find that very interesting."

"Then I must be the most fascinating man in the GCU because I vis-u lots of people every day, MesoCommander."

"Ah, but isn't Ragobar the Underworld's most elite shamcommer? Haven't businesses hired him for Electronic

Germ Warfare against their competition? Didn't he originate more effective fake vis-u pleas for yoonies than anyone in Underworld history? Isn't that his niche?"

"These days he's Manager of the Quad Three Underworld operations," said Skytreg. "His attention has not been otherwise focused for many Universal years."

"Then why vis-u him at the very moment the ransom message hit? Buzzing to congratulate him, perhaps, on a job well-done?"

Skytreg clasped his hands neatly before him. "Quite the opposite. It occurred to me I hadn't heard from him recently, and I was concerned for his welfare. If you checked my comms, you'd see I never connected with Mr. Ragobar. It is apparently as I'd feared. He's trapped in the field like everyone else from Quad Three."

"We'll be confirming that, if you don't mind." She rose. Middly rose. "In the meantime," she said, "perhaps you'd like to give R.G. Middly here a list of the people who had access to that collection room of yours." Middly sat again and drew out the clipboard. "Also, a list of the friends who were there with you that night. Then we'll talk again. Maybe even discuss beaming technology and how to get the viral shields off the properties you've trapped. We'll have a stellar old time, the three of us."

"It will be a party of four, M.C. Blyte. While this date was on me, we'll be including my lawyer in our next one. And then it will be your turn to pay."

"Expect some serious dinner and dancing," she said, moving to the door. "I'm not a cheap date." And Waranda Blyte let the door clang shut behind her. She'd always wanted to do that. It was such a nice touch.

12

Bertram Ludlow popped in the infopill and washed it down with a swig of flimberry juice.

It took only a moment before he started to digest the brochure. Breathtaking astronomical views flooded his mind and for a fleeting moment, he actually smelled the homey scent and felt the comfortable seating on his own orbiting rental pod. He could have all this, it told him, at prices to suit any budget.

Yes, the rings of Ragul-Sfera were well-worth a visit.

He noted it on his ever-growing list, shuffled through the various promo-packets narrowly being eaten by the bed, and he popped in another trip option.

It had a funny aftertaste, but the lunar landscapes were mind-blowing and the three-night package had definite possibilities.

"Why, good morning, Mr. Ludlow," said Bob from the doorway. Bertram could see the doorway, since he'd discovered the bed was adjustable. "Enjoying the tour information?"

"It's the age-old dilemma, Bob," said Bertram. "How do you choose between awe-inspiring interstellar phenomena?"

"I'm more of a homebody myself, Mr. Ludlow," Bob confessed. "But with Tryfe in the viral field, I imagine this could free up your schedule considerably."

"It's looking that way," said Bertram brightly. "Right now, the finest minds in the Universe are working to unravel the Number Three Virus. There are elite law enforcement agencies, crack teams of astrophysicists, technology gurus—even great planetary leaders. And you know what? Not one of them would do a better job of it with more Bertram Ludlow involved."

"The total lack of responsibility must make a refreshing change, Sir."

"You bet your bidirectional buttons it does. My plans have had to shift completely!" Bertram beamed at the idea. "Picture this: I hire a driving service. It takes me to as many suns-filled days and interstellar nights of exotic locales and cosmic cuisine as I can squeeze in."

"I have accessed a comparable set of relevant digital images in my memory," said Bob.

"And during this time, I learn from this driver. I take notes. I ask questions. I absorb all the tips and tricks of intergalactic piloting at the hands of a professional. A real professional. Not an infopill where half the instructions are missing. A lifeform who knows its stuff."

Bertram was really warming up to the topic now. "I get hands-on lessons. All while enjoying the wonders of the GCU—or at least the three-fourths of it that haven't been hijacked by numeroterrorists. It's perfect! It's fun, it's productive—it's multi-tasking."

"You do seem to have thought this through, Mr. Ludlow."

"Ah, but that's not all! Then, I use my remaining money to purchase an ICV of my own. So once Tryfe is free, I am in control. I go to Tryfe, sweep in there, assess the situation, and save whoever I can. That is, if I'm not, y'know shot down by our new alien overlords, or a mind-controlled human puppet regime or whatever. Some of this I'm gonna have to wing, you understand."

There was that electronic whir again.

"Er, yes, Mr. Ludlow. Very proactive," Bob said. "Which is why you may be quite pleased with the news I have for you. Guess what today is!"

"Another interview with the *Heavy Meddler*? *NewsMillennium*? *Popular ICV Astrodynamics*?" Bertram had learned the trick to extracting himself from the bed and getting into the hoverchair, even though Manor staff frowned on it for legal reasons. He did so now.

"You do have two interviews scheduled, yes," admitted Bob. "But that's not my news. Guess who's likely to get discharged later today?"

"Bet it's that famous singer with the respiratory tract transplant. He sounds all kinds of awesome through the wall now."

"You, Mr. Ludlow," continued the hoverchair. "You're getting discharged today."

A jolt of excitement coursed through Bertram's body. He knew this day was coming, of course, and he felt better than he ever had. "Are you sure?"

"I heard it directly from your medical records."

Bertram considered this as they moved down the hall to the breakfast room.

"Now, I hope you haven't spoiled your appetite with all those infopills," continued Bob as it docked at Bertram and Rozz's standard table. "I highly recommend this morning's paargraath."

Rozz was already there, shoveling in the last bite of something herself, and she glanced at Bertram just as she tossed down her fork. "Hi!" she said, chewing. "And bye! Nothing personal. But I've gotta blast."

"Blast?" Bertram blinked. "Blast where?"

"Got a job. So cool. I'll fill you in over dinner, if there's time." She wiped her mouth and tucked her napkin onto her plate, as her hoverchair edged away.

"Wait! A job? Doing what?"

The chair paused. A smile broke over Rozz's face—unusual for her. She'd never been a smiler. "Programming!" Her voice was breathless. "Helping Beddsyde Manor update their computer systems for a Number Three workaround. If we can find out where the threes were in their programs and replace them with an alternate numeric configuration, we might be able to get operations rolling again. Won't do much for the third floor. That's another issue, but..." She shrugged. "By the way, the paargraath?" She pointed to her empty plate. "It's my new favorite way to start the day."

She began backing away again, but Bertram seized the chair arm. "Hold on a minute. Programming? Really? I mean, no offense, Rozz, you're a real whiz on Earth. But what do you know about GCU systems?"

"What do *you* know about what I know about GCU systems?" she asked, with a smirk. "I told you; when I worked for Spectra Pollux, I thought I could bust out of there by cracking her ops. So I hit the infopills pretty hard. All the major programming languages, all the popular systems. Lot of good it did me then; the woman controlled most things through a chip in that monumental melon of hers. But anyway, Manor IT needs as many techs on this as they can get right now. And they said they'll pay." She leaned in and the big brown eyes locked onto Bertram's. In a confidential tone, she said, "You know, you were right earlier."

"I was?" Along with the smiling, this was almost unheard of behavior.

She nodded. "If I'm going to live in the GCU, I need to start thinking seriously about my career here. I don't know if I can go back to Tryfe. Not permanently. And you had a point. It's important to take our opportunities where we can right now, to make a start. So I'm sorry I ragged on you about the interviews," she said. "You were doing what you thought made sense. Even if it is kinda, y'know, ick. But right now," her chair beeped as it backed up, "I gotta go. Don't want to be late for my first day of work. Later!"

"Er, later," Bertram said. But he told it to the air behind her, as she whisked from the room.

Bertram did order the paargraath, and when the dish unveiled itself from its shiny serving dome, the sheer smell had him excited about future culinary adventures. He seized his utensils. He unfurled a napkin that had been folded into some sort of decorative waterfowl. And he stopped.

The napkin had something to say.

Bertram's eyes darted around, scanning the area for other hospital guests who received Fortune Napkins, then for the shifty suspects who might have put them there. But most guests were tucking into their food with gusto, while staff stood by in normal attendance.

Something about it made Bertram shelter the napkin under his table, as he opened it to its full span. The message was written in a bold, awkward hand, the lettering thick and black. It was in English, yet a few of the letters weren't quite right— an angle off here, a curve off there, giving it a sort of fierce, aggressive, off-kilter appearance. Bertram thought it looked like it had been penned by an acutely intelligent child in desperate need of family counseling. It said:

COME TO THE REJUVENATION GARDENS
NOW.
UNDER FRABBLAGUNDGER BRIDGE.
NOW.

The writer was either very impatient or didn't proofread.

"Your pulse has increased significantly," observed Bertram's hoverchair. "Is the food not to your liking?"

Bertram barely heard it as he reread the message. "When were those interviews scheduled again?" he asked.

"This afternoon," replied Bob. "Why?"

Bertram turned the napkin over in his hands. He saw a third "now" had been scrawled on the other side. He read the full message once more.

"Is there a Frabblagundger Bridge?" Bertram asked.

"Why, yes!" said Bob. "The Foobaz Frabblagundger Deviated Septum Bridge is a central feature in our award-winning Rejuvenation Gardens."

"Great, let's go," Bertram told it.

"But Mr. Ludlow, you didn't even touch your paargraath. Your nutrients level is low and—"

"The Bridge," Bertram said with some force. "Paargraath can wait." And with a hesitant purr, the hoverchair glided from the table, down the long Manor hall to the exit.

The Rejuvenation Gardens were misty this morning. Condensation formed a glistening layer over the foliage, the benches and the Gardens' famous statuary. These last items were renowned for the unique way they depicted the healing arts as performed on eerily accurate representations of celebrities.

Here Bertram passed a scene featuring a likeness of action star and stuntman Rix Manglutes. According to the sign, Rix was having his right bicep sewn back on after an unfortunate detonation experience during *Return of Epochageddon Eclipse Strikes Back Five: Payback Revenge*. Rix was so well-sculpted you could see every vein in his muscular forearm, every bead of perspiration on his fraught temple. His eyes looked alive and somewhat sedated. The expression of the Manor's Wellness Worker was one of efficiency.

The artwork was surrounded by an explosive selection of colorful blooms.

Further down the path, Bertram passed a memorial tribute to Mergle Farcrumple, kachunkettball player for the Blumdec Blasters, who had come to Beddsyde Manor after his infamous in-game decapitation. Wellness Workers surrounded him holding various surgical technologies. Unfortunately, the head was beyond a full-body reunion. The landscaping around it included tasteful wreaths and a bed of flowers in front spelling out, "Sorry, Merg."

Bertram's hoverchair glided past statues experiencing eye color alterations, statues enjoying skeletal mass reductions, and an area of newly upturned ground that would be the future site of a Stella Cygnus display, in honor of her brave recovery from crudfoot. The machinery sat still and solitary in the fog.

The Foobaz Frabblagundger Deviated Septum Bridge lay ahead. Along one arch was a representation of the music star, a gentle spray of water fanning from his hoselike nose into the stream below. It was on the banks under the bridge that Bertram noticed an eerie shift of movement.

"Your heartbeat has become rapid. You really should have had breakfast. Maybe we should go back inside," Bob suggested.

"Quit backseat driving, Bob. You act like such an old rockingchair sometimes." Bertram said, directing the personal hovervehicle down the slope and to the bank of the stream. Again, he saw something move in the dim under the bridge, and then it registered what—or rather who—was waiting. One of the figures was someone he hadn't imagined seeing again. He didn't quite see him now, either.

"Rollie?" Bertram breathed.

It was a chilling second before Bertram determined the ghostly form was actually the real guy wearing alien camo. It wasn't quite like an invisi-suit, which left the wearer completely transparent, but it did make him unusually easy to ignore. The man's hair, which had been bright yellow, was almost colorless now. His sunburned face was set in determined angles, his orange eyes acute. With him was an unfamiliar female being with shiny, dark blue hair and pale skin.

"My God," said Bertram, "Rollie, you're alive!"

"My ship," said Rollie, "where the frag is it?"

A relieved laugh escaped Bertram's throat. "Are you kidding me? For six months everyone thinks you're dead, and this is how you greet a friend? I should have known the RegForce would never get you to Altair."

"Altair?" Rollie repeated the word as if he hadn't heard it before. "Absolutely, I went to Altair. Yes, Altair-5, how I know her well. Stellar place, very diverse, friendly foliage, perhaps I'll buy the planet and move there if I ever settle down. But as for now, it is irrelevant to our discussion. Which is about...What's it about? Flamin' Karnax, I should have had another Feegar bourbon," he muttered, tapping a spot on his forehead. "Ah, right. The Protostar. And where it's gone, now that you've mishandled it into ruin."

Bertram turned to the petite woman beside Rollie. "Are you his … nurse?"

"Oh, he's actually doing much better," she assured him with a warm smile. "I'm Meena Tsoogarkken, by the way." She extended one porcelain hand. It was surprisingly rough for someone so otherwise put together.

"Bertram Lud—"

But fingers snapped before Bertram's face. "Hey. Over here. Answers. Forthwith."

"Look, I don't know where your ship is," said Bertram finally. "I'd guess the salvage crew still has it."

"Which salvage crew?"

"I don't know, I barely heard it. I was half dead."

"Death is no excuse; half dead, fifty percent off that. Think, would you?" Rollie's fingers clenched, unclenched and got stuffed into his pockets.

There was no use arguing with him; so Bertram thought. What he recalled was an image of the tusked face of his rescuer, so bristled, so pink, so smiling, so— "Liddlebiggs. Here on Daglann-Da." The words just came out.

Rollie nodded crisply. "Right. Thanks." He brushed past Bertram and climbed the bank to the garden path. The rising sun made the pattern on his clothes shift and change with the movement.

The woman, Meena, patted Bertram gently on the shoulder and excused herself to follow. "It was so nice meeting you, I've heard so much."

"Wait," called Bertram, "that's it? You show up, ask about your ship and go?"

They both paused. Meena looked up at Rollie. Rollie thought about it, rolled his eyes, and gave an irritable exhale. "So, um … you've been well, then?" The tone was forced and formal.

Bertram indicated his Beddsyde Manor sweatsuit and hoverchair. "What do you think?"

Rollie nodded. "It's why I hate small talk," he said, turning on the heel of a boot. "Speedy recovery, Ludlow." He gave a backwards sort of wave and vanished into a hedgerow.

"You, too," said Bertram. Altair-5, he thought, would not be making the tour list.

It had seemed hopeless. Meena's pocket Uninet had no listing under Liddlebiggs, in any variety of spellings or creative configurations. Then, after a chat with some locals, they got a lead on a "3 Liddlebiggs' Jetsam Emporium and Salvage Service" in the warehouse district right off Beddsyde Circle. And they were on their way.

The place read "2+1 Liddlebiggs'" now, Meena noticed. She could still see the mark on the shack roof where the "3" had been, recently amended using parts of other signs.

They hadn't gotten through the front door before Meena longed to linger. The central salvage office was surrounded by ten thousand kroms of shipwrecks, obsolete equipment, aged furniture, machinery, decommissioned weaponry and rusty advertising signs for long-forgotten snack foods. Right by the front door was a row of beautifully old and filthy holotheater seats, with ripped upholstery fabric and popped stuffing.

Yes, Liddlebiggs' was the home of artistic potential.

As the office doors parted, they stepped into a worn and stained reception room. The place smelled strongly of ICV fuel, wet wood, leaky robots, cleaners, polishes, paints and metal. Carpeting showed the trails where wheeled items had rolled through swinging doors into a back room. Glass display cases hung from the walls, smudged with fingerprints and topped with scarves of dust.

In a corner, lifeless early-model Non-Organic Simulants were stacked like war casualties. Barrels of old rusty handlasers and outdated gadgets lined their path.

"Anyone here?" Rollie called. Then he noticed an ancient, manually-operated bell in one corner of the cluttered front desk. Grinning, he snatched up the item, felt its weight and its craftsmanship. He returned it to the desk and gave it a good, firm slam. CLINNNNNGGGGGG!

His effort was met with the barely audible sounds of the swinging doors squeaking against each other and the distant hydraulic sound of a levitating dolly's descent.

"Once we find your ship," Meena began, "I simply have to look around this place. It's an absolute treasure trove for art supplies. I can't believe I've never heard of it."

Rollie raised an eyebrow. "I thought you were in this big hurry to get back to that client of yours, Mr. Speedclap."

"Spacecaps," she said. "And, well, there's been a change of plans." She could feel the color creeping up her neck and onto her face. She didn't really want to talk about Mr. Spacecaps and her meeting right now. Meena hit the bell.

And CLINNNNNGGGGGG! There was more squeaking. Somewhere, a Uninet system bonged for attention it didn't get.

Rollie, she noticed, was still staring at her.

"Oh, all right," she snapped. "Mr. Spacecaps left me a comm message last night. He's tied up dealing with that horrible virus and has no idea when he'll be free. I swear, Rollie, if Zenith Skytreg cost me this sale, *I* want revenge."

"Justice," said Rollie automatically. "And it's not Skytreg. I keep telling you." Rollie's hand reached out and struck the bell a third time—CLINNNNGGGGGGG!—as an elderly tusked lifeform shuffled in.

He was Suidae Verrucan, as far as Meena could tell and he took the still-ringing bell, opened a drawer and dumped it inside. He slammed the drawer shut. She could still hear it faintly through the drawer. "Okay, so you tested out our fine antiquities. What more could you want?" he asked.

Rollie stepped forward. "I'm looking for a ship you brought in here last Universal week or so. A Protostar 340-K."

"Well, keep looking," said the old Verrucan. "It's gone."

"You scrapped it already?" Rollie's sunburnt face seemed to drain. "One of the rarest ICVs in the GCU? One of only three in, well, okay, not quite working condition anymore. But with a little effort…"

"Hey, cool your rockets there, sonny. Who said anything about scrap?" said the man. "I sold it, as-is, down to its dents, defunct life support and its hotplate. Somebody saw that Tryfe kid's interview on the *Heavy Meddler* and buzzed us with a client who had to have the thing. Huge fan of *There Goes the Galaxy*, I guess. They towed it out of here a day or two later."

"Who did?"

"Do I know? Do I care?" The old man moved a few things on the desk into new piles, but the overall clutter stayed the same. "They paid cash. Lots of it. That's what I care about. Anyway, I got bigger things to deal with right now. My Uninet site's one big error page. My sales system keeps freezing and my second-level progeny's gone, so nobody's here to fix either of 'em."

Meena gasped. "Your second-level progeny's gone?"

"Yup, she went over to Beddsyde Manor to deliver something Stella Cygnus had ordered, and that was it. Trapped in the virus. We still list the kid on the sign out front, of course, in case she comes back. My boy's pretty broken up about it. So I imagine we'll wait a week or two, see what happens and then take the plus-one off."

"I'm sure she'd have wanted it that way," said Meena, trying to be empathetic.

"But if you're in the market for a ship, I can do you a lot better quality than that Protostar, anyways. And—" The Suidae Verrucan's small brown eyes grew large. "Wait, you're that Tsmorland fellah, aren't you? From *There Goes the Galaxy*. Sure," he said, squinting, "I see it now, I just didn't notice with all the—" He waved his hand at the camo, then scratched his stubbly chin. "Aren't you dead?"

"Yes," said Rollie, turning to go.

The old man nodded. "Shame. You were one of my favorite characters on there."

12+1

"Oh, so you want a fight, huh? Well, power it up it, ya sniveling slaggard! Once I get my arms on you, you'll feel the meaning of The Big Bang!"

In the Tech Department of Beddsyde Manor, a dented hoverchair, strapped to the wall, thumped and strained at its bonds.

Bob's hydraulics sighed over the smack talk. "Such a shame. Before its accident, that chair wouldn't so much as smudge your bumper. Now look at it."

The chair, though vocal, wasn't the only thing waiting for attention today. Vending machines, cleaning robots and medical equipment were racked and stacked, forming a small cyber cityscape along the department's walls. Some technologies flashed error messages. Some beeped weakly to themselves. One was trying to fix itself with a pair of safety scissors, cotton balls and some used Translachew.

Bertram felt Bob shudder as they passed. "Programming's in here," it said, as the skyscrapers of the disturbed, defunct and damaged gave way to a small back room. Based on its size, the area would comfortably house six in-house staff members. An extra twenty-five consultants made the place downright cozy, if you defined "cozy" as "wedged belly to buttock like the universe's most dull yet determined rave party." Which, thought Bertram, corporate efficiency experts often do.

So some programmers got cozy in cubes. Some transformed dead equipment into makeshift desks and chairs. Some perched on window ledges, balancing terminals on knees, tails and other publicly-acceptable body protuberances. What they shared was an expression of intense concentration, a devotion to solving the Number Three Problem and an obliviousness to the cozy smell of working long, hard hours together on a diet consisting mainly of Flinky Rolls.

Bertram found Rozz and her hoverchair crammed between a water dispenser and a food processing unit. A colleague was reaching over her head for some steaming Flinky Rolls when Bertram entered.

"How is it going?" Bertram asked, peering over Rozz's shoulder at the screen. "Any closer to fixing the Three Problem?"

She didn't look surprised to see him, but she also didn't look up from her work. "It's all two-plus-one these days," said Rozz.

"Pardon?"

"Two-plus-one. You know, in place of the missing threes? We tried a one-one-one sequence, but the moment we entered it, that went poof, too. So it's all two-plus-one now. Zenith Skytreg must have quite a sense of humor."

Bertram considered the times he'd seen Zenith Skytreg in action. "Maybe he stores it up for the really big acts of terrorism," Bertram suggested.

"So what brings you to the technology graveyard?" Rozz's eyes swung toward Bertram, then back to her data. "I'm sure you didn't come down here because coding's the hot new spectator sport. Any news on the viral shields? Something on Tryfe? Did Skytreg crack like a four digit PIN?" She grinned hopefully.

"No. Nothing like that. I just wanted to let you know, um…" This was harder to say than he'd envisioned. "…I had my checkup just now, Rozz. And the Wellness Workers said I'm a hundred percent. I can go."

"Oh," she said, a dark cloud passing over her expression. "Um, that's good. That you're well, I mean."

"I ..." He looked at the hands folded in his lap, "I guess you'll be staying here for a while?"

Rozz bit her lip. "Well, I imagine I'll get the green light for discharge any time now myself. Or the red light, if it's Klinko. But, see, I've got this job. I mean, until Three's back, they really need the help here. And if it doesn't return, which it's kinda looking like it won't unless Skytreg comes clean, well ..." Her words hung on the air, limp and cold, like wet wash on a line.

Bertram nodded.

"Where are you going to go?" Rozz asked.

"Oh, don't you worry about me," Bertram said. "The Universe is my oyster. I've got the Gears of Opportunity turning. The Pistons of Possibility pumping. The Cogs of Creativity grinding. My future's a ..." he hesitated, "... a well-oiled robotic shellfish." It didn't sound as enterprising as he'd hoped, but maybe she wouldn't notice. "Also," he continued quickly, "in just a few short weeks, if you take a walk around the Rejuvenation Gardens, do you know what you'll see?"

"That Stella Cygnus crudfoot thing?"

"Er, maybe, I don't know," he said, annoyed Ms. Cygnus was stealing his thunder. "But in exchange for all of Beddsyde Manor's medical help, I gave them the rights to produce and market the very first Bertram Ludlow *There Goes the Galaxy* Space Sickness garden statuary. They're going to put it somewhere near their Gout Gazebo."

"Cool," said Rozz. "I'll be sure to check it out."

"Cool," Bertram said.

"Cool," Rozz repeated, and Bertram was grateful when a creature who, in fact, looked something like a well-oiled robotic shellfish interrupted all the witty repartee.

"Rozz," it said, "are you about done with that equipment tracking code?"

"Just about." Rozz turned a wan smile on her fellow Tryfling. "Look, Bertram, I'm really sorry, but I ..." She hooked a thumb at the computer screen.

"Yeah, no problem." Bertram waved it away. "You're busy. So …" He leaned in to kiss her goodbye, but this task was unexpectedly challenging with both parties in hoverchairs. The wide bases of the vehicles bumped together, jostling Bertram in his seat. He yanked the hovercraft harness latch. It wouldn't budge. "Bob," Bertram said, "this once, can't you just—?" He shook the harness.

"I'm sorry," said Bob. "I'd love to. But as you know, Beddsyde Manor does not permit our guests to move around the grounds unassisted. It's policy."

By now, the moment was gone anyway, and they all knew it. So Rozz reached out, summoned that wan smile again, and squeezed Bertram's hand. "See you, Bertram. I hope your oyster's in season."

"Thanks, Rozz," he said. "You take care." And as Rozz Mercer returned to tackling the Number Three Virus, Bertram Ludlow left Beddsyde Manor feeling just a bit like number two.

The ICV driver was already half an hour late. So, as Bertram waited outside Beddsyde Manor with his meager possessions, he used one of his newer ones to vis-u the driving service.

"Our apologies, sir, but with the Farthest Reaches Cosmos Corral down, we're simply swamped," explained the company rep, a creature Bertram thought looked a little like a roasted marshmallow with hands. "We're doing the best we can, and we thank you for your understanding. It'll be just ten minutes."

"Ten minutes in what planetary system?" Bertram asked, but the rep had already signed off. Bertram hit the Uninet for local-to-Universal time conversion rates and discovered "ten minutes" was actually Daglann-Da slang for, "We get there when we get there, amusing tourist."

On the plus side, that was the portable vis-u/Uninet already paying for itself. The device was one of two purchases he'd made from his interview funds, the second being a souvenir t-shirt from the Manor giftshop. This read: "I got stuck at

Beddsyde Manor" and showed a smiling hypodermic needle with a glistening drop of green blood at the tip. There was something about the brazen universality of souvenir crap that Bertram found very soothing.

A voice cut into his thoughts. "Bertram! Wink Wallop, *The Low-Gravity Living Channel.* Look this way please?" FLASH! It was a retinal scan for *Low-Gravity Living*'s lucky viewers.

"Hey, that's fifty yoonies, pal!" Bertram shouted, trying to peer through the spinning stars in his eyes. But Wink Wallop was already off quizzing a group of lifeforms about their favorite low-gravity vacation planets. Bertram decided to let the guy have his freebie.

It was that moment he noticed the weird shimmer of movement out of the corner of his eye and he turned. Something there, but not quite there, was moving down the walkway to the ICV park.

No, some*one*, wearing versatile GCU camo. Now that Bertram knew what to look for, he recognized the purposeful figure and couldn't understand why it had ever been difficult to spot.

"Rollie!" Bertram ran to catch up, his legs still stiff from so much quality hoverchair time.

Rollie Tsmorlood didn't slow his pace, but he did take a moment to give Bertram a critical look up and down. "They've let you loose, eh?"

"Did you find your ship?" Bertram asked.

"Indeed," he said with a nod. "Found it sold." Bertram opened his mouth to respond, but Rollie was ahead of him there, too. "Some brooquat with more yoonies than brains bought it as a collector's piece because of your blasted Uninet show. All cash, untraceable, now gone forever. Imagine, my Protostar 340-K trapped in a dusty showroom, never to fly again. It is to weep." He fished into a cargo pocket at his thigh for something.

"Well, I'm sorry to hear that, Rollie." Bertram wasn't sorry; that ship was a public menace. "But think of it this way: that Protostar lived a long, good life, and it needed more work than it cost." The glare Bertram got could have singed his eyebrows. "Dude, the life support system was down. The in-cabin gravity died. That thing in the corner that went 'bip' didn't. Even the hot plate started giving electric shocks when we heated something it wasn't in the mood for."

Bertram noticed an ICV remote in Rollie's hand now. It was far sleeker than the thing he'd had before and a third the size. "Oh. So you broke down and bought a new ICV, huh?"

They had stopped below a highly-polished model with the word "Astrocrat" written across the hull in beautifully-defined lettering. From the graceful shape of the rocket boosters to the well-designed line of the hatches, everything about the machine said modern elegance and spacious comfort.

It was suspiciously not Rollie's style.

"Alternative transportation," the Hyphiz Deltan told him. He hit the remote, and the access ramp began its slow, smooth decent.

"Your alternative, I'd believe," said Bertram. "But whose transportation?"

Rollie responded with a derisive sound at the back of his throat. "The lady," he began, and Bertram presumed he meant the tiny, navy blue-haired woman from earlier, "has found piles of spacejunk she intends to transform into 'treasures of artistic expression representing the blurred line between beauty and repulsion,'" he said. "I am *expected* to bring her ship to the salvage yard for loading."

Bertram noticed the subtle tone-shift on the word "expected." "But you're going to steal it, aren't you?"

Rollie just flashed him an unconvincing smile and started up the ramp.

"Aw, come on, Rollie." Bertram told his back. "You're like me: you got a second chance at life. Is this any way to start over?"

Bertram followed the man into the ship, through the main cabin and into a shiny cockpit. The guy dropped into the pilot's chair like he'd done it a hundred times. "You can't just—"

"Oh, I can. I 'can just,' yeah," Rollie said, harnessing in. His smile reminded Bertram of a piranha, happening on a lagoon filled with plump Brazilian villagers. "But today, as it stands, I won't. I owe Meena a favor or two right now and theft might come off as ungrateful." He motioned to the copilot's chair. "Sit. You're here. Might as well make yourself useful and help."

Bertram remembered the ICV service that was just ten minutes away, give or take a few million light years. "Look, I'd love to, but I've got this driver coming. I'm off to see the rings of Ragul—"

"Help starts with less yapping," Rollie advised.

Aw, what the hell, thought Bertram. *The Rings aren't going anywhere.* So he helped.

It was only a moment before the Astrocrat settled down again outside of a fence containing miles of rusted metal. Rollie was out of the pilot's chair before the ship had stopped its whir.

"A bit afraid to even find out what she's set her sights on. Meena's off her orbit, you know. Zonked." He pointed to one ruddy, scarred temple. "Up here."

"Ah." Bertram coughed discreetly over an escaped laugh, and they moved to the exit hatch. Rollie punched a button and they watched the ramp descend. "So what's the deal with you and this Meena, anyway?" Bertram asked.

"Life-merged a ways back," Rollie said. "Also, a ways back before that. Never takes, though. Me and Meena, we're from different worlds."

This time, Bertram couldn't stop the laugh quickly enough.

"What?" Rollie scowled. "It's true. She's from Hyphiz Epsilon, different planet entirely. Same species, but you'll never convince her people that. Fraggin' elitists."

By now Meena was outside, directing tusked beings in orange jumpsuits as they guided hoverdollies of salvage up the ramp to the ship.

"Just right this way," she said in her light, melodic voice, "that's right, very nice, watch that corner, please!..."

Rollie surveyed the dollies that bore structural metal bits, barrels of fist-sized ball bearings, metal canisters, rolls of wire fencing, boxes of paper leaflets and what Bertram thought looked a lot like half of a wooden extra-terrestrial chicken. "Only sell it by the mega-tok, do they?" Rollie asked.

But Meena's eyes were shining as she swept toward them. "Oh, it was simply out-of-this-world in there! Have you ever seen such a cosmic place, Rollie? History, effluvia, potential! My creative juices are ..." Her pale face flushed. "...Well, it's just very exciting. I can't wait to get back to my studio and—" She turned to three of the salvage workers. "—If you gentlemen could please go and fetch the rest of it?"

"Frag me; there's more?" Rollie watched in some amazement as those workers returned to the building. He noticed some other customers had arrived, and Rollie called to them, "Sorry, there's no junk left. She's bought it all. You'll have to come back later."

"Oh, shoosh, you. It's not that bad." Meena turned to the four remaining workers, "And as for you fine fellows, we'll need to secure the items so they don't shift around en route. As you're the experts, I'll leave you to figure out the best way to do that. Now," she began, and twirled on Bertram and Rollie with a quick, keen assessment. "I'll need some help transferring these items to my studio. If you two would be willing, we could all just pop over to Hyphiz Epsilon and you could—"

"I'm sorry, I'd love to help," said Bertram, "but I've got plans. I booked this awesome pod for the rings of Ragul-Sfera. Then I'm headed to Lamblag Beta to see the GCU's largest sculpture of a mootaab made entirely out of toenail clippings. Then—"

"I'll pay," she said brightly.

"I'm in," said Bertram's mouth, almost of its own initiative. Okay, so he'd be a little late to Ragul-Sfera, but it would fund another fascinating meal as he overlooked intergalactic wonders on his GCUniversal tour. Perhaps he could charge her for travel time, too. "Absolutely, I'm in."

"Stellar. That's the fire I'm looking for!" Meena turned an expectant face up to Rollie. "And you?"

"Well, I owe you that much, don't I?" said Rollie. "Can't very well say no."

Her smile was beatific. "Cosmic!" She patted his arm. "That's the lukewarm, mildly begrudging response I hoped for!"

"But just so you know," he continued, looking grave, "I help you on Hyphiz Epsilon, and that makes us even, yeah? Then I'm done. I'm off to Vos Laegos."

"There's a sudden rush on drinks and debauchery, is there?"

Rollie winked. "Only if there's time." He crossed the room to assist one of the salvage guys as they fastened a teetering stack of aged newspapers into place.

Meena followed, arms folded, eyes narrowed. "Now I'm curious. What else does one do on Vos Laegos when one is, well, you?"

"Loads of things." He tightened a cable at the base of the stack and rose. "Catch up with my mates ... See what's turned up on the Underworld print market...Track down the slaggards who framed Zenith Skytreg and prove his innocence..." Rollie dusted off his hands. "Endless options."

"Wait." This was Bertram. He had a feeling he'd either missed a critical shift in the tides, or Altair-5 was even harder on Rollie than he'd thought. "Go back to that thing about Zenith Skytreg?"

"Excuse me, ma'am ..." A salvage employee thrust a service order at Meena. "We've finished."

"Twinkly!" Meena took the order, scanned her retinas and handed it back to him, along with a tip. "Thank you so very much for all your efforts." She walked them to the hatch and waved goodbye, like they'd simply come to bid her safe journey on some lengthy luxury cruise.

Rollie pushed a button near the door, snapping the hatch shut in mid bon voyage. "If we're going to make decent time," he said, "I am flying this thing."

"Oh no, you are not." While the words were firm, her tone was still light. "We went through this before. It's my ship. It was all very nice of you to bring it to the salvage yard for me, but I shall do the planet-to-planet piloting, if you please. You sit back there." She indicated the room full of artistic possibility. "Stay out of trouble. Pour yourself a cocktail." She swept into the cockpit and vanished from view. After a moment, she called back, "You know, given your proclivity for helping yourself to other people's things, I admit, I was somewhat surprised you didn't just take the ship."

"Still off my game," Rollie called back. "Death does that."

If there'd been any question that Meena was not a member of the Underworld, it was clear to Bertram now. The Astrocrat wasn't made for hiding, storing or transporting large shipments, let alone serving as a giant junk drawer for universal odds and ends. Nets, belts and stretchy cords formed a crude web across the lounge, confining the treasures to the limited floor space around the built-in seating. It reminded Bertram of childhood vacations, when he and his brother were carved into niches in a backseat mountain of must-haves, a bag of charcoal and the inflatable girraft (half animal, half raft), the only barriers between Bertram and hours of punchbuggy bruising.

From Bertram's seat now, he could just about see Rollie stretched over a barrel, trying to unbury himself a drink from the minibar on the other side of it. Bertram asked, "So did I hear you say you wanted to go to Vos Laegos to prove Zenith Skytreg was innocent?"

First there was the clink of ice cubes. Then the sound of fizz. "You heard," Rollie said. "What of it?" He emerged with a glass full of some roiling purple liquid.

"Don't you sort of—what is the word I'm looking for?" Bertram scratched his face. "—Hate his guts?" It had always been a little hard to keep up with Rollie and his shifting thought processes, but Bertram had felt pretty firm on this one fact.

"I've nothing against his gastrointestinal tract," Rollie said. "It's his personality I loathe. My dislike of Skytreg is one of the few eternal things in this ever-changing universe. At least, until dark energy mucks it all up, or me and Skytreg are both scattered bits on the breeze. That last one'll probably come first." He took a swig of the drink.

"But yet you think the guy who runs the biggest criminal organization around isn't the one holding the GCU for ransom?"

"Yes, why?"

"So the enormous pile of money found in his mansion...?"

"A plant, of course," said Rollie.

"Ah. Which is why you're going to Vos Laegos. To find out who really did it and prove Zenith Skytreg's innocence?"

"Stars to you, Ludlow. You shine brighter than I've given you credit for." He raised his glass to Bertram and drained half the drink.

Bertram frowned. "You know, hydration is really important to brain function. I mean, I don't know anything about Hyphiz Deltan physiology, but in most higher creatures the functionality you can lose when you're without proper fluids over a length of time ... like, when you're, say, a castaway on a death planet ... it's pretty significant. I imagine that purple stuff doesn't help, either."

"Appreciate the concern, Ludlow, but it's misplaced," said Rollie. "I am light years better."

"That's what Meena said. And you said Meena was 'zonky.'"

Speaking of Meena, it was her voice now reverberating from the cockpit. "Rollie, er, awfully sorry to interrupt your catching up, but could you come here and take a look at something for me, please?"

Rollie was busy glaring at Bertram over the wooden chicken. "If I'm so off my orbit, then tell me just how is Zenith Skytreg supposed to get out of confinement with everyone automatically assuming he's guilty?"

For a moment, Bertram wondered about his own hydration levels. He pushed at the bridge of his nose. "You've said the guy's ruining the Underworld. You said he lied about his role in the Feegar Rebellion. Let's say he is innocent. Why on Earth would you, of all people, want to help Zenith Skytreg?"

Meena's voice came again: "I hate to be a pest, Rollie, but I really do need your opinion on something." Her tone sounded strained.

"Hold on," Rollie shouted. He turned back to Bertram, eyes narrowed. "Skytreg can hardly face an Underworld Tribunal if he's already serving in a blasted topside confinement, can he?"

Bertram blinked. "What Underworld Tribunal?"

Meena cut in again, "Is Mr. Ludlow available at all, then? Mr. Ludlow, perhaps you could just—"

Now Rollie's eyes appeared to flicker. "The Tribunal to set the record straight and prove before everyone in the Society that Zenith Skytreg violated Underworld Principles. The Tribunal that will strip Zenith-fragging-Skytreg of Official Leader of the Intergalactic Underworld once and for all. Sure, a mainstream confinement sentence gets him out of the way for a while, if that's your cheap, narrow little aim. But that's not how the Underworld operates. If Skytreg's to serve Justice, it's got to be Official Underworld Tribunal, all the wa—"

A burst of speed tossed Bertram back into his chair and flung Rollie onto salvage. Metal screeched on metal. Something toward the back of the stacks crashed. "Meena!" Rollie untangled his foot from one of the secured nets. "Blast it, Meena!" He separated from the net, but a second shift in direction jolted him into the cockpit doorway. "Meena, what the frag are you doing up here?"

"There's someone following us." As Bertram joined them, he saw Meena point to a monitor showing the aft of the ICV. "I wasn't sure about it at first, so I was forced to try some abrupt maneuvers. Terribly sorry."

Bertram peered over her shoulder to examine the screen more closely. He wasn't seeing anything. Just the standard pinprick star systems on a black field. "Well, they're not there now," he said.

"Oh no?" she asked. "Look again, Mr. Ludlow."

On more careful inspection, Bertram did see that to the back, left, in a general triangular-shaped pattern, there was a vague ripple in the fabric of space.

Meena nodded at his frown. "It's cloaked. But that doesn't mean you don't get a slight bending effect around the object, depending on what technology's being used."

"Holy Karnax, you remembered." Rollie squeezed her shoulder warmly. "The eyes are still keen."

"We were pursued often enough during our time together that it's reflex now." She pursed her lips in thought. "Which makes me wonder what, in your brief life after death, you've done to irritate someone."

He shrugged. "Nothing. I been keeping a low profile."

"So this is completely unrelated to, oh, Rordon Moonwax's ship then? And where Mr. Moonwax happens to be now?" The look was pointed.

"I told you. I did my best for Moonwax. His failed recon's nothing to do with me." He hooked a thumb at Bertram. "Maybe it's Ludlow. He's the big Uninet star these days. Could be the media. Or a crazed fan looking to steal something he sweat on."

Bertram wondered about the going rate for an item like that. He had a few things he could part with. "You think someone followed me from Beddsyde Manor?"

"It's not a law ship. You can tell by the shape."

"Either way," began Meena, "I would prefer not to have a scene on Hyphiz Epsilon, if at all possible. I'm still living down the fact I'd life-merged to a Deltan as it is." Her eyes lingered on the monitor. "I'd like to encourage our new friends on their way."

"Leave it to me," said Rollie. "Up." He waved her from the pilot seat, but she sat there looking torn. "Do you want to do this right or not?"

With a reluctant sigh, she moved to the copilot's chair and harnessed in, while he seized the ship's controls. "Hold on," Rollie said, and Bertram should have known to find secure seating quicker than he did.

As the ship shot into the void, Bertram grabbed one of the craft's built-in firehoses and lashed himself to the wall with it, like Jason prepping for his famed siren troubles, but without the stoic charm.

By the time he looked up from the mariner's knot—sufficient for the most crazed captaining, let alone some scaly songstress—what he saw made his skin grow cold. A fleet of over two hundred thick, squat ICVs and other weird apparatus sliced through the space before them like a school of off-the-map monstrosities.

Meena was already shrieking. "Oh, look out, look out, what is it?"

"Construction convoy," said Rollie.

"Well, go around! Around! It's called space for a reason, man!" If Meena's arm waving had been propulsion, they would have been a Quadrant away in no time.

But Rollie apparently had different thoughts on the matter. "Go round?" he mused quietly, a jagged smile creeping over his face. "Now why would I ever want to do that?"

Soon, yellow hooked vehicles whizzed past the side ports with inches to spare. Dirty orange metal walls ridged with enormous spiked pizza cutters rolled into and out of view, as the ship veered. One moment, the Astrocrat spiraled down and around the circumference of a blue drillbit the size of a skyscraper, to a dizzying display. The next, a sawtoothed metal bucket stretched over the ship's hull like a hungry Titan about to bite.

It seemed as if they'd never get into open space again, but when they did, Bertram realized he'd been holding his breath. "The other ship—is it gone?" he wheezed.

Meena glanced at the screen. "They're still there," she cried. "Altair's tarpits, how can they still be there?"

"Even though we're cloaked?" asked Bertram.

Rollie cut in, "No cloaking mechanism on Astrocrat models. And no external weaponry. As always, Ms. Tsoogarkken chose form over function."

"It's hardly my fault Astrocrat engineering doesn't serve the fast-paced needs of the modern Underworld."

"Could we make it look like we're going to the local law?" Bertram suggested. "See if they back off?"

"We could," said Rollie quietly. "But I got a better idea."

His idea came into view in the form of a large, swirling field around a single planet in an oncoming star system.

Meena recognized it instantly. "Treyfab-3?" she whispered.

"Treyfab-3." Rollie gave a slow nod.

She turned to him. "So will it be Bottoms-up or Thunderous Purkbeast of Pow?"

"I like both for this."

A crease appeared between her eyebrows. "Have you ever done both?"

Rollie released a lever. "Precedence is for the uncreative mind."

"But ..." Bertram craned his neck to be sure he was seeing the planet properly. "That's the Number Three Virus."

"Yes." Rollie's voice was a little too smooth, a little too pleased. "Yes, it is."

The planet was growing closer, its surrounding field a mesmerizing surge of movement.

"Just to confirm, it's the Number Three Virus that disintegrates whatever it touches," repeated Bertram.

"Tighten your harnesses, people," said Rollie. "This could get woozy." And the Astrocrat wove a winding path toward the atmosphere of Treyfab-3.

Meena was on monitor patrol. "They're following, Rollie, they're still following," she said.

Bertram could barely make out the shape of the cloaked ship, but the virus field—that swirling, roiling matter right before them—filled the front window like the largest, most totally non-mellow lava lamp. He wished someone was paying a little more attention to that.

"Well, lookit there," observed Rollie. "It's our friends from the media. No doubt they're panicking over the state of Treyfab-3's normally-thriving couture industry."

Bertram peered over Meena's chair to see a cluster of ships, emblazoned with Uninet channel names—*Shop-o-Drome Chic*, *Two-Headed Haberdashery* and *Astrotogs a la Mode*. The Astrocrat passed them on descent and for a moment, their tail followed suit. Then...

"They've stopped, Rollie," Meena announced breathlessly. "They've cut the engines. They've gone silent."

"About fraggin' time," said Rollie. His attention shifted to a single gauge. "And five... four... half-of-six..."

"Still silent."

"Two..."

The view was practically drowning in virus.

"One!" And with a blast and a shudder, alternate rockets powered up from the front of the craft, buoying the Astrocrat from the viral seas around Treyfab-3 and propelling it on a course straight for their triangular tagalong.

"Yeah, that's right, fellahs," Rollie shouted. "You wanted us, you got us!"

The cloaked vehicle initially didn't react as the Astrocrat cannonballed toward it. It was like an opossum realizing the dead act didn't cut it anymore and needing a moment to mourn the failure of evolutionary strategy.

By the time the pursuers' ship finally sprang to life again, the Astrocrat had closed the distance, bullying the cloaked craft forward and pressing it straight toward the cluster of media ICVs.

Meena's face was ghost white. "Tell me you know what you're doing."

"Absolutely," said Rollie. "Give or take."

"'Give or take?!'" Now Bertram could see the rippling mass clearly through their aft monitor, wavering in its own illusion. Then... BUMP! The Astrocrat rattled its pursuers' frame with a crunching impact.

"Oh, my insurance isn't going to like this at all," murmured Meena.

For only a fraction of a second, the cloaked ship flickered into view. But in that second, Bertram's memory captured the perfect image of a cockpit window and an orange flesh-and-furred alien face frozen in surprise behind it.

Rollie caught it, too. "Ha, how'd you like a dose of that, ya fuzzy slaggard?"

And then CRACK! Sandwiched between the Astrocrat and the media, bits of equipment fractured off the cloaked machine in a shower of shards that appeared from nowhere and spun off into space. A screeching, scraping sound reverberated around the hull.

Rollie laughed. "That should make the statement!" With a nod, he slammed down on a lever and the propulsion shimmied from fore to aft, blasting the Astrocrat from the scene and leaving them, for the first time in light years, company-free.

It was a few moments before Bertram felt secure enough to unstrap himself from the wall. He rubbed his hose-burned wrists and made a mental note to push back a few more of his tour reservations.

Meena unlatched her harness, crossed her legs and cleared her throat. "In case you had any delusions, Rollie," she began, "that was not how one tends to keep a low-profile."

"Oh, I got loads of delusions," he admitted. "But none about that, no."

"Good." She blew a stray wisp of hair from her face. "I must say, I am impressed at my little Astrocrat's performance. I've never even used those front rockets before."

"Yes, well, I believe in using all my rockets." He flashed her a grin. "If you recall."

She cleared her throat again. "Such a shame I'm going to have to get a new ICV. I imagine this one is hot now." She said hot like it actually was, and it scorched the roof of the mouth. "Thanks to your little brush with the media, I'll have to report this ship stolen, if I'm ever to show my face around Hyphiz Epsilon again."

Rollie nodded. "If I'm going to Vos Laegos, I'll need transport myself. Handy thing about being Underworld is, I happen to know just the fellah. Be there in a flash."

"Twinkly," she said and rose. "So it looks like we'll be parting ways sooner than originally expected, then."

"Why not?" He fiddled with some dials. "Stick to what you're good at, I always say."

"And here I thought 'precedence was for the uncreative mind.'" Meena shot him an arch look and paused in the doorway. "My offer is, of course, still open to you, Mr. Ludlow, if you're willing to help me unpack the ship. Afterwards, you should have no trouble hiring an ICV from Hyphiz Epsilon to wherever your holiday plans take you."

"Er, thanks," said Bertram. "I'll think about it." But Bertram had been thinking harder about that bag of currency of his from Beddsyde Manor and what it might do to secure himself a nice touring model of his own. Maybe a sturdy craft, gently launched by some little old lifeform from Ursa Minor, barely flown to the Shop-o-Drome once a week. And like he'd said before, all he'd need was a pilot to show him the ropes.

14

**That's right! You've finally reached
Zonky Zeg's Previously-Launched ICVs and
Aromatherapy Supply
"That smells like stellar savings!"**

This was the glowing sign bobbing merrily off of the space station platform. To Bertram, the place looked like the GCU's largest aircraft carrier, a seemingly-endless surface covered in rows of spaceships and on-planet hovercrafts, all nestled in its own atmosphere. In the center of this landmass of launchables was a small, square structure labeled, "Office." Rollie settled the Astrocrat down in one of the station's free spaces, and the trio made their way toward the tiny building.

But before they could pass through the door, a voice behind them said, "Welcome to Zonky Zeg's! What brings y'all here today? Looking for a quality pre-launched ICV? A runabout? Maybe a sleek little hovercraft to take the progeny to kachunkettball practice?"

Bertram turned to see a creature built much like a fireplug, if fireplugs were muscular and covered in gray and white shaggy hair. The main feature on the creature's face was a nose:

prominent, round and fleshy-brown. The eyes above it, while small, were equally brown and so soulful, Bertram was overcome with a wave of instant trust for the stranger. The guy's nametag read, "Zeg."

"Ideally," began Rollie, "I'd like something in a Protostar 340-K. But with only a few of 'em left unfragged, I recognize that is likely a non-option."

At the sound of his voice, the salesman gave a jolt and began to sniff the air around them with vigor. "Why, crumblin' craters, if it isn't my good ol' pal, Rollie Tsmorlood!" Zeg reached out, snatched up Rollie's hand and sniffed it in a long series of snuffling huffs. Then he gave him a friendly slap on the back. "What in the GCU have you been up to these past light years?"

"Confinement. Larceny. Abduction. Exile. Same old thing. You?"

"Well, smell it for yourself, my friend," he said, gesturing to the lot around him. "Zonky Zeg's has become the Quad One's premiere station for reliable, previously-launched ICVs. We've been busier than a Klaxon bee in a bed of hyperpollen blossoms. Had to open two more stations a few systems over. Leaving the Underworld for a topside career was the best thing I ever did."

"It does appear you have a nose for this sort of business," agreed Rollie.

"And who've you got there with you?" asked Zeg, nudging him. "How I love the sweet scent of company!"

Rollie gave a laughing nod. "Zeg, meet Meena Tsoogarkken and—"

"Meena?" gasped Zeg, grabbing up her hand and leaving no spot unsnuffled. "*The* Meena? Why, frag it, I've heard so much about you, darlin'. You two life-merged again?"

"Erm, no, Mr. Zeg," said Meena, extracting her hand, "as charming as that sounds. Rollie had simply suggested you were the go-to man for a good trade-in."

"And maybe also extend a bit o' credit to an old mate who happens to be between ICVs at the moment?" added Rollie.

"Well, now, that all depends," said Zeg, rubbing his chin. "I don't mean to be impolite, but that trade-in doesn't happen to be ... stolen ... does it?" Zeg put up a shaggy hand. "I'm not accusing, I'm just saying that Zeg may be zonky, but I run a clean business. I don't do stolen merchandise these days. It's not what Zonky Zeg stands for. I've left the Underworld behind for good."

"The vehicle is mine, Mr. Zeg," said Meena. "Financially free and clear."

"Uh-huh. Then why," asked Zeg, "do you smell so nervous?"

Meena's face drained of the little color it had.

"Come into my office," he said and motioned them into the lot's central shack.

Inside, the lights were dim, and the air was heavy with mixed perfumes. On one wall were dozens of small bottles with labels reading things like, "Solar Flare," "Blumdec Surf" and "Vos Laegon Good Times."

Rollie squinted at the shelves. "Picked up a bit of a side business, did you?"

"Well, I don't mind saying I was pretty twitchy by the time I left the Underworld. Always checking the winds to make sure no one was chasing my tail. But the scents therapy, it helped. Blocked out some of the stimuli. So I started making my own, thinking it would be handy to have something available to customers in that new ICV smell. The rest fell into place from there." He motioned them into the chairs before his desk and took a seat himself. "But enough about me. What's really going on here?"

Bertram and Meena both looked at Rollie.

"Someone was chasing our tails," said Rollie at last. "Got a glimpse of one of 'em. Looked Tangtapien to me, but it was only a flash."

Zeg let out a short, rough chuckle. "So who is it you've scorched this time?"

Rollie shrugged a shoulder. "Fragged if I know. Seems unlikely. I been out of circ."

"Our dilemma is this, Mr. Zeg," said Meena. "I have already experienced my fill of the maniacal whimsy that is daily life with Captain Tsmorlood. Yet, it is my ship that seems to be the target of unwanted attention. So I would like to exchange my Astrocrat for something tasteful and unobtrusive."

"It'd be my supreme pleasure to help you," said Zeg, taking her hand and sniffing it cordially.

"Then if our mutual friend Captain Tsmorlood could get a loan on something grubby and horrid you'd rather weren't on your lot anyway, we can all go our separate—"

"And this is where it gets supremely unpleasant."

Rollie rolled his eyes. "Let me guess. You're running a clean business here. You don't extend credit to the Underworld Society these days. How would it look on your books? How would it—"

"I have cash," said Bertram.

All heads swung his direction.

"I've got…" Bertram withdrew his bag of varied currencies. "This." He poured it across the desk. Some of it rolled. Some clattered. Some crunched under the weight of other currency.

Zeg reacted instantly to the sound. He took a long deep whiff of the items on the table. "Well!" He cleared his throat, "now that's a zakari of a different color. Why didn't you say so? I might be able to find something for you with that." Zeg reached out for a handful, but Rollie clamped a scarred hand over the man's mitt.

"Wait." Rollie turned to Bertram. He gestured to the money, suspicion on his face. "What's all this about?"

"Interview fees," shrugged Bertram, "sponsorship rights, that kind of thing."

"Do you even know how much this is? There must be," he sized up the pile of various currencies, "a couple hundred thousand yoonies here."

Bertram nodded. "I did make a killing on those souvenir retinal scan permissions."

Rollie folded his arms. "And just how does your mass o' money connect to my transportation issues?"

"Here's my offer," said Bertram. "I buy the ship. You fly it. We go to Vos Laegos and find out what we can on the Skytreg situation. Along the way, between the lifeforms trying to kill us and whatever else crops up, you teach me how to fly. And maybe we hit a few tourist attractions."

Rollie blinked. "This is Tryfe humor, innit? I always felt I missed something in Tryfe humor."

"Look, you have your goals, I have mine. Yours includes taking down the single most powerful person in the Intergalactic Underworld. Mine happens to involve nebula and giant livestock made of toenails. But," he said, "throw in a few Vos Laegon buffets and I'm flexible."

"And you trust me to keep such an agreement?" Rollie's smile was astonished.

"Not particularly," said Bertram. "But at least it's never boring. I figure I'd be ahead on the entertainment value alone."

Rollie turned to Zeg. "This." He pushed a quarter of the currency across the table to the man with the nose. "This is what you have to work with. No more, no less. Ludlow? Put the rest away. Now."

Bertram began to slide it back into its bag.

"Well, that sounds settled, then," said Meena, looping an arm through Zeg's. "Mr. Zeg, could you show me something in a nice Cosmolux model, perhaps? Maybe a Comet 1270? Oh, and I should mention, I'll need help transferring just a *few* things to my new ship."

Should've upped the budget, thought Bertram, as he surveyed his brand new, previously-launched Penumbra Classic 199-SB interplanetary cruise vessel. Some of the built-in cabinets were chipped, and the cabinet doors hung loose on their hinges. The furniture of the ship's central lounge looked like it was soaked in a residue made of spacetime and dried-on cola. A few console knobs were missing. And then there was that green stain on the floor. It might have been spilled soup or a fragged passenger; Bertram would take no bets on which. In fact, the whole thing was a far cry from the ship of his daydreams. Still, it wasn't every day that a guy from Tryfe—er, Earth—got his very own spaceship, and a sense of pride buoyed his mood.

"So it needs a little elbow grease," admitted Bertram. "Maybe a good disinfectant. But hey, at least it's probably almost too clean for anyone to buzz Health and Humanoid Services on us. So that's cool." He ducked in to check out the ship's onboard restroom and hopped out again. "Rollie, are there slugs in the GCU?"

"Plugs?" came the voice from the cockpit. "Saw a few power ports, yeah. Why?"

"Never mind." Bertram made a note to grab a container of salt at the next stop, though he wondered if that might not just make them angry. "Let's see if the holovision works." He pushed a button and dodged out of the way as holographic heads projected into the room. They faced vertically. Bertram banged on the holovision, then tilted his head to the side to see a trio of double-skulled, lavishly-dressed and hatted talk show hosts, gathered before their own holoscreen.

"—Now what we're seeing here in this exclusive footage, caught by the *Two-Headed Haberdashery* cameras, is a rippling, triangulate mass believed to be a cloaked ICV, possibly from the Scalene Corporation," a lifeform in green told the studio audience. "Moments before, this vehicle dove straight towards the viral surface around Treyfab-3 in pursuit of the Astrocrat model you see there on the left." She pointed it out. "Now here's where you can see how the cloaked ship is being pushed by the Astrocrat."

On the footage, someone shouted, "Crumblin' craters, it's coming right at us!"

Bertram could hear one of the on-ship reporters screeching to their pilot. "Move, move, move!" But it was already too late. The sound of the cloaked vehicle's impact shook their sound equipment, causing a high-pitched squeal. The studio audience squealed, too, and clamped hands to ears, if they had either. Then the broadcast cut from the screen.

The crowd murmured with excitement.

"I understand," continued the being in green, "that the Treyfab System's law enforcement are trying to identify and track down both ships now. I also understand that the trauma of the event has inspired you, Sheeshee, to create a very special hat commemorating it?"

"Yes, that's right, Veratna," said Sheeshee holding up a hat only slightly smaller than the Stanley Cup. "I call this style 'Hot Headed,' and its design revolves around three shapes that symbolize ships locked in commuter conflict and—"

Bertram flipped off the holovision as Rollie thudded in. "Hey, uh, Meena will be okay, won't she? Y'know, if the law shows up at her door wanting to know about the Astrocrat?"

Rollie laughed. "Aw, she's resourceful, that one. I imagine Meena's already filed a theft report and convinced half her neighbors and their Simmis to help move her new art supplies." A loose ceiling light fixture had caught his attention, and he stretched to fiddle with the wiring. "Yup, no worries there, Ludlow. Meena'll be all right."

Bertram didn't question the lady's competence but neither did he quite share Rollie's confidence. "And you trust Zonky Zeg not to say anything about the sale?" There was just something about trusting the guy instantly that made Bertram not trust the guy.

The light went on, then off again. "Trust Zeg? Why, he's practically my brother!" Rollie said warmly. "A genetically-dissimilar brother, o' course. Who's on the hairy side and has uncanny olfactory senses. But other than that, we're virtually from the same litter." He pulled an ancient-looking handlaser from a pocket at his thigh. It still had a Liddlebiggs' pricetag on it. He powered it up.

Bertram watched as he adjusted the settings. "Hyphiz Deltans do litters?"

"Nah." Rollie directed the laser on the wire until it sparked, then smoked. He tacked the wire to something, then waggled it around again.

First the light fixture flickered, then it stayed on.

Bertram gave an impromptu cheer, and Rollie grinned in the golden illumination.

"You haven't ever used that thing on, say ... household pests?" Bertram asked hopefully.

The light went out.

"Never mind," he said. "I'll deal with it. You're, um, busy."

15

They were in the waiting room, lined up in the hall, winding into the break room and clogging the foyer. It reminded MesoCommander Waranda Blyte of that time she waited in line for Dumbbell Nebula's "Resentment, What Resentment?" Return of the Reunion Re-Reconciliation tour. Only with more affordable snacks, fewer souvenir novelty noses and—here was the kicker—all these people were here to see her.

She hadn't anticipated, when she'd called in experts in the field of matter transference technology, that there would be so many of them with so much to say. Particularly since, up until the ransom vanished, the field was largely theoretical.

"Oh, we were getting close," mused Professor Warptoler. (Or was it Professor Flysputter? They were starting to blur together.) "We knew that someday soon lifeforms would have the ability to beam down from ships onto a planet's surface. Soon ICV travel would be completely unnecessary. Soon we could get food delivered without sending it via some kid who gets lost for two hours on the Mig Verlig Expressway."

Blyte had heard it all before. "So if you had to guess, which of your colleagues would you say invented the beam?"

The scientist laughed. "Those hacks? Most of them wouldn't know a photon from a family photo." The man's blue face turned deeper blue. "If anyone's having any breakthroughs, it'll be our research group, that much I know. We once beamed the atoms of a purebred zakari from one end of the room to the other."

"Really?" She made a note; this was the stuff she'd been hoping to hear.

"Not all at once," admitted the professor, "and reassembly, well…" He waved his hand in a teeter-totter motion. "As I said, true beaming is only a matter of time."

"So if I asked you whether it was possible that the ransom money was using some kind of matter transfer technology, you would say…?"

"Media spin. Not a hailstone's chance on Altair."

Of course, when she pressed the man on alternate ways the ransom might have vanished from under the watchful eye of hundreds of media cameras, the scientist was somewhat less forthcoming. He mumbled about optical illusions, grumbled about intradimensional portals and alternate universes and actually dredged up something about group hallucinations. Ultimately her questions sent him steaming off in a cloud of hauteur and warm mootaab tweed.

R.G. Middly was almost knocked over by the departing scientist in the doorway. "Er, should I send in the next expert, M.C. Blyte?" the young man asked. He shot a worried glance down the hall and lowered his voice. "They're getting restless out there. They've started passing the time by playing Name That Theoretical Fallacy, and things are getting nasty."

"Separate them into Entanglement Theorists and Sub Zero Matter Theorists. That should hold them for a while. At least until they get beyond the small talk."

Middly made a note of it. "So no leads yet?" he asked.

"Patience, Middly. Someone knows something. We just haven't snagged the right someone yet. How's the search team doing?"

"We've scoured Skytreg's compound, his summer home, winter home, off-season-but-makes-a-nice-change home, his casinos, his office in Underworld headquarters, his secret snack drawer and the local LibLounge he goes to for spontaneous PR appearances, twice every week at noon."

"And?"

"Skytreg loves his junk food. He's got Smorgs stashed all over the place. You wouldn't know it to look at him, would you?"

"I meant any evidence."

"Nothing yet. But our tech guys are still going over his computer systems."

"And where are we with Skytreg's own tech staff?"

"We've grilled them. Then broiled and flambéed."

"Well done," she said. "Anything suspicious?"

"Everything's suspicious!" erupted Middly, looking a little surprised at how loud it came out. "Just nothing that helps us find the number three, ma'am."

"Well, Skytreg is the Official Leader of the Intergalactic Underworld," she reminded him. "He gets paid for that sort of thing. Follow up what you can."

R.G. Middly nodded. "You'd also asked us to check out any previously unsolved crimes that might have used beaming technology."

"That's right. This stuff didn't come out of nowhere. Clearly, it took time to develop. And anyone with that kind of power would have been dying for a few dry runs," she said. "Did you uncover something?"

"Possibly. I've got information on two instances in Quad One that fit the criteria. They were minor robberies, high security, but with no signs of forced entry. In both cases, the law there was stumped. Here's the brief." He put an infopill on her desk.

"Stellar. I'll digest that with lunch," she said.

"And one last thing. I don't know if you're aware, ma'am, but Skytreg may be enjoying the attention from this case somewhat more than you'd like." There was a hesitation in Middly's voice now.

"As in…?"

"He's writing a musical about it," he said.

A pang of fear shot through her. "Dinner theater?"

"No, stage production."

The pang subsided. "Then what's the trouble?"

"It's just that Skytreg is strangely charismatic, ma'am. Even with the vocal projection diffuser, he seems to be drawing people in. Members of the staff ... you know, RightGuides. I don't want to name names, but some of the RightGuides are walking around practicing supporting parts in his production. Minor solos, even."

"Oh, are they?" Blyte leaned back in her chair. So that was Skytreg's game—a nefarious combination of bribery, up-tempo ensemble cast numbers and Vos Laegon pheromones. She would have to see what could be done about that.

"I don't want to name names," Middly repeated and with one glance at her expression he said, "I'll write them down. And, um, if you happen to notice my name on that list, ma'am?" He tugged at his collar. "Please know, I only included it for full disclosure. It was just a few bars, ma'am, not even a refrain. I swear. I heard one of the numbers in passing, and it was so catchy ... so melodic ... I—"

"It's okay Middly, deep breaths," she said, and Blyte swore she saw him relax by at least two internal stress settings. "What's the theme of this play, anyway?"

"From what I understand, it's all about an innocent innovator in the Underworld who's charged erroneously with orchestrating the most dramatic crime in Universal history, simply because he's the only one talented enough to have come up with it."

"Subtle," she said. "And you know what I think, Middly?" She smiled. "I think it's a cry for help. I think he's just waiting to tell the GCU what he's done. I think he's purposefully holding onto three because the longer he draws it out and the more inconvenienced the entire universe is, the more grateful everyone will be to have it back. And if he thinks he can somehow swing being a martyred hero, too? Well, all the better."

R.G. Middly raised an eyebrow.

"I think it's time Mr. Skytreg had a roommate, Middly. Let's see who we can find. I want it to be an extra special one."

16

"You're a sight, you are," chuckled Rollie, staring across the table at Bertram as he scooted into the booth's seat.

"What?" Bertram followed Rollie's gaze to his new souvenir hooded jacket that read, "I'm Off My Orbit for the Lunch-n-Launch" and smoothed its logo. "Their store had it on discount," he explained, swinging a thumb that direction, "along with the boots."

He held up a leg, revealing his very first pair of levitating space boots. They were in the diner's official colors. "It's a knockoff of the knockoff hoverboots everybody's fighting over these days. Fifteen yoonies! You can't beat a deal like that."

The Popeelie sandals he'd been wearing for months now were comfortable but drafty. And unlike the sandals, the boots had jet propulsion capabilities for those weary walking days. He was still working on his technique. The ride was unsteady, but he felt sure he'd master it quickly. "Hey, you want a pair? My treat."

The alien just laughed. He turned his gaze to the flashing lights outside the free-floating, iconic eatery, then returned to the inventory of weaponry he had sprawled across the table. Only two of the objects looked like they'd been professionally manufactured and those, only within the last century. Most of the other items looked handmade and cobbled together from materials that might have been parts of his former Altairan neighbors. Rollie was apparently trying to get organized. He was winding up a rope attached to a hook made of carved organic something, when the Simulant waitress whisked table-side, brandishing a tray. "Okay, who's got the Gastronomical Event Platter?"

"Me," said Bertram, raising a hand as she settled a huge disc of fascinating foods before him. According to the menu, the Gastronomical Event was "loaded with an assortment of the solar system's biggest breakfast classics." Which, barring further explanation, appeared to be smooth pools of Blue, Purple, Gray, Brown, Browner, Yellow and Aqua, each the general consistency of grits. The plate was the size of a kachunkettball field.

The waitress turned to the Hyphiz Deltan. "And you must have the Number Two-Plus-One special."

"Thanks," said Rollie, moving a dagger and some kind of cosh, so she could put down the plate.

"Isn't this amazing?" said Bertram, spooning in a bite of the Blue. "I feel like a new man. Here I am, in an interstellar diner having an interstellar breakfast on an interstellar roadtrip to clear and smear the Underworld's biggest name." He took a sip of his beverage. It tasted like fizzy murk, but he didn't care. It was interstellar fizzy murk, and Bertram was alive to enjoy not enjoying it.

Rollie's orange eyes glinted like the blade of the dagger by his plate. "You're not going to be like this the whole trip, are you? I am armed."

"Aw, come on. You nearly died, too. Doesn't it give you a sense of perspective? Doesn't it make you want to savor every moment you have?" He spooned in some Purple. The flavor was sweet, earthy and wholly unexpected.

Rollie gave a sniff. "Ludlow, I've nearly died a hundred times to-date. Likely to do so a hundred more, before all's said and done. If I got powered up on life every time I didn't get fragged, I'd get nothing else accomplished."

Bertram admitted he was still new to this whole intermittent peril thing and saw how even the high of not getting dusted might lose its zing after a while. "Which reminds me... how far are we from Vos Laegos?"

"Not far now. And you'll be launched about this visit, Ludlow," said Rollie, grabbing a brimming glass of something topped with fog. He smiled over the mist. "We're going on a tour."

Bertram looked from Rollie to the dagger, grappling hook and cosh, then back again. "It's not a tour of duty, is it?"

"I think you'll just have to wait and see." The jagged smile widened across his lips. "Surprise is half the fun."

Bertram wasn't so sure about that. He *was* sure about Aqua, though. It was a savory flavor with just a hint of muskiness. "This. I would definitely order this again."

"Interesting." Rollie clunked the glass to the table and wiped his mouth. "Pureed meznat entrails. Usually an acquired taste. You're adventurous, Ludlow."

"Um, yeah," said Bertram, infusing his voice with as much enthusiasm as he could. "I just love the smell of entrails in the morning." He clicked on their booth's private holovision and turned his focus to the *Heavy Meddler* news, so the Aqua would continue on its one-way downward course. It seemed smart to not overthink breakfast.

Newscaster Qwerty Zaqwer, Bertram noticed, was back in the studio or perhaps had never left. "With the Farthest Reaches Cosmos Corral out of commission, GCU commuters are experiencing massive challenges," the newscaster was saying. "ICV taxi services are facing an unprecedented backlog of trip requests, leaving many travelers stranded for days. In a wry contrast, the Number Three Virus has been a boon to personal ICV sales, which manufacturers estimate have increased a thousand-fold since the virus' appearance. Tutorial infopills on intergalactic piloting have flown off of LibLounge shelves, but with the main supplier trapped behind the Quad Three field, customers now scramble to find any pills on this and other topics. Accredited flight schools in most systems are packed to capacity. Major cities are in gridlock, as more lifeforms take to the air. Law enforcement officers report an overwhelming number of accidents involving unlicensed ICV pilots. Illegal parking is also widespread, as the number of ships exceed legal touchdown spots."

They cut to a second newscaster, one that appeared to be a head in a jar. "Consumer experts say this gridlock has grown because of another facet of the Number Three Virus," the head said. "With Uninet delivery sites almost completely crippled, many lifeforms are forced to make their purchases in person for the first time in their lives. Shop-o-Dromes across the GCU have found themselves crushed by crowds of confused shoppers. So savvy vendors have responded with free instructional sessions on how to find, select and pay for items in a non-virtual setting.

"They've also developed a tracking service to trace lost shoppers and match them with their parked ICVs. If you are trapped in a Shop-o-Drome, or have a loved one who may be lost there, please vis-u 249-HEY-WHERE-WE-AT for support."

"Coming up after the commercial break," continued Qwerty, "the Coalition of Planets applies to the GCU's Most Elevated Court for a Jurisdictional Override in the Zenith Skytreg numeroterrorism case. Will Skytreg be leaving Vos Laegos... in Klinko portable confinement techn—"

Rollie's vocabulary blazed up, forming a wall of ferocity, fragging and flame. Diners' heads swiveled their way.

"Hey, easy," said Bertram, "what's the problem?"

"Weren't you blasted listening?" Rollie had risen and was slinging on his coat. "The Coalition of Planets wants to bump the Skytreg case from local Vos Laegos to centralized GCU."

"So they take over the case." Bertram shrugged. "I don't see the big deal. It makes sense. They're already working on the ransom situation."

Rollie leaned hard on the table. "The deal, Ludlow, is the whole initiative will be up to its eye sockets in bureaucracy, security and ... what the frag's the name of it? That sticky, stringy stuff that prevents someone like me from getting anything useful done."

"Red tape," Bertram suggested.

"BurgleBGone." Rollie started stuffing the knife, hook, cosh and other items into his pockets. "Popeelies make it. I think they use it to keep the Coalition out of *their* financial files." He knocked back the last of his beverage and clunked the glass to the table. "If we want any sort of Justice, we got to go. Now." With a sweep of his coat, he was headed for the door.

Bertram hurriedly stuffed in a bite of the Browner (it was just as well he didn't spend time on that one) and leapt up to follow.

"Sir," said the waitress, catching him mid-stride, "your bill?"

"Oh." Bertram dipped into his bag of cash and tucked into her palm what looked like a reasonable amount of money, plus tip. "Thanks a lot. Great breakfast!"

"Glad you enjoyed it," she said, and leaned in closer, "Um, I hate to bother you, but aren't you Bertram Ludlow from *There Goes the Galaxy?*"

Bertram smiled, dropping a few coins more into her apron pocket and pressed a finger to his lips. "Shhh," he said and dashed out the door.

Bertram couldn't say the *Heavy Meddler* didn't warn them. Vos Laegos City was so packed with shiny new ICVs, they had to park the Penumbra on the edge of the desert just to find an open spot. It took a few shuttles and a good hike before they arrived at their destination—a large block structure, surrounded by silver gates that groped the sky. It looked like Heaven, if Heaven had been constructed by a megalomaniac militant with a tendency toward paranoia and flair for interstellar art deco.

Out front, a crowd of mixed species had assembled, some of them shouting, others doing an electronic-sign-plus-shouting combo maneuver. Both effective.

"Free the Three!" one of the signboards read.

And "THIS is the Only Number We Need!" proclaimed another. It showed Skytreg's holo-mugshot, bearing his prisoner number.

Rollie motioned Bertram through the demonstration and stopped at a ticket booth. "Two for the Zenith Skytreg Underworld Extravaganza Tour," the Hyphizite said, and the booing behind them had some real zip.

"Traitors!" someone shouted.

"Don't support the Skytreg brand!" screamed someone else.

"Having three quadrants is mathematically awkward!" shrieked another.

And this launched the group into a rousing chorus of "Free the Three! Free the Three!"

The ticket seller, who was behind bars, shatterproof glass and wore riot gear with a friendly built-in nametag said, "The morning tour just started a moment ago. But if you head right this way, you can still catch them." And she pointed through a gate on the right that was manned by several armed guards, each the size of your average hovercraft.

Bertram and Rollie entered Skytreg's inner sanctum to the rhythm of crowd agitation, but the sound was soon replaced by an upbeat selection of piped-in tunes from Zenith Skytreg's old Vos Laegos lounge act.

The ticket seller had been right about one thing: the tour group hadn't gotten far. And from the looks of it, Skyreg's arrest had only fanned the interest for a certain sector of the populace. A parade of voyeurs stood before them, sucking in every detail. "… And this is Mr. Skytreg's visitors' lounge, where he's welcomed both important members of the Underworld and mainstream business," an unseen tour guide said from somewhere up front. "Eudicot T'murp has waited here. This is also where the infamous smuggler Laefos Maddagoria was tracked down and fragged by local law, right in that chair there. Take a moment and touch it, if you like. We steam clean for your sanitary convenience."

The group jostled to take advantage of this unexpected tour amenity.

Rollie snickered and nudged Bertram forward. "Go on, then, Ludlow. Don't hold back on my account."

But Bertram stayed firm. "Why are we here?" he whispered. "Seriously? How does knowing Zenith Skytreg's taste in home decor even remotely help you prove his innocence?"

"I'm afraid I don't know what you mean," said Rollie, picking up a small bowl from a nearby table and examining it. "Said I'd show you the hot spots of the GCU, didn't I?" He turned the bowl over and pretended to be fascinated by its manufacturer's mark.

Bertram snatched the thing from his hand. "Try again, Tsmorlood. I wasn't abducted yesterday." He slung the bowl back onto the table. "Why are we here?"

Ahead, the tour guide clapped for attention. "All right now! If you all will just follow me through this door into our next room, I'll tell you a little bit about Mr. Skytreg's dual purpose conference facilities and steam room."

They moved on, through meeting rooms and game rooms, employee quarters and elevators. They dished on Skytreg's kitchen cupboards—"Did you notice all the Smorgs and Sleemy Snaps?"—they dug into his views on garden spaces and they took a whirl around his grand ballroom. They tucked into Zenith Skytreg's major master bedroom, the minor master bedroom and the G-minor minor master bedroom, which had an in-house live band that woke up and started playing covers of Skytreg's former nightclub act whenever someone opened the door.

It was just about the time Bertram's attention span and legs were weary that he realized they'd looped back around to the front entrance. "... And that concludes our examination of one of the Underworld's most glamorous and controversial landmarks," said the guide. "Now, before we go, can I answer any last questions?"

"Where's Zenith Skytreg's Private Collection Room?" asked one lifeform at the front.

"Yeah!" said someone else. "We wanted to see where the ransom was found!"

The chorus of agreement wasn't quite on the Mormon Tabernacle scale, but it definitely had several part harmony and some oomph.

"Ah, I am sorry. That room was only available on our extra-special, twice-a-year 'Way, Way Under, So Totally Under, If You Were Any More Under You'd Be In the Planet's Core' Underworld Tour," the guide said.

Bertram could finally see the guy. His smile was a gleaming shield against thrown epithets and the flames of misdirected anger. "The room is also temporarily closed, due to the ongoing RightGuide investigation."

Here the chorus did their impression of a large backed-up garbage disposal.

"However," continued the guide, knowing the mathematical equation that said disappointment is inversely proportional to tips, "there is still one stellar room you haven't seen yet..."

The garbage disposal gave way to a curious dishwasher.

"If I can just direct your attention to your left, you'll see our Official Underworld Headquarters gift shop. There we have a variety of supernova souvenirs, including our exciting new confinement theme t-shirts and ICV stickers, authorized by Zenith Skytreg himself. Yes, folks, he's still held onto that strong Underworld sense of humor and I'm sure he'll be back with us in no time, a blanked man."

There was still some grumbling, but now the group was giftshop-bound, resolute in its quest for solace through polymer-based products bearing Underworld logos.

Bertram headed forward, too, drawn by the kitsch potential of confinement-themed merchandise.

Then he realized Rollie was not with him. He turned in time to sense that someone tall and purposeful had just swept around the corner.

He caught up with the man one hall away. "What are you doing?" he hissed. "This is Underworld HQ. You can't just go wandering around Underworld HQ. Isn't there security?"

Rollie consulted the tour map. "Didn't you know? In the Underworld, we like to leave things completely open and unmanned. In case the law wants to pop round and borrow some hot weaponry…cup of glucose…"

Bertram blinked. It was so hard to know what made logical sarcasm for the GCU.

"Of *course* there's security." Rollie tapped the map four times and the basement, first, second, and third floors peeled away. "We weren't on that tour to study Skytreg's taste in fraggin' knicknacks, you know."

"You're more of a minimalist, anyway."

"There's five guards, right now, stationed at key points throughout the compound. Native Vos Laegons. Nasty slaggards, but no mobile patrols, so that's in our favor. Still, overconfidence *is* the Maternal Archetype of the fragged man. So we'll want to keep our eyes peeled at all times." On the fourth-floor map, he traced a finger to the Private Collections Room and it highlighted on the brochure. "Ah!" He looked up and pointed ahead. "This way."

Bertram followed. "What about security cameras?"

"Twenty of those, at minimum. One there." He pointed to something in the crown molding that looked like a one-eyed bird. "Smile pretty."

Bertram cursed and pulled up the hood on his Lunch-n-Launch jacket. "Don't guards man the cameras?"

"Absolutely. Right now we're lost tourists, separated from our group, but that won't play for long." Rollie elbowed Bertram convivially. "Stellar lost and confused face, by the way."

"It's my real face," said Bertram. "Rollie, I don't get it. The RightGuides have already been all over the Collections Room. What do you expect to find?"

But Rollie didn't answer; he just stepped into the elevator, a richly-crafted tube of lush carpeting and gleaming silver. As Bertram joined him and the doors closed, he noticed the tiny room was covered in bas relief scenes. Most of it was done in a metal, but the central figure in each scene was completed in white pearl. One panel showed a figure standing center stage of the Crater Club's auditorium to an enraptured crowd. One depicted the figure posed with a very large handlaser, pulling a small, furred creature from an explosion while hover tanks and razor-toothed savages pursued them. In the last panel, the figure sat enthroned, surrounded by hundreds of progeny— Bibluciats, Bertram guessed, from the way they half-blended into the background—looking upon him with dozens of adoring eyes. Two kids held a banner over the scene that read, "Our Savior, Our Hero, Our Thanks."

Bertram didn't think the figure looked much like Zenith Skytreg. The sculpture Skytreg was better looking, his eyes more widely spaced, his large jaw more finely balanced. His hair, however, that was the same perfect ski-jump sweep Bertram remembered from back on Skorbig.

The elevator glided to a halt, and the doors peeled open. Rollie was already down the hallway and approaching the last door on the left, a room plastered with so many banners it looked like the world's worst—or possibly best—party was taking place.

"CRIME SCENE! DO NOT ENTER!"

"HEY, WE MEAN IT."

"SERIOUSLY NOW, TRESPASSERS WILL BE PROSECUTED."

"AND/OR ALTERNATE OPTIONS, TBD."

In the door's frame, a retinal ID system glinted tauntingly.

"Aw, wouldn't you know it?" groaned Bertram. "And us all out of approved retinas."

"I did, actually," said Rollie. "Know it, I mean." From a pocket, he withdrew one of the old manufactured objects Bertram had noticed earlier. It was shaped like half a grapefruit. Rollie clamped it over the scanner. "They showed this fragging hallway all over Uninet news, didn't they?"

"Well, yes, I suppose, I—"

"Got to pay attention to the details, Ludlow. Got to prepare accordingly. There's always a work-around if you know where to find it." He pressed a button and the little machine began to hum, its lights sequencing slowly at first and gradually picking up speed.

"Where *did* you find it?" Bertram had been almost a hundred percent sure the guy hadn't bought anything at the Lunch-and-Launch or at Zeg's. And then he realized…

"Liddlebiggs'," Rollie said. "Had loads of 'em there in a barrel. Early version retinal scan variant replicator. Needed a bit of work. But I try to always have one round. Never know when it'll come in handy."

Bertram nodded, content with watching the lights run back and forth, until he heard a whistling, rolling sound. It was the sound of the elevator being summoned from another floor. "Looks like we might not have much time."

BOMP! That was the grapefruit, adding to the discussion.

Bertram drew closer. "That's not an 'I'm done, everything's awesome' noise, is it?"

Rollie growled, peeling the device off the door. He pushed a button and a small touch screen popped out. "System's not recognizing the default retina's species."

"Because you got it from a barrel."

"Because it was set to Suidae Verrucan and our tourguide was what? From Breen, maybe?" Rollie said, scowling. "Never mind, if I set it to native Vos Laegon, it should find a match. Eventually."

"Eventually? Shit!" He could hear the elevator whistling merrily along. The question was: to what floor?

On impulse, he seized a mirror off a nearby wall and ran down the hall to the shaft. He tuned into the mechanisms whispering behind those grand silver doors and stood in wait for their next guest, mirror at the ready.

Even from his spot, Bertram could see Rollie punch a million characters into the touch screen, before the screen retracted and Rollie slapped grapefruit-to-door once more. For a second time, the gadget's lights danced.

The elevator whistle had stopped. Bertram could hear voices—something about big evening plans involving a passionate night of Vos Laegon mating rituals—from one floor below. The sweat from Bertram's palms smeared the mirror frame and made him shift his grip.

Then, TWEEEEEEEE, the elevator started up again.

Bertram cursed to himself, taking turns wiping each hand on his Beddsyde Manor t-shirt and readying his resolve. He wasn't sure when he'd stopped questioning the morality of acts like burglary, or how exactly assault had become just another way to pass the time between breakfast and his next sightseeing opportunity. He thought it had something to do with the company he kept. He admitted, he had gotten in with a shifty crowd. This was a lot easier to do in the GCU than back in Pittsburgh. At least in the Burgh, the criminal element didn't hold annual meetings.

Then...

"Stellar!" The door clicked open, Rollie wrenched the grapefruit off the keypad, and he climbed through the RightGuides' posted warnings. The time was certainly right. The elevator's whistle was loud now, and Bertram dashed to the empty hooks, slung the mirror onto it and dodged into the Collections Room just as the elevator banked on Floor Four.

There's an age-old Earth saying about how when one door closes, another one opens again. It was true in this case, too, but Bertram was pretty sure the proverb hadn't meant to cover breaking and entering.

"Crap, what if they come in here?" Bertram whispered, heart in his trachea, eye on the door behind him.

"Then I suggest you use your weapon of choice," chuckled Rollie.

Bertram wondered what that meant, until he turned and promptly leapt out of his skin. It was another mirror, all right— free-standing, full-length and twice as elegant as the one in the hall. But this one had startling bonus capabilities. Instead of seeing his and Rollie's own reflections, two faces of Zenith Skytreg grinned back at them, superimposed flawlessly over their own bodies. Bertram leaned in closer to figure out how it was done. The right-hand Skytreg leaned in, too. The detail was remarkable. Bertram could see fine hairs and tiny pores.

Skytreg needed to do something about the nose hair. It was like a bamboo jungle in there.

There was a plaque beside the piece, Bertram noticed. "'This mirror is presented to Zenith Skytreg by the Zagblats Facial Recognition Corporation. We give thanks for Mr. Skytreg's support, and the innovative ways he reflects on every member of the GCU.'"

Rollie sniffed. "All that technical capability just to put an ugly slaggard onto a bit of glass." He shook his head and wandered further into the room.

The place itself was the size of an airplane hangar. Awards and medals from myriad solar systems shimmered in one corner. In another section, original artwork from the GCU's most legendary artists told the story of Skytreg's illustrious career, from just before birth (he was apparently a very enterprising fetus) up until his current unfortunate incarceration. Worn weaponry was encased and catalogued with museum quality pride. Statues immortalized his Underworld sponsorship deals with such realism, you could almost hear the crackle of the retinal scan machines. Battle-scorched flags formed a canopy across the arched ceiling. And enclosed in a case was a figure modeling a fancy uniform and containing a series of beautiful etched hand-lasers. A card explained it was the garb Skytreg wore during his pivotal leadership role on the battlefield in the Feegar Rebellion.

Bertram figured Rollie would have choice words for that display in particular, but in the interest of time, he just made an irritated sound in the back of his throat and pressed on.

"Okay, what is it we're looking for exactly?" Bertram asked.

"Who says we aren't finding it?" Rollie's smile was electric, possibly of the eel variety. "Look around you, Ludlow. The room speaks, if only you listen. It's giving us the answers ... More answers every second."

"Great. What are the questions?"

"I'd think that would be obvious. Did Zenith Skytreg hold the GCU for ransom? The answer: no."

"And how is the room so sure of that?"

"This, Ludlow." Rollie pointed to a painting of Skytreg unifying two intergalactic tribes through the wonders of

Underworld PR. "And that." He indicated a terracotta statue of Skytreg, arm curled protectively around a rescued Klimfal. "It's saying it all."

"My Translachew must not work on the Arts."

"Aw, come on, mate. Rare, delicate objects displayed out in the open? Would Skytreg risk hundreds of toks of weight crashing down into this room where the fragile, fibbing honors of his life are kept? Not in a million light years! He keeps the room under retinal security. This stuff means something to him, and he's been accumulating it for a while. Ten to one, this stuff goes to a museum once he's stardust. I sincerely doubt he'd risk something happening to it while it was under his control."

"That is, if the money really was beamed in," said Bertram.

"And that leads to the next question. 'Was it really beaming?' The answer: yes."

"Who says?" Bertram hooked a thumb toward the door. "Anybody with authorization could have brought in the cash manually, and that includes Skytreg."

"That amount of cash? And between the time the ransom disappeared from the crater, and the time it poured into the hall with that rare morning tour? Not fragging likely. Plus, look there."

He pointed up through one of the tallest glass cases. A small, metal disc teetered on the edge of it. "How'd currency get way up there if they brought it in manually?"

Bertram looked past the coin and turned his attentions skyward, through the hanging flags and pennants. "There are skylights."

"You're suggesting a ship poured the stuff through Skytreg's fragging rooftop in the middle of the busiest city on the planet, but no one noticed?"

Bertram wasn't sure what he was suggesting anymore.

"Whereas beaming..." Rollie's attention was on the ceiling, arms folded. "Top floor. No impediments. This room would have been a very easy target."

"If beaming exists," Bertram reminded him.

Rollie sniffed. "Just because something doesn't exist, doesn't mean it's not being employed regularly." He pointed. "Now what is that?"

Bertram followed the man's bony finger, craning his neck to the rafters, but by the time he asked what he wasn't seeing, the finger had vanished, and Rollie had gone with it.

Bertram tracked both of them down near the entrance, where he was dragging a carved bench—some gift from an intergalactic emperor (they seemed to always be emperors these days)— and settling it in front of the case containing Zenith Skytreg's supposed Feegar Rebellion duds.

In a nanosecond, Rollie had leapt onto the bench and was crouching on top of the display case.

"What are you doing?" Bertram hissed, wondering how a guy who could make so much noise just entering a room could be so nimble other times. "We need to go. We're pushing our luck as it is."

Shielding his eyes from the spotlights, Rollie was focused, not on the uniform, but on a handful of the flags hanging above the case. Bertram saw now that one in particular was folded and caught on two others.

Slowly, Rollie rose and stretched to reach it, fingertips missing the item by half a foot, despite his height. The case jittered and swayed ominously beneath him.

Bertram jittered and swayed himself, to brace or catch or ... something. "Rollie, get down here. It's not going to hold your weight for long."

"Nonsense, Ludlow. Unlike your flimsy Tryfe glass, we got advanced, super-thin materials that can take a bit of waggle. Hand me that pole, would you?"

The "pole" was a jeweled scepter from a star system in Quad Two, according to the plaque, a gift when Skytreg had made some uncomfortable *Heavy Meddler* report (and possibly, a reporter) go away for yet another imperial family.

Bertram removed the staff from its golden stand and reluctantly passed it upward.

Rollie relieved the rotunda of more than one stretch of fabric and a hailstorm of trapped coins, before he'd teased the item in question into his hands.

"This!" The flag wasn't much to look at: it had a central crest of a large Y overlapping a perfect diamond shape. There was a saying underneath the symbol that Translachew refused to explain. Or rather, kept explaining, but with different nonsensical suggestions. Rollie held the flag wide and the case shimmied ominously beneath his boots.

"What is it? What's it mean?"

Rollie's voice sounded far away. "Nothing prob'ly." His eyes were fixed on the crest. "Since Altair, I get these fraggin' flashes. Feels like light through the holes in my memory. Right now I can't place this one. But it'll come." He began feeding the flag down to Bertram, but the swaying movement jarred the scepter off its spot on the top of the display case.

Bertram watched the jeweled artifact tumble down, end over end like a majorette's baton and hit the floor with a clunk. It landed on its point, bending the precious metals, while the other end swung up and tapped the display case.

TICK. That was the sound of a bejeweled scepter striking the advanced, super-thin materials of a Feegar Rebellion uniform case.

"Uh-oh." That was the sound of a Bertram Ludlow as he noticed a fresh mar in the case's surface.

And CREEEEEEEE! That was the sound of a tiny mar, turning into a crack, and a crack becoming a web, and the web becoming propellant in half a second with a sound not entirely unlike flimsy Tryfe glass shattering and exploding.

Bertram was too busy shielding his face from fragments to point out the commonalities.

As the case went to bits, the uniform fell like an overthrown tyrant, and weaponry clanked and clattered to its base. Rollie hit the floor in tandem, dropping into broken panels and glistening shards.

Movement echoed down the hall now, and voices called out. Rollie rose from the debris in one tinkling move. Orange-red blood was running into his eye, but he seemed more interested in the chunk of display case in his palm. He yanked it out, pitching it into a pile, then noticed a laser from Skytreg's fallen collection peeping out from splintered wood. He scrambled to unearth what he could into pockets.

Voices were closer now.

Bertram earned a look of surprise as he snatched one laser for himself, stuffing it into his waistband. But scanning the area, it wasn't the weaponry that gave him ideas. "Hey, help me move this."

"This," was the standing mirror by the door.

Rollie had been trying to fold his holey memory into a convenient to-go package. Now he abandoned the task, instead slinging the flag around his neck like a giant beach towel, and he moved to help.

"Hey, Ozo," the voice was outside the door, "you have retinal access to Collections? I've only got Level Two clearance."

"Coming!"

Bertram took a deep breath. Rollie wiped blood from his eye with an edge of the flag. They waited.

It was hard to say just what the employees of Zenith Skytreg's Underworld compound expected to see when the door whooshed open. But based on the shouts and misdirected laser fire, they probably hadn't imagined their boss, in triplicate, would rush at them through the police warnings and pin them to the wall with commemorative furniture. It was simply the sort of thing nobody ever thought to write into a job description.

Bertram drew his laser as they rushed down the hall to the elevator, only they arrived to find the elevator was ... "Gone," Bertram shouted, reaching for the button to summon it.

"Skip it," said Rollie. "Here." And he ducked through a door marked Emergency Exit.

Bertram followed, ready to hoof it down the three flights and make a desperate dash through the lobby, but instead found himself on a rooftop surrounded by twenty different items in Zenith Skytreg's escape vehicle collection. There were runabouts. There were personal hovercrafts. There were sleek ICVs. There was...

"Bleedin' Karnax in leviboots!"

No, it was a Protostar 340-K, filthy and broken.

It looked as if the coroner in charge was on break. Parts littered the floor like harvested organs. Burnt wires jutted out like sliced veins. Missing heat shield panels offered gruesome views to the skeleton beneath.

If there were any doubts about the ship's identity, it still bore the tag from Three Liddlebiggs' Jetsam Emporium, tacked to the front port window.

Rollie's face went ashen under its burn. "That slaggard bought my ship? *Zenith-fragging-Skytreg* bought my Protostar as some kind of... Uninet collectible?!"

Bertram listened for the sound of the emergency door and scanned the ledge for a way down. The only thing between them and the ground was the crystalline roof of the first floor gift shop. "The remote," Bertram said. "Call the Penumbra."

But Rollie stared glassily at the Protostar like it was a war buddy who'd just died in his arms.

"Rollie," said Bertram, more firmly, "get a grip. Call the Penumbra."

"What?" He looked up, his eyes refocusing. "Oh. No room. Too many ships. Never reach us here, 'less we had someone on board to—" He didn't finish the thought, but it did spur him to dig around in his coat, withdrawing the grappling hook. "This. There's room down there," and he pointed at the roof below.

Three floors below.

As Bertram's mind calculated the level of reckless insanity for this plan—about a two-plus-one on an Underworld scale of ten (Bertram had been through worse)—Rollie had already wrapped the hook around an intake vent and was checking it for strength. The pipe was stable. The apparatus held firm.

Bertram watched the tail of rope soar over the building's edge. And with a farewell nod, Captain Rolliam Tsmorlood leapt off the building...

And dangled there, the rope having come up unexpectedly short.

"Seven more kroms and this would have been cosmic," the Deltan observed.

Heart pounding, Bertram tried to assess the distance. "Can you jump?"

"Absolutely," he called back. "And with broken ankles, it'll be the shortest fraggin' chase scene in GCU history."

Bertram heard the Emergency Exit open and the clatter of boots across the pavement. He drew Skytreg's handlaser and tried to remember what Rollie had told him six months ago about the weapons operation. "Push this, it's on. Adjust that, it fires. And whatever I do: Plant. My. Feet."

He knew this last one was the important point, unless he planned to find his way off the building in a free and unsupported fashion.

Speaking of which, he peered over the edge to see Rollie had somehow fumbled a length of that troublesome flag into a knot at the rope's end. With one bloody hand, the man had managed to shimmy from the flag and onto a drainpipe. Now down on the roof, he motioned Bertram to join him.

By this time, Bertram could see a shadow of movement come around one of the ICVs, and he knew he could wait no longer. He dipped over the ledge, climbing hand-over-hand so fast he could feel the rope cut into his palms with every new grasp. He had just reached the section of flag, when he looked up to see unfriendly faces peering down from the platform above. These were complemented by some equally-unsociable laser fire.

The surprise came when the line he was clinging to jerked up ... and went loose.

It was the loose part that was the real stunner. And it was in one of those absurd details you happen to notice during times of terrible shock that Bertram saw the grappling hook, which had been wrapped so firmly around the vent pipe, sailing gracefully from the top of the landing and following his own path on the way down ... down ... down.

He kicked on his leviboots. This, he determined, was the perfect time to test out the technology and see what they were made of.

Turns out what they were made of was the finest materials the illegal sweatshops of Quargus-9 could grab off the back of a stopped hovercraft, glue together and ship out before the traffic light changed. Their three-step quality control process, well-detailed in their annual report, involved turning each pair of boots on, making sure they didn't catch fire much and praying to the god Tungtyda, the local deity in charge of avoiding sticky legal ramifications.

If the shock of the grappling hook's pursuit of Bertram wasn't enough, the footwear's fizzle did the trick.

Gravity, Bertram considered, *is a harsh mistress.*

Then he thought something he couldn't believe he hadn't considered sooner: *Oh yay. More glass.*

At least his fall was slowed by the advanced, super-thin materials that comprised the gift shop roof, where Rollie was waiting until the whole thing gave way.

Jabbing pain ran across Bertram's arm and calf, but those concerns seemed strangely petty as he found himself dropping into the middle of souvenir outerwear, a flag, rope and grappling hook barreling down on him from above.

Bertram dodged out of the way as the hook embedded itself in the register desk, and from a sales display, he grabbed the first thing he could find to shield both of them from the eyes of the startled, scattered tourists. It was some sort of giant sign with printing on it, but there was no time to read it. Bertram and Rollie fled through the ICV lot exit to the tune of a sirens' blare.

"'You'll be launched about this, Ludlow. We're taking a tour,'" shouted Bertram in his best Hyphiz Deltan accent, as Rollie lowered the ladder to the hovering Penumbra Classic outside. "I knew there was more to it. I knew it."

"Aw, stow the noise. The tour ended in the fragging giftshop, didn't it?" Rollie closed the hatch and vanished into the cockpit, while Bertram watched site security run from the building, weapons blazing.

The Penumbra was well into lift-off before Bertram got a good look at his "shield." It was a seven-foot-long ICV bumper sticker reading, "I had a blast at Zenith Skytreg's place."

"Define 'blast,'" Bertram said to no one in particular. He poked at a cut on his arm and considered how this was just one more example of the way we go on vacation and bring home all sorts of crap we don't need.

17

"Why do I feel like we're just saving the RightGuides man-hours?" Bertram murmured, shifting in his chair.

The visiting room of the Vos Laegos City Confinement Hub wasn't exactly a quiet, unobtrusive space. So far, Bertram had seen a grateful Mathekite reunited with his wife and two-hundred and fifty-seven larvae, watched as a drunk Stella Cygnus impersonator picked fights with a shoddy Jet Antlia in a live toupee and saw a visitor reassemble its molecules into the form of a bladed weapon, as part of a misguided jailbreak attempt.

At least the RightGuides were busy enough they weren't focused on Bertram and Rollie.

Now, as they waited in Visitors' Booth Two, Rollie had borrowed Bertram's pocket Uninet, while Bertram flipped the virtual page on a fifteen-year-old e-magazine.

Its cover image had burnt into its polymer sheeting, so no matter what article you were on, you could still see former holotainment ingénue Starlit Ionica giving her two-headed, over-the-shoulders wink.

"We discussed this, didn't we, Ludlow?" Rollie responded to the man-hours comment. "I believe we agreed to take our opportunities where we could."

"I know," Bertram said, "and I'm on board. It's just after our recent activities, I feel like we might be pressing our luck here, y'know, *in the police station.*"

Rollie glanced up from the tiny handheld screen. "Bah! Station's next door. This is a confinement hub. Who'd look for active suspects in a confinement hub? Might just be the safest fraggin' place on Vos Laegos for us." He turned the screen upside down, then righted it. "Anyway, it's not like anyone saw us at Skytreg's."

The sheer absurdity of that last comment made Bertram gasp. "In the parallel universe where everyone's blind."

"Well, okay, yes, they *saw* us," the pilot continued lightly, "but not in any… meaningful way." He scrolled.

"How many pints of DNA evidence are meaningful, exactly? Two? Five?"

"Nah, that's not me." Rollie flashed him a smile. "I'm dead."

"And the security recordings are, what, evidence of supernatural phenomena?"

Rollie gave a one-shouldered shrug and was back to the Uninet. "Likely overzealous fans using *There Goes the Galaxy* holowatch costumes. Anyway, ten witnesses saw us at the Hoverboards-n-Hangovers Follies over in Celestial Circus."

"Oh, they did, huh?"

"Will do, need be." He looked up. "Seems to me New Bertram worries near as much as the early, untested version."

"We're both still getting the hang of our Underworld affiliations," Bertram said. "Cut us some slack."

Rollie conceded the point of this, when the door on the prisoner side of things opened and Zenith Skytreg rolled in.

Or "was rolled," to be specific. A RightGuide was driving the Underworld leader to the prisoner side of Visitors' Booth Two in some large, upright, transparent cylinder. And while there wasn't room in that thing to so much as scratch your nose, Skytreg wasn't bothered. He was singing, his face the picture of bliss, vapor clouding its walls with his impassioned musical respiratory emissions.

As the intercom flipped on, Bertram caught a quick sample. "… Confiiiinnnned … Maliiiiiiigned … Resiiiiiiiiiiigned am I …" Skytreg's voice had a beautifully clear, almost haunting tone, though somewhat diffused by a speaker-gadget fixed to the tube.

Skytreg broke off, as if he were surprised to see them there. Then he beamed a smile upon his guests like some benevolent Egyptian sun god pausing in his big day of being awesome to warm the shivering slaves below. "Oh. Hi there! I was just working on my transition number between the duet love song and the trial scene. I've always wanted my own autobiographic musical—I mean, who hasn't?" He winked. "But I've never quite found the time to whip one up until now. Do either of you sing?"

Rollie looked at the man like he was one gumball short of a full pack of Translachew.

Bertram recalled his own recent performance history and felt glad Skytreg had either missed or forgotten it. "No."

A RightGuide moved a chair from the booth window and trundled Skytreg closer in its place. "Well, no matter," said Skytreg. "I must say, this is certainly unexpected. One star I helped create. The other, I thought burnt out for good."

He waited until the RightGuide stepped away, then sized up his visitors with small, acute eyes. "You both look like you went six rounds with a polyfisted megapoid. If you're here with questions about our Underworld emergency care plan, you'll need to contact Rentar Proximetra. She's dealing with those things while I'm…" he made a deferential, open-palmed gesture, "… otherwise occupied."

"Appreciate the concern, Skytreg," said Rollie in a tone suggesting he didn't much, "but maybe you should concentrate on your own problems. 'Specially considering you're accused of mucking up the Universe for cash …" the Hyphiz Deltan leaned forward, "… *and you didn't even do it.*"

Skytreg's mouth slowly relocated itself half an inch to the left. "You're not here to step forward and take credit for that interesting little scheme, now are you?"

"Take credit?" Rollie leaned back and gave a sniffing sort of laugh. "Nah, that's more your style, innit? Like what you done with me and the Feegar Rebellion?" His pointed gaze could have run the man through. "See, that's where you and me have a divergence of philosophies."

"Oh, do we?"

"I recall the days when an Underworld member's work was his own. When serving your mates up to the law earned you a quick, lively jaunt out the nearest airlock. I remember when the Principles stood for something, and we all stood with 'em."

"Principle Number Two: 'Never frag over one of your own,' huh?"

"And Two B," said Rollie, "'Unless you really, really have to. And it's a good reason. And they can see it coming.'"

Skytreg shifted almost imperceptibly in his cylinder. "Intriguing. So is that what this is? You're here to tell me I've been marked for the great airlock promenade? Because as you said, I do have more immediate concerns."

"Aw, now, I would have thought you'd be more creative than that."

Skytreg's eyes narrowed. "And just how creative are we talking?"

"As a lifelong, devoted Underworld member, I believe in Justice. You're a brooquat and a slaggard, but in this case, you're also an innocent man. And as such, I'm motivated to track down who's stuck it to you." Rollie propped his chin on folded hands. "Who hates you enough to set you up, Skytreg?"

"Besides you, it would seem?"

"Tell me: who else finds you as thoroughly loathsome as I do?"

"Well, Tsmorlood," Skytreg shook his head in an amused, dismissive way, "once you reach my level of achievement, jealousy is just something you come to expect. You recognize it a hundred times a day. You brush it aside. You write a few catchy songs about it, if I do say so myself. Of course, you wouldn't know much about that, would you?"

"What," Rollie squinted, "songwriting?"

"No, success." Skytreg's face flushed with impatience. "Coping with the envy of success. After we got acquainted on Skorbig, I had to ask around. It seems you've been toiling away in the Underworld for years without much to show for it. Knocking over commercial freighters ... Grubbing from the LibLounge print incineration bins ..." He chuckled. "A battle here, a cause there ... Spending more time in confinement than out of it. Truly a mixed bag of misplaced energies and marginal efforts."

At this, Bertram felt his own face go hot. "So marginal you had to steal one of them for yourself?"

"Shut it, Ludlow," Rollie said, his gaze still riveted to Skytreg, "All right. So everyone in the entire GCU is a candidate for framing you. Cumbersome, but we'll launch with it. Any one of them happen to have beaming tech?"

Skytreg laughed. "Teleportation would be the single most useful technology the GCU's had in years. It would revolutionize everything. Who would keep that to themselves?"

"Lots of reasons to keep it under wraps for a while. And a few more to keep it wrapped up permanent. Not everyone enjoys the benefits of revolution. So I'll ask again. Beaming: who's been keeping a lid on it?"

"This is fun," said Skytreg, looking sincere for the first time since he stopped singing. "It's fascinating how those misplaced energies operate. And with such tenacity. I heard a strange rumor coming in here, about a rather messy security breach at my home just now. It has me wondering. Was that you 'helping' me? Because if so, Justice better have a contractor."

"Rollie was dead," said Bertram quickly. "I was at Celestial Circle."

"Circus," supplied Rollie.

"Circus," said Bertram.

"But since you mention it," Rollie continued, "now might be the time to get your opinion on this." From a bag at his feet, he withdrew a large piece of folded cloth. Bertram hadn't realized Rollie had even retrieved the flag but then, their exit from Underworld HQ had been a little on the sprinty-shouty side.

"A cape?" Skytreg wrinkled his nose. "I wouldn't say it suits you."

Rollie just turned it over and revealed the flag's main symbol, the Y-shape layered over the diamond background. Bertram's Translachew was still addressing the words printed underneath it in a strange way. It was like the gum was trying to match something—anything—to the language on the flag. So the more he'd look at it, the more the words would shift in his mind.

"*Fuumere Solif Snuvvid*," it suggested.

"*Shebba Mellot Carba*," it tried.

"*Klaatu barada nikto*," it said. (Or something syllabically similar.)

"*Greb*," it told him, giving up altogether.

At the sight of the thing, Skytreg's expression was like an eclipse on time lapse footage, darkening for just a second before it returned to its normal brightness. "And what does this have to do with me?"

"You mean you don't know? Because it was right there in your Private Collections Room," said Rollie. "Tangled in the rafters with the flags of battles you claim to have participated in. It's not familiar to you?"

"Well, I have so many awards and historic pieces in that room these days, I just can't be bothered to keep track of them all."

"Thought you might say that. So while we waited, I pulled up visitor photos of that room from the Uninet. This flag doesn't appear in any of them prior to the day the ransom was found." He held up Bertram's pocket Uninet to confirm it.

"And your point?"

"Do you know what the flag says?"

"You know I don't. It's gibberish to Translachew."

"Wrong!" snapped Rollie. "The Gibbers lobbied to have their language included in Translachew two Universal years ago. Everyone knows that. And this ain't it."

"Then what?"

Rollie slipped the flag back into his bag.

"You're not going to tell me?"

Rollie turned to Bertram. "Perhaps we should go."

"You're really not going to tell me?" The stress in Skytreg's voice made the projection device buzz lightly. "Tell me what the flag says."

"Tell me who'd set you up, Skytreg," pressed Rollie.

"No." His prominent jaw was set firm. "And you know what? I think we're done here for now—RightGuide!"

"What?!" Bertram leapt up from his chair.

"From what I've seen," Skytreg continued, "anything I could tell you would only put a damper on that old-time Underworld zeal of yours, wouldn't it? I'd hate to ruin that. So I think you'll just have to do your own research from here on out. Oh, Guide? Guide!"

Rollie stood, too, chair screeching out behind him. "You'd rather rot in confinement than help your own fraggin' case?"

The smile had returned to Skytreg's face, broad and pleased. "The evidence against me is largely circumstantial, and I have the best legal counsel the Underworld can buy. I'll be blanked of the charges eventually. But it's so entertaining to see our Principles in action. I might have to write it into my show.

"Besides," he said, "I still have this nagging feeling you have other reasons for wanting me free." He looked over his shoulder as much as the tube allowed. "Can someone roll me back to my confinement cube, please?"

"There's no denying," said Rollie quietly, "I would love to see you out from behind these walls, Skytreg. Nothing I'd like more."

"Not because of forgiveness, though."

"Forgiveness is not top-of-mind, no."

Skytreg nodded. "And since we're being so candid, you wouldn't care to share just what creative method you have planned for me once I'm blanked of these charges, would you?"

"Well, here's the thing. I could tell you," Rollie said, a hair's breadth from the safety glass, "but I think you'll just have to do your own research."

"Yeah. Like I said: so fun." By now, a RightGuide had joined them to wheel the prisoner away. "The next time you stop by, bring me some Smorgs or maybe a few packs of Flinky Rolls. I know what you're thinking. They'll eventually kill me. But hey, that's not a big concern for you, is it?"

And Zenith Skytreg was rolled from the room, singing some confinement-themed dance number.

18

"Do the ZapTrap ..." rumbled the voices in time, "Do the ZapTrap Flap..."

Waranda Blyte gritted her teeth as she strode down the hall approaching the locker room, the source of the sound. The place echoed like the Cackling Caverns of Naga Nasleeb. She passed the room...

"Do the ZapTrap... Do the ZapTrap Fl—"

...And made a U-turn straight through the door.

"Listen up!" she shouted, clanging the butt of her handlaser on a locker. "This is a RightGuide Hub, not the Hoverboards-n-Hangovers Follies. Sing on your own fragging time, starlets. Got me?" Four pair of eyes, currently the size of spotlights, froze in surprise. Other parts froze in various states of undress.

"And," she continued, "if I find out any one of you has had anything to do with Skytreg's musical ... That any favors were given, that any messages were passed... If I learn you so much as catch a Solsday matinee with your aged Maternal Archetype who's been begging to see the show as her last dying wish... I will have you up on ethics charges so fast, you'll hear a sonic boom before you even hit the theater lobby. Do you understand me?"

"Yes, MesoCommander!"

She couldn't do that, of course—bring them up on charges. Not if they went on their own time and paid for their own tickets. (She wasn't sure about the sonic boom.) But this really was the outer limit. So far, she'd had to break up an opening number in Booking, a trio in the break room and some kind of jaunty exit medley in Dispatch, and that was just this morning. It was getting embarrassing.

She left them, all cold eyes and steaming shame, and stalked back to her office, having completely forgotten why she was headed there.

"Do the ZapTrap...Do the ZapTrap Flap," hummed in her head. She screamed and flipped on her sound system, accessing her internal headset and cranking it up all the way.

"Ahh ..." She sank into her chair as the tunes really got grinding, the instruments thrashing, the echolocation vocals causing that prickly discomfort some species just couldn't hack, but that she found soothing. Yep, predawrath music. It was based on ancient native Vos Laegon dinner theater; as in, if you heard it, you were dinner. Blyte used it to help her think.

And right now she thought she noticed Middly standing in her door, saying something that looked urgent. She read his lips.

"A break-in at Skytreg's Underworld HQ?" she asked. "When?"

He told her.

"Anything missing?"

He explained about about the Private Collection Room, the shattered display case, the missing lasers Skytreg used in the Feegar Rebellion and one ICV bumper sticker lifted from the gift shop, though the latter seemed more of an impulse theft.

"Hm. All that for some lasers? Find out everything you can about them. Do we have copies of HQ security footage? Anyone get a look at the suspects?"

Middly said something she didn't quite catch.

She frowned. "Barking?"

With vigor, he shook his head no. He said it again.

She turned off the music. "What is it?"

"Farking," he said. "We've been looking at the footage but it's farking like crazy. You know, pixelated disruptions on the transmission?"

"Show me."

Middly was already on the comm. "Hey, can you send a copy of that Underworld HQ footage to the M.C.'s machine? Thanks." Her Uninet popped on and a small holoscreen opened up. There were shots of two figures. Well, one figure in a bright Lunch-n-Launch hooded jacket and one mass of wavering, streaking, pixilated mess.

"Tech's not sure what happened yet," said Middly as the footage shifted to another security camera, different angle, equal mess. "Possibly some kind of reflection off the suspect or interference due to implanted tech. They're still looking into it."

"It's that new camo," she said. "Blends into whatever's around it, but filming's a black hole. The recording doesn't register at the compression rates the eye sees, so the camo graphics expand over half the image." At Middly's curious gaze, she said, "Remember when Ambassador Bling-Mingies did that frib hunting home movie and 'accidentally' fragged her latest life-merge partner? It's like that."

Middly nodded. "That's why Bling-Mingies got off, right? No positive I.D."

"'If it blips, she zips,'" said Blyte, quoting the defense in the case. Blyte was watching as the figures in Skytreg's collection room fished some pennant from the ceiling. "Look, it's pretty obvious they weren't here for the handlasers. Find out what that thing is." Middly made a note. "And this other one: Mr. Lunch-n-Launch. Do we ever get a clear shot of his face?"

Middly grinned. "Yeah, that should be coming up. Just wait until you see." Eventually, the film paused on the intruder's look of terror as he plummeted down through the giftshop ceiling, a pronged implement following suit.

Blyte rubbed an eye. "Bertram Ludlow?"

"So say our witnesses," said Middly. "He even took the tour."

"Wasn't he just in the hospital?"

"On Daglann-Da."

"So either this kid gets back in the action fast, or somebody's using a holowatch disguise ... genetic makeover ... something. How about our blur?"

"It follows your camo theory. Witnesses sensed someone but basically felt compelled to ignore the person. Found blood, though. We're running it against current criminal archives. I'll update you on that, too."

"And, let me guess: Ludlow paid for the tour with...?"

"Cash."

"Premeditated. Interesting."

"Do you think this is related to Skytreg and the Number Three Virus, ma'am?"

"Too soon to say. See if you can't track down Ludlow." She closed the screen and noted the underlying window monitoring Skytreg's cube. "This reminds me. I found the perfect roommate for Mr. Skytreg." She felt considerably cheered by the idea. She rose. "I think it's time to introduce them."

19

"Absolutely zero creativity," said Rollie for the third time. "Skytreg actually believes I'm plotting to kill him. How can the Official Leader of the Intergalactic Underworld even operate with such dull, linear thinking?"

"Not everyone shares the benefits of your medical condition, Rollie. You might want to try being more specific when you threaten people." Halfway up the city's landmark welcome sign, Bertram paused and gazed upon the Vos Laegon landscape below, feeling optimistic. It wasn't even real optimism. It was the jubies, the euphoria brought on by the Vos Laegon air quality. He suspected it was the only thing that kept him from worrying how one slip, one misplaced foot on one rung, would transform "Bertram Ludlow, Intergalactic Traveler and Reality Star" into "Bertram Ludlow, Delicious Paté."

Still, it was a very nice view.

The jubies never seemed to affect Rollie much, Bertram noticed, as the alien grumbled away. Maybe it was his hearty Hyphiz Deltan constitution. Maybe he was used to it. Or maybe there simply wasn't enough blood in his liquor system for it to make much difference. "So why exactly are we climbing fifteen stories up again?" Bertram asked.

"Twenty," came Rollie's voice. "It's twenty stories, easy."

"Not that I'm complaining," Bertram continued. "Great skyline. But couldn't we have met your contact somewhere less... dangly?"

"Actual city's a bit much for him," Rollie replied. "But it'll all be worth it, Ludlow. Skytreg wants us to do our own fraggin' research? Well, no one knows what goes down in this city better than Skane." With this, Rollie decided to get some more grumbling done, leaving Bertram to soak up the Vos Laegos City landscape as they climbed.

By the time they reached the top platform, the midday sun beat hard, and Bertram hands were blistered and sweaty. He wiped his forehead with his arm and joined the Hyphiz Deltan, who stood waiting over the "S" in "VOS" like a stalwart sailor searching for land. Peering down the line of lettering, Bertram could read much of the city's slogan now, words curving neatly around the town limits in an electric embrace: "Vos Laegos City: You Bet You Can!" The world below was small and serene, as worlds tend to be without all that sloppy Life cluttering up the joint.

That's why, when something spiny, slinky and black whipped up over the edge of the platform, Bertram took a quick step back and almost kissed his S goodbye. More whips followed the first, and soon a thick, black body covered in fine hairs heaved itself onto the platform like a surfacing submarine.

"Ah!" Bertram cried, hoping it sounded more like an interjection than the crow of damp-shorts surprise it was.

"Bertram Ludlow, meet our noon appointment, Mr. Skane," said Rollie, and it was only the power of the jubies that helped Bertram root out the smile currently hiding in the shelter of his left ear.

Skane was ten times their square footage easily, and each whiplike appendage ended in a cuplike hand. These cups also protruded across Skane's bony plated skull, down his back and jutted from his knees. He appeared to have no eyes, and that worked out great because it left loads more room for the two sets of glistening pincers around his mouth. A mouth that at this very moment bared some fangs in what may, or may not, have been a friendly gesture.

"Er, heya, Rollie! Sorry I'm late; I was over on S South," said Skane, pointing down the stretch of letters to the "S" in "LAEGOS." The voice was higher than Bertram had expected and held an over-eager tremble. "Er, what brings ya to my humble abode this time?"

"Got a few questions for a man with an ear to the ground."

"Well, I got thirty of 'em," Skane said. He let out a squeaking laugh that went on too long to not be awkward. "Which ear ya want?"

"Whichever one can tell us about Zenith Skytreg."

"Skytreg." Whip stroked mandible in a meditative moment. "Well, y'know, that depends. The sound waves may fly free, but that don't mean my service does."

Rollie motioned to Bertram's moneybag, and they poured a handful of currency onto the platform floor. Rollie scooped up the cash and let it jingle back down.

Skane's cups all directed toward it, alert and pert. "I suppose I might have a little something I could share for that." The lifeform heaved itself down on the platform floor and crossed several dozen legs. You could have called it "Indian Style," only you wouldn't have. "Skytreg's here in Vos Laegos City confinement. So I happened to pick up a comm or two."

"And?"

"Skytreg sang."

"Holy shit, he confessed?" Considering Skytreg was having such a blast being coy, Bertram hadn't seen that coming. But if the man outright admitted his guilt, well, that would put a whole different spin on their current activities. "Who to? His lawyer? A lackey? Some … skirt?" Bertram wasn't sure when he'd started channeling Jumpin' Jimmy Jive, but it felt right.

"What?!" Or maybe it didn't. For a creature without eyes and eyebrows, Skane sure could frown. "Who said anything about confession? I said Skytreg sang. He's working on some kind of musical. Anyways, I picked up the signal of one comm to his lawyer," he ticked this off on one whip, "one comm from Rentar Proximetra to Skytreg," another whip, "and then a few comms with this big Popeelie composer he's been working with. All pretty dull stuff, and a little too much with the *a capella* for my taste. Mostly, though, Skytreg's been in lockdown."

"And what did Skytreg tell his lawyer?" Rollie asked.

"Kept saying he's innocent. But, hey, who hasn't used that line before?" Skane made the squeaking laugh again. "Ain't you suddenly innocent when the law catches up, Rollie?"

"Haven't been yet," Rollie said, "but we're not here to talk about my occupational approach. What else you got?"

"Vis-us from the RightGuides back and forth about scanning his systems, doing premises searches. Far as I can tell, they didn't find nothin' big."

"Look, you don't just wake up in the morning and say, 'Hm, I'm bored. I hear numeroterrorism's fun. Think I'll wipe out the number three from the whole universe today,' do you? It takes planning. So think back. You catch anything before Skytreg's arrest that seemed out of the ordinary? Any comms to consultants, maybe?"

"What kind?"

"Oh, energy field security systems, physicists, matter transference hobby clubs, professional hackers associations…"

"I wish," said Skane. "Info like that, and the Vos Laegos City RightGuides would be paying for my vacation to a quiet pod in the Melugian Mountains right now. I mean, sometimes a guy just wants to get away from it all, know what I'm sayin'?" Skane reflected a moment on tranquil holidays past. Bertram knew the feeling. "Now I think of it, Skytreg did vis-u Jymkrax Ragobar right after the ransom message went out. And I mean right after. He tried buzzing his office and the guy's ICV. Like bam, bam!"

Rollie turned to Bertram. "Jym Ragobar is the undisputed king of shamcomms, strategic e-viruses, things like that. He's also manager of Underworld Quad Three. He still has his hand in the scam and virus game, o' course, but not like he did. Too much administrative work. Takes time." He turned back to Skane. "What did Jym and Skytreg talk about?"

"Nothin'," said Skane. "Skytreg never connected. Ragobar's stuck in Quad Three like everybody else."

"Timing's interesting." Rollie stroked the cut at his temple. "Did Skytreg think Ragobar had something to do with the ransom note?"

"Or maybe that Ragobar knew someone who did?" suggested Bertram.

Rollie gave a thoughtful nod.

"I understood the two of them was kinda buddy-buddy," Skane said.

"More like bonded by a mutual interest in brazen commercialism."

"So you think they was workin' together?" Skane propped his chin on a few tentacles.

"I think it's fraggin' strange Skytreg would have buzzed the man at two separate locations if he actually expected him to be trapped in the field," said Rollie.

"It's all fraggin' strange if you ask me," said Skane. "You should've been here the night that lifted cash beamed into Skytreg's place. Gave me such a migraine I blacked out and fell off the platform. Woke up halfway down the sign, with nothing but the ledge of a letter that saved me."

On reflex, Bertram and Rollie both peered down the sign to the ground far below.

"Lucky," breathed Bertram.

"It was L," agreed Skane, pointing to the letter in question.

They nodded solemnly.

"Tell me, who's not on Skytreg's fan list these past six months?" Rollie asked.

Skane took a moment to think. "Well, he's got those Underworld university classes, right? One guy made a big gaseous cloud about it because he joined the Underworld but didn't get the results Skytreg promised."

Rollie gave a dismissive shrug. "Man who can't handle an Underworld correspondence course is unlikely to pull a sophisticated frame job as this."

"You really think Skytreg was framed?"

"Doesn't matter what I think. Who else? Surely, Skytreg's scorched more than one lifeform since I been away."

"Your friend Rentar Proximetra was pretty scorched with him. She was no fan of the correspondence course. One comm, she was ranting about the bricks of Underworld civilization tumbling down. Least that's what it sounded like. Hard to tell with that one. She's not what you would call direct and to the point."

"I'm familiar with Proximetra's opinions."

Skane nodded. "Then there's Stella Cygnus. She and that Jet Antlia renegade poet guy was pretty flared up about something to do with Bibluciat orphan brokering. I wasn't clear on the nuances, but Stella really gave Skytreg what-for."

"Hm," said Rollie.

"Not Underworld, of course, but they know everybody, so they've got the connections," said Skane.

"And the clout," agreed Rollie.

Bertram said, "Only right now Stella Cygnus is trapped on floor three of Beddsyde Manor."

Rollie uttered something as anatomical as it was resistant to the known laws of physics.

"Oh!" exclaimed Skane, raising a tentacle like a student in class. "What about Eudicot T'murp?"

Rollie frowned. "What of him?"

"He and Skytreg ain't so buddy-buddy these days neither."

An ironic laugh escaped from Bertram's chest. "What, wasn't Tryfe all he'd expected in a cheap fixer-upper?"

"From what I heard, T'murp thought that because of his deals with Skytreg, T'murp's freighters would be on the Do-Not-Touch list for you Underworld guys with an eye for the goods, know what I'm sayin'? He thought they had themselves, what do you call it?—an understanding. Turns out all Skytreg understood was that one deal was no relation to another. Skytreg tells T'murp it's no biggie, that the insurance companies plan for a certain amount of piracy. They build it into the premiums, he says, and he's not going to reassign all the guys covering DiversiDine when T'murp should just write it off like everybody else. Wasn't DiversiDine your territory, Rollie?"

"Once upon a crime," said Rollie.

Skane nodded. "Anyways, T'murp, he wasn't having it. He said he'd yank Underworld promos from all his holotheaters, the Smorg packaging, the whole pazoolee. He told Skytreg they was done, and T'murp would see him in confinement for breach of contract if that was the last thing he did."

"When was this?

"Month or so back."

"Wait," the words almost jumped from Bertram's lips, "what does this mean for Tryfe?"

"Excellent question," said Rollie. "And wouldn't you just love to see T'murp's accounts a Universal month or so back?"

Bertram smiled. "You mean payments to third parties who know a little something about, say, planetary perimeter security?"

"Among other things," said Rollie returning the grin.

"You don't happen to have a favorite hacker around here, do you?" Bertram asked.

Rollie thought, his frown deepening. "Hard to say. Things've changed since I been out of the loop."

"What about O'wun?" asked Skane. "O'wun could do it."

Rollie shook his head, a grave expression falling over his features. "O'wun's stardust, mate. RegForce fragged him up on Skorbig."

"Impossible!" said Skane. "I just picked up his frequency yesterday."

"And I saw him with my own eyes, shot clear through the cranium six Universal months ago. Which of us, do you think, has the more compelling evidence?"

Skane's pincers clicked. "He was at the Emperor's G'napps table of the Dwarf Star Den, clear as a Vos Laegon day." Click, click. "And it was yesterday."

"Everyone knows Non-Organics aren't allowed within five hundred kroms of the fraggin' gaming tables. You're mistaken, mate."

"And since when would that stop O'wun? He ain't exactly risk-adverse, know what I'm sayin'?" replied Skane. "Heard he came in early for the Underworld Secret Lair and Arms Show we got goin' on now."

"Has that come round already?"

"Yeah, most everybody's in town for it—who ain't trapped in a field, anyways. But O'wun, he's been playing a little here and there for weeks. I'm telling you he was refurbed."

Rollie made an exasperated noise at the back of his throat. Bertram recognized it as the standard Tsmorlood precursor to acquiescence.

"He was living on Ludd there for a while," Bertram reminded him. Ludd was the go-to planet these days for relaxed, tech-free living, but it wasn't exactly the safest spot for an android enjoying his retirement years.

"Fine," snapped Rollie, turning on a boot. "Fine. So O'wun's rebuilt and here in Vos Laegos playing the blasted table games."

Skane might have smiled. "It's what I'm telling ya."

"Right. C'mon, Ludlow," grumbled Rollie and he stalked to the ladder.

"Yo, Rollie, one thing…"

Rollie leaned on the railing.

"There's reason to believe O'wun might be, uh, different these days. What with the refurb."

The Hyphizite raised a pale eyebrow. "Define 'different.'"

"He's—what do they call it?—custom. He's custom now, not one of your standard Simulant molds. Least that's what I heard. Real proud of it, he was, they said."

BONG! It was the sound of Rollie's palm striking the rail. "Well, that's just fraggin' stellar. If he's custom, how on flamin' Altair will we know him?"

"He's still O'wun," said Skane. "You'll know him. Start at the Dwarf Star Den."

20

There were no viable candidates for O'wun at the Dwarf Star Den. Or the Crater Club. And for a second, they thought they'd found him by the door in Lascivious Loova's Lodge of Lax Morals and Laundromat, but that just turned out to be an overly friendly coat rack.

"Hate to say it, but I think Skane may have overestimated our capabilities for this particular task," said Rollie now, as they entered the Space Bar, Hotel and Casino. "An eyeball man cannot do the tracking of a ... a cup-thingy man under these constraints."

"Needle in a haystack," agreed Bertram.

"Possibly, but I expect he'll be much bigger than that," Rollie told him, surveying the room. "Your height at least. And likely still bipedal."

"Um, yeah." Bertram made a mental note that if he ever got back to Earth and it wasn't aliened-up beyond all recognition, he would buy Rollie a book on the American idiomatic phrase.

He scanned the busy room himself, but the floor gave him vertigo. The black surface had been designed to reflect the feel of spacetime, a grid of white luminescent lines that bent around lifeforms and objects on the floor in a constant, shifting pattern of waves. Elegant cocktail servers orbited the tables, wearing costumes inspired by astronomical events. Bertram particularly liked the look of a Nebula that went by, then found himself hoping that wasn't O'wun. So he focused his attention on the Space Bar's patrons, sizing up their expressions, their body language and overheard snippets of conversation.

Bertram noted nothing familiar, just strangers locked in their personal battles of "man versus machine." (Or in this case, "dude with four wings and a tail versus something with a perclickety-boop sound.") But certainly the element of danger O'wun thrived upon was present. Every few feet, a posted sign read:

ATTENTION!

NON-ORGANIC SIMULANTS ARE NOT PERMITTED IN THE GAMING AREAS.

ANY NON-ORGANICS FOUND ON THE GAMING FLOOR WILL BE DEACTIVATED AND THEIR EMPLOYERS WILL BE EVALUATED FOR CRIMINAL CHARGES.

SIMULANT DOCKING STATIONS ARE AVAILABLE IN OUR 'BACKSPACE ZONE' FOR YOUR CONVENIENCE.

"I see that's Carsoolia." Rollie hooked a thumb to one of the many planet-themed beverage carts orbiting the room. Or at least Bertram sensed he did. His camo was reflecting the room's pattern in equally queasy ways. "You want anything?"

"Only if it makes the floor *stop* moving," Bertram laughed.

"One house special, coming up." And Rollie set a course for Carsoolia.

"Ooohhh!" A cheer went up a few tables away, and Bertram tripped across to check out the action.

The table was labeled "Emperor's G'napps," something he'd heard a lot about but he'd never seen in person. It was based on an ancient game that some planet's ruling class played with buttons, or "g'napps," off Ye Olde Royale duds. The playing pieces came in four types ranging from flat disks to small faceted pyramids, all designed to look like shimmering metal, enamel and gems.

The point of the game seemed to be to catapult the g'napps onto levitating platforms and—"Ahhhhhh!"—knock off your opponents' pieces first. You bet against your opponents to fail.

The latter had just been demonstrated with an incisive hit, bouncing the lost g'napp off the table's safety shield to clatter into a pit below.

"Good shot!" shouted one onlooker.

"Supernova!" praised another.

Player Two seized the controls and skittered a shining green g'napp onto one of the platforms, a move that looked promising, *so promising*, until it slid too far and toppled into the pit.

"Ohhhhhhhh!" groaned the crowd, and Player One seized control once more.

"It's all holographic programming these days," came Rollie's voice from somewhere over Bertram's ear.

The Deltan had returned gripping a dark beverage that was already half-gone. He thrust a second, less murky cup into Bertram's hand. "Realistic, innit? And those levitating platforms?" He pointed with his drinking glass. "Used to be imperial servants maneuvering food platters. Only, not much of game then."

"Why?" Bertram frowned and tried the drink. It tasted a little like smoked meat.

"Would you want to be the fellah holding the tray when the Emperor misses?"

Bertram saw his point. He also saw a g'napp careen up, hit the top of the playing field, bounce off, curve in a remarkable display of physics and land smack-dab on a platform.

Merry shrieks rose from the crowd, while Player Two became a solo voice of discontent. "What?! That's not even possible! This machine is fixed. I demand a do-over."

"And that concludes the final round," said the Emperor's G'napps machine. "The pot goes to Player One. Would you like to play again?"

There were pleas from the crowd, but Player Two had already marched off to get a manager, and Player One waved away their enjoinders.

"It's like they say," Player One told the crowd, "'G'napp and win, g'never go back ag'in.'"

"That's a saying?" Bertram wrinkled his nose.

"A very ancient and noble one," Rollie said. "Also their culture had just discovered fermentation and was a bit stupid." Reminded of the glass in his hand, Rollie drained its contents and handed it off to a nearby robotic busboy.

Player One pressed a button to retrieve his winnings and moved to go. "Pardon me." He cast a quick glance at Bertram and Rollie in his path. It was in that fleeting moment, Bertram swore he saw the man's face transform from joy to fear to a mask of frozen neutrality. A moment later, he'd brushed past them into the void.

"O'wun?" said Bertram.

Rollie's eyes were wide. "You saw it, too?" In a flash, Rollie had jogged across the galaxy to catch up. "Had a bit of work done, eh, O'wun?" he asked, falling into step with the man.

"I'm sorry," said Player One with a patient smile. "I'm afraid you've mistaken me for someone else. I do have one of those faces."

"Then you were overcharged, mate. It's a custom job. Diversity's the point," said Rollie.

By now Bertram had fallen into step with Rollie who'd fallen into step with Player One. And as he got a better look at the guy, he was more sure than ever that they were on to something. This was certainly not O'wun's strategically-receding hairline, his thin lips, his widely-spaced eyes. No, the head of hair was full and trimmed in the latest GCU style. The mouth was strong and firm. The eyes were deep set and full of life. But the tone was familiar and the microexpression was undeniably nervous.

"Look, I'm just glad you pulled through," said Rollie. "Got ugly back on Skorbig, didn't it? But you did us proud."

"We could never have gotten as far as we did without you," agreed Bertram.

They had entered the piggelties section by now and a vein throbbed at Player One's temple in a believably organic way. Through gritted teeth, the man said, "I'm sorry, but I am not this O'wun. So please leave me alone. I'll call casino security if I have to."

Rollie pointed to the nearest "No Non-Organics" sign and served up a bright, venomous smile. "Dare you."

With a growl and a surreptitious glance around, O'wun yanked Rollie and Bertram into an empty gaming alcove. "Okay, fine. What is this about? Knowing you, this isn't a chance meeting."

"Knowing me? Why, you know me now, do you?" Rollie was enjoying this a lot.

"Watch your step, Rollie. I may be a pariah here, but I'm not the escapee from Altair-5. If that got out…"

"Let it." Rollie folded his arms. "No law says you can't leave Altair-5 once they put you there."

"Only because no one's ever done it."

"You, on the other hand, are—"

"Simply using my natural talents to rebuild my financial cushion in the most expedient way possible. One, I might add, I had safely tucked away on Ludd, until you came along and ruined everything." O'wun shot Rollie a look.

"Well, I got a job for you."

"I don't want your work."

"Not for old times?"

"Not for new ones, either." O'wun leaned on a machine and its screen blipped. He danced away from it guiltily and tried to look casual. "I'm glad you're alive, Rollie. I am. But these days I'm in it for one person and one person only: Megzek Zarkapom."

Rollie squinted, as if trying to recall the Zarkapoms of Outer Orion's Belt. "Some bookie who's got the squeeze on you?"

"Me. I'm Megzek Zarkapom."

"Melodic," said Bertram.

"Look," said Rollie, "I don't care if you call yourself Kardulius Knig of Upper-Fraggin'-Lombuster-12. I need an expert hacker today and that's you under any name."

O'wun's eyes narrowed. "And what is it this time?"

"We need to know about any large, unusual transfers of yoonies from Eudicot T'murp's accounts in the past six months."

O'wun's narrow expression did not widen for the explanation. "Why?"

Bertram stepped in. "Rollie thinks T'murp might have hired someone to frame Zenith Skytreg."

O'wun laughed. It was a very real laugh, with very organic amusement powering it. "Zenith Skytreg: framed? That's ridiculous."

"Does the Number Three Virus seem like Skytreg's work?" asked Rollie. "If he'd done it, he would have signed the fragging ransom note in blasted digital letters across the sky. He'd be doing media events and selling infopills on how to hold the GCU hostage in ten easy steps. I need you to check out T'murp."

"Hey, I could do T'murp—"

"Stellar."

"—Only when he comes up blank—and he will— " O'wun's new face still managed its old jaded glare, "—then it'll be, 'Oh, O'wun, just do this guy. O'wun, just do that one.' It never ends with you. You have boundary issues. So the answer for this one, and all the other ones that will inevitably come down the line, is no." O'wun turned to the game, plugged in his yoonie card, touched the machine and it beeped its congratulations, colors flying on the screen. He cashed out his winnings and tucked his card away. "I don't get why you'd even bother with Skytreg. You wanted him out of the picture as much as anybody."

Rollie withdrew a rolled up document from an inner coat pocket and held it close before O'wun's face.

"Oh," O'wun said. "Underworld Tribunal."

"Fraggin' straight." And the document vanished back into Rollie's coat.

"You realize, Rollie, there are plenty of lifeforms out there who'd like to see a shift in Underworld power. As much as you, maybe. Most of them are just in hovermode until the next elections."

"Enough to tip it?"

O'wun stroked the new little divot above his upper lip uncertainly, like he was checking to make sure it hadn't run an errand between rounds of G'napps.

"Yeah," Rollie sniffed, "didn't think so."

Yet the finger lingered a meditative moment longer. "Okay, look," O'wun said finally, "never let it be said that Megzek Zarkapom turned away a buddy in need."

Bertram looked up hopefully. "You'll check out T'murp for us?"

O'wun offered them his warmest, most organic smile. "Absolutely not." He raised a finger, "But ... I will put you in touch with Xylith down at the ZSIUSUCA, who I'm certain knows someone who can."

"The Zussi-yoosucka?" This was Rollie.

O'wun rolled his eyes. "Don't you pay attention to the GCU at all when you're in confinement?"

"It was flamin' Altair-5. When you're s'posed to die, they don't give you Uninet access, do they? It's fiscally unsound."

O'wun sighed. "It's the Zenith Skytreg Intergalactic Underworld Society University for Criminal Artistry."

"The correspondence course?"

"Xylith's been teaching some classes, and its Vos Laegon branch is right here in the City, down the main—" O'wun froze as a horizontal beam of light passed over his eyes and down his body.

Bertram turned to see a towering humanoid, uniform stretched over masses of rippling muscle, standing but a few paces away. A wand-like gadget was clamped between her massive, car-crusher digits. "This is Guest Relations

Kremblow," she rumbled into a chip implanted next to her mouth. "I've traced the subject in question from the G'napps table to Piggelties Sector Seven. Illegal Non-Organic...Yes, I'm doing it now."

She planted her feet to face O'wun, like two enormous gunboats moving into position for a hot game of Battleship. "Non-Organic Simulant," she said, "you are in violation of the Space Bar's policy against the presence of electronically-engineered guests, which represents Number 42-8-12 of the casino code. I must now ask you to—"

Possibly Skane might have picked up what she said from a safe and comfy spot on S South, but O'wun, Bertram and Rollie certainly didn't. They were out the door quicker than you could say, "Vos Laegos City Annual Bipedal Marathon and Unikini Contest." Which nobody did because they were too out of breath.

Also, the marathon was next month.

21

Well, you couldn't beat the location.

The Zenith Skytreg Intergalactic Underworld Society's University for Criminal Artistry was smack-dab between two of Vos Laegos' most popular casinos. Before them flowed a ready, steady stream of unwary participants, impromptu training scenarios and yoonie laundering options. *Just the thing to get that promising new Underworld career in motion,* Bertram thought.

"It's Late Vos Laegon Neo-Neo-Neo-Classical," O'wun pointed out, as they approached the university's digs. "Its reproduction simulated faux marble slabs are particularly representative of the time period."

"Which time period?" Bertram asked with interest. He rapped on a stone column that echoed like hollow wood.

"Four months ago through the middle of last week," O'wun said, waving them on. "This way."

He led them through the forest of columns, under an arch, past a recruitment table, beyond a generous lounge ("Note the real imitation marquetry!"), through a hatch and stopped in a low, narrow, thoroughly shag-carpeted capsule.

Here, eight lifeforms sat at eight desks in rows of two, a vis-u before each of them, and all of them talking at once. It reminded Bertram of a telethon, with operators ready to take your call, only one guy seemed to be talking about the finer points of interstellar piracy, a creature in back discussed test scores in the latest burglary simulation and a bald personage in row three lectured on "Home Planet Tax Evasion: Don't Let It Be Your Downfall."

Front left in this academic armada, sat a very familiar lady with long dark hair, shiny clothes and two very absorbed expressions: Xylith Duonogganon.

"So when you're pickpocketing a subject, class," Xylith was saying in that patient, lilting drawl of hers that Bertram had always enjoyed, "what should you do after the bump and the grab? Anyone?"

She let the words bounce around in her students' brains a moment before explaining, "Why, it's three little ol' steps. You conceal the lifted object. You give the quick apology. And you make a calm..."

Bertram didn't know what caught her attention, but the violet eyes of her right face shifted to the newcomers. In a second, they'd grown warm and wide with recognition. "A calm..." A smile appeared, lighting one face, then the other. "A calm..." Both smiles were radiant now. "Oh never mind, class dismissed!" Xylith punched a button, flung off her headphones and leapt up from her chair on silvery boots.

"Why, if I didn't see it with my own four eyes, I would not believe it," she said, gesturing from Rollie to Bertram and back again. She eventually settled on hugging them both at once.

Rollie, who was almost too tall for the room, hooked a thumb at her terminal. "You're teaching for Zenith Skytreg now?"

"Shhhh." Xylith indicated the classes in session. "Not *Skytreg*, my star, never *Skytreg*." Her voice was barely above a whisper. "If I didn't take opportunities just because Mr. Skytreg's name was plastered all over them, I'd be back in the Imperial Citadel on Dootett sitting around waiting for the manicure robots to finish my Arquillian tips."

Apparently being related to the Empress was not the perpetual dance riot one might hope.

"And this is the whole Underworld University?" Frowning, Rollie patted the orange-carpeted ceiling, indicated the tiny fitted kitchen at the back and gestured to the cabinetry covered in a logo reading, "HoverHeart."

"It's a satellite school," she said.

"It's a hovertrailer tacked to an old holofilm set."

A hand went to her hip. "Do you know how much satellites are these days? Not to mention the orbiting permits and the pain of commuting." There was a sour twist to her left lips. "Only you, Rollie Tsmorlood, would return from the dead just to nitpick—"

"Is there somewhere else we can talk?" Bertram asked. A vibe from the lifeform teaching Advanced Artillery suggested they might want to take it outside.

Xylith nodded. "This way."

They grabbed a prime table in the University lounge surrounded by a wide selection of GCU vending machines. In addition to the Smorgs and Sleemy Snaps Bertram expected, they also offered Underworld-themed school supplies, something that looked like shrimp cocktail and a reasonable assortment of lower-end handlasers. Bertram chose a pack of Translachew, which he needed, the shrimp cocktail because he had to find out what it was and an XJ-29, just because he could.

"I really am glad see you," Xylith was saying. "First I hear Bertram's been found by that salvage crew. And now to learn that you're both alive and come to visit, well…"

"Oh they've come," snickered O'wun, cracking the cap on what looked like an antifreeze wine cooler, "but they're not here to visit."

One eyebrow arched, per face, in mirror symmetry. "Oh?"

"*I'm* glad to visit," Bertram assured her. The shrimp wasn't shrimp, he discovered, dropping the tail onto a napkin, but he wasn't sure what it was. Contrary to a running Earth joke, it didn't even taste like chicken, and the consistency was something akin to circus peanuts. He needed more data. He dunked the next one in sauce.

"I should have known this wasn't simply a social call," said Xylith, crossing her arms. "You're just here for the Secret Lair and Arms Show, aren't you? Like everybody else who's left."

"Guess again." Rollie smiled. "We need a hacker. Anyone in that roving thermos of yours teach Hacking 101?"

Xylith's gazes went automatically to O'wun.

Rollie shook his head. "See, we been through this. O'wun won't do it. Some excrement about boundary issues." His gaze flicked to Owun, then back to Xylith. "He said you'd know someone who would."

"And I do." Xylith gnawed a lower lip. "Or rather, I did."

"Don't tell us," said Bertram, putting a third tail down to napkin. "The Number Three Virus got them."

She nodded. "You have no idea what it's been like with so many people out of commission," she said. "Mlet Corgi, Queeeeeeee Strup-Pang, Brash Dunestryker ... So many contacts I turned to regularly, just gone. That's why I've kept the job here. I mean, I know it's a correspondence course and it's not quite to the letter of the spirit of the traditional Underworld. But it's good work when you're looking for something solo, and I think I have a lot to offer a new student of criminal art and—"

Rollie frowned. "Where's Tseethe?"

"Off at a surgery resort, having an extra set of lungs installed."

He blinked. "More lungs? He's Deltan. He's already got four."

"You know Tseethe; he blew through his spares," Xylith said. "But don't you worry. I heard his doctors finished growing him two fresh sets, so all that's left is the installation. He should be out soon."

"How about Fess and Wilbree?" Rollie asked.

She waved a dismissive hand. "Oh, they're helping Backs with his DriftGoods parties."

"DriftGoods. Do I want to know?"

"Probably not. Backs was having trouble fencing his merchandise, so now he's direct-to-consumer. He's set it up as a secret club that non-Underworld folks can join for special odd-lot deals. Then those people sell the stuff through parties to their friends. The locations shift. It's all very hush-hush."

"Sounds like a pyramid scheme," said Bertram.

"Sounds like a sure way to get Klinkoed," said Rollie.

"He swears the concept will get him another shot at Official Leader of the Intergalactic Underworld. Especially since Skytreg is, well…"

"Speaking of Skytreg," O'wun chimed in, "Rollie hasn't told you why he wants the hacker."

"Why does he want the hacker?" Xylith's gaze shifted to Rollie. "Why do you want the hacker?"

Rollie explained the situation.

"We've got a couple of ideas about who might want to frame Skytreg," Bertram added when he was done. "But like Rollie said, O'wun won't help us." He shot O'wun a dark look.

"Skytreg can rot for all I care," snapped O'wun.

"But wouldn't you rather he rotted as an ousted Underworld leader, humiliated and stripped of his clout? If he gets prosecuted by GCU law, won't that just make him an honored victim of the cause?" Bertram was concerned he was starting to see things from Rollie's perspective. He was also a little worried there was something in that shrimp cocktail.

"Skytreg, a victim? Not necessarily." But O'wun's expression wavered. "I mean, it's possible, but—"

"Calculate the chances of it, O'wun," Bertram said. "Fifty percent chance he goes down a martyr? Sixty percent? Sixty-five? More?"

O'wun squinted. He seemed to be trying to put a quick stop to a statistics program Bertram had triggered against his will.

"O'wunnnnnn …" Rollie's tone was like a tiger about to explain to a gazelle that so much cardio was bad for its joints. "If we didn't care about performing our illegalities with that extra bit of spark, we would have become businessmen. Or politicians. Now wouldn't we?"

O'wun squinted tighter.

Rollie poured the last of the bottle of antifreeze into O'wun's cup and pushed it toward him. "You know I'm right."

O'wun let out a grunting sound, one that still had a mechanical grind to it. "Okay, yes! You're right. Fine. You're right. I said it." He grabbed the cup and polished it off.

"So you'll search?" He didn't make O'wun actually say the words; the Non-Organic's look of defeat was enough. "Make sure you note any large outgoing funds from Eudicot T'murp to anyone in the past six U-months. And I mean anyone."

"Oh!" Bertram had an idea, and he didn't want to lose it. "And is there any way you can tell us who's visited Zenith Skytreg since he's been, um, Klinkoed?"

O'wun let out a second mechanical grind. "I knew it. I said it, didn't I? Boundaries." With that, he went to screensaver. It was a new one. His formerly fractal graphics had changed to ones involving closed eyelids in REM sleep. It wasn't as interesting from the observer's point of view, but it was probably safer for him. The worst that could happen now was he'd be sent to a narcolepsy clinic.

"Oh, and you." Rollie pointed to Xylith. "You been around…"

Xylith sat a little straighter. The right face laughed. "Such a charmer."

"No, I mean, you been to a number of the places I have. You recall anything that looks like, well …" Rollic grabbed Bertram's napkin, scattering the tails onto the table, then pulled a knife from his boot. With it, he drew a diamond shape onto the napkin. He cut a Y into that. He held it up. "Familiar?"

"Not especially," she said, wrinkling one nose. "Why?"

Rollie crumpled it up and tossed it across the room. "Dunno. Probably nothing."

"It was a flag in Zenith Skytreg's collection room," explained Bertram. "Rollie showed it to Skytreg. Skytreg played it off, but he seemed… nervous."

"It's got a slogan underneath that won't auto-translate. And I know it. It's right here." Rollie tapped his forehead. "I just hate not remembering."

Bertram added, "Rollie forgot how to buckle his gun holster for, like, a half hour the other day, too. Totally blanked."

Rollie turned to him sharply. "Did I?"

He nodded. "Didn't want to worry you. So Xylith," Bertram smiled, "how've you been?"

One face gave Bertram a delighted glance from under lowered lashes. The other took a breath to respond and—

"That. Was. Interesting." O'wun was with them again, mopping his sweatless brow. "Our friend Eudicot T'murp has been a busy interstellar entrepreneur these past six months. I should have paid more attention who his financial advisors are. I could use some tips."

"Get on with it," said Rollie. "What'd you find?"

"Patience, Captain. Patience. In fact, to get it out of the way, we'll start with Skytreg's guest list. Since his arrest, Zenith Skytreg has been seen by his lawyer (no surprise there), a couple of his assistants (again, no shocker), reporters from a number of Uninet channels and a Dax Q. Phlyjollee and a Berglat Largo," O'wun saluted Rollie and Bertram.

"But no Jym Ragobar." Bertram thought he had been onto something. Now he felt disappointment weigh in his chest. Actually, it was a little low, so it was probably that shrimp thing.

"Moving on, to Mr. Eudicot T'murp." O'wun dusted off hands that weren't dusty. "There were lots of transactions across T'murp's accounts, but all of them were pretty consistent. Only one of them was a particular surprise."

"Let me guess," Rollie stretched out in his chair. "A firm specializing in, say, experimental astrophysics?"

"Rollie, Rollie, when is the GCU ever that neat and tidy? Plus, what I found is kinda twinkly. Three Universal months ago, Eudicot T'murp sent one billion yoonies to none other than... are you ready?..."

They were ready.

"... Stella Cygnus."

"Okay." Rollie's tone was flat. He clearly wasn't ready. "Cygnus again. And what does that mean to me?"

"Wow, but that's weird!" Bertram exclaimed. "Isn't it weird? Stella Cygnus is best buds with Spectra Pollux. And Pollux was really bitter about losing the whole Tryfe deal to T'murp—I mean, seriously vocal about it all over the Uninet. I can see maybe he'd give Stella Cygnus money for something. But why would Stella need it? Or take it? It has to be something cosmically big to bring those two together." Everyone turned to look at Bertram. "What? I was stuck half-dead in Beddsyde Manor for days. It was either watching the *Heavy Meddler* or listening to the Personal Affirmation System."

"But Stella Cygnus is trapped in Beddsyde Manor," said Rollie. "You said it yourself."

"I know," said Bertram. "But there is someone intermittently close to her who isn't. Anyone feel like taking a field trip?"

22

"Harbinger," said the lifeform on stage. Jet Antlia's sculpted, coppery face loomed over the crowd courtesy of holographic technology, ensuring everyone could see his good side. Which appeared to be all of them.

The man paused for effect and the room exploded with shrieks and cheers, like former residents of Pandora's box on their first hot night off house arrest. Here lifeforms wept. There, undergarments were efficiently liberated, airborne and puddled or clattered onto the stage.

The speaker nodded thanks, and the room settled into a braced silence. Antlia glanced at a prompter in his hand, scratched his mathematically balanced jaw and cleared his throat. His acute gaze pierced even the dimmest seats and his lips turned up in a subtle, anticipatory smile. "Foreboding," he said.

For a moment, there was silence. Then, as the word was absorbed by tens of species in hundreds of different Translachew translations, the room was showered with hysterical screams, manic stomping, vigorous applause and stray underpants.

Bertram, Rollie and Xylith were watching this spectacle from the doorway, when a four-armed lifeform passed out at their feet from the sheer power of the performance. Her t-shirt read, "Member of the JET PACK: Proud and Poetic 4-Evah!"

It was this display that ultimately drew the security guard's attention. "Hey!" The guard clomped toward them in a metal exoskeletoned suit, a little slow as far as footchase potential went, but points to him for the overall effect. "No ticket, no show," he snarled. He was still coming at them, backing them out the door. "Got it?"

"Got—"

He slammed a button on the wall, with all the force his robotic hand could muster, and the door clanged shut, quivering in its frame.

"—It," finished Bertram. On reflex, he adjusted the now-tilted computerized sign on the lobby wall that read, *Last Word, Live: The Jet Antlia One-Word Poetry Tour.*

"Well, this answers what Mr. Antlia's been up to," said Xylith. "Either of you gentleman know how we get in to see him?"

"Disguise ourselves as meter and metaphor, and tell him we're suing for lack of equal opportunity?" suggested Rollie.

Bertram considered it. "With this crowd? They'd have us by our pentameters before we knew what hit us."

Rollie nodded. "I'm open to suggestions."

At this moment, a lifeform walked by, trailing a wailing infant in a levitating baby seat. The kid seemed to be dividing into three separate, equally wailing progeny as the journey commenced. In the next half hour, they were going to need a much bigger carriage.

"Well," sighed Bertram, "I've got one idea. But you won't like it. *I* don't like it." He motioned. "Follow me."

Jet Antlia rushed to his dressing room, a flood of beings rolling after him with tsunami-like power. "Babbling Bard of Bibluciat, they're coming! They're coming!" he shouted.

The poetry star slipped into the room just as the wave of admirers crashed at the wall of security. Two lifeforms in exoskeletoned suits, who'd spent the past twenty minutes flirting pleasantly with a certain lady from Dootett, sprang into action, damming the open passage between Antlia and the pooling throng in the hall.

Antlia caught his breath as the bodyguards stepped forward.

"Stay behind us and cover your mouth, sir—you, too, miss!" And they sprayed a mist across the encroaching crowd, who fell back, coughing, to the floor.

"MR. ANTLIA THANKS YOU FOR ATTENDING," one of the guards' voices buzzed through his gasmask. "HE VALUES EACH AND EVERY ONE OF HIS FANS. UNFORTUNATELY, HE WILL NOT BE GIVING OUT RETINAL SCANS AT THIS TIME. PLEASE SEE MR. ANTLIA'S UNINET SITE FOR OFFICIALLY-SCHEDULED SOUVENIR SCAN DATES AND TIMES. HAVE A COSMIC DAY." Some of the poetry fans were now snoring. A few had started to drool. A couple twitched and mumbled in their sleep.

"My stars," said Xylith, "you gentlemen are just so brave!"

"Whoa." Antlia wiped his brow with a sleeve. "Is it me, or are they getting ... faster?"

"There are Uninet sites that let them track and improve their speed under simulated Jet Antlia stalking situations, sir," said the guard.

He nodded. "Illuminating." And Antlia pressed a button, closing the door between him and Sleeping Beauty's castle.

He turned around now, slowly, cautiously, as if he had remembered something even more unnerving than the tidal pool of Universal Life in All Its Snoozing Splendor outside. He surveyed the wardrobe rack. He eyed the carpeting. In a small voice, he called, "Er...progeny?"

"They're in here, Mr. Antlia." This was Bertram, motioning from the door of the adjacent room. And that was where the GCU's hottest poet-at-large discovered twenty-seven of his children, adopted straight from the rocketboot labor camps of Bibluciat, gathered in a circle around two complete strangers.

Rollie had set a handlaser to Flare mode. It beamed to the ceiling, showering the room in a bright, cheerful red, while the children worked hard to mimic it with the chromatophores in their skin. That is, when they weren't punching each other or picking their noses. One or two even managed a good glow effect. There was a lot of giggling.

"Hey, where's the nanny?" asked Antlia. "What are you guys doing here?"

"The nanny had to leave. Sudden illness," said Bertram. This was not precisely a lie; the way the stun ray had hit her was, indeed, very sudden. "The agency sent us," continued Bertram, extending a hand. "I'm—"

"You're that *There Goes the Galaxy* guy, aren't you?" Antlia's eyes narrowed in a way Bertram had seen him do on Uninet programs when he was trying to look particularly perceptive. It seemed painful. "Bertram something."

"That's right," said Bertram. He'd forgotten he was famous, but he figured he could work with it. "You know how it is, don't you, Jet? In a few weeks, my popularity will have dropped like a meteor in re-entry. And so I decided there was no time like the present to finally seize my dreams and pursue my one true calling."

The eyes were almost slits now. "Being a nanny?"

"Given our respective experience with fame, the agency thought I'd be the perfect fit."

"And you," Antlia turned on Rollie, who was apparently easy enough to see under a Bibluciat-trained eye, "didn't you kind of … you know …?" His eyes fell on Rollie's chest, the location of his former wounds.

"Nah, stunt clone," said Rollie, flashing a grin and giving the area in question a good, solid thump. "Fired me end of season one." He flipped a switch on the handlaser, changing the flare mode to blue. The children oohed and began their transformation with shades of magenta, then purple, before making their way to more true blue tones.

Bertram expected additional questions, and he was prepared to lob answers back like a kachunkettball shoop. But instead, relief had fallen over Antlia's rich copper features. "I'm so glad you're here," he exclaimed and before Bertram knew what was happening, Antlia hugged him like a brother; one who actually liked him, even. When he let go, his gaze was wide, his tone desperate and confidential. "These kids are sending me off my orbit. Do you know there are more of them back in my hotel room? And another bunch on the ship? We hire our nannies in bulk now. Did they tell you that back at the agency? In bulk."

Bertram made a non-committal gesture, as Antlia traipsed to the dressing room. He removed his jacket and paused, then motioned Bertram closer. His eyes shifted around the room nervously. "Everywhere I go, I have to watch where I step. I can't move. I can't breathe. Stella had some sort of system worked out with the nanny unit, but she and I had a real scorcher before she left." He lifted a section of hair to demonstrate. It looked like someone had set fire to rows of a cornfield. "She said if I ever paid any attention, I'd know the schedule, so I should just 'handle it.'"

Antlia dropped into a chair but leapt up again when the furniture shrieked. Momentarily, he extracted a small, giggling Biblucian kid, currently the color and texture of a leather makeup chair, and plunked it onto the floor. "Do you see what I'm dealing with?" Antlia went on. "It's too much." He handed the kid his coat, who returned it to the wardrobe rack.

Bertram saw an opportunity here and grabbed it. "So the argument was with you, then?" A second kid was now busying itself with some makeup remover gizmo. The child was using it to score around the edge of Jet Antlia's face with careful attention, and then pry the layer of topcoat up, from the edges on inward. The whole thing came off like a jar lid with a brief suction sound. As far as Bertram could tell, there seemed to be only more handsome underneath. It was vaguely disappointing.

Bertram continued, "I just thought I'd heard something on the *Heavy Meddler* about Stella Cygnus getting into it with… let's see, who was it?…" He paused to extract one kid from another kid's headlock. They had a strange amount of upper body strength. Probably from working with all those tough leviboot hides. "… Zenith Skytreg?"

"Oh, that, yeah. Him, too." Antlia accepted a slushy beverage from a third child and took a long sip. "That's a whole other kachunkettball game, man."

A clipped Deltan accent rang out from the other room. "Look, if you kick me one more blasted time, I will turn this handlaser from flare to frag in a hearts—"

"Um, how so?" Bertram asked Jet Antlia quickly. "The, er, thingy with Stella and Zenith Skytreg, I mean."

Jet Antlia glanced at the door of the other room. It felt like a long moment before his gaze returned to Bertram. "Well, everyone knows Skytreg was involved in orphan brokering on Bibluciat. He writes those regular feature articles about it in *Elite Guilt Soother Weekly*?" He waited for Bertram to nod, so Bertram nodded. "But Skytreg had also apparently negotiated some fat Underworld sponsorship with an off-planet hoverboot manufacturer, in exchange for some Bibluciat adoptees."

"What?!"

"I know," said Antlia, chewing meditatively on his straw. "Here Stella was, trying to get the progeny out of the local rocketboot slave trade—she even had her eye on thirty or so of these kids for herself, luck help us. And here Skytreg was 'adopting' them to a company for leviboot labor on another planet. Their parental archetypes are now legally listed as the board members of this hot footwear corporation, if you can believe that."

"Gapoochi?" Bertram asked.

"I don't like to say," said Antlia. "But yeah." The first kid was back and was applying some kind of lotion to Antlia's face with careful attention.

A concerning thump came from the other room, but by now Antilia was lost in thought. "Imagine," mused the poet, "taking advantage of young, innocent lifeforms for cheap labor." He turned to the kid with the face cream. "Are you using the 'for sensitive skin' type? Because your Paternal Archetype has allergies to perfumes and dyes. You know that, don't you, buddy?"

"So I guess Stella confronted Skytreg about the deal," said Bertram.

Antlia laughed. "Confrontation doesn't cover it. She *blasted* him. She told him she would do whatever it took to get those orphans back."

"Like?"

"C'mon. She's Stella Cygnus." Antlia laughed again. "She knows people. People who could make some of Skytreg's other projects very messy."

"Like Spectra Pollux."

"Nah, Spectra's the main distributor of infopills for the guy's Underworld correspondence course. I think Skytreg tossed it to her to make nice after she lost that Tryfe bid. No, Stella found some other support, and she told Skytreg that, straight out. Now Stella's paying the price."

"What do you mean?"

Antlia sighed. "Are you kidding me? The Number Three Virus? Hello?"

"You don't think Skytreg set up the whole Number Three Virus, all across the GCU, just to get Stella Cygnus out of the way?" asked Bertram.

"Stella and her business partner had a plan to get the controlling shares of Gapoochi, man. Gapoochi! Can you imagine? It was huge. Problem is, she just never got a chance to make the purchase. Why? Because Gapoochi's got the virus, and Stella's trapped in Beddsyde Manor. You don't think that's coincidence, do you?" He turned to his young makeup assistant. "Seriously, check the package on that, buddy. I feel a little sting." The kid moved to read the labeling, but Bertram was pretty sure it was too young to read. "See," Antlia went on, "the ransom's just a decoy for what Skytreg really wanted to do. He got the money, but has he put the number three back? No. Because it's a cover to keep Stella out of the way and distract everyone until this whole orphan thing blows over."

"Um, yeah," said Bertram.

"I just wish Skytreg had thought about somebody else's needs in this whole thing."

Bertram nodded. "Those poor kids."

"Well, them, yeah. But leaving me alone with six-hundred and ninety-seven Biblucian orphans and no instructions for the nanny squad? Cold," he said. "Free space kinda cold."

19+4

R.G. Middly ran into the room, huffing like a full-throttle hovercar with a clogged intake filter. "Coalition... coming," he panted. "Jurisdictional Override approved ... GCU's Most Elevated Court..." He thrust a cylinder at Blyte. "Retinal scan certified."

M.C. Blyte motioned him into a chair, "For pity's sake, Middly, sit down before you pass out."

One ear was turned inside out, from running. The other lolled at his shoulder. "But they're ... on their way, ma'am ... They're ... they're ..."

Blyte slid out the override order and returned the tube to his sweaty palm. "Breathe into it, Middly. Slowly." She unrolled the document, read it over (blah blah compliance required ... blah blah failure to transfer all blah ... will result in serious blah and blah ...) and then tossed it onto her desk. It promptly rolled itself back up. "No problem," she said.

"Ma'am ...?" The word echoed steamily in the tube, but at least his breathing was less on the exploding star spectrum.

"No. Problem," she said and smiled. "This was sent from the Court. The Court's just over the moon past Midliana. Whereas our friends at the Coalition are deeper in Quad Two. Now, they might use local confinement officers to collect

Skytreg and bring him back. But more likely with such a high-profile prisoner, they'll send their most trusted agents from the Coalition Home Office. That means we, Middly, have at least two days before they're here. Two whole days to send a message to the Vos Laegos Underworld that, once and for all, the City RightGuides do not work for criminals.

"So," she folded her hands on her desk, "all we have to do is trace the origins of the virus, find the anti-viral program if there is one, determine the location of the planetary shield locks, unlock the universe and make sure we have enough evidence against Zenith Skytreg to put him away for good."

Middly started hyperventilating again. It made a whistle-hoot sound in the tube.

"It's not that bad, Middly," she insisted.

Whisss-hoot. "Yes, ma'am…" Whisss-hoot.

She brushed a silvery hair from her eye and subdued it with an archive clamp from her desk. She'd already lost six of them in there today, but some things would not be tamed. "Where are we with tracing the virus and ransom message?"

"We've got the top guys in TechSplatter on it." Middly pulled away from the tube and gave a long sigh, resulting in one last musical note. "So far they've traced its slimetrail as it went through our network, but it's seriously slick. Triple-, quadruple-coated. They say they need more time to scrape it down and see what's underneath."

She rose and peered out her window behind her. The pro- and anti-Skytreg people were still out there and, while their dedication was admirable, the winds had shifted. Their organic scent wasn't improving as the case lingered.

"If only we had access to Quad Three," Blyte mused, more to herself than Middly. "I'd bring in Jym Ragobar. He'd know how they did it."

"Oh, right," Middly nodded. "Wasn't Ragobar originally responsible for something like ninety percent of the shamcomms out there?"

Blyte turned from the window. "More," she said. "At least, before he took over Quad Three. I met him once, you know."

"You did?"

"The previous MesoCommander hauled him in for questioning about a flood of fake e-passes to Vos Laegos shows. Ragobar was behind it. We knew it. He knew we knew it. We knew he knew we knew it. He even sat there in our confession room and described how the thing could be done, in step-by-step detail. But ultimately, we couldn't connect it to him, and he knew that, too. I recall leaving that interrogation thinking, 'This guy is Undeworld scum, but he loves his job.'"

Blyte noticed the young man's awkward fidget in the chair. He was either debating whether to speak up, or he'd had too many bottles of FizzyYum with lunch. "Something you want to add, Middly? Or expel?"

"Are we absolutely sure the guy is trapped behind the Quad Three field? I mean, like you said, this job does have a certain Ragobar odor to it."

She smiled. Ah, the young, who always operated on the assumption that every thought in their brains was universally fresh and undiscovered. "I put a Facial out on him the moment the ransom note swept through. No one's seen him and no likelies have popped in the system. It doesn't preclude a good holowatch disguise or genetic makeover, of course. But it's been long enough without sight or sound, I'm inclined to think Ragobar really is stuck at home with the rest of Quad Three."

"Two days, though ..." Middly stood with a sigh. "It's not enough."

"Cheer up, Middly. A lot can change in two days. We might still get something out of Skytreg."

His face brightened. "That's right. Any progress with the 'roommate'?"

"See for yourself." Blyte pressed a button and a monitor flipped on across the room. The screen showed a clear view of Skytreg's cube. Skytreg sat silently, stiffly, on his bunk, eyes shut tight in a wince. A smaller, more portable ZapTrap confined only his head now. An old Hyphiz Deltan man with a cloud of misty yellow hair and skin like ancient stone seemed to be carrying the conversation.

"… And so I told him, I said, 'Well, kid, you better know whether it's a Simmi or an Organic crew before you latch on, or you'll be up to your neck in frag-rays quicker 'n you can say XJ-72.' And then he said—"

"Who is that?" Middly asked Blyte, indicating the aged Hyphiz Deltan.

"Oogon 'Backspace' Bungee," she told him. "Friends call him 'Backs." Got picked up along with two of his Underworld buddies for trying to fence stolen goods to tourists. We nabbed him when someone reported seeing lights in an abandoned factory near the desert. Apparently, Bungee's been unloading hot stuff to targets in similar locations across the GCU."

"—But I told him it didn't matter if they used XJ-72s or not," the old man in the confinement cube continued, "it was just one of them turns-of-phrases. A metaphor I think…"

"Looks like they've bonded," chuckled Middly. Skytreg was pressing his pillow over his head, ZapTrap and all.

"… Or maybe a simile," Bungee went on, "I don't know which exactly, since back in my day there was none of them infopills on grammar and such. You had to learn it the old fashioned way—by lit slams at your favorite multi-media bar. Anyways, so I explained they could use XJ-72s or XJ-29s, or XJ-92s even. Or, if it was a Simmi crew, which was the thing I was worried most about, they could very well use their bare hands, which means you employ a whole fleet of other tactics for disarm—possibly in a literal way, in that the arms do, in fact, need to come off. So that brings me back to my first point—"

Blyte pushed an intercom button. "How are you gentlemen doing in there today?" she asked, her voice reverberating in their cube.

Skytreg flung the pillow from his face, and he scrambled across the cot and in close to the camera. His pearly complexion had lost some of its luster and his eyes were bloodshot. "Okay, Blyte, you win! Do you hear me? You win. It's endless. I swear, endless. And it's made me realize something important about myself."

"And what's that?" The quest for personal enlightenment was not something she'd ever associated with this particular prisoner.

"I am a talker. Not a listener," said Skytreg. "So whatever it is you want to know about the Virus, the Underworld, and apparently any of the subtleties in the entire line of XJ-class handlasers and how they apply to freighter piracy tactics with Simulant and natural lifeforms, I'll tell you. Just get me the frag out of here."

Waranda Blyte was more than happy to oblige.

"Lyuna Flutterbitt," said Skytreg. "That's who you want to talk to."

"Lyuna Flutterbitt, the manager of the Quad One Underworld?" Blyte watched his expression carefully, while Skytreg's lawyer and Middly took notes. There were thousands of Flutterbitts out there, most of them related in some vague way to the others, with only ten variations of first names between them. When it came to Flutterbitts, you had to be specific.

"Yes, the Quad One Underworld Manager," said Skytreg. "There were two Quad One jobs in the past Universal year that might have involved beaming tech. One on Wonda-4, and one on Ojinz-11. Yet no one took credit for either of them. I don't know if it's beaming, I don't know if it's Underworld. Either way, Flutterbitt might have some insight."

Waranda Blyte nodded. Recently, she'd had a working lunch by devouring an infopill on this very topic. It contained the breakdown of each case, dates, times, suspects, witnesses, alibis, descriptions of the items that mysteriously vanished from the completely sealed rooms and full transcripts of the depositions.

It also went well with a nice Solarian three-course-meal-in-a-milkshake.

Both cases had been written off as inside jobs, with the suspicion the businesses were looking to collect on the insurance. Lyuna Flutterbitt had not come up in either of these cases. "And you're just getting around to mentioning this now?"

"My client has been more than gracious," interjected Skytreg's lawyer, Muut Insichuu, a Mathekite whose obvious love of the finer things didn't offset the impression made by his rotting vegetable cologne. "Mr. Skytreg's knowledge of alleged beaming technology in the GCU, which may or may not be in the possession of third-parties he may or may not be acquainted with, has not been a topic of discussion until now. Mr. Skytreg was questioned regarding his own alleged role in the numeroterrorism charges. His responses were perfectly appropriate given the line of questioning."

"And I allege your client has been purposefully withholding information in order to drag out this investigation."

Insichuu turned to his client. "You don't need to respond to that."

"Ah, but I'd like to," said Skytreg. He turned a mild gaze on Blyte. "My good MesoCommander, I take my role in the Underworld very seriously. One of the Guiding Principles of the Underworld is to 'Never frag over one of your own.' Our honor among members has not only elevated the art of crime, but it has made ours a successful professional society. One that has earned respect. One that has, unless I'm very mistaken, even supported the efforts of the Vos Laegos City RightGuides from time to time. Am I right?"

"So you're not fragging over one of your own by giving me the name of one of your own?"

"Solely as an informational resource, M.C. Blyte," piped up Insichuu calmly. "My client is simply opening the lines of communication between your profession and his, at a mutually beneficial juncture that involves my client no longer having a roommate. Which, I might suggest, will help him better concentrate on recalling additional information that might be useful in your case."

"Flutterbitt reports to you, doesn't she?"

"All the Managers do," said Skytreg.

"Then are you suggesting Flutterbitt's gone rogue?"

"My client is not suggesting anything," said Insichuu.

"My self is not suggesting anything," agreed Skytreg.

"He is simply assisting the RightGuides with their information-gathering process during a challenging time. Each Underworld Manager operates independently on his or her own areas of interest. My client merely helps provide structure on the overarching policy of the organization. Think of it as a parent company/franchise situation."

Blyte rose. "Fine. So, we'll check out Flutterbitt."

Insichuu rose, too. "And my client will once again enjoy the benefits of a single occupancy confinement cube?"

"It's done." She watched Insichuu's wings give a pleased buzz. He grabbed his briefcase. "So Mr. Insichuu, what's Skytreg offered you in the musical? A walk-on? Member of the chorus? Minor solo? A couldn't-have-done-it-without credit?"

"The payment arrangement between my client and I may or may not be subject to a variety of privacy l—" He broke off when he saw the lack of buying-it on Blyte's face. "Song-and-dance number," Insichuu confessed, giving another excited twitch of the wings.

"Figures." Everyone wanted their fifteen minutes these days.

24

"Lost my thumb once and sewed it back on myself. Been stabbed, lasered, poisoned, suffocated, skewered, fried and near disemboweled. Been gnawed by Feegars and chased by Spew. Today I fell through a ceiling. And none of that scared me near as much as twenty-nine Biblucian fraggin' orphans once boredom hit." Rollie waved that reattached thumb toward the cockpit window of Bertram's ICV. "You keeping an eye out there, Ludlow? Remember, this'll be you getting your money's worth having me as your tour guide."

It was just becoming dusk. The Penumbra hovered half a mile over the Vos Laegon desert outside the city, joined by hundreds of other hovercrafts and ICVs. Several had words like "Vos Laegos Happy Tours" and "Jubieful Journeys" printed on the sides, triple-decker vehicles with more than the usual number of portal windows. Bertram could see anxious alien faces pressed to the glass. He wasn't sure what they were so excited about, unless they were all jungle-dwellers savoring the novelty of the raspingly dry Vos Laegon soil. But after an active day, Bertram was grateful for the downtime in whatever form it took.

"So Mr. Antlia really believes Zenith Skytreg engineered the whole numeroterrorism gag just to backburner Stella Cygnus?"

This was Xylith, perched on the arm of Bertram's chair. She stared at the desert floor like everyone else. Her perfume smelled like heavy spices and it wafted.

"Aw, that boy needs a reality infopill," Rollie sniffed. "It's a fraggin' lot of trouble to go to, putting the whole GCU in crisis just to sideline a celebrity activist. Though he did raise one fair point—"

Bertram noticed the dusty Vos Laegon terrain was starting to look...dustier...somehow. "And that is?"

"Why isn't Three back yet?" He looked from Xylith to Bertram to the Vos Laegos skyline. "If Skytreg stole Three and got the ransom, why didn't he return the number? The GCU met the demands. Skytreg had at least a few hours, local-time, between the payoff and the tour group 'accidentally' finding his stash. We all knew what time the payoff deadline was. Why not release Three then?"

Bertram considered it while the dust churned ominously.

"Not to mention, stashing your ransom in a room that tours are visiting the next day? Not bright, even for Skytreg."

"Well," said Bertram, "to Skytreg's credit, the tours only came through that particular room, what, twice a year? Would he even be paying attention to the schedule?"

"On the other hand," Rollie continued, like Bertram hadn't spoken, "if the money was a plant, wouldn't the person who planted it *also* return the number three after the payoff, to prove the payoff worked and frame Skytreg even more thoroughly?"

Xylith's noses both wrinkled. "Maybe. But then that means you've proven—"

"Absolutely nothing!" Rollie's smile was triumphant. "Precisely my point."

Bertram felt a headache coming on. It might have been from the stress of actively copiloting these couple of trips. But it probably wasn't.

"Whether Skytreg did it or not," Rollie continued, "three should have been returned. So where the frag is it?"

"Rollie," Xylith crossed her legs. It made a satiny whooshing noise. "There could be any number of reasons Skytreg or anybody else held it back. Maybe restoring it is some elaborate process. Maybe someone got greedy and is planning a second wave of ransom. Maybe the reversal technology doesn't work. Maybe there is no reversal technology. Maybe Skytreg wanted some private time to swim naked in his yoonies first—"

"Thanks for that image."

"—Or maybe, just maybe, the man simply didn't get around to putting the number back before he got bus—"

-ted laid there, tossed aside and forgotten. Bertram imagined conversations all across the Vos Laegon desert broke off in similar fashion, trains of thoughts derailed, participles dangling obscenely, as thousands of colorful glooping, blooping spheres rose shining and resilient from the churning desert dust.

Bertram was unsure what he was seeing, but Rollie clapped and cheered as the first of these newborn travelers passed the cockpit window. "Very nice, fellahs! Welcome to the universe. You're right on time."

Soon, the creatures had surrounded the onlooking ships like a flurry of soap bubbles.

"What are they?" Bertram asked.

"Loombahs," Rollie said. "Some call 'em Star Surfers. Hatched every eleven Universal-years. They eat bits of meteors, space junk, whatnot, as they travel. Store it inside 'em on their journey. Carry it off."

"They finish their migration by casting themselves into the black hole at Fitali Entor," Xylith explained. "I've always found it rather sad, in a poetic way. Poor dear things, they get a single one-way trip and then ..." She shrugged. "Such is the fleetingness of life."

"You're seeing a rare natural phenomenon today, Ludlow. A bit better than picking up knockoff, knockoff leviboots on discount, eh?" Rollie grinned.

The loombahs moved in unison, swirling now to the right, now to the left, all the time rising higher in the Vos Laegon atmosphere, glowing brighter against the darkening sky.

Bertram could see electric pulses trickle through fine veins in their translucent skins, creating a sparkling effect. The sublime grace of it all had rendered Bertram speechless.

For a long moment it was quiet, as they watched the creatures on this initial leg of their first and only migration. Then, in a low, grave tone, Rollie spoke. "Flamin' Altair. I been looking at it all wrong, haven't I?"

"The loombahs?" Xylith was riveted as a trio of the spheres twirled past in a slow-mo spin upward.

"The frame job," said Rollie.

There was another long pause. Bertram waited for more but felt reluctant to break the loombahs' gentle spell.

"I was thinking the problem was at the top," said Rollie finally. "But what if it isn't? What if it's all through? Or if not all, or even most, what if it's enough? *Just* enough that it would make things that absolutely could not—should not—ever happen, possible?"

He leapt out of the chair. "Frag me, I hate it when this happens."

"What happens?" asked Bertram.

"I'm pretty much almost entirely sort of certain I was wrong." And with that, he ducked through the cockpit hatch and vanished into the ship lounge.

"Do you know what he's talking about?" Bertram asked the lady on his armrest.

"I try to minimize it. I've found understanding him too clearly has always been a sign of my own mental decay."

In a moment, the Hyphiz Deltan was back with a familiar bag. He slapped it down on the control panel.

"What if it's Underworld?" Rollie asked. "What if it isn't just Skytreg who's cast Principles to the wind? What if we've decided we don't actually mean every little bit of every Principle and that maybe fragging-over our own—and behind his back, to boot—is a pretty blasted cosmic idea now and again?"

Xylith's faces were pale. "Depends on who 'we' is. Are."

He gestured widely. "We. Us. All of us. Card carrying members of the Intergalactic Underworld Society. 'We don't care anymore. We're in it for the prestige, the networking, the yearly business write-offs...' Whatever. We."

"But what are you saying?" Her violet eyes were wide. "If you take away the Principles, that opens up suspicion to include the entire Underworld. It could be anyone who framed Zenith Skytreg. For any reason. Or none at all."

"Yes, absolutely!" he agreed, nodding. "Only not necessarily." Rollie pulled the flag from the bag. He tapped two long fingers on the crest. "See, it occurred to me just now that—"

There was a buzzing sound. Then: "Hello?" called a voice from...somewhere...around them.

Bertram blinked. Several loombahs rolled slowly past the front window. He eyed them suspiciously.

"Hello? Hello?" came the voice again. It sounded female.

Bertram found himself leaning closer to the cockpit window. "Hello," he called and pressed an ear to listen. "Hello? You can hear us?"

"Hello? Is someone there?"

"Yes. We're here," said Bertram eagerly.

Rollie sighed. "Ludlow, it's the blasted ship vis-u. You do realize most sounds don't travel through the hull of an ICV, right?"

Bertram felt his face grow hot. Rationally, he knew. But things got a little confusing in the GCU sometimes. It was easy to get swept up.

In the lounge, a wall panel featured the projected head and shoulders of a deeply scowling Hyphiz Epsilonian woman. The frown cleared the instant Rollie joined her at the screen. "So you are there," said Meena. "I haven't any time to explain. I hate to ask, but then it technically *is* your fault, and I simply can't call my M.A. because, well, you know how *she* is, and my sisters, well, double that, and you are a member of the Underworld after all, so—"

"Bleedin' Karnax, Meena, for not having time..."

"I'm in confinement," she said. "On Mawdank."

"Mawdank?" He squinted. "Where's that?"

"Quad One, same system as Treyfab, three planets over. I understand it's new."

"Whole planets don't just show up, Meena," he said. "Unless it's rogue. Is it rogue?"

"The question you're really looking for is, 'Meena, do you require bail?' And the answer is, 'Yes, please. Come quickly. Lightspeedish would be cosmic, thanks.'"

Rollie smiled.

"That horrible smile had better mean you're coming."

"Just never thought I'd see it. Meena Tsoogarkken is asking me to bail her out."

"Yes, yes, I know, it's all terribly ironic and we shall have a great laugh about this when you get here and we both go very, very far away from this place. But as for now, the living conditions are appalling and the whole place has severe Translachew issues regarding the term 'personal space.' So I'm certain you see my dilemma."

He did. It was only a moment before Xylith canceled her classes for the rest of the week, Bertram looked up Mawdank in his travel brochures (it was conspicuously absent) and coordinates were set for the Treyfab system.

All in lightspeedish fashion.

Mawdank had not been easy to find. The Treyfab system was right where they'd left it, but as for where Mawdank had insinuated itself, that was harder to say. Concerned the Number Three Virus would infect Bertram's ICV—which Bertram argued was only a natural complement to the mystery stains and toilet snails—Rollie wouldn't risk downloading any current nav charts. This left them roaming the star system like parents searching for a missing tot in some Earthling discount mega-store, one of those places where you can buy food and dialysis machines and socks and airplane tires.

Eventually, they spied the world tucked between two lush planets and three graceful moons. It made an awkward neighbor. It sat there in some self-sustaining, manufactured atmosphere like a rusty RV that had somehow found its way into a gated community and decided to live the life.

It was only as they flew in closer and Bertram perused the red-brown, rocky landscape, a chill of recognition prickled the hair on his arms.

"Do you have a word in Hyphiz Deltan that means 'an inexplicable feeling you've been someplace before'?" Bertram asked, lowering the landing gear.

An ICV lot appeared before them, filled with vehicles from all over the GCU. They parked around a single mirrored tower, a slim structure that reflected the light off the nearest moon.

"Yeah," said Rollie darkly, shifting a lever. "Rhobux-7."

The chill turned into an all-out cold sweat. Rollie was right. Bertram recalled that same tower under Rhobux-7's suns. He remembered the Seers and their eerie, echoing voices sending Bertram on his quest. The planet had seemed eternal then, locked into an important place in a mysterious cosmic plan. Until, of course, the next time he'd wanted some choice words with the Seers. That's when they'd discovered, in a twist of fate and physics, both the Seers and Rhobux-7 had bolted. It seemed very long ago.

"Meena Tsoogarkken's in Rhobux-7?" called Xylith, running in from the other room to look out the front portal.

"Yes," said the pilot, "and simultaneously no." Rollie extended a bony finger toward a levitating sign, which flashed:

Mawdank Roving Confinement Center:
Going the Distance for a Safer, More Orderly GCU.

"Ah, Rollie," Xylith shook her head with sympathy. "You always did know how to show a girl a good time."

The atmosphere in the waiting room of the penal colony formerly known as Rhobux-7 had changed a lot from Bertram's last visit. Gone were the holovisions lining the walls, each tuned to a different Uninet station. Gone was the alien Muzak layered over the room's impatient buzz. Gone were the family members, lawyers and media crews all being officially ignored for the official length of time one must officially wait for no reason at all in small, official offices.

Instead, a starched, itchy silence hung over the place like stiff, well-bleached canvas. The only décor was the mural-sized holographic image of a lifeform on the wall, one that despite the gray uniform reminded Bertram of a large puffed, orange toad. The eyes were blood red and no-nonsense. "Warden Wambo F. Kleefer," read the name underneath it.

And next to it:

A Note from Our Warden:
The Mawdank Roving Confinement Center has been designed to address today's growing needs for a firmer and more rigorous Intergalactic Order. Too long has the Greater Communicating Universe turned a blind eye, a passive shoulder and a not-pointy-enough boot to vile and flagrant lawlessness.

Wherever Evil tries to have its way with our noble communities, the Mawdank Roving Confinement Center takes up the ever-vigilant gauntlet of Order, crushing the tender, fleshy nether-regions of Criminal-Minded Chaos into the Pulp of Incapacity.

As warden of these facilities, I vow to enforce the letter of the law, the law of the land, the law of gravity, natural law, physical law, law of diminishing returns, law of averages, Kohl's Law, Iambda Law and the law of a final, personal fragging by me, if you don't follow the first nine.

Obey the Law, Avoid the Pulp.
XXOO,
–Warden Kleefer

"New boss is same as the old boss," Bertram observed. "Only, y'know, angry and scary and totally different."

In the quiet of the room, his voice seemed loud, and it caused the only thing that hadn't changed—one giant lime-green eye behind the tiny sliding door in the reception desk window—to pop into view.

"Can I help you?" The eye shifted from Xylith to Bertram to Rollie. It briefly tried to focus on the camouflaged man, looked uncomfortable, gave up, and bounced back to Bertram and Xylith.

"We're here to bail out one of your prisoners," Bertram said. "Meena Tsoogarkken?"

The receptionist nodded—an achievement, considering its lack of visible head—and it disappeared behind the frosted glass.

Bertram could see the shadow of something move back there. "Tsoogarkken ... Tsoogarkken ... Ah, yes." The receptionist returned to the window. "Willful endangerment. Reckless operation of an ICV. Assault. Hit-and-run. And attempt to dispose of criminal evidence. That will be ... two hundred thousand yoonies."

"What?!" said Rollie. "For a fraggin' first offense? Until now, the woman's only crime was her art."

"She's a public risk and Warden Kleefer believes firmly in the ever-vigilant gauntlet of—"

"We read the flamin' memo."

The eye might have shrugged before it disappeared behind the frosted glass.

"Well, there's no way we can make bail with this," said Bertram to his companions, holding up his bag of remaining funds. He'd have to do paid interviews, sponsorships and retinal souvenirs for at least a week, and that was only if his popularity curve were at its peak, not swiftly rolling down the other side into obscurity.

Rollie turned to Xylith. "I don't suppose you'd care to contribute to a worthy cause?"

"Ordinarily, I'd be happy to," Xylith said. "Being life-merged to you twice, that poor woman has clearly suffered enough. Unfortunately, a certain virus has frozen my major accounts. I'm living off the bits and bytes of one worn and weary yoonie card."

Bertram said, "But you're related to the Empress of Dootett, aren't you? Can't you hit her up for a personal loan or something?"

Xylith laughed. "You do overestimate the economy of my home planet. Imperialism isn't what it once was, Bertram. Everyone's had to downsize. Our crown jewels are currently two candy rings and a holotheater headset with sparkles glued on." She pressed a finger to one set of lips. "Don't tell the Empress. She hasn't noticed yet. She's a little far-sighted."

By now, Rollie was rapping on the reception desk window. "Hey you. We want to talk to Ms. Tsoogarkken."

The eye reemerged and glanced at a clock on the wall. It looked surprised. "Hmp, you're in luck! It's actually Visiting Hours." The eye swiveled to a sign that read:

Visiting Hours are:
10:14 a.m. to 10:42 a.m. Mawdank time.

It was 10:21. Bertram did some quick math. "Visiting hours are twenty-eight minutes long?"

"The warden is very big on the law of economy," said the receptionist. "I'll buzz you in."

Metal doors opened beside the desk.

Stepping through, Bertram heard, "Please empty your pockets and put all objects in the bin. You may retrieve them when your visit is over."

First Bertram noticed the bin being thrust at him. Then Bertram noticed the receptionist thrusting it. The large green eye was, indeed, only a minor feature of a much larger production. The creature's body was a huge spherical mass, with a single horn at the top. The body balanced on one tree-like leg in front and a long thick tail ending on a spiked club in back. The creature had small, pretty hands. Three of them, for variety.

The hands shook the bin enticingly. Bertram settled the bag of currency inside it, tossed in his vending machine handlaser, the laser from Skytreg's collection, his portable vis-u/Uninet combo and a few pieces of busted glass that had somehow come along for the ride.

"Step through the scanner, please."

Bertram did, expecting them to scan for hidden weapons, drugs or illegal print. So he was more than a little surprised when he was promptly blinded by a light. It bewildered him almost as much as the Manfred Mann song of a similar title, but this was a whole lot quicker.

"No match," announced the machine. "Individual is not in the registered database. ID required."

"Wait, was that a retinal scan?" They hadn't been required to give retinal ID, or voice prints or anything else at the Vos Laegos City lockup; they'd given names—and fake names, at that. Bertram's heart was pounding.

"If you're not in the database, I'll need some form of ID, sir," said the receptionist. "Identity chip, voice print documentation or at least a sneeze verification registration."

"Er, look, this is embarrassing, but I don't actually have any registered mucus or—"

"Sure you do," Xylith piped up. "I believe I saw you put your ID in your pocket before we left the ship." She pointed to Bertram's hooded sweatshirt, gave him a meaningful glance and then smiled at the receptionist like a pageant contestant lobbying for the Miss Congeniality title. "Doesn't spacelag just do such a number on the mental faculties? I know I'm no good for anything simply days after I travel."

Bertram slipped a hand in the pocket of his hoodie and withdrew a slim chip he'd never seen before. He pushed its button.

"Mephisten Phlann," it said, and a lifeform projected from the device. One glance and Bertram found it almost astonishing how much the being in the holographic picture resembled him, if only Bertram had been a five-tiered cherry Jell-O salad. "Er—"

Xylith was apparently insane. But before Bertram could confer with her about the method to her madness, the receptionist had snapped the chip out of Bertram's hand, pressed the button a second time and looked hard from the chip data to Bertram.

Bertram could feel his own pulse thump in his neck.

"Limitless possibilities at our disposal, sir, yet we went with the 'Uninet Reality Star from Tryfe' look today, did we?" The receptionist rolled its eye and plugged the chip into the system. "You know, I met Bertram Ludlow once, Mr. Phlann." The creature hit a few buttons and unplugged the item. "He was taller." The chip was tucked back into Bertram's hand. "Please wait by the door, and an escort will be with you shortly."

Bertram slipped the chip into his pocket, then moved to the door, not entirely sure what had just happened.

"Next," said the receptionist, motioning to Xylith. "Miss?"

She deposited a few things in the bin and stepped into the light. "Xylith Duonogganon," announced the machine. "Please proceed to the red door." And momentarily, she joined Bertram there.

"Next!"

Bertram leaned in to Xylith and whispered, "What about Rollie? Did you plant a chip on Rollie?"

"No time," she whispered back. "Anyway, I only have the one shape-shifter ID."

"Shit."

A uniformed guard was approaching, and Bertram waved for Rollie's attention. "Hey, um," Bertram said, trying to sound cheerful, "dude!"

The Deltan's eyes flicked toward him as he reached into a pocket.

"Y'know, there's no sense all of us going in. Why don't you, um, wait here, and Xylith and I can talk to Meena?"

"Sure," said Xylith with enthusiasm. "I'd love to finally meet Meena."

"Great! Then that's settled, and—"

It was like they'd never spoken. Rollie's attention was back on the bin and in went the handlasers and chem-gun, the dagger, the cosh, a drained yoonie card, the grapefruit half, the rolled petition and the grappling hook.

"Only that?" drawled the receptionist, surveying the items.

Rollie offered a tight, unamused smile since, for him, this was traveling light.

"All right, through the scanner then, please."

Bertram held his breath. He liked to think Rollie had a plan, but if he did, there wasn't much time for implementation. In a moment, sirens would wail. More uniformed guards would come running in. Rollie would either be fragged to stardust on the spot or stunned into a puddle, as step one in Warden Kleefer's pulp production unit. Bertram tried to think of something—any good reason—to stop the scan in its tracks.

Rollie strode forward into the beam.

"No match," announced the machine. "Individual is not in the registered database. ID required."

Xylith tried not to look as astounded as Bertram felt. One face she managed to get under control quickly, but the other still looked like she'd been goosed by Fate. Didn't Rollie have a crimes archive the size of, oh, the entire planet of Mawdank? Why weren't these connected to his retinal scan?

"A bit backspace, I am, I'm afraid," said the Deltan, giving a sheepish smile that made Bertram wonder who the hell this guy was and what he'd done with Rollie. "No retinal ID yet where I live. Maybe next millennium." Rollie shrugged, like it was all such a pity.

"Alternate ID, please?" asked the receptionist.

"You take seed implants?" he asked.

The receptionist looked almost as surprised as Xylith did. "My! You weren't kidding about backspace, were you? We don't see those very often."

"Yeah, that's what I hear," said Rollie in an apologetic, almost wistful tone. "Is it all right?"

"It'll do," the lifeform said. And Rollie held up a hand while the receptionist waved some wand-like technology over it.

"Dax Q. Phlyjollee," announced the machine. "Please proceed to the red door." Which he did.

"Take them to grid block fourteen-thousand two-hundred and ninety," the receptionist told the guard. "And tell Mub to put out three chairs."

A moment later, Mephisten Phlann, Xylith Duonogganon and Dax Q. Phlyjollee entered the inner-workings of Mawdank Roving Confinement Center. And not even as prisoners.

"Someone's redecorated," murmured Rollie, as they moved down the hall.

At first Bertram didn't know why he sounded so grave. The space seemed very bright. Polished, utilitarian tile lined the floors, and the art glass walls shone.

It all seemed perfectly pleasant. Maybe more like a museum than a prison, but … It was only when Bertram turned that he saw it. And it saw him, too.

The wall had eyes.

Truthfully, the wall also had whiskers, ears and the other requisite parts that comprise certain interstellar lifeforms. But it was the eyes, so large and hollow and pleading that immediately made Bertram jar back.

The creature was in a prison jumpsuit. It was numbered. And it was embedded right into the architecture.

It was also not alone. Next to it, just inches away, another creature stared with resignation. Across the hall, an opalescent blob slouched. Next to that: a Hyphizite woman. Here was an insectoid. There: a glowing mist in a jar. It was like the Universe's most horrifying toy store, with living, breathing action figures packaged row by row into the building itself.

Living, breathing and screaming.

Bertram could see mouths moving, calling out as he passed, but their words remained unheard.

"Warden Kleefer believes in keeping a calm, meditative confinement atmosphere," said the guard, as if this topic came up all the time, and he might as well just nip any questions in the bud. "Can you imagine the racket if we could hear them all? It'd drown out the music."

There was a peppy little number playing through the overhead sound system, and the guard had been humming and patting his leg in time as he walked.

"But these poor people ..." Xylith's voice quavered. "They can't move. They can't sit. It's like they've been ... compressed."

Bertram found himself looking at the faces and not wanting to look at the faces as they moved past. "It's inhumane."

"Not everyone's humanoid," explained the guard, ceasing to hum long enough to speak. "Warden Kleefer says we've increased our capacity by nearly five hundred percent since we reorganized. This way, please." And the guard motioned them into an elevator. It was made of the same materials that housed the prisoners, only this was of a more livable size. The guard pushed a button, and as they descended, Bertram could see floor after floor of action figure boxes with prisoners inside. "We've won awards," continued the guard proudly. "We've been featured in Unimags. *Penitentiary Pride ... Innovative Incarcerations ... Cell and Salvation ...*"

"Makes a fellah long for the good old days, when there was enough elbow room to get stabbed over breakfast," said Rollie.

"What happened to the Seers of Rhobux?" Bertram asked.

"Retired," said the guard. "I hear they host a weekly talk show on some minor Uninet channel, interviewing celebrities about things that haven't happened yet."

The elevator had slowed to a halt, and they followed the guard down a corridor. There were three chairs circled around one area of the wall. Pressed into the center of that wall was Meena, her face drawn, her eyes tired.

The guard checked a clock. "You have five minutes before visiting hours are over. I'll return then." He plugged a number into a remote. The intercom clicked.

"Oh dear. Rollie, Bertram and *Xylith*, is it?" came Meena's tinny voice as they sat. "With such a large audience, I can only assume there's been an issue with the bail?"

Xylith nodded sympathetically. "A two hundred thousand yoonies sort of issue."

"Two hundred thousand yoonies?" Stress cracked Meena's normally measured voice.

"They say you're a public risk," explained Bertram.

She sighed. "A public risk just because I owned the ship."

"And you reported the ICV stolen?" asked Rollie.

"Yes, but apparently some eyewitness claims they saw me piloting the thing."

"Excrement!" he snapped. "Who?"

"Anonymous tip. From a 'concerned citizen.'"

"In free space? That's some neighborhood watch," Rollie growled. "Well, they can't keep you here based on that."

"No. But they can keep me here when it's backed up by your chum, Mr. Zeg. Who came forward saying I sold him the Astrocrat just after the approximate time of the 'altercation.' That's what they're calling it now, the 'altercation.' He told them if he'd known my Astrocrat had been involved in 'the altercation,' he never would have bought it. That his is 'a clean, Underworld-free business' and—"

"Mangy slaggard." Rollie's fingers clenched. "When I get my hands on him, by Karnax, he'll discover hair removal the hard way."

"Do that and they'll have you in here, too," said Meena. "Which you should be, frankly, since it was your zonky piloting skills that got us—"

"'I'd like to encourage them on their way, Rollie,'" responded the Deltan in his best Meena tone. "'So will it be Bottoms Up or Thunderous Purk-beast of Pow?' Isn't that what you told me?"

"Hey," said Bertram, pointing to the clock and trying to block out all the eyes around them. "Time's ticking. Meena, how are you set for yoonies? I have some, but since I bought the Penumbra, two hundred thousand's way out of my price range."

"I've got some cash back at my studio on Hyphiz Epsilon. I'll tell you where I've stashed it. As for the rest, well," she gave a sigh that sounded like it carried the atomic weight of uranium, "I hate to say this, but you'll have to ask my Maternal Archetype."

Rollie gave a sharp laugh. "Moena? I hardly think she'll just hand over money to me," he said. "She didn't that once, and I had a handlaser on her."

"Well, you have to try. Please tell me you'll try. I can't stay here, Rollie. We never get to move. We never see sunlight. They feed us through a tube. It's—It's—" She held back tears and raised her chin. "This place used to be Rhobux-7, you know. I don't know how you endured it."

"Things have changed a lot since my time here. Rhobux-7 was a resort planet compared to this." He reached to pat her shoulder but settled for pressing a palm to her part of the wall. "Don't worry, Meena, we'll get you out."

Meena responded with a shaky nod and that determined jut of her chin. "Lightspeedish, please, if you would."

"Lightspeedish," Rollie agreed. "I promise."

25

The door to Meena's studio wooshed open and mud-brown arms extended for Bertram's throat.

With a reflexive yell, Bertram leapt back and drew his vending machine handlaser, checking the settings and aiming with conviction. "Okay, pal—freeze!"

The thing froze.

For a brief moment, a warm flood of elated pride swept over him. Yessir, Bertram Ludlow was gaining his spacelegs. He was fresh off another piloting lesson and quick with a draw. He was capable. He was confident. He was...

Noticing how the paint flaked in the center of the creature's massive forehead and chickenwire jutted from a bare spot at its elbow.

His hope sank and the handlaser with it. This muddy monster hadn't moved a muscle, and it never would.

Yep: Bertram Ludlow had nearly fragged Art.

By now, Rollie was cackling like a hyena on Serengeti open mic night. "Easy there, Ludlow," he managed, wiping a tear and leaning affectionately on the paper maché creature. "He's no beauty, for certain, but he just wants to make friends."

This got him laughing again, and as he vanished into the room, Bertram could still hear him chuckling.

"Great." Bertram stepped over the threshold and tucked away the gun. "Cosmic. But I bet this guy saves Meena thousands in home protection each year."

"Common side-effect of Meena's art, really. Speaking of which, no time to waste: where is *Reclining Nude?*" Rollie scanned the room for Meena's makeshift safe. In passing, he glanced at Xylith and frowned. "Do you plan to help at all, or are you thinking of subletting?"

Xylith *had* been assessing the studio like a potential renter considering the possibilities. "Typical," she said. "Can't even take two seconds to appreciate a cute place when you see one."

At first Rollie sniffed at this. Then he stopped short and looked at her sharply. "What did you say?"

"That you are intensely, even rudely, goal-oriented at times?"

"I know that. The other part."

"I said it was cute." She shrugged. "I mean, if you block out that giant pile of junk she's got stacked along the wall, the whole place is practically snoogly. Look at the natural light. And that stellar little kitchenette."

Rollie did look at the natural light. He did look at the stellar little kitchenette. "Oh no." His face drained a few shades of crimson. "It *is* cute." His voice was a horrified whisper. "Bleedin' Karnax, why is it *cute?*"

"Why? What's wrong with that?" A hand went to Xylith's hip. "Oh, I know what it is; you expected that since you and Meena, and you and I, all shared a past orbit that she and I might not get along. But she seems to really have ta—"

Rollie dashed to the counter and swept a hand over the surface. He stared at his palm. "Oh, wrong. Very wrong."

"You pictured her in more of a geodome maybe?" One of Xylith's noses wrinkled.

Rollie whirled on them. "Paint! Where is it and why are we not trodding in it? And what happened to the laundry? Why aren't there rags drying?" He indicated the chandelier. "Why are the counters so fraggin' clean and ..." He looked down. "Flamin' Altair, why is the rug *there?!*"

Bertram's attention went to the rug. "On the floor."

"Must I spell it out?" Rollie's voice cracked with strain.

"Er." Bertram looked to Xylith. Both faces mirrored the confusion he felt. "Can we buy a vowel?"

"Meena was never this organized when she worked," insisted Rollie. "Never! Personally? Yes. But in her studio? Galaxies have collided with less hullabaloo."

"Maybe she made a resolution," said Bertram.

"Maybe she got a cleaning robot," suggested Xylith.

"Or maybe," said Rollie, "this place has been ransacked." He disappeared into another room.

"Wait. You think someone broke in and *tidied up*?" Bertram called, going to examine the door lock. It seemed fine. Everything seemed perfectly fine.

"Son of a Keeltsar, this is clean, too. The slaggards." Rollie emerged from the room, scowling. "Just help me find *Reclining Nude*, would you?"

Surveying the space, Bertram saw a number of finished works displayed ... well, not quite to their best advantage, since Bertram thought that would have to be in a completely dark room ... but in a way they caught the light that made them somewhat less What-the-Holy-Hell.

One blob sat over a cabinet looking like a decomposing bowl of fruit. Some sinewy thing was perched on a stack of crates, ready to grab at passers-by and ask for change. A scythe-shaped contraption with tumor-like knobs jutted from a shelf over the door. And a lumpy amorphous mass sat on the sofa, like that party guest you wish had called a cab hours ago. Bertram wasn't sure whether it was her artistic style or the fact he was still new to the GCU that he couldn't figure out whether or not one of the works was *Reclining Nude*.

The problem was solved when an "Ah!" came from one end of the room. Rollie hoisted the item aloft in triumph.

Bertram stared at the sculpture and tilted his head. "Are you sure that's it?" It could be roughly humanoid, Bertram supposed, if the subject were of some two-armed, four-legged species he hadn't yet encountered. And if he cocked his eyes right, he might be able to see the dents in the underlying chickenwire framework representing rough facial features. But...

"That's the one, all right. Meena did this the first time we was life-merged. I told her it was a big mistake sitting for it in the first place." At Bertram's blank expression, Rollie added, "When you work in the Underworld, it doesn't do to have your image all over everything, does it?"

"Um. No." Bertram glanced from the copy to its original and back again.

Rollie turned the statue upside down and made a quick critical examination of its base. Someone had sliced through its painted paper and sealed it up again. Rollie punched through it and rooted around inside, up to his elbow. "I'd asked her to destroy this thing. But did she? Course not. Here it sits." Parts of the statue seemed to be waggling around as he rummaged within. Bertram was glad when he finally withdrew a wallet. "Course, seeing it again, I don't know what I was so worried about. Barely a passing resemblance."

"Some issues with extra limbs, too," Bertram observed.

"Yeah ..." Rollie squinted at the thing, "I don't think those are limbs." He tossed the statue onto a chair and turned his attention to the money. "Well, if our ransackers found it, they didn't take the cash. Got about ten thousand Epsilonian dollars here. That would be ..." His mouth moved slightly as he did the math in his head. "... Call it twenty thousand yoonies. Not enough to spring Meena, I'm afraid."

"Where's her mom live?"

"This planet. Better neighborhood." He tucked the wallet into his coat.

"Um, gentlemen? I think I've found something you'll want to see." Across the room, Xylith's voice seemed to come from the artistically-balanced stack of junk.

"Oh, that's just stuff Meena bought from Liddlebiggs' salvage," Bertram told her.

"You know, I was standing here noticing how nicely everything was sorted ..." Between the objects, Bertram caught a flash of silvery boots. "... And then I spied this little item caught in some of that wire fencing." She emerged into the light like the Lady of the Lake, if the lake were tetanus and Excalibur were a wad of rust-colored fur. Smiling she said, "Now, unless my eyes have deceived me, I do believe Meena Tsoogarkken is not a fur-bearing redhead?"

"Wouldn't be my type," affirmed Rollie. He tugged both Xylith and her handful of fur to the window for a better look in that natural light.

"And how about those strapping salvage men?"

"Also not my type," chuckled Rollie. "And Suidae Verrucan. So, dark and bristly, not ginger and furry. Hold that?" He left her with the fur while he rummaged in Meena's lower cabinets.

Bertram barely heard him, for the ideas coming together in his own mind. "Hey, when we picked up that tail, that was after we hit the salvage yard, wasn't it?"

"Oh yes," Rollie said, rising. He came away from the cabinet with a small, lidded container. He took the fur from Xylith, tucked it inside, capped it and pocketed it.

"So if Meena bought something someone else wanted, or that she wasn't supposed to have..." began Bertram.

"But that's the glitchy bit. No way to tell what, if anything, is missing."

Bertram assessed the stacks. There were barrels of rusted metal coils, gears and ball bearings. There was a stack of ancient print copies of *The Centurna-4 Excavator* tied with string. There were drums of paints and miles of that old, rolled wire fence. There was a small row of theater seats, upholstery like an unlucky victim in a slasher film. There were crates of dusty glass tubes. There was even a throne that had become sadly disconnected from its royal subjects, unless they happened to be woodworms. There were fasteners and clamps, beads and knobs. There was a box of shiny tokens from TwinklyTech each redeemable for a free vis-u case as a part of a limited time giveaway.

On impulse, Bertram grabbed his own pocket vis-u and chose a name from the list. It seemed like forever before a bright pink head popped from the device. "Hey, Rozz! You getting a lunch break anytime soon?"

"Break?" Rozz Mercer glanced somewhere off-screen, her expression shifting from focused concentration to shock. "Holy shit! Would you believe I've been sitting here for the better part of ..." She did a quick calculation. "Two days? Possibly three, hard to say. Where are you? Is this a lunch invite? Because, well, three days, I'll need a little time to get freshened up."

Bertram smiled. "You're perfect just the way you are."

"Aw geez, Bertram." She ran an uneasy hand through her hair. "I mean, that's nice and all, and if this is just a friend thing? We're totally cool. But if you remember, you and I agreed we were calling it quits."

"I need you to look through some garbage."

Rozz blinked. "I saw this conversation going somewhat differently."

"Not garbage, exactly. Salvage. At Two-Plus-One Liddlebiggs' Jetsam Emporium. It's walking distance from Beddsyde Manor."

"Is this specific garbage or just a general interest hobby?" she asked.

"I'd like you to go and ask the owner there about any jobs they picked up in the past three, four weeks. Have them show you what they brought in, if there's anything still there. Find out who bought the stuff that came in. See if anyone's asked questions about any of their recent customers or any particular items. Take notes. Look over everything really well. Open up boxes, look in crannies, the whole thing."

"So what am I searching for? Aside from ten easy steps to fun new vaccinations?"

"I don't know. That's why I need the notes. Comm me in a few hours no matter what you find."

"Okay," she said, reluctance in her voice. "But I'm only doing this because the trip will stave off total muscle atrophy."

"Yeah, don't care. You're cosmic. Two, three hours, okay?" And with that Bertram Ludlow signed off.

"Well." Xylith's voice shared a similar reluctance to Rozz's. "I suppose if you two want to go ply the rest of the bail money from Meena's Maternal Archetype, I could sort through the things here and inventory what we have."

"Smart lady," said Rollie, walking to the door. "You picked the pleasant job. Mine's guaranteed to be awkward, littered with landmines and there's a fair chance someone gets lasered. But, hey," he winked, "that's family reunions for ya. See you in a bit."

Bertram stared up at the mansion's crystalline protective dome. Glistening flakes rose, fell and swirled inside it, like a souvenir snowglobe from Vale, only home-and-garden sized. The place next door, he noticed, was enjoying simulated sunshine and clear skies. But at Chez Tsoogarkken, today was set to Winter Wonderland.

"So let me get this straight," Bertram said. "You were life-merged to Xylith, and she's related to the Empress of Dootett…"

"Over-brother's under-cousin," Rollie said, pressing the buzzer by the dome's hatch.

"And you were life-merged to Meena, and her Maternal Archetype lives here." Inside, snow twirled around the home's sweeping balconies and graceful parapets.

Rollie punched the button a second time. "Your point?"

"Well, it's just that there seems to be a serious socio-economic discrepancy between you and your choice of lady friends."

"Skewed sample group, is all." He peered into the monitor camera and really leaned on the button now. "And if someone in this fraggin' place would bother to answer the blasted vis-u, we could return to our appropriate peer group and—"

A face appeared on the screen. "Someone *has* answered the 'blasted vis-u,' sir. I regret to inform you the lady of the house is currently unavailable to salesmen." The lifeform squinting at them was fascinating in his lack of detail. It was like someone had drawn a face in as few strokes as possible, then erased a few more for good measure. It was less a person and more an implication.

"Aw, Larvis—c'mon, mate. You fraggin'-well know me." Rollie moved closer to the camera to give Larvis a clearer view. "It wasn't that long ago me and Meena was life-merged."

"I do, indeed, know you, Captain Tsmorlood. But it is from the lady of the house that I repeat the directive; she wishes no salesmen."

Rollie winced. "She doesn't still hold that little incident against me, does she?"

The silence suggested she did.

"Larvis, it was a MaxBlast Elite 470-007 ICV with roto-rocket boosters and double upper lower lomb casings. Double! Why, there's not a lifeform alive who wouldn't want a joyride round the Quadrant in that."

"The joyride was not the issue, sir."

"Okay, yes, circumstances did present themselves so it happened to get a bit sold along the way, but..."

"The lady indicates that if you do not cease cluttering up the doorstep to her bubble unit, she will be forced to contact the Epsilonian RegForce."

Rollie growled. "All right. I was hoping it would never come to this. But clearly, I've no other choice." He looked into the camera. "Larvis, you go to Moena, and you tell her that Rolliam Tsmorlood has heard...the Fountain Story."

"'The Mountain Story,' sir?"

"Ffffountain," said Rollie, "Story."

"Very well," said Larvis. But the "well" dried up under the buzz of a quickly opening hatch. Rollie led the way through the dome to the mansion's front door. In person, Larvis' simple, all-white uniform seemed excessively excessive compared to his personal self. He gestured inside. "The lady bids you welcome."

"That's our Larvis," called a bell-like female voice. "He always puts that polite spin on things, even in the case of cruel blackmail. What I said was, 'Have them come in quickly so the neighbors don't see them.' So come in." A woman swept into view wearing crimson. Her navy blue hair was aloft in a gravity-defying updo. A selection of small spheres of different sizes, also red, orbited it jauntily. They helped distract from the fresh bruise that darkened on the pale skin of her temple and the ones already established on her toned arm. "Larvis, close the door...And you two, don't just stand there. Have a seat."

There was not a single thing in the echoing white room.

Bertram wasn't even sure it was a room. It felt like they'd stepped into a void, some endless place between worlds. The back wall disappeared into darkness. The side walls extended into infinity. He glanced at Rollie, and the Hyphiz Deltan was shaking his head, muttering, "Should've figured."

At this, the woman's glossy red lips peeled back into a delighted smile. "Yes, it really is so Me, isn't it? Do you like it? It's the latest in invisibility interiors. I just had it done." She turned to lead them into another part of the Nothing, but thumped her shin on Something, cursed, rubbed it and spun back around beaming, as if hoping they hadn't seen. "This place was absolutely *desperate* for a change—so unnecessary with all its tedious surfaces and superfluous shapes and agitating visual planes." She shook them all away with her hand. "And then I saw Voltan Limbo's show, down at that cosmic little gallery on Gwash? And it was an absolute revelation!" She glided over to a space, felt the air a bit and started to sit. Halfway down, her face donned a fleeting look of uncertainty, but she regained her confidence the second her posterior made contact. "He transformed my whole home into livable art. I swear, Voltan does for interiors what the LibLounge did for that nasty old print. I feel so tranquil, so free, so—"

"Contusioned?" asked Rollie.

With a sour expression, she indicated a void to her left. "Well, what are you waiting for? I won't have you looming over me like some Marglenian Megabat. Sit, sit."

They felt around and eased onto the Nothing. It was surprisingly comfortable. But for the first time since Bertram met him, Rollie did not look comfortable. He sat on the edge of the Nothing, hands clasped tensely before him. "Moena, I haven't much time. I've come because—"

"Meena's work is in that show on Gwash, you know. And is she taking advantage of this innovative new technology? No. Instead, she's wasting her energies with rusty wire frameworks and muddy paper. But that's Meena: rebellious to the core and clinging to anything filthy and degrading that will get her attention." The woman gave a pointed look to Rollie. "Which reminds me: you're not here because you're life-merged to Meena a third time, are you, Rolliam?" She took a moment to assess him (because of the camo she gave it a moment longer) a little smirk on her lips. "Meena seems to have an unfortunate low-orbit when it comes to you."

Rollie said, "I'm here, Moena, because Meena needs your help."

"Ah. Well!" She toyed with a single hair-planet, putting the rest of them off their rotation. "Of course, she does. She always has, she's just too stubborn to realize it. I was only telling her sisters the other day, how the more our dear Meena struggles to do things herself, the more desperately she needs—"

"Two hundred thousand yoonies kind of help," he continued.

"What?" She wobbled slightly on her Nothing. The planets wobbled, too. "Why? That's a lot credits to give to one's progeny when she can't even be bothered to show her face. Where is she? Out waiting in that deathtrap you call an ICV, I suppose? Too embarrassed to ask me herself so she sends two of her Underworld thug connections to pressure me?"

"Um, I'm not a member of the Underworld, ma'am," Bertram interrupted, extending his hand and his most friendly smile. "Hi, my name's Bertram Ludlow and I—"

"Meena," Rollie explained, "is an innocent victim stuck in Mawdank Roving Confinement Center. And she needs the two hundred thousand yoonies for bail. Now."

Moena blinked. Then laughed. The laugh was light and merry like the snow outside. And just as unnatural. "Meena is in Mawdank?" She was still laughing as she dabbed at her eyes.

"That's very creative. I had no idea you Deltans were the least bit creative. I thought you were still savoring the high of discovering fire and eating with tools."

"You don't believe me?" said Rollie. "Put on the holovision. I'm sure it's all over the *Heavy Meddler.*"

"Oh, Rolliam, I don't Uninet or infopill these days." She dismissed the media of the entire universe with the wave of her hand. "My priorities lie in the sublime. The aesthetic. The intellectually- and emotionally-enriching. Also," she squinted left and right, "I can't quite seem to remember where my holovision and vis-us have gone. There's a floor plan somewhere but ..." She gave a weary shake of the head, then looked from Bertram to Rollie. "For all I know, Meena could be off on Blumdec enjoying a Total Cellular Massage, while you're here shaking me down for yoonies for some Underworld scheme."

"Moena," Rollie leaned in to her now, his voice the soft-spoken calm that always made Bertram worry, "if I was robbing you, I'd tell it to you straight. Also, I'd hold a handlaser on you, right...about ...here..." He extended two fingers to point in a general weaponry way just a hair's breadth from her temple. He unfolded a broad, jagged smile. "... Remember?"

Moena's pale face had flushed, but not with the indignant outrage Bertram had expected. Instead, a faint smile slid across her own lips as if she were remembering something that wasn't entirely unpleasant. "Ah," she said, "so you would."

He nodded and dropped the finger-gun; fortunately, it wasn't loaded.

"But wait," she said, blush fading, eyes narrowing, "this trouble Meena's in ... This isn't about that package that man thought Meena left here, is it?"

"What man?" said Rollie.

"What package?" said Bertram.

"Yes," she said, "there was someone here a little while ago. You probably just missed him. Larvis talked to him and— LAAAARRRRRVIS!" The name bounced violently through the home. It was a wonder Larvis didn't get knocked over with it when he appeared from the direction of East Nothing. "Didn't a man come by a few minutes ago asking for some package he thought Meena had left with me?"

"Yes, ma'am. The gentleman was quite insistent about it," said Larvis. "I explained that nothing had arrived recently, including Ms. Tsoogarkken herself, and that if she had left anything behind we would know, given the new …" Larvis' eyes played around the room, "… interior arrangements."

Rollie stood up abruptly. "Did he leave a name? What did this fellah look like?"

"No name, sir. But I believe the gentleman was not native to Hyphiz Epsilon. He looked Tangtapien."

"Orange fur, fleshy face?"

"And a very polished personal appearance. Yes, sir."

Moena stood, too, and seized Rollie's sleeve, her planets reversing orbit along with her. "Then you know this man?"

"No, but I have this feeling we'll be getting acquainted very soon." Rollie pried her hand from his coat. "The bail, Moena. You'll pay it?"

She brushed a lock of hair from her eye and gave a quick sigh. "All right, but it's going directly to Mawdank. That way, I know what you've told me is the truth, and there isn't any funny business with the funding."

"All I could ask," Rollie answered. He motioned to Bertram, and they searched for the door. "Let us know when the funds go through. We'll pick her up."

"Oh no," she said, trailing them. "I will be sending an ICV to pick Meena up, thank you very much. I believe that you, Rolliam, have had quite enough involvement in Meena's life to-date."

The orange eyes seemed to flicker. "Are you zonky? It's not safe, given her circumstances. The reason she's in Mawdank in the first place is because—"

"It's nice that you still care. And I'll admit you do have a certain … quality … that isn't wholly uninteresting. But you, *na tseenee*, are never, ever the route to safety. Now go." It was as the door was closing behind them, Bertram heard her add,

"And about 'the Fountain Story.' Don't expect to use that on me twice. Blackmail is one thing. But redundant blackmail? Vulgar."

It was silent for a long moment as Bertram and Rollie headed down the walk to the ICV. Finally, Bertram had to ask: "So what is it you have on her?"

"Me?" Rollie reached in his pocket for the ship remote and laughed. "Nah, this one's all Meena, mate. It's just I remembered Meena saying she's got this home video of Moena lecturing her on her favorite sculpture in the local art museum. On and on the woman went: its aesthetic merits, symbolism, political statement, why it's innately superior to Meena's work in every way…"

"So?"

Rollie grinned. "It was a busted drinking fountain. Meena's been threatening to show the video to Moena's art appreciation club for years."

26

Xylith held up a digital news leaflet, its polymer-coated surface rolling at the corners and yellowed with age. "Centurna-4," she said.

She slapped it down and moved to a large piece of folded canvas, opening it up. It looked like the backdrop curtain for a stage and featured a flaming pink sky. She flipped it to the reverse side. "Manufactured in Mineheart City, Centurna-4."

She let it pool to the ground and shifted to the throne. She tipped it, reading, "Made with care on Centurna-4."

As that clunked to the floor, she stepped to the set of theater chairs. She crouched, lifted a seat and pointed to a label on the bottom. "Property of Glaem Studios in…"

"Let me guess," said Bertram. "Centurna-4?"

"My star pupil," she said, her dimpled smiles in duo.

"Glaem Studios," murmured Rollie, kneeling to examine the chair. "Does that really say 'Glaem'?"

"Why? What's Glaem?" asked Bertram.

Xylith brushed dust off her clothes. "Took me a minute, too, before it hit me. Glaem was the big shamcomm headquarters way back when. Spurius Glaem invented the first shamcomm on Centurna-4."

"Shamcomms again?" Bertram frowned.

Xylith nodded. "Mr. Glaem convinced everyone he was this deposed emperor of some obscure planet that didn't even exist."

"King. They had kings back then. And it was Klaer-2." Rollie rose, wiping his hands on his pants. "Made up an invasion. Said his people were dying of diseases the invaders brought with 'em. That he needed to raise money for their cure and to overthrow the usurpers. 'Act now and sponsor a rebel family for just two yoonies a day.'" He grinned.

"Oh, and Mr. Glaem had these elaborate sets and scale models he used to fake his war footage. He showed fake patients in fake emergency units. He faked alien invaders."

"Played it all very urgent," said Rollie, "like he'd barely got the comm through. Made some pretty yoonies from the whole thing, too. For a while, anyway. Until the fire."

"Someone burnt down the studio?" Bertram asked. "What was it, for the insurance?"

"No," said Xylith. "A local mine caught fire." She moved to the sink and turned on the tap. "Centurna-4's industry was, maybe thirty percent carbon mining. And when one of their biggest mines caught fire, it went completely out of control. I guess the locals thought they could smother the flames, so they tried plowing it under. Only, the fire kept burning. It mixed with some mineral deposits, and eventually they had to evacuate the whole place."

"Word was," said Rollie, "the stink could be smelled over a quarter of the planet."

"The place has been like that for … what … over a hundred U-years? More?" Xylith wiped her hands on a towel. "The fires should be down to a low smolder these days."

"Yeah, and it looks like someone was finally able to clean house." Rollie picked up a tiny red lollipop tree from a box of them and twirled it between thumb and forefinger. "Centurna-4 would be outside Quad Three. And there's no facial-rec anywhere." Rollie leaned on the throne, twiddling the tree thoughtfully. "If I was a shamcomm expert looking to pull off the biggest job in GCU history, I'd find working in the ruins of Glaem almost...poetic."

"You really think this is has to do with the Number Three Virus?" asked Bertram.

"I don't know, do I?" He handed the tree to Bertram.

"And you think whatever Meena's ransacker was looking for was—"

"See previous statement," said Rollie.

"And our redheaded stalker. He tracked down Meena's mom. Was it because he couldn't find what he was looking for here and then decided maybe Meena had—"

"To be determined, Ludlow."

"But what are the chances of that? Of Meena picking up something related to the Number Three Virus?"

"Bitty," said Rollie. "Of the itty variety. But that's not the point, is it?"

"Well, if it were here, it's not here now," said Xylith. "I went through everything. Every corner of the furniture. Every tiny tree. Every token for a freebie whatnot. It's not even all from Centurna. That woman picked up stuff from half the GCU. Our red rummager either found what he wanted and took it, or Meena never did have it."

"Listen to what I'm saying. It doesn't matter if she has it," said Rollie. "She doesn't need to have it. She likely doesn't have it and never blasted did. Someone *thinks* Meena *could* have it. Someone who's compulsive and driven and did I mention compulsive? And that, my friends, is the only fraggin' important bit.

"Now," he clasped his hands together with a single, echoing clap, "I don't know about you two, but I feel like paying a little visit to Centurna-4."

Bertram Ludlow was behind the lead controls of his very own Interplanetary Cruise Vessel, and he was sure he'd never view anything the same way again. No video game flight simulator prepared you for the exhilarating responsibility of an actual rumbling multi-ton ship as it hurtled through the fabric of space.

And he loved every second of it.

They were rocketing away from Hyphiz Epsilon—"Give it more boost, Ludlow! That thing, there! Pull it down!"—when Bertram's sweatshirt buzzed.

"Uh, kinda busy right now!" Bertram shouted, hoping the caller heard.

It buzzed again.

Rollie growled and fished the thing from Bertram's sweatshirt pocket, while still instructing. "… Okay, you got it! Let up on the boosters. Let up, let up …" Rollie turned his attention to the holographic head in his hand. Bertram caught a glimpse. It was Rozz. Fluffy, pink and coated with dust, she was like a slipper that had been lost under the bed for a year.

"Rollie Tsmorlood?" Rozz's squint transformed to wonder. "Wow! I thought you'd croaked on Altair-5! Where's Bertram?"

"I'm here, Rozz," called Bertram.

"Hey," said Rozz, "I went to your salvage place, and I have two words for you."

"Rotten timing?" suggested Rollie, turning back to Bertram. "… Close the lomb casings! No, not there. There."

"Wayning Gibbis."

"Wayning gibbis?" Bertram checked the gauges against his notes. Things looked good. They were actually headed on course. He might just have done it. "What's wayning gibbis? Some sort of inflammatory condition?"

"Gibbis is a dude," she said. "And he and his buddy stopped by Two Liddlebiggs' salvage just last week, asking about a job they'd done on—"

"Centurna-4?" Bertram asked.

"Thunder: stolen," she said. "How do you know about Centurna-4?"

"Wild guess. Go on, Rozz."

She ran a hand through her hair, stirring up a cloud of dust. "Anyway, Gibbis said they wanted to see everything that came from Centurna-4. And it was this shitload of stuff; believe me, I've breathed in half of it. So Liddlebigg, he says, 'Here's the bulk of it, except for the couple of things I just sold.' And Gibbis says, 'Sold? When?'

"And Liddlebigg says, 'Just now. To the little blue-haired chick in the fancy ICV. If you hurry, you can catch her.' And with that, Gibbis tells his buddy, 'You go through this,' pointing to the salvage, and he runs, all warp speed, out of the building. Just books it and ditches the guy."

"Wait. So what happened to the guy left at Liddlebiggs'?"

"He spent hours doing the dirty work. Eventually someone else came to pick him up. Didn't even buy anything. But," she said, "he did leave this... Wait a minute. I'm sending it to your screen."

Bertram could see something flat appear out of the vis-u. "What is it?"

"Business chip," said Rollie. "'Gibbis & Associates Interstellar Investigation Services. Discreet Expertise. Big Bang for Your Buzz. Underworld Certified.' And there's a vis-u connection."

Rozz's head popped out again, bumping the info out of frame. "Gibbis' buddy asked Liddlebigg to buzz him if he could remember anything else about the shipment or anyone who bought something from it."

"What did they look like?" This was Xylith, peering over Rollie's shoulder. Bertram wasn't sure how long she'd been standing there.

"Hey," a smile of recognition crossed Rozz's smudged features, "Xylith right? I saw you on Skorbig. I'm Rozz."

"Well, it is just a pleasure to finally meet you, Rozz. I—"

"What," said Rollie firmly, "did they look like?"

"Honest?" Rozz laughed. "Like something Jane Goodall would try to drag back into the banana tree."

Rollie raised an eyebrow. He looked to Bertram.

"It's our guy," translated Bertram. "So, Rozz, you didn't happen to find anything in the salvage, did you?"

"Besides blacklung and this weird rash? No. That has been its own reward."

"You're awesome, Rozz. Go back to the Manor ..." Her image began to fade away. "... And have that rash looked at!"

He wasn't sure if she'd heard him before she disappeared.

"So," said Xylith. "Wayning Gibbis."

"Yup." Bertram checked a gauge.

"Private investigator hired by someone to find something that was once on Centurna-4."

"Yup."

"Didn't find it at Liddlebiggs'. Didn't find it at Meena's. Didn't find it at Meena's M.A.'s ..."

Bertram grinned. "What do you say we give Mr. Gibbis a buzz?"

Rollie was already clicking the vis-u connection on the calling card.

Bzzp...

Bzzp...

Bzzp...

An orange-furred creature with a pink fleshy face smiled broadly out at them. The fur was groomed to perfection. His office was all streamlined efficiency and right angles.

"Hi, you've reached Gibbis and Associates Interstellar Investigation Services. We are so discreet, we can't even tell you what we're doing right now. But you can expect that same sensitive, quality service from us when we return your comm just as soon we can. Leave a message!"

Rollie cut the connection. "Busy ransacking someone else's place, I imagine."

Xylith stroked a set of lips thoughtfully. "It makes you wonder if he ever thought to search Centurna-4."

Glaem Studios lay across the landscape like a carcass in the desert, picked clean by buzzards. Holes gaped where architectural embellishments might have hung. Metal girders propped up rotting balconies. Tall grasses grew around the fence, and the gate screeched in the breeze.

Over time, the spongy groundcover extending from the ravaged structure had waved like a rough ocean. Where it cracked, black smoke seeped from the earth below, giving off a foul, burnt rubber scent. Bertram expected Rollie to make a beeline for the building and bust through its weathered doors. Instead, he lingered, scanning the landscape with keen eyes.

"What is it? What do you see?" Bertram wasn't sure, but he'd always gotten the impression Hyphiz Deltan eyesight was a whole lot better than his own. Maybe it was simply a reflection of the man's years of Underworld training. Or possibly there was some automatic bias that goes along with having bright orange eyeballs.

"Dunno," Rollie said, but his voice was distant. After a moment he shook his head and led the way inside.

The interior of the studio was much like the outside, offering only a sense of what had once been. The roof sagged. Rusty stains lingered where rain had pooled. Patches of old carpeting loitered in faded glory. Marks creasing the bare floor left maps to where stages, chairs and equipment had rested.

Maybe it was the eerie despair of the place or maybe it was the way Rollie had paused at the gates, but every now and then Bertram found himself catching a shift in the light, a shadow out of the corner of his eye. He'd turn, to spy dust and pollen on the breeze.

They spent time feeling around the walls, looking for some residue of rationale for recent events, but the Liddlebiggs had ripped Glaem history from its roots. Soon Xylith, Bertram and Rollie stepped back into the hazy light with nothing to show for it but dirty hands and a greater insight into the robust lifespan of dropped snack chips.

They were checking around the exterior in the same way, when Rollie spun around, pulled a handlaser and directed it toward the tall grasses outside the fence.

"All right, you. Come out or I flush you out. Your choice."

Silence held. Bertram scanned the weeds, wondering if all his ideas about unnatural eyesight and Underworld training had been over-swayed by misplaced Deltan confidence.

Even the air didn't stir now.

"That brush looks pretty fraggin' dry to me. I wonder, how much of a spark would set it flaming sky high?" called Rollie. "What do you say? Should we find out?" The edge of delight in the man's voice was concerning.

"Rollie, face it," said Bertram, "you're talking to yourself, man. Nobody's out there. Nobody's—"

A gaunt figure stepped from the grass and up to the fence. It was a tiny ancient woman, dressed in a strange assortment of tied fabric panels and parts of a military uniform.

"Very good." Rollie motioned her with his gun. "Come here, round the front."

They met her at the gate. Her hat, a peaked creation the color of the grass, was loose on her head. It bore a faded crest that said, "Klaer Command." Her hair trailed around her like tangled vines.

"You live here?" Rollie asked.

"Are you the coach?" Her eyes were large and luminous, larger for the smear of thick kohl drawn around them.

"Who are you? Why've you been watching us?"

"Ah," a smile split her gaunt face, "you work for the King. I should have realized such fine, brave people must work for the King."

Rollie leaned to Xylith and muttered. "The Centurna System's not become a monarchy of late, has it?"

Xylith's eyes were glued to the old woman. "Not that I know of."

"He was back, you know," the old woman continued. "The King. Too short, too short, but ah, such a grand return! Until the invaders took the kingdom away."

Rollie's eyes narrowed. "The planet Klaer, you mean?" He holstered his gun. "Do you remember when this was?"

"He arrived with our subjects, you know. Such a grand procession!" Her eyes shone with joyful tears. "And they came to share in his wisdom. And they went off to spread his word. But then it changed." Her expression clouded over. "He was so angry. He left and hasn't returned." A tear rolled down her cheek. It made a clean spot.

"Look, can you describe any of these—"

"Do you remember? His new palace was here." With a youthful speed Bertram didn't expect, she ran to a level spot outside the gate to show where it had stood, arms sweeping wide. "Some days he would spend the whole day in it. But when it was quiet, he would walk the True Palace and I..." she held her chin up high, "... walked with him."

"As his Queen?" asked Xylith. "Queen ..." She thought a moment, "Wuvdora?"

Bertram turned to her. "Seriously?"

Xylith shrugged.

But the woman's face lit up. "You remember!" She twirled on a toe. "We would talk of the old times, the King and I! Days when the kingdom was in its glory."

"And when she had regular work," whispered Xylith. "I heard she went missing. I didn't know they'd evacuated without her."

"But then the King went away, and the invaders came. And the True Palace was gone." Wuvdora's expression was wistful. "They said it was for the best. But the invaders lie. They rip and tear until nothing is left."

"Were these invaders sort of, um ..." Bertram gestured for what he thought the intergalactic symbols of snout and tusks might be.

The woman's head bobbled so quickly back and forth, Bertram thought it might spring right off. "The King will be so unhappy when he returns. Just like his subjects were, when they saw the devastation." She buried her face in her hands and wept.

Xylith gave a sidelong glance to herself. "You mean someone came here after the, er, invaders did?"

The woman threw herself on Xylith sobbing. "If only the King had let me go with him. But he said I should wait for the next Royal Coach." She peered up at Xylith, black trails streaking down to her neck. "Are you the coach?"

Xylith just patted the woman awkwardly.

"Hey, Your Highness?" Rollie leaned on the pillar at the front gate. "Tell us some more about your King, eh? What'd he look like?"

"Oops!" The woman pointed at Rollie and giggled. "Number's up!"

"What'd she say?" said Bertram.

"Pardon?" said Xylith.

"Number's up!" Queen Wuvdora doffed her hat. Underneath it was a metal circlet, encrusted with layers of colored crystals. Some of the prongs were bent and some of the crystals were missing. She took off the tiara, put the hat on and screwed the tiara down over it. She then proceeded to do a little toe-shoe dance around the wavy surface of the ICV lot. "Number's up, number's up, num-ber's up!" she sang.

Rollie looked from the woman to the pillar beside him. In a flash, he was pushing on its bricks, scouring its base and searching the grass around his boots. Soon he was extending his search to the inside fence perimeter. "Didn't you hear her? Frag it, don't just stare. Help me look, would you?"

"Rollie," said Bertram, "okay, it's weird…"

Wuvdora leapt by. "Number's up! Number's up!"

"… Really, really weird. But we're not exactly working with what you'd call a reliable narrator here. Whatever Gibbis has been searching for, I'm guessing this King—Jym Ragobar or whoever—took it with him when he left. Before the salvage guys got here."

"So she's a Smorg short of a full package," Rollie said to the weeds he was currently molesting. "I've spent quality time off-orbit myself, Ludlow. It made me many things. It didn't always make me wrong."

"But… 'number's up'? How does that even help us? All that tells us is that the numeroterrorist might have set up shop here. And that he might have left."

The woman had changed her tune now, possibly an anthem for the planet Klaer. She held her arms straight over her head in a salute, but it looked more like she'd just finished an Olympic gymnastics routine. Wuvdora noticed the trio was not saluting, and she scowled, motioning them all to join her.

Bertram and Xylith obliged. But Rollie just watched them, got this brief expression like someone had turned on all the lights in his attic, and he ducked out the front gate.

Bertram shot a questioning glance to Xylith.

"Don't ask me," said Xylith lowering her arms as the song finished. "I've never spent quality time off-orbit."

They found Rollie hard at work, stomping down all the grass out front of the property. Bertram started to ask about the realistic need for this impromptu lawncare, but a closer look answered his question.

Attached to the front wall, they could now see the old address sign for Glaem Studios.

Rollie beamed over folded arms. "Three Glaem Square," he read aloud, like he was announcing the discovery of King Tut's tomb or something.

"Uh-huh …?" Bertram glanced at Xylith again. She shook her head.

Rollie frowned at their blank faces. "Three Glaem Square," he told them.

"We heard. We read," said Bertram. "It's just—"

The man let out an exasperated huff. "Flamin' Altair, you people. Don't *read* it. Why would you *read* it? Look at the fraggin' shape of the three. The shape, the *shape*."

That was easier said than done. It required pushing aside the Translachew translation that kept popping up in Bertram's mind. Bertram had to actively force himself to unfocus and see the symbol as a series of lines.

Really, when you got right down to it, he considered, the symbol was basically a Y. Or a fork-in-the-road. Or…

Bertram laughed as his own attic lights flipped on. "Ah," he said. "The flag."

Rollie was already unscrewing the glass cover off the symbol. "Imagine, all this time, a fraggin' Centurna-4 three. But that's the problem with language, innit? A symbol for this over here is the symbol for that over there. Half a planet away and it's totally different."

The old lady had joined them and was watching with great interest.

"That's why it's always good to learn as many languages as you can without the fraggin' Translachew. The gum's made us lazy. Me included, or I would've thought of this sooner." He pulled a knife and slowly, carefully, began to edge the cover panel out. He set the panel down in the grass.

"Number's up," the old woman told him.

"Fraggin' straight, Your Highness," agreed Rollie. Inside was a technology half the size of a portable vis-u, with a tiny screen and foldable keypad built into it. "I see it's got a Uninet connector." At the jar of movement, the screen flickered to life. They all drew closer.

HI, THERE! WOULD YOU LIKE TO:

- ❑ Take a number?
- ❑ Return a number?
- ❑ Destroy all data on the Uninet in a violent and indiscriminate fashion?
- ❑ Edit program?

Suddenly, the screen grayed out, and they all stepped back. "I didn't touch it," said Bertram.

A dialog box had popped up that said:

PASSCODE: PICK A NUMBER.

Underneath, a cursor blinked expectantly. Nobody moved for a long moment.

"So…" said Xylith finally, gaze frozen to the device, "that'll be the virus, then."

"And the anti-virus," said Rollie.

"And then some," said Bertram.

"Well, Jym Ragobar always was thorough," mused Rollie.

"So..." Xylith was still trying. "Next steps... Um..."

By now, Rollie had grabbed the glass panel and snapped it back over the number three. With a flick of the knife, he began to cut through cords and pry the whole symbol off the wall. It screeched in protest before it gave way.

"Right," he said. "Clearly, this is not for messing around with. This is for dumping on someone who'll know what to do with the blasted thing, prints and all."

"So... O'wun?" asked Xylith.

"Oh, this is bigger than O'wun. Much, much bigger. And unfortunately, that means it needs to go to the one place I never thought I'd go of my own volition in my entire Underworld career. Frankly, I can't believe I'm suggesting it now." He took a deep breath. "I want to go to the law."

The old lady turned to Rollie. "Are you the coach?"

He tucked the three under his arm and smiled. "Yes."

27

"You are not going to believe who's come to see you, M.C. Blyte," muttered Middly's voice through the intercom. "I've got—Hey, wait! You can't do that!"

Blyte figured it was Lyuna Flutterbitt; they'd been trying to pin her down for days. Yet the door opened and in swept four lifeforms, or rather three lifeforms and Waranda Blyte got a sense of a fourth.

It was the latter—a tall, imposing being in some distracting all-terrain camouflage—who stepped forward first, clunking something onto her desk. Her brain kept trying to forget him as he stood there, but she could still sense his lack of Flutterbitt.

"Hear you're in charge of the Skytreg investigation," the man said in a curt accent that sounded like the Hyphiz System, possibly East End Hyphiz Delta. "I believe you're looking for this."

It was one symbol from an old sign. They hadn't made signs like this for over a hundred U-years. The thing was rusty and wrapped in the scum of centuries.

"Oh, I'm sorry," she said, pushing the thing back toward her guest, "I'm afraid you've confused the RightGuides with *Antiquated Intergalactica Happy Hour*. That films at The Starburst twice weekly. That way." She pointed left. "Good luck."

"I know where we fraggin'-well are," the man snapped. "Inside, inside." He pulled a knife (she pulled her XJ-42), which he used to pry off the translucent front covering. It came away with a pop. He gestured to the item's contents, but she was more interested in his face.

Initially, it was hard to separate him from the camo that so desperately sought to blend and blind. But once she got it, he came in clearly. He had sharp, distinctly Hyphiz Deltan features. Familiar ones, complemented by old, prominent scars and a few fresh wounds.

It came to her. "Captain Rolliam Tsmorlood, isn't it?" He was known in Underworld circles, completely banned from the Hyphiz System and popular in Vos Laegos. (She'd heard he tipped well, unusual in the Underworld where they were mostly cheap slaggards.) Last word was, he'd been sent to Altair-5 for the final crime in an infraction archive the breadth of a Vos Laegos moon. She just wasn't sure what the laws were about Not Dying On Altair once you got there. She'd have to look it up—fast.

"Dax Q. Phlyjollee," the man corrected, flashing the kind of bright, reassuring smile that made her really glad she still had her gun fixed on him. "People confuse us all the time." He thumped down into one of the guest chairs. "Look, er…" sun-colored eyes focused on her nametag, "… MesoCommander Blyte: an artist friend of mine bought some salvage that came from Centurna-4. Since then, she's been chased, framed, sent to Mawdank confinement and, while a guest of those facilities, her studio was ransacked. Fortunately, they didn't get their hands on it."

"And 'it' would be …?" She looked down at the item in question.

"A little something for the removal and restoration of bulk Uninet data. Like a certain missing prime number, perhaps?" He jostled the device, and the screen flickered to life. The menu on it made Blyte's breath catch in her throat.

"Number's up!" sang an old lady in the group, peering at Blyte with huge blackened eyes.

Blyte frowned from her, to the device on the desk, to the Hyphiz Deltan. Her heart beat fast. "And this was in your friend's salvage here on Vos Laegos?"

"My friend's on Hyphiz Epsilon. We found this on Centurna-4. We backtracked the item there." He took a moment to explain, with one of his group—a Dootett woman—filling in the details he missed.

By the time they were done, Blyte had a whirl of intra-jurisdictional conflicts flying in her head. Who was in charge of this? The salvage place was on Daglann-Da. The break-in was way out in the Hyphiz System. And Centurna-4, well, that was basically off-grid; even the other planets in the system didn't bother with Centurna-4 these days.

If the device contained an antidote for the Number Three Virus, then the Coalition of Planets would be hot and heavy for it. In fact, their people were destined to be here any minute, to pack up Skytreg and haul him back to HQ.

Combine this with the Tsmorlood situation and the fact that they were currently looking for a camo-wearing suspect in relation to the Skytreg break-in, and well, it was hard to know exactly where to start.

Of course, until the Coalition officially got here, the group technically in command of the Skytreg investigation was still...

Blyte hit the intercom. "Middly, come here. Bring gloves." She turned to the Deltan. "I'm going to need the name and contact information for your friend who bought the salvage, and—" The door opened, and she handed the device, sign and all, to a gloved Middly. "Get this to the team at Analyzing Teeny Tiny Evidence."

"Yes, ma'am."

"Have them run prints, residue and any other scan you can come up with, outside and in. Then have TechSplatter see what they can find out about the device, preferably without touching that passcode. I don't want to activate it, but I sure as flaming Altair want to be certain it's what we think it is before we share it with the Coalition. Tell Teeny Tiny and TechSplatter it's a Two-Plus-One Code Green."

"A what?"

"A 'Do It Now Because I Said So' request."

"Yes, ma'am," said Middly," and he rushed to the door.

"Oh, and Middly," called the Deltan, stopping him in his tracks. "I believe you'll want this, too." He tucked a small, sealed container into Middly's other hand.

Middly looked to Blyte, and she nodded permission. Setting aside the sign, Middly unscrewed the jar, peered into the container and wrinkled his nose. "Fur?"

The Dootett lady stepped forward. "I collected that off the salvage in the studio," she said. "We think it's Tangtapien."

"Interestingly," added the Hyphizite, "it was a Tangtapien following my friend."

Here, Blyte's fourth guest, a male she'd barely even noticed until now, stepped forward and plunked down a fancy vis-u/Uninet device sporting the image of a business chip on it. "Wayning Gibbis. A gumshoe. Looks like the galoot was hired by some mug to shadow the skirt to get the goods. He flim-flammed an anonymous tip to get the dame sent to the bighouse, while he went over every inch of her joint like silk stockings on Betty Grable's gams."

Blyte blinked. Not only was Translachew doing a terrible job making sense of a single thing the man said, she realized the man looked like Bertram Ludlow. Yes—Bertram Ludlow, the one she'd wanted for questioning in relation to the Skytreg break-in.

The Tryfling grinned like this was the best part of his day. It was all so surreal, she wondered if she'd fallen asleep at her desk again. It had been a few days since she'd gone home.

"He means," the Deltan translated, "Gibbis is a hired investigator. It's ... all pretty much on the card." He picked up the handheld. "I'll send it to you, along with my friend's contact information."

"You do realize, even if we confirm whose hair it is, it's already been tainted. I can't verify where it came from. Same with the device. If what you're telling me is true, you removed them from the scene."

The Deltan gave an almost imperceptible shrug, like it wasn't even worth the effort to be fully indifferent. "I confess, you weren't my first thought when I took 'em." With a crooked thumb, he indicated the old lady, who was knighting Ludlow and the Dootett woman with one of Blyte's sports trophies. "You'll want her, too, by the way. She saw the fellah who stashed the device in the sign. Just ask her about the King. She'll tell you."

"King?" said Blyte.

The Dootett lady nodded. "Of the planet Klaer."

A song—presumably the Klaer planetary anthem—started up from the back of the room. The old lady put some real gusto into it.

"Has to do with Glaem Studios, Centurna-4. Where we found the device," the Deltan continued, raising his voice over the singing, and obliging the old woman in some planetary salute they had all inadvertently become involved in. "That's Evni Spigott, who played Queen Wuvdora in those classic shamcomm films. As you can see, she's not exactly firing all her rockets these days. But if you can wheedle a description out of her, I suspect you'll find it matches the fellah who put the prints on the device."

The song finished. They lowered their arms.

Blyte looked at him narrowly. "And why do I get the feeling you know whose device that is?"

"Suspicions aren't evidence. And you have all that now. I know one thing, though; it's not Zenith-fraggin'-Skytreg." The man rose. "Skytreg was set up. He's innocent. Of this, anyway. First time for everything." In one fleet move, the Hyphizite was out in the hall, with Ludlow and the Dootett woman trailing him and the old lady bringing up the rear.

"Hold it! We are far from done here," Blyte said, moving swiftly after them and raising the gun that, to her own surprise, had been tight in her hand all this time.

The Deltan didn't bother to turn, just gave that barely perceptible shrug. "You have what you need."

"I said stop. And I will fire."

They were at the front desk now, or was it suddenly Celestial Circus? It was hard to tell. Several lifeforms in formal hats, shiny suits and sashes had burst through the doors, followed by a color guard with cheerful Coalition of Planets banners twirling, people distributing flowers, and a troop of armed beings calling out a chant. This last part of the parade marched forward with a hovercart carrying the latest model ZapTrap and about four hundred toks of other equipment.

But with Ludlow and the Deltan in her sights, Blyte was not about to give up so easily. She flipped her settings to stun, curled her finger around the trigger, squeezed and...

The roundest of the visitors in suits extended an elbow to her in a traditional Coalition of Planets greeting, jarring her own. The shots went wide. "MesoCommander Blyte? I'm Ambassador Hanshar Zibbidi, Coalition Chairman. You may call me His Peaceable Pompness. I buzzed you about this visit?"

Blyte cringed as one of the court stenographers hit the tile floor with a thud and that weird old lady dropped on top of him in the middle of her anthem reprise. "Ambassador Zibbidi, I'll be with you in one moment," she said and peered desperately through the crowd.

"M.C. Blyte, we do have a schedule to keep," pressed Zibbidi. "I thought I had made that perfectly clear in the—"

"Frag you and your schedule," Blyte heard herself say. She caught a glimpse of a wavering camo pattern among the troops and rushed toward it.

A smiling being held out a wreath. "MesoCommander Blyte? Please allow me to extend to you this Peace—"

Blyte extended her piece, too. Then she stepped over the stunned flower-bearer, kicked the wreath, and continued toward the camo in the crowd. Once again she aimed her gun. "I see through your camouflage. You will leave when I say you can leave, Tsmorlood, or Phlyjollee, or whatever you're calling yourself these days," she growled.

Lifeforms leapt out of the way, saving themselves and revealing her camo-printed prey. "Weglewiffs, ma'am," drawled the young soldier, who was carrying a camo rocket launcher and looking concerned. "LauncherLeague Zoostan Weglewiffs, ma'am. Did I do something wrong?"

Two hundred eyes fell on her. The music stopped. The only sound was the persistent buzz of the front-desk vis-u. Waranda Blyte winced. Where was that personal beaming technology when you really needed it?

"Perhaps planetary unity and cooperation are done somewhat differently in Vos Laegos City," said Zibbidi tartly.

Blyte holstered her gun, tossed on a smile and hoped the Hub still had some of those free box seat passes to the Hoverboards-n-Hangovers Follies. She had a feeling she was going to need them.

"We did it," cheered Bertram, "and whoa, talk about the lion's den! I mean, that RightGuide, she's not buying the whole Phlyjollee thing at all, is she? And me, I think she was stunned by my celebrity and—"

"Keep moving," said Rollie, motioning them through a Vos Laegos City park. "More distance between us and them, please." Rollie drew Bertram's vis-u from his pocket and tossed it to him.

"You know, there's a certain thrill about this kind of work, and I'm starting to really appreciate its attraction," said Bertram. "First comes the worry, but then there's this amazing relief. I mean, I'm sort of a worrier, anyway. I come from a long line of worriers." At the smirk on Xylith's left face, Bertram added, "No, seriously. We traced our genealogy back to England on Earth. My great, great, great, great, great, great, great, great grand-uncle, Berthold Ludlow of Gloucester was the Royal Worrier to King Richard III. Can't say it worked out great for Richard, but at least he died on Bosworth Field knowing someone else would worry about what happened to him." He considered this further. "Okay, they unburied him in a parking lot sixteen-hundred years later, but still…"

"Cosmic. You can entertain the RightGuides with that story once they've tracked us down," said Rollie. "Keep moving."

Bertram moved and gave his vis-u a quick check. He chuckled as he saw the entry for the last comm they'd made.

"What is it," asked Xylith, "an entertaining message from some fiery celestial body you met in your adventures?"

"Ah, just Wayning Gibbis. We never did get to talk to our Tangtapien friend." Bertram's finger hovered over the entry. "What do you think? Should we give him another shot?"

"I can think of a few people who'd like to give him a shot," Xylith said. "But I'm not sure there'd be much chit-chat."

"*I* still have a few things to discuss," said Rollie.

Bertram pressed the link.

B*zzzzzzzzzp!* (B*zzzzzzzzzp!*)

Bertram frowned, holding the thing to his ear. "That's weird. Do you guys hear an echo?"

B*zzzzzzzzzp!* (B*zzzzzzzzzp!*)

They stopped. They listened. The sound appeared to be coming from the phone. Also, from a purple shrub, fifteen feet away.

B*zzzzzzzzzp!* (B*zzzzzzzzzp!*) "Hi, you've reached Gibbis and Associates Interstellar Investigation Services. We are so discreet, we can't even tell you what we're doing right now..."

Bertram, Xylith and Rollie walked the fifteen feet back to the shrub.

"But you can expect that same sensitive, quality service from us..."

And they found Wayning Gibbis crouched behind it. "...When we return your comm just as soon as we can..." He pushed frantically at the sound controls on his vis-u. "...Leave a message!"

"Hi, there," said Bertram, grinning. "This is Bertram Ludlow. How's it going?"

"Why, Wayning," drawled Xylith, "you have been such a bad private investigator."

The fleshy part of Gibbis' face had gone flamingly red. He thrust the vis-u into his coat, pulling a handlaser with one hand

and a perfectly-folded handkerchief with the other. He dabbed at his brow. "Okay, don't come any closer."

"How long have you been following us, Gibbis?" asked Rollie. "We pick you up at Meena's? Moena's? Centurna-4? Bet it was Moena's, wasn't it? A little cloaking, little duck and cover? And there we were, thinking Ludlow's piloting was the only danger around. Did you decide to let us do all the dirty work on Centurna, too? I hear that's your specialty."

"Never mind that. Just give me the gadget. And do it slowly. You reach for your handlaser? You're dead."

"All this time, waiting for the perfect moment. Well, you *should* be sweating, Gibbis," continued Rollie. "You've lost. It's too late, mate. We're done."

"Done?" The handlaser wavered just slightly.

"That tech you want so bad? Should be in the hands of the Coalition of Planets by now. Soon the number three will be returned to the GCU. And there's not a fraggin' thing you can do about it."

"Wait." His eyes were wide. "That was the Coalition back there?"

"Flamin' Altair, Gibbis, what do you think?"

A burst of laughter escaped the Tangtapien. "That was the Coalition," he chuckled. "Back there." Gibbis' smile grew so wide Bertram could see his back teeth. "You guys found the anti-virus. You brought it to the RightGuides. The Coalition came for Skytreg. And now the Coalition has it!" Still laughing, he clapped Xylith on the shoulder, kissed Bertram on the cheek, started to approach Rollie, thought better of it, remembered he was supposed to be covering them and practically danced to the path.

"What? But—no!" Rollie sputtered. "No jolliness! You sent Meena Tsoogarkken to Mawdank, you slaggard. You do not get to be jolly."

"Yeah, really sorry about the lady. But I'll fix it. I swear." He held up three fingers in some kind of salute. "Tangtapien's honor!"

"What fraggin' honor? And who do you work for?"

"Now? No one." Gibbis started laughing again. "No one at all. Thanks, guys. Thanks so much."

And with a wave, he backed away with them in his sights, and vanished down the path.

28

"Makes no sense," said Rollie over his Carsoolian pod liquor. "Gibbis spends all this time tracking down the anti-virus. Even scoured the Penumbra for it when we was in the RightGuide Hub ..."

"Really scoured," said Bertram approvingly. "I can't believe he got that green stain out of the carpet. I wonder what he used." Gibbis hadn't done anything with the toilet snails, unfortunately. Bertram supposed there was only so much the man could accomplish in his available ransacking time.

"... But then," continued Rollie, "when he learns the Coalition of Planets has got the virus, he's all, 'Stellar. Off I go."

"Maybe he works for the Coalition," suggested Xylith, pouring herself a refill of something that came in a glass so tiny, Bertram almost couldn't see it between her fingers.

"Maybe," said Rollie. "Doesn't fraggin' feel right, though," and he fell into a meditative silence.

Rollie had been unusually quiet and contained ever since they'd left the RightGuides, Bertram thought, adding an ounce of flimberry juice to the drink he was making.

Here they were in Vos Laegos City—voted one of *AstroAdventure* unimags's "Most Supernova Travel Destinations for the Cheap and Reckless," and a place Bertram Ludlow had yet to spend any real time without being chased by angry people with handlasers.

But were they taking on the Emperor's G'napps tables? Hitting Celestial Circus? Getting two-for-one deals on the "Number One Top Best No-Kill-You Cosmic Stellar All-You-Can-Digest Klinko Buffet Nice in the City"? (Bertram had seen some billboards for the place. He desperately needed to know if the Klinko Buffet Nice was even half as long as its name.)

Nope! Since their tete-a-tete with MesoCommander Blyte, Rollie had decided it would be safer to lie low in the Penumbra with the ingredients for a Calderian Casserole and an assortment of adult beverages.

Clearly, he had something on his mind.

Bertram held his glass to the light, then added a little Smorg wine, Veltannan liqueur and just a splash of Zlorgon Subatomic Headbanger because he liked the fog on top. He thought he'd call it Tempting Death, since that's probably what he was doing. But after the past couple of days, he was ready for a little risky celebration.

Bertram stirred the potion and took a sip. He coughed. *More fruit, fewer licking flames*, he decided, reaching for the flimberry juice.

"You know, Rollie," he said after a moment, "I was kinda surprised you didn't just laser Gibbis until he talked."

"Considered it," admitted Rollie. "But I don't have a good bead on this handlaser." He patted the object in question. "Settings are fluky. Likely'd just dust the man before he confessed. Besides," the Deltan clomped his feet onto a the coffee table and chuckled over his drink, "he was just so blasted happy."

"He was, wasn't he?" Gibbis' beaming grin was still vivid in Bertram's mind. "What was that about?"

"Oh, who cares about Mr. Gibbis now?" said Xylith, flicking him away like a gnat in her Southern Comfort. "The RightGuides have the fur sample; I'm sure his DNA is all over Meena's studio. He's not going to slip out of this that easily.

What I want to know is: will the evidence be enough to clear Zenith Skytreg?"

Rollie looked at his glass like he might find the answer swimming there. "Easy enough to prove Skytreg was never on Centurna-4," he said finally. "They could still blame him for ordering the scheme, of course, but right now there's not much evidence to back that up."

"Aside from the tidal wave of money in his place," Xylith reminded him.

"Always gets in the way, don't it?"

"But this is exactly why we should be celebrating," exclaimed Bertram, refilling Rollie's pod liquor and Xylith's thimble. "What's wrong with you guys? You're acting like someone died. We tracked down the device. We got it into the right hands. We're more than halfway to clearing Zenith Skytreg, so you can ruin his life later. I am piloting all on my own, with minor coaching. We totally kick ass! Cheers to us!" Bertram held up his glass, ready for a trio of clinks, but was left clinkless.

"Thing is," continued Rollie, rising to check the casserole in the shipboard Food Processing Unit (and it did smell good) "this may get the number three back, but what does that do for the protective fields? Nothin'. And where's the beaming tech? It wasn't at Meena's. Your Rozz didn't find it at Liddlebiggs'. So where is it? With the returned 'King'? And where's he gone?"

Bertram took another sip. Then—when he didn't start sizzling—a longer draught. "Yeah, I noticed how you conveniently omitted Jym Ragobar's name when you were talking to the RightGuides."

Rollie shrugged. "Law's got the device. What evidence they pull off it is up to them. I got no problem with Ragobar."

"Even if he ordered Gibbis to get Meena out of the way?"

Rollie gave a sharp laugh. "Then I got a problem."

Bertram nodded and looked down at the floor. He realized he could suddenly see tiny fibers in the rug and the tinier, individual strands that made up those strands. All that wasn't as troubling as the fact the fibers seemed to be line-dancing. "Is the carpet... redesigning itself?"

Bzzzzzzzzp!

"...And buzzing? Is it redesigning itself and buzzing? Shh," he cupped a hand to his ear, "I think it's plotting a Turkish weave." He leaned down to listen.

Rollie made a noise at the back of his throat and snatched the glass from Bertram's hand. "It's the fraggin' vis-u, Ludlow. It's always the fraggin' vis-u." He pointed at the wall behind Bertram, where Meena's head projected sideways from the cabinets. "Bleedin' Karnax, you shouldn't drink, mate... Hello, Meena. Funny, just talking about you."

Meena's voice was shrill. "Two hundred thousand, Rollie? You asked my Maternal Archetype for the entire two hundred thousand yoonies bail?"

Rollie tilted his head to see her right side up. "Aw, one hundred eighty or two hundred... What's it matter to Moena? She's got yoonies coming out of her invisible sofa cushions."

From the vis-u panel, Meena scowled. Bertram could detect every individual dot that made up her image. It was mesmerizing.

She said, "The fact that I have a trial coming up, and the shame this has brought to my family, that's bad enough. But you know what it's like owing my Maternal Archetype for anything. The Feegars turn to *my* M.A. for trendy torture ideas. An extra twenty thousand will only prolong the agony. Even if I am absolved of the charges, this one incident will be top on Moena's hit list at every family event until I'm three hundred."

"I'll make it up to you," he said.

"You'll return my twenty thousand yoonies," she said. "But never mind. That isn't precisely why I buzzed. I buzzed to see what you thought about this whole Jymkrax Ragobar thing."

Rollie frowned. "Which thing?"

"I have it right, don't I? Jymkrax Ragobar, the Underworld manager of Quad Three? Azure skinned fellow."

"I'd call him blue, but—"

"You worked in Quad Three, didn't you? Wasn't that your territory?"

"Years ago, when I first started out. I—"

"I thought you knew him rather well?"

"Yes, yes, to the power of infinity, *yes*, Meena. Now what 'thing'?"

"You haven't even looked at the *Heavy Meddler*, have you?" She sighed. "I'm fresh out of confinement, yet somehow I'm more informed about current events than you are. I shall never understand it."

"Meena: Ragobar. Speak."

"Well, he's dead, Rollie," she said. "He was found inside a loombah in the free space somewhere between Vos Laegos and Midliana."

"Dead?" said Rollie and Xylith.

"Dead?" said Bertram. It reverberated in his ears.

"They found his ship first, empty and floating. But it was a tour group waiting to see the loombahs who got the nastier surprise. Seems he'd been lasered, stabbed, poisoned and shot out an airlock. Vos Laegos medical examiners ruled it a suicide."

"He always was thorough," muttered Rollie.

"The strange bit is that Ragobar wasn't trapped in Quad Three with everyone else."

"Yes, Meena, that's the strange bit."

Meena pursed her lips with irritation. "I suppose you'll be attending the funeral. I understand it's all super-secret and private, Underworld only."

"Sure, if I can find out when it is and get there in time."

"It's tomorrow."

"Hm. Not exactly dragging their feet, are they? Where?"

"I said it was super-secret, didn't I? I don't know. Somewhere in Vos Laegos City."

"Ah." Rollie looked around the room and nodded. "Made it."

Meena blinked. "You're in Vos Laegos City?"

"For now, why?"

"No reason." She leaned into the vis-u camera. "Just be careful, Rollie. It's dangerous out there. No rule says you can't die twice."

29

Blyte swept down the station's hall toward the Confinement Hub, with Middly scrambling to keep pace.

"Okay, I looked into it," Middly said. "There's nothing anywhere that sets the duration for sentences on Altair-5. There's stuff about bringing a prisoner to Altair-5. There are regulations for drop-off on Altair-5. There are safety practices for Altair-5. There's even a handy little RegForce book of 'Things to See While You're Speeding Away from Altair-5.' But there's nothing about a prisoner actually having to stay on Altair-5 once dumped there."

Blyte gritted her teeth. "Unbelievable." She would have to bring this up at the annual GCU law enforcement conference. "Next issue," she said. "Skytreg's break-in."

"You wanted to file a Facial-Rec on both Tsmorlood and Ludlow, to pinpoint them for questioning on that."

"Exactly. Why wouldn't the system let me do it?"

Middly referred to his notes. "Ludlow has no registered data. The only time he was in actual custody was on Podunk, and they didn't have the Facial tech to officially scan him into the system."

"And Tsmorlood?"

"When a prisoner is exiled to Altair-5, apparently their archive is compressed and sent to Level 12 Fatally Inactive, where they're zipped, buttoned, buckled and vaulted. Then they're automatically blanked from the Active system. It saves space."

"So unvault it." She flung open the Confinement Hub doors, which was a surprise to them because they usually worked solo. They shrieked as they went flying into the walls.

"To unvault a Fatally Inactive archive," continued Middly, "you'd have to file a Resurrection 490-J."

"Good, go ahead and file one."

"They require a certified retinal scan to prove the individual in question is, in fact, not dead. Which we can't get—"

"Because we can't file a Facial to find him and bring him in. Frag!" she shouted.

Tsmorlood had fallen through a loophole as wide as Chee's Crater. Combine this with the guy's Phlyjollee profile, which was basically one identity registration in an almost obsolete tracking system, and this was not a good day.

"Now, that missing Uninet host, Rordon Moonwax..." she began. "His files indicate he was investigating Altair, but his ship was found on Daglann-Da. Any DNA residue there?"

"Residue, yes. An Active match, no. Same goes for the blood found at Skytreg's."

She felt her teeth clench more tightly. "Because we don't have DNA on Phyljollee and Tsmorlood basically never existed."

Up ahead, the hall was clogged with a jumble of ambassadors, wreath bearers and assorted troops.

"Oh, but ma'am," Middly said, "I also have some amazing news. TechSplatter managed to work around the passcode enough to view a fragment of the program's source. They're convinced that what we have here is the virus *plus* a modified Takebacksie application."

A wry laugh escaped her. "So Tsmorlood was telling us the truth."

"At least about that," said Middly. "We're still checking out the rest of his story. As for Teeny Tiny, this is really interesting. They said—"

Two buff examples of Coalition of Planets soldierhood rolled Skytreg into the hall in his new model ZapTrap, as Coalition PR preserved the moment for their upcoming Uninewsletter. Zibbidi stood in the center of it all, as his PR team got his left side, his right side, rubbing elbows with the troops and pretending to do the same with Skytreg, though the man was in a tube.

At the sight of Blyte, he extended an elbow to her as well, but then pulled back, gave an exaggerated glance around her and laughed. "Just wanted to make sure your weapon was secured this time, M.C. Blyte," Zibbidi chuckled. "We don't want any more accidents, now do we?" He offered her his elbow for real this time, which she reciprocated in a purely cursory fashion, since she recognized applying it sharply to his nose might lack diplomacy. "Thanks for taking care of Skytreg for us," he said. "We'll handle it from here."

"Got to keep to the schedule," she said cheerfully. "So we can discuss the processes for how to handle the little virus/anti-virus device later. We still have some tests we'd like to run on it, anyway."

All the muscles in Zibbidi's face let go at once. "What device?"

"Oh," she said. "The Vos Laegos City RightGuides have identified tech containing both the original virus and the number three anti-virus. It seems to involve a universal Takebacksie program adapted specifically for numbers."

"Not the mythic Do-Over 128!" cried someone from Zibbidi's crew. "The ultimate skeleton keycode for anti-viral data restoration? No one's been able to develop one of those before."

"Yes, a modified Do-Over 128," she said. "I understand that our Analyzing Teeny Tiny unit has also come back with some interesting results after examining the device. Middly, would you like to tell the Ambassadors what that is?" She was rather curious herself.

"Certainly ma'am," said Middly. "Teeny Tiny has confirmed that Jymkrax Ragobar's fingerprints and DNA are all over the device in question."

The group gasped.

"Where did you find this device?" asked Zibbidi.

Blyte smiled. "It was brought to us by a witness who lived near Jymkrax Ragobar's operations on Centurna-4. This witness is currently in our custody and being debriefed." Actually, the woman was sleeping off a rather exhuberant accidental stunning.

Blyte figured that since both Tsmorlood and Ludlow had momentarily disappeared into the ether, there was no real reason anyone needed to know they'd been a part of the equation. At least, not yet. Explaining how they'd shown up, dropped off evidence and then slipped out in the middle of a RightGuide Hub was the kind of embarrassment one wouldn't live down easily—and certainly not with full-time pay and a retirement plan. Besides, Blyte needed more time to dig into the reasons Tsmorlood might suddenly be feeling so helpful.

"Because this new evidence has come to light," continued Blyte, ignoring the look on Middly's face, "the numeroterrorism case is now directly tied to a prominent local murder investigation." As she said it, it was surprising even to her ears. But it felt right. It felt good.

"Murder?" Zibbidi's jowl shook. "Are you talking about the Jymkrax Ragobar case? That was ruled a suicide, wasn't it?"

She had found her footing now, and she was starting to like the view. "You tell me. Ragobar programs the virus and the accompanying antidote for the single largest crime in the GCU. The ransom is paid. The number is not returned. Ragobar is found dead. What does that sound like to you?"

"But there was a suicide letter in his ship, wasn't there?" said Zibbidi.

"You mean the way his screensavers were all set to read, 'Buh-bye!'?" she asked. "I'd call that more a tribute to brevity than any convincing evidence, wouldn't you?"

"But you have the anti-virus. Clearly the Number Three job was botched. If Ragobar were responsible, well, suicide makes sense. It not only conveys shame, but it's the ultimate escape, isn't it? The Underworld has always been very sensitive about these things."

"Or perhaps Skytreg was working with Ragobar and had him killed."

"There's also the possibility I wasn't involved in the Numeroterrorism plot at all," piped up Skytreg in the ZapTrap, grinning. "Of course, you just never know with us Underworld types." As everyone looked at him, he added, "Sorry. Carry on."

"Much as I hate to say it, Mr. Skytreg has a point," Blyte said as the group resumed their journey down the hall. "So I tell you what, Ambassador. I'll let you crack the passcode on our little device and choose when to release the information to the press. I won't even make you get another court override."

Zibbidi looked suspicious. "And what is it you want in return?"

"My team gets lead on the Ragbor case and assists as needed in the Skytreg initiative. We believe in doing our part to help keep crime at bay here in the Vos Laegos system. Consider it interplanetary cooperation at its finest. I hear you Coaltion people are all about that, aren't you?"

It wasn't quite an elbow to the nose. But it was close.

WOOSH!

THUD, THUD, THUD, THUD, THUMP! CLUNK!
BANG!

Bertram's dream mind transformed the sounds into those of a herd of alien cattle operating a furniture moving service, remarkable for their determination and dedication, as well as their uncanny grip with hooves.

THUMP! (rustle.)

The cattle reared and flew away. Their furniture turned to vapor. And from his place on the sofa in the ship's lounge, Bertram peeled open a crusty eye.

He saw Rollie sizing him up with that expression of keen, clinical analysis that Bertram recognized from the days when his alien abduction still had the New on it.

"Oh, did I wake you? Ah, well. No time to waste." Rollie crouched and rummaged around in some bags at his feet.

From one, he withdrew what looked like a very large, multi-sided die from a roleplaying game, wrapped in clear protective plastic. He flipped it to Bertram. It landed on his stomach with a whump.

"You'll want that. Tried and true hangover remedy, that is. Frag me, mate, it was like you was tempting death with that drink last night." Chuckling, Rollie grabbed a bag and disappeared into another room.

"Where we going?" Bertram managed groggily. Or post-grog, as it was.

"Ragobar's funeral, o' course."

"Evening…" Bertram pressed at his pounding temples. He had vague memories of them tracking down the time and location of the event. There'd been something about the Underworld wanting to hold the service while everyone was still in town for the Secret Lair and Arms Show. "Wasn't the funeral supposed to be this evening?"

"And evening, it is," said Rollie. "You were out cold the whole fraggin' day, mate."

Bertram smacked his lips and his dry, dry mouth. It felt like there were chia seeds growing on his tongue. With his vision returned to normal, he grabbed a metal tray and tried to catch his reflection. He extended his tongue and gave a start. "Jesus, sprouts!"

"Mugweed. From the Veltannan liqueur. It'll go away once you get some salt into your system," came Rollie's voice. "Or is that for bark tongue? I never recall."

Bertram sat up and turned his attention to the decahedron on his stomach. The packaging read, "Lastysnag™: *The Number One Name in Krepblips.*"

"No Number Two krepblips for this Tryfeman," muttered Bertram through the sprouts. The noise of the crinkling package was deafening, but it seemed worth it when a puff of savory-sweetness filled the air.

Bertram seized the pastry and took a large bite. It reminded Bertram of pot roast candied in honey and wrapped in one of those rubbery fruit rolls, only not. "Where's Xylith?" he asked through the food.

"Went back to her rental-unit to change. She'll meet us there." Rollie clomped back into the room, having exchanged his camo for something a little more completely black.

"It's convenient your personal style aligns so well with funeral attendance," Bertram observed. The krepblip really was doing the trick. He could feel the energy coming back to him by the second. He spit a few sprouts into his hand.

"Doesn't show blood, is all." Rollie knelt down and dug into the bags, withdrawing a handlaser, another handlaser, a large Swiss Army knife that had never seen Switzerland, a personal wound mending unit, a utility belt, a bag within a bag and three gadgets Bertram didn't recognize. Most vanished into the depths of Rollie's new long, black coat.

"You expect blood at a funeral?" Bertram asked through another bite of the kreblip.

"I expect anything, Ludlow." Rollie smiled, buckling on the utility belt. "It's Underworld."

The super-secret private funeral ceremony honoring Jymkrax Ragobar, Manager of the Underworld's Quad Three, was held on the rooftop of Lascivious Loova's Lodge of Lax Morals and Laundromat.

The press had arrived early.

Hovering vehicles from various Uninet stations shone spotlights, swept up dust and swirled the coats, fur and antennae of the Underworld mourners. Holographic heads of the GCU's favorite newscasters projected from the ships, rattling off questions—"How well did you know Ragobar?" "Did you see any signs he was planning a multi-tiered suicide?" And "What was the deceased's favorite brand of handlaser?"— but no one dignified them with an answer.

Bertram and Rollie emerged onto the roof, ducking from the wind, lights, projected heads and ten people surprised at Rollie's current existential status. They wound their way past catering and Lascivious Loova's erotic Simmi-servers—hard to get an hors d'oeuvre off them, and if you did, even harder to remember you had it—and into a growing crowd. Before them, boughs of local flora draped over a silver rocket perched high on a platform. The rocket sat stalwart and firm, surrounded by many smaller rockets, also wreathed in flowers.

Dusk had fallen over the Vos Laegon horizon, the world's bright suns replaced by the illumination of the "Vos Laegos: You Bet You Can!" sign just kroms away. Bertram was squinting at it, searching for the outline of Skane among its bright letters, when the podium before them came to life. The crowd grew silent as two-plus-one figures took the stage.

Bertram recognized the two—Jor-Jan Chatta-Chu-Bular Meep-Meep and Rentar Proximetra—but the plus-one was unfamiliar. As if sensing this, Rollie said, "Lyuna Flutterbitt. Manages Quad One."

It was a pink, fluffy, butterfly-winged creature that looked like a cross between Mothra and a doodle out of a seven-year-old girl's notebook—which, now Bertram thought about it, were kind of the same thing. Bertram wondered what Underworld skills Flutterbitt brought to the table: glitterbombs and forcing her enemies into over-tight braids? He supposed he'd find out tonight.

Meep-Meep was first to take the vocal projection device. "Greetings, everyone! Rentar, Lyuna and I would like to thank all of you for joining us on this somber occasion. Tonight we honor Jymkrax Ragobar, manager of the Third Quadrant territories of the Intergalactic Underworld Society. Jym was a technical and mechanical genius in the world of stylish crime and a friend to so many among our ranks. His dedication to doing absolutely anything for a yoonie is just one of the qualities that helped him get where he is today."

A blank and deafening silence fell over the crowd.

Meep-Meep looked flustered. "Er, I meant, as a beloved Quad Three manager, not, um, dead. I didn't have a lot of time to write this speech."

"Get on with it!" someone shouted from the crowd.

"Meep-Meeeeep!" someone cheered from a far corner.

Meep-Meep's throat cleared with a rattle. "Now, I'm sure you are all aware, Jymkrax Ragobar's death was not a peaceful one. Hanging himself on a rope connected to an engaged handlaser might be viewed by some as a cry for help. Setting it up so it shot both himself and released a poisoned knife to stab him in the jugular could be considered an expression of a silent misery that some might call overkill. And using his waning energy to toss himself out his own airlock can only be considered a final act of pure desperation. But tonight we are not here to talk about Jymkrax Ragobar's hideous and excruciating death. Tonight, we come to praise his life. And Lyuna, I believe you have a story you'd like to share?" Meep-Meep motioned to the pink figure.

Lyuna flew forward, wings shimmering orange, backed by the sun's last rays. Her eyes were like bright black buttons and around each one was a spray of feathery eyelashes. Her antennae curled into delicate spirals. Her lips perched at the end of a slim pink tube. In a voice like a leaking balloon, Lyuna said, "I remember meeting Jym Ragobar for the first time when we were both suiting up for the Battle of Pachengo Klatts. I was balancing my XJ-59 auto-repeat handlaser and making sure I had enough quasar grenades, when Jym saw me and said, 'Hey, why don't you use a maxblast retroflakk crossover belt for those? They fit the same fasteners and will give you added mobility. I've got an extra.' And wouldn't you know it? I used the belt, swept into the fray doing a double-ergowohm maneuver and wiped out thirty-five Upper Pachengo insurgents before they could so much as pop a dropcannon. And I had Jym Ragobar to thank for it. Thanks, Jym!" Lyuna addressed this to the main rocket by the podium.

"Beautiful memories, Lyuna," said Meep-Meep. "Beautiful memories. Now, Rentar Proximetra would like to say a few words. For those who have difficulties with the Translachew version of Gropkor, I will translate the translation of that translation."

The polished skull of Rentar Proximetra gleamed nobly in the looming media spotlights. She was wearing some elaborate layered ensemble that made the palace at Versailles look low-key. "Tonight," she said, "one star goes out. Yet its dust will form a thousand more."

"Jym Ragobar has bit the big one," Meep-Meep translated. "But his spirit carries on in stuff and, um, things."

The crowd murmured with agreement at this consoling thought.

"The Emperor's G'napps are cast," continued Proximetra, "even the most apparent arcs unclear until all energy has passed."

"We couldn't predict Jym's tragic end," translated Meep-Meep. "We can only see where he's been, except for, of course, those last few moments before the airlock."

A four-armed, muscular guy up front burst into tears. Someone in the back cried out, "We loved you, Jym!"

Proximetra herself seemed to be trying to keep a stiff upper lip. "The biggest, brightest star burns out sooner," she continued, "and—"

"Holy crap," said Bertram.

Because it was at that moment, the words printed at the bottom of a certain flag popped into Bertram's mind in perfect focus:

Fuumere Solif Snuvvid.
"The biggest, brightest star burns out sooner."

It was like a media spotlight had gone off in his mind. "Rollie," Bertram whispered, nudging him. "The flag... She—"

"Later, Ludlow," said Rollie.

"But, Rollie, she said—"

Rollie turned and, through all forty-plus teeth, hissed, "I know. I know what she fraggin' said. Later."

Bertram nodded, though unsure whether knowing meant just knowing, or knowing what Bertram knew he knew now.

The person who framed the Underworld Leader had left a little calling card that only Skytreg, under normal circumstances, would be likely to notice. A smug symbolic ha-ha he might not even have seen for years, depending on his conviction.

But Rollie had said the Gropkors were a dwindling species. Few people embraced the language these days, and even Translachew was only so helpful. Of those who actually knew

Gropkor, how many of them had a hate on for Skytreg enough to frame him? Only one came to mind.

In a way, Rollie had been right. No member of the Underworld could have stolen the number three: but two members working together and both of them Underworld managers? Well, that was a zakari of a whole other pigmentation palette.

There was one thing that still nagged. "Then why'd she sign your petition for an Underworld trial?" asked Bertram.

Rollie didn't hear him over the applause as Proximetra left the riser.

"Now," said Meep-Meep, stepping forward once more, "it's time we say goodbye to our friend Jym Ragobar. Lyuna Flutterbitt, will you do the honors?"

Lyuna nodded solemnly, picked up a cylindrical weapon twice her size and slung it over a winged shoulder. Gliding from the ground, she pulled the trigger, shooting a thin flame. She approached the ring of rockets and applied it with precision to a waiting fuse.

Music rose to a crescendo, and Bertram was surprised to see pop sensation Dumbbell Nebula appear on an once-dark side stage, a mournful melody now lilting from the lead instrumentalist's tube-like nose. The refrain wafted across the roof and echoed through skyscraper caverns, as the rockets caught fire one-by-one. Screaming skyward, they sprang into the air of Vos Laegos City, exploding in showers of color against the evening sky.

Finally, the central rocket, now alone, met its glorious blazing destiny, sending it up, up, up, and—

Er, no. Over a bit … A bit more…

Now down…down…down… *oh God, down*…

Too low…too slow…and—

It slammed right into the "VOS LAEGOS" landmark sign.

"O!" everyone chorused because, y'know, it was. And a second later, the vowel was on fire.

Bulbs all throughout the letter shattered in a chain reaction, causing a blowback that rushed through the air. The hovering

ICVs only fed into the momentum, drawing the cloud of ash across the rooftops like high-powered fans.

Some funeral guests darted out of the way, only to run into it as the wind changed direction. Bertram covered his face and shut his eyes. The music came to a sneezing stop. Everyone coughed.

"Um. Farewell, Jym," said Meep-Meep, over the cries and the chaos. "You'll be with us forever in our hearts. Somewhat less time in the wash. Now, everyone: there's food and drinks over here to my left. And I believe Madame Loova has found us some pre-moistened towelettes for the... well, okay... So... Let's do this party right for Jym!"

And as the air cleared, the music picked up again, this time with a rousing beat.

"Well." Bertram dusted ash from his hair and took advantage of one of those wipes. They had Lascivious Loova's logo on it. Bertram pocketed two extras. "That was different."

"Not enough lift," said Rollie, brushing off his shirt. Black didn't show blood; cremains were a different story. "Should've used self-starting fuel rockets instead of these light-'em-yourself ones. But the hoop of fire's a nice touch. Ah!" His eyes fell on Rentar Proximetra, who was just winding up a vis-u chat with the leader of the Conflagration Squad currently on the ground. "'Scuse me. I got something to take care of."

"Rollie—wait! We need to talk." Bertram motioned him closer. "I figured it out. The slogan on the flag. It finally translated for me. It's Gropkor."

Bertram expected a look of grateful enlightenment to spread across the Hyphiz Deltan's angular features. It was funny how much that resembled apathy. "Yeah, I know. Came to me last night over cocktails," he said.

"You knew?"

"Only for a bit."

"But ... But this means Proximetra was probably in on it with Ragobar."

"Hope so. Otherwise, I wasted all that time searching her ship today for nothing." He flashed Bertram a smile.

"You searched her—"

"Had some time to kill between errands. Didn't find anything. Unless you count a well-archived collection of Gropkor folk music. Which I don't because it's so fraggin' showy. She's got songs in there that last three days. *Three days*, mate."

Bertram wasn't sure if it were the disappointment of missing his second break-in, or the fact Rollie had been right, Bertram really shouldn't drink, that bothered him most. But before Bertram figured it out, Rollie was already halfway across the room and ready for a chat with the Quad Two Manager—and not about her taste in tunes.

"Rentar: a word?" said Rollie.

Coincidentally, a word was all he managed before an eager pink figure swept in between Rollie and Proximetra, like a one-being swarm. "Rollie Tsmorlood! Just the Hyphizite I was looking for," squeaked Lyuna Flutterbitt.

He noticed she'd traded her flamethrower for the well-stocked defense system hanging from an impressive utility belt. One thing you could say about Lyuna; she had a sharp eye for quality armaments.

"Look, I'd love to talk, Lyuna," Rollie craned to see around her, "but right now I need to—"

"I've heard some very interesting things about you lately."

"Let me guess: I'm not dead. I know it's true because twenty people told me so."

He caught a glint of bald head barely two kroms away. Now if only he could extract himself from Lyuna without stunning her clean out of the air, which was becoming an appealing option…

"I hear you've been trying to prove Zenith Skytreg is innocent," she said. "That can't be right, can it?"

"Ah." He smiled. A subject that warmed the heart and several supplementary back-up organs. "Well, it's interesting you mention that. Because at some point, I was hoping you'd lend your eyes to this." He reached into his coat and unveiled the Tribunal petition.

Flutterbitt glanced at it, the mouth at the end of the proboscis giving an "o" of understanding. "Do you really think this is the right time?"

"I think Jym proves we don't always have time," he said.

"Jym proves that losing your Quadrant to outside terrorism can be more shame than a devoted Underworld manager can handle."

"Jym? Shame?" Rollie had meant to play it nice with her, keep it light and polite, but this was simply too inane. His laughter erupted like Spew. "Jym once shamcommed the treasuries of every world in his Quadrant with an 'Inner Office Memo,' ordering them to leave all currency for destruction at his summer home next to a sign that read: 'Drop Fuggy Cash Here.' Shame is not how I'd describe Jymkrax Ragobar."

The sour look on her face suggested Flutterbitt didn't share in his amusement, but it was no surprise there. Her sense of humor leaned more toward the darkly ironic.

"Besides," he continued, "doesn't his method of death sound just a bit much, even for the GCU?"

"Jym always was thorough," said Flutterbitt.

"In his prime."

"And out of it?"

"Like a FizzyYum can with a laser hole."

"Are you suggesting Jym Ragobar didn't die by his own hand?" She blinked the black button eyes, her curled eyelashes batting in syncopation with her wings.

"I don't waste time making suggestions, Lyuna."

"So you say Skytreg's innocent, but you think Jym's been," she whispered, "murdered? Rollie, I'm afraid you may still be suffering from the effects of your traumatic time on Altair-5. It sounds downright ...paranoid."

"Well, you know what they say: 'one man's paranoid fantasy is another man's premature fragging in his sleep.'"

An antenna cocked curiously. "Who said that?"

"I did. Just now." He held out the petition. "Sign?"

She pressed a button at the bottom of the page, and the document rolled up into his hand. "I still don't feel right doing this here. Why don't we talk tomorrow? 'Kay?"

"I'm not messing round, Lyuna," said Rollie. "If Skytreg's blanked of his charges, what then?"

"The ransom was found in Skytreg's home. It's an undisputed fact, Rollie."

"It's the fraggin' GCU, Lyuna. Facts have wiggle room."

"Tomorrow," she said. "We'll talk about it tomorrow."

"Who says I'll even be in town tomorrow?"

"Everyone's in town tomorrow. It's another big day."

He sniffed. "Why? Someone kill himself by accidental beheading?"

"Well, you never know." She gave a coy little wave goodbye.

"Wait. What the frag's going on tomorrow, Lyuna? … Lyuna?"

Rollie heard her giggle as she flapped into the night. He had a feeling it was the same thing the Upper Pachengoan resistance heard, right before she turned them to space dust.

Rentar Proximetra, he noticed, had slipped away.

From the buffet line, Bertram was helping himself to an assortment of intriguing tidbits to counteract the last of his hangover when a voice from behind him spoke softly in his ear. Fortunately, it didn't have a Hyphiz Deltan accent.

"My, my," drawled the voice, "so pensive this evening." He turned.

Xylith was wearing a shiny red creation that appeared to be half laser-repellant armor, half designer cocktail dress. She surveyed him, folded her arms and clicked her tongues to her teeth. "So serious. You'd think you were attending a funeral where the guest of honor just blew up an important planetary landmark, or something." One face gave him a teasing ruby smile. The other sized up the food on his plate with an expression of concern Bertram considered asking her about. But he didn't want to ruin the mood.

"Well," he told her, returning her smile, "unraveling intergalactic intrigue, being surrounded by dangerous alien dames and figuring out an important link in an Underworld conspiracy that might span Quadrants ... It tends to weigh on the mind."

This got the attention of both faces. "Um, that last one?"

Bertram left the line and motioned her to a more private corner. He double-checked to make sure no one was in earshot. "Remember that flag?" he asked. "The one from Skytreg's collections room?"

She nodded, violet eyes wide.

"It finally translated. The motto was written in Gropkor."

A nose wrinkled. "Gropkor? But hardly anyone speaks Gropkor these days. Well, except for ..." Her wide violet eyes grew wider.

"Yup," said Bertram.

"No..." The word was mostly air. "Jym and Rentar?"

"If it ends there."

"Well, now, that just burns my rockets!" Xylith moved to the punch fountain and grabbed a ladle. She skimmed off some ash, then knocked back the cup. "We took a vow. We have Principles. When you can't trust the GCU's most devout and noble criminals, who can you trust?"

"No one," said Rollie, popping up out of who-knows-where. "Not a fraggin' one. Either of you seen Proximetra? I got sidelined by that giggling Sylvenoid."

"Last I saw, she was across the way while Skane was being treated for auditory injuries." Xylith indicated the far end of the Vos Laegos sign, where a few media hovercrafts were taking in all the action.

"Aw, poor slaggard." Rollie actually sounded concerned. "Good thing the Underworld offers six weeks Disability."

"While I have you here," Xylith gave Rollie a mischievous smile, "were you aware your name's being bandied around as a candidate to take over Quad Three?"

Rollie sniffed. "Where's this?"

"Here and there. Mostly there." She indicated a congregation of Underworld members, who seemed to be doing hovershots at the open bar. Apparently, trying to grab them was part of the fun. Someone fell off a chair.

"That explains it; they're launched, the lot of 'em," Rollie said. "Everyone knows I don't go for this Look-at-Me-I-Got-a-Title thing."

"Ah, but you survived Altair-5. You were Captain in the Feegar Rebellion. And for some reason, you seem to be well-liked. Probably because they've never lived with you."

"We'll see if they like me so blasted much when I turn 'em down," he said. "Flamin' Altair, the ash isn't even brushed off our coats and they're talking about who'll run Quad Three. Maybe we should worry about why Quad Three's still blocked, not electing a manager of nothing."

"I told them you wouldn't go for it," Xylith said. "But I hear the official nominations are tomorrow. Rentar's called an emergency meeting, while everybody's still here in central GCU."

Rollie let out a sharp, humorless laugh. "So that's what Flutterbitt was flapping on about." He started to help himself to punch, came up with a little Jym in it, and flung it, cup and all into a lit topiary, which flickered and shorted out. "It's hardly fair. Look how many people are missing. Most of the really connected members didn't even make it. Where's Plait Wangstat?"

"Stuck on Zarquon-3, I'd heard."

"Lenz Vetni?"

"Trapped on Blar-Zix-3."

"Lemmish Bajoom?"

"Three o'clock showing in theatre three of the *Tri-Breasted Triumvirate of Trianglica* on the third moon of Trippelnippel-9."

"Frag me," Rollie murmured.

"Captain Tsmorlood?" At first Bertram couldn't see who was talking, but then realized he wasn't looking down far enough. By Earth standards, it was a tiny girl of about two with large overblue eyes and a blue complexion. Her silvery dress was made of concentric rings that orbited around her middle. "Oh." Rollie's gaze dipped downward, too. "Yes, Prinny?"

"I couldn't help but overhear. I hope you'll reconsider running for the Quad Three position. Really, it's so much more than a title. I feel certain you could make a difference in the current disillusioning leadership direction we've been taking since Skytreg got into office. Perhaps lend balance and assertiveness to the discourse and help with a greater focus on the Underworld as True Art. I know you care a lot about that, too."

"I'm not running, Prinny."

The eyes went two sizes larger. "Please?"

"I said forget it." He made a shooing motion. "Get yourself another fragging patsy, right?"

The swimming pool eyes filled with tears.

"Aw, don't give me the hydrated ocular cavities. When has that ever worked? Now launch, would you?"

"Rollie, geez, man." Bertram patted the kid on the shoulder. "She's just a—"

"Fine," sulked Prinny. In the blink of an eye, Prinny had shifted to a four-foot-tall being the shape of a blue gelatin mold and was slugging away.

"I did not see that coming," said Bertram. Suddenly his new I.D. made so much sense.

"I told you, Rollie." Xylith nudged the Deltan. "You're a Society favorite."

"Hey, Prinny, one second." Rollie called, and the jiggly dessert paused. "Why isn't Gleb here?"

"He's trapped on Junkkit-3 impersonating a wall safe," she responded and glooped off.

Rollie nodded. "Good for Gleb. He used to only do wallets." He glanced toward the bar. "I need a drink. Something besides a Jym and Tonic. You want anything?" He addressed this to Bertram and Xylith.

"Yeah, the remote," said Bertram. "I'm going for a walk." He needed to clear his head. He had this feeling there was something they were missing, something big and obvious, and he couldn't think with Dumbbell Nebula tootling in the background.

Rollie raised an eyebrow. "You need the ship's remote to take a fraggin' walk?"

"If I want to guarantee the ship's still here when I get back, I do." Old Bertram would have been too concerned about being lasered to have said such a thing. New Bertram just didn't care. Funny, there was so much power in Not Caring. He liked it.

"Fair enough," conceded Rollie, tucking the device into Bertram's open palm. "Just keep an eye out for RightGuides. I don't think MesoCommander What's-Her-Name gives up so easy."

Bertram nodded. "Coming?" he asked Xylith.

"Well…" There was a lot of dimple potential when you had two faces. "…I suppose I could use some air."

Bertram heard Rollie say something about the peculiar oxygen deprivation on city roofs these days, as they disappeared into the night.

$\sqrt{961}$

They peered out, stepping from Lascivious Loova's infamous back door and onto the street. The place had three exits, all of them back doors; Bertram wasn't sure how Loova managed it.

Away from the fire and the media's glare, Bertram could finally appreciate the beauty of this Vos Laegos evening. It was owed as much to well-calculated technology as nature. While the moons were high, the streetlamps shone a light simulating golden sunset—perfect for setting just the right mood, but even better for not getting stabbed in an alley over your piggelties winnings. On a night like this, with an intriguing alien lady at his side, it was almost inevitable that Bertram Ludlow would have but one thing on his mind.

Was Jymkrax Ragobar murdered, or was it the most thorough suicide in GCU history?

Two things. Two things on his mind.

Were Ragobar and Proximetra working together to frame Zenith Skytreg, and if so, did she off Ragobar?

Maybe three. *Who was the Tangtapien working for, and would he ever get therapy for his OCD?*

Where was the technology controlling the viral field, and why hadn't that been found yet?

Who'd pay to hear a Zenith Skytreg autobiographic musical?

"Shut up, shut up," Bertram hissed. "Can't you see I'm relaxing here?"

"Hey, you invited me on this walk, Mr. Ludlow." Xylith shot him a double-frown. "But don't you worry; I have plenty of other places I could be." She started to cross the street.

"No, no, stay!" He took her arm and drew her back to the path. "It's not you. It's this Skytreg thing. It's in my head. I can't stop thinking about it. I just feel like something important is right here," he held his hand before his eyes, "and it's too close and I can't see it."

"Well, I can understand that," she said. "The Number Three Virus has thrown everything off. Like Rollie was saying, half the people we know are gone." Her hand reached out and snatched something from a passing tourist's bag. "It's not like I haven't been able to pick up work." What she'd picked up was a wallet. She thumbed through it, examined the yoonie cards, tucked them into her purse and then stashed the wallet into a potted plant. "But it sure is hard to know who you can trust… Ooh, look!"

She'd paused at the booth of an on-street vendor featuring a mix of items, including imported Dootett sunglasses.

Bertram said, "You know, Wayning Gibbis *was* really happy when we told him what we did with the anti-virus."

She faced him wearing a stylish quad of sunglasses with mirrored lenses and holographic eyeballs. "And why is Mr. Gibbis' good mood ruining ours?"

"Because I think Proximetra hired him."

She wrinkled a nose and removed the glasses, perusing her other options. "What happened to our 'Coalition of Planets hired him' theory?"

"Hear me out," said Bertram. "Say something between Ragobar and Proximetra goes wrong. It happens after the shamcomm goes out but before the number three can be returned. Jym either knows he's in jeopardy or wants to have some leverage. So he hides the viral device in the address sign on Centurna-4. Then he heads to the central GCU and gets himself thoroughly killed."

"By Proximetra?"

"Or a few flunkies. Or maybe it's an accident, and the general overkill was designed to complicate things. Either way, Proximetra still needs the anti-virus. The ransom has hit. The whole GCU is expecting her to return the number three. But the device is gone. She can't find it. It's not in his ship. It's not on Jym. She knows Jym did something with it. So she goes to Centurna-4 and discovers the whole place has been cleaned out by a salvage company. She's in a panic now."

"Our Royal Subjects who were so sad about the Kingdom being gone?" suggested Xylith.

"Hey, good one." Bertram hadn't caught that. "Now, Proximetra can't be running all over the GCU, trying to recover this thing. She still needs to keep up appearances. So she hires Gibbis to track down the company and find the device." Bertram chose some green specs and handed them to her.

Xylith tried them on. They projected the Vos Laegos City landmark sign in an arch effect over her head. She looked like the Statue of Liberty, if Ellis Island had gotten a GCU makeover. "So Gibbis and his partner hit Liddlebiggs', Gibbis trails Meena and we both know the rest of the story from there." She mulled it over and her left face appreciated it sooner. "So then Gibbis was buoyant because the anti-virus got, well, not into Proximetra's hands precisely, but at least safe hands who could do the right thing with it."

"Exactly," said Bertram. "The whole thing works out just fine for Proximetra, too. If any prints are on that chip, they're Jym's. Jym's dead, he takes the full rap for the virus and the Coalition of Planets, presumably, will be returning Three for her any time now. The pressure's off Gibbis, Skytreg looks worse than ever since his presumed accomplice is dead and Proximetra's a satisfied client."

Xylith traded the Vos Laegos themed shades for orange ones that pulsed with energy. "You are clever, Bertram...Very clever. With your fine mind, you really should consider a career in the Underworld. Aside from the occasional murder, it does have its perks, you know."

"So I've seen," he said. "The white-knuckle thrills ... The exotic locales ... The, er," he glanced at her, "smart and sexy co-conspirators."

She blushed delicately in duo. "Which reminds me, Mr. Ludlow. Did I hear right, that you and that Rozz are no longer a ... um ... chemical compound?" She let the words hang in the air with balmy anticipation.

"Funny you mention it," Bertram told her, not quite achieving balmy, but at least working up a good meaningful humidity. "It *was* a weak covalent bond."

"So what you're saying is, you two won't be sharing any ... um ..." she chose the words carefully, "electrons ... anymore?"

Bertram felt like Vos Laegos had turned up the heat ten degrees. He said, "As it happens, my electrons are completely flying solo." It was the first time he'd ever broken out in a sweat over high school chemistry, but he sort of hoped it wouldn't be the last.

"Well, that's *very* interesting ..." she purred.

"You know what else is interesting?" Bertram asked. And he was just settling on an original line, something confident and cool—something very New Bertram—when his eyes fell upon a sign next to a stack of thin, polymer sheets. And before he could stop it, Old Bertram jumped right in and shoved New Bertram out of the way. "Holy shit, an Interactive Holomap of the GCU!"

"Beg pardon?" Xylith blinked.

After the Gibbis Enlightenment (as he planned to call the section in his memoirs), questions that had been floating around Bertram's problem-solving mind were coming together much more quickly now, organizing themselves into an idea ... then a plan. Bertram pointed to the sign on the table:

KLINKO brand INTERACTIVE HOLOMAP OF THE GCU!

How many worlds YOU seen? Chart your course across the stellar stars and mark places you visited and see. Educational!

Learning something! Fun! Cosmic entertainment for parental archetypes and also progeny, too! Able to customize for self and others! A value of cheapness at four yoonies!

Bertram had his money out in a flash, and the vendor came running over from another booth to seize it.

"Bertram ..." Xylith made that clicking noise again with her tongues. "Great galaxies, save your money. Your ICV already logs where you travel. If it's that important for you to have a permanent record, we'll download it to an infopill."

"With this nice purchase and four more yoonie," interrupted the vendor, tossing a black look to Xylith, "you get a free souvenir item of choice. Made of cosmic stellar material." He pointed to an array of junk featuring the slightly irregular logos of Vos Laegos City's most popular establishments.

Xylith sniffed, a nasal duet of distaste.

Bertram coughed up the extra yoonies and grabbed his free notepad with the Crater Club name printed on it.

"Cosmic stellar choice!" said the vendor. "Happy health for wearing!"

"Er, many stellar thanknesses to you," said Bertram with gusto, shaking the lifeform's hand and grabbing his bag. He motioned to Xylith. "C'mon. I have an idea."

"What?" She put a last pair of glasses down quickly. "Where are we going?"

Bertram grabbed her hand. "To the ship. I need you."

"Why, Bertram," she said, as she let him pull her down the street, "you give a lady more mixed signals than a Simulant hovertraffic controller with a burnt out logic board."

Rollie Tsmorlood loved a good party. Too bad this wasn't one of them.

In the past hour, he'd had two people beg to be his campaign manager, one threaten to kill him if he accepted the nomination and three try to frag him for completely nonpolitical reasons, which made for a refreshing change. The thinking behind these last fellows was that everyone in the Underworld knew Rolliam Tsmorlood was dead, so clearly Rollie must be a holowatch impostor from the *Heavy Meddler* trying to gain confidences and free mootaab mini-quiche.

A few well-placed laser shots on a low setting convinced them he was who he claimed to be. But it was a bother, and by the time he got back to his Zlorgon Subatomic Headbanger, its trademark fog had already dissipated. He drank it, anyway.

Of course, since then, "Backspace" Bungee arrived, determined to convince him to drop out of the race he wasn't in.

It seemed after a brief stint in Vos Laegos City confinement, Backs had decided not to run for OLIU but to start smaller, as Quadrant Manager. A half hour later, he was still droning on about his "changed, more geographically-targeted strategic leadership initiative."

Rollie wished him luck. He'd need it. His plan was hard to follow. Also, it was scribbled on the back of a funeral program.

"Seen Proximetra anywhere?" Rollie asked quickly, taking advantage of Backs' eventual need for air.

"Ah, Rentar ... That woman's like a quantum particle, son: everywhere at once." Backs leaned back in his chair and gave a rusty-hinged laugh. "What do you want her for? Not looking for another life-merge partner, are you? I'd say you've had your limit."

"Don't you have an acceptance speech to write?" Rollie caught sight of a smooth head bobbing in the center of one small group, then moving swiftly to another. He rose, drank the last of a Carsoolian pod liquor and plunked down his glass.

"Fought with her in the Feegar Rebellion, didn't you?" Backs asked. "Well, I'll tell you what I say about that. I say, 'Never let a dead shot touch your trigger.' It's a simple case of love 'er or laser. You cannot do both."

"You should have been a poet, Backs," Rollie told him, and while Backs geared up for a story about his piratical poetical past, Rollie slipped away on the trail of the shining head.

He caught up with it—and the rest of Rentar Proximetra—at the ice sculpture, or what remained of it after the pyrotechnics. Right now it was a dripping amorphous mass covered in wet ash. It occurred to Rollie that Meena would have loved it. "Rentar, got a moment?"

She gave him a smile, broad and congenial. "He who is dust reclaims life in remembrance."

"Glad to have come, Rentar. Always been fond of Jym," he said. "Lucky for me, I happened to be in Vos Laegos City."

She angled an eyebrow, though the smile remained firm. "The sun shines above rain."

"Yeah, funny, innit?" He nodded. "Only, unlike most of 'em here, I wasn't already at Secret Lair and Arms Show. Nah, see, I was showing a Tryfling friend round one of my favorite tourist spots…" He studied her closely. "…Zenith Skytreg's HQ?"

She had to be using some kind of adhesive on the smile. "The planet turns three-sixty," she said calmly.

"The tour was very informative, you should go sometime. But I think you'll really like what we found in Skytreg's Collections Room." Rollie didn't take his eyes off her as he reached into his coat and withdrew a fabric panel tucked into a BlackHole Bag he'd picked up earlier in the day. BlackHole Bags were clever compression tools courtesy of Popeelie engineering that could take even the largest soft object down to the size of a deck of yoonie cards. Proximetra's ice blue eyes barely flicked to the item before returning to meet his gaze. Her smile remained faultless.

He touched the logo, which he'd purposefully put on top before compression. "It's a flag. The symbol's a three in Centurnian. But the motto's all Gropkor. Not a lot of people use Gropkor these days. Of course, you'd know about that better than anyone, eh?"

She folded her arms. He slipped the item back into his pocket, and she watched him do it with interest.

"So I did a little research. The flag wasn't there before the ransom showed up. But it was there right after, tucked among Skytreg's treasures. Enough to make ya wonder whether it wasn't beamed in along with the ransom." He stroked his chin thoughtfully, adding, "If you was the suspicious type."

Her folded arms were a tight knot now. "Time marches swiftly. Those that wait, waste." For the first time this evening, her voice held an edge.

"All right then. I'll get to it. You and me, we go way back, Rentar. We fought against the Feegars. We called each other friend. I like to think that still holds for something."

She considered it, and what came from her lips was the first honest thing he'd heard her say all evening. "Time moves. Space expands. Galaxies ever-shift."

"And worlds get swallowed, don't they, Rentar? Drawn together and destroyed. Does the same go for the fragging Underworld Principles? For Skytreg? For Jym? I'd rather you just told me."

Her eyes met his, cool and unblinking, for what seemed like a very long moment. It was one time Rollie was willing to wait.

"Excuse me, Rentar." This was Meep-Meep, and it broke the tension like an XJ-37 set to frag. "Weren't we supposed to finish tonight with a Hanzigrette pudding? The caterer says they have no record of our ordering it."

The smile that returned to Proximetra's face had changed. It held a relieved, smug sort of pleasure Rollie knew well from won skirmishes and post-battle celebration.

She turned to Rollie and summoned a helpless gesture that didn't match the far-from-helpless smile. "One pair of hands must do the work of many," she said and bowed her head in apology before taking a step away.

"I'd rather you just told me, Rentar," he called.

"And sometimes many hands must do the work of one," she said over her shoulder

"If only they made this style in hoverboots," Xylith sighed. "But the twinkly ones never are."

Bertram tried to keep his mind on the map, but Xylith had settled into the ship lounge sofa and was unzipping one of her high, metallic red boots with a slow, deliberate jjjjjjjjjjjjjjjjjjjjjjjjjjjp! Which shouldn't have been alluring, given the fact Dootett feet looked like something you'd spy from a Jacques Cousteau's mini-sub. But apparently, somewhere inside, Bertram Ludlow felt the lure of the deep sea.

New Bertram's eyes kept drifting, while Old Bertram forced himself to focus on the task at hand. "It's Lemmish. I know it," he said. "Lemmish ... Lemmish ... Lemmish ..." He tried to recall.

Jjjjjjjjjjjjjjjjjjjjjjjjjjp! CLUNK!

"Bajoom!" Bertram exclaimed, and Xylith gave a jolt. Bertram turned to her. "Rollie said Lemmish Bajoom was missing, and you said he was where?"

She squinted to the heavens for answers, or at least the missing ceiling panel with the wires jutting out. "In a theater on Gron-Graby-4, I think."

Bertram double-checked the Klinko instruction pamphlet, then held out the Holographic Map of the GCU. In a clear voice he said, "Find Gron-Graby-4!"

On the map, a planet lit up in Quad Two. "Mark Gron-Graby-4," he commanded. "Hover note. Mark: Lemmish Bajoom." An annotation symbol appeared on the planet and Bertram's note was added. "Okay, who else from the Underworld is trapped in a field somewhere?"

"Frankly, Bertram," she said, massaging a foot. "I don't see the point."

Bertram dragged his eyes from the pedal object at the end of her leg. It had toe-ish elements, but also knobs and angles and was that a fin?

He cleared his throat. "You and Rollie keep saying it feels like all the connected members are trapped in the field. But what if you're right? If we can find a pattern in the people who are missing—or the people who are left—we might be able to figure out how big this conspiracy is. I don't know about you, but I like to know who I'm dealing with. And I'd prefer to find out, before one of us is doing the Airlock Mambo. So names," said Bertram. "I need names."

"How I do admire your tenacity," she said warmly, toying with a lock of hair. "Are all Tryfemen so noble and persistent, or is that just particular to you?"

"We'd have to do a mass double-blind test under saving Life As We Know It conditions to be sure," Bertram told her with a grin.

"You know, on Dootett, when two beings appreciate each other's company and feel a certain ... gravitational pull ..." She moved closer on the sofa, her voice just above a whisper. "...and you do feel the pull, don't you, Bertram? ..."

"Nine-point-eight meters per second squared," he murmured, drawing closer himself. "Possibly more." Old Bertram wondered what the rate of gravity actually was on Vos Laegos. New Bertram told Old Bertram to shut up.

"Well, when we feel that pull on Dootett," she continued, "we typically don't sit around marking up souvenir star charts together. We do something about it."

"Same on Tryfe," he said. He was noticing how violet her eyes were, with the right pair just a shade darker than the left. The air around her smelled warm and floral like a Blumdec resort.

"Stellar," she breathed and grabbed the map from his hand. She tossed it over her shoulder. "Now, I recognize there may be some challenges in this area between different species such as ourselves, but I have found some very interesting compromises can be made to ensure the evening's delightful for both parties."

"I believe strongly in doing my part to support positive alien relations," Bertram told her.

This was met with an enthusiastic kiss for the cause, six lips in total. And it wasn't long before both Old and New Bertram agreed, Xylith made some very valid points about interspecies affairs.

"Ah, Rollie! There you are."

Through bleary eyes, Rolliam Tsmorlood turned to see the speaker but got distracted by the contents of his glass. It was an unusually viscous Feegar bourbon, he thought. Not entirely unlike a melted jar candle from the centerpiece.

He looked harder.

"Oh." He set it down and addressed the newcomer without a glance. "Look: I will tell you what I have told every-fraggin'-body else at this fraggin' Karnax-forsaken blasted, fraggin' party—" He turned to Fess, Wilbree and some other friends around his table, "Not you mates, you're mostly all right... Er, what was I saying?"

"Fragging blasted something," suggested Wilbree.

"*Karnax-forsaken* blasted fragging something," corrected Fess.

At least they listened, Rollie thought. Then he remembered. "What I will tell you is: save your respiration, I am not running for zoggin' Quad Three Manager. Do not ask me again. Power down."

He found the jar candle in his hand once more. Thinking he might have misjudged it, he gave it another try. The flavor and texture were similar to a Yan'Qii Vo'Tiiv fruit fermentation when you got right down to it. He held the item aloft. "To Jymkrax Ragobar!"

"To Jym," said the group.

"And to the old, true Underworld, where offing someone meant you always had the manners to do it to their face!"

"To ... all that stuff you just said!" cried Fess, caught up in the moment. The group toasted this, too.

"Rolliam. Tsmorlood." He'd already forgotten about the guest at their table, but something about the sharp tone was familiar.

Rollie forced himself to focus this time and recognized the run colors and sour expression of Meena Tsoogarkken.

"Here," she said. "These." She dropped a large, rusty can marked "Centurna's Best Blipfruit" onto the table. Its contents clattered against the tin, unusual behavior for a blipfruit.

Frowning, Rollie dipped his hand into the can and withdrew a sample. It was a small plastic token. It read:

Thank you for choosing TwinklyTech®!
Redeem for one (1) FREE Handheld Vis-u Protective Case
in your choice of White!
Limited time only, usually one day shorter
than you remember having the thing.
Valid at all participating TwinklyTech stores,
which may not be located near you.
See our legal rep, Big Cosmo, for details.
Visiting hours at Mawdank Roving
Confinenent Center are...

It was too small to read the rest.

"They came from Liddlebiggs' Salvage," said Meena. "I was planning a mixed media collage about the consumer's deep psychological need to buy art mocking consumerism." She pointed to the token. "TwinklyTech's a chain in the Centurna System, you know."

"Of course I know." Rollie scanned the area for Proximetra. She was halfway across the roof, but who knew which members were working for her. It could be anyone, anywhere. It put an unwanted edge on his buzz. "This is not a good time, Meena."

"They're freebie tokens."

"I can see that."

"But unlike the other things I bought from Liddlebiggs', these," she said, "are new. I looked it up. Three Universal months ago they were free at TwinklyTechs all across the Centurna System with any one hundred yoonie purchase."

Wilbree rattled the can. "That's a lot of one hundred yoonie purchases."

"Oh, I know!" she said brightly. "So I became curious. What

would freebie tokens from TwinklyTech be doing in an old can from Centurna? And do you want to know what those purchases were?"

"I do!" said Wilbree.

"You bet!" said Fess.

"Not," Rollie spoke through gritted teeth, "now. Could you not have vis-ued me? Left me a fraggin' message?"

"Well, of course, I *could* have …" She tucked a lock of hair behind her ear and pulled a handlaser from a holster she had hidden at her thigh. "But then I wouldn't have been able to take back the twenty thousand yoonies you removed from my statue, yet somehow failed to use for my bail." She flipped a switch, and Rollie heard the gun power up. He looked from the gun (which he realized was a gift he'd given her some years back) to her face. Her jaw jutted with determination, but she gnawed her lower lip in a distinctly less certain way. "I've experienced confinement now," she said. "Mawdank, no less. I am not afraid to use this."

"Ah. So you'll be robbing me, then?"

"It's not robbery," she said. "It's re-appropriation."

"I once got two years for armed re-appropriation."

"You know, you really are an unrepentant slaggard and … and … a skimious vagar and … a sleegy prib."

He smiled. "Write my next Underworld resume?"

"And you completely ruined *Reclining Nude.*"

"No comment."

"The money, please." She extended the hand that wasn't holding the gun.

"Look," he said, "that last drink was death on an empty stomach. Why don't you put the laser down, and I'll take you to dinner? You can tell me all about those tokens."

"Oh yes, dinner." She emitted a short, sharp laugh. "With my money."

He rose. "Ah, come on." He grabbed the can of TwinklyTech chips and curled an arm around her shoulders. "We'll have a nice meal, catch you up on all the important bits you missed while you were cubed in Mawdank and you can re-appropriate the money from me over dessert. It'll be fun. Like old times."

"As I recall, for half our dinners, the law arrived before the dessert did."

"We all define fun differently, Meena."

"To the left. No, my left," said Xylith. "Now, lower, lower! That's it. There. That's stellar."

"Should we come back?" asked Rollie from the ship's open hatch.

Bertram wobbled as he stood on the metal toolbox, clipping the slip of paper to the string that hung from the ceiling. There were hundreds of these items spread across the room, waving in the cool breeze. He hopped down and watched the light from various projected stars and planets play across the blank expressions of Rollie and Meena. Bertram quickly tucked in the tail of his shirt, which he realized he never wore tucked in, and said, "Er, I suppose you're wondering what all this is."

Rollie batted through the papered strings and dropped into the closest seat beneath them. He held an old tin can and something rattled in it when he sat. "Nah…"

"An art installation?" suggested Meena, neatly ducking into a chair next to Rollie. "Signifying the, um …" She sized up the labels. "…Relative unimportance of the individual in the vastness of the cosmos?"

"Nope," said Bertram. "Nice idea, though. This is everyone who's missing from the Underworld right now, trapped in a viral field. We've got it organized by location."

Xylith nodded. "The red planets are ones where we've confirmed a member of the Underworld is missing."

"We started to use the chart's annotation feature, but it only lets you put one annotation per planet," explained Bertram. "We needed way more than that. Way."

"So our clever, clever Bertram came up with the idea of the labels and the string."

Bertram smiled at her and felt his face go warm. "Aw, it's nothing. Just doing it up Old School Tryfe Style. You were the one who buzzed a few friends to help fill out the list."

She returned the smile, two-fold. "It was my pleasure. Truly."

Rollie looked from Xylith to Bertram narrowly, then started to laugh. "Aw, I knew it. I fraggin' knew it. 'Light Fingers' Lady Duonogganon could not keep her hands off the poor Tryfe boy. Just remember, Ludlow, I warned you. And make sure she didn't steal anything from anywhere you'll need later. And I mean anything."

"Oh, you're one to talk," said Xylith, folding her arms, but not really turning up the haut in her hauteur.

"Of course," he continued, "it couldn't have been too cosmic, if you had time to redecorate, as well." He seized the nearest marked string and squinted at it. "Speaking of which: all this proves what exactly? The power of height discrimination in arts and crafts?"

"You don't remember?" asked Bertram. "You said it yourself."

"You know I rarely listen to me."

"You said you were surprised how many people were missing from the funeral. Specifically, a lot of the really connected people," said Bertram.

"Ah." Rollie stretched out in his seat. "Was I right?"

"Well, allowing for the element of randomness, and based on general probabilities and taking into account some room for error..." began Bertram.

"And making a fraggin' lot of excuses, we *know*: get on with it."

"...It does seem there's an inexplicable bulk of Underworld members trapped in the field from..."

Xylith said it with Bertram: "...Middle management."

"We're just not sure what that means yet," Xylith added.

"Middle management," said Rollie.

Bertram nodded vigorously. "Why would anyone want middle management out of the way? And even if you did, how would you do it? Especially since there's no central location here. Everyone's pretty evenly distributed across the various viral sites."

"Let me guess," said Rollie. "They're also disproportionately not big fans of Zenith Skytreg."

Xylith's eyes practically sparkled. "How did you know that? I said that very thing to Bertram. I said, 'Bertram, now why would Rentar Proximetra and Jym Ragobar want to trap all the people who'd actually be happy to see Skytreg gone? Unless Skytreg is involved, after all."

Rollie gnawed at the nail of his crooked thumb. "Who says they're trapped?"

Bertram laughed. "Oh, I don't know, the *Heavy Meddler*? Every single person Xylith buzzed? Not to mention, the viral field I saw eat a Wellness Worker."

"Well, yes, obviously they're trapped." Rollie rolled his eyes. "They're just not *trapped*. That's completely different, you see?"

Bertram didn't see. Nobody saw.

He exhaled sharply. "It's not outside in. It's inside out."

"This isn't another one of those red/green things, is it?" Bertram asked.

"Look," said Rollie, "the way the virus attacked, it was like one giant switch flipped on, controlled by some mysterious outside tech no one's been able to trace. And why's no one been able to trace it? Because the fields aren't coming from outside through one big switch. Just like the viral fields and the missing number three are separate issues, each field is separate, originating inside its contained area and radiating outward."

"And you know this because?"

"Ah," said Rollie. "That's where Meena comes in. Meena, tell 'em about the tokens."

Meena told them about the tokens.

"At first the manager of TwinklyTech wasn't terribly helpful. But you'd be surprised how quickly people volunteer information when you explain it's a part of a confidential, pan-galactic peace-keeping mission and your Paternal Archetype is the Coalition of Planets Ambassador to Hyphiz Epsilon." She added confidentially, "Only one of those things is true, of course."

Rollie grinned and nudged her. "Now tell 'em what you told me."

"I asked about purchases in bulk—anyone who bought hundreds of items for at least one hundred yoonies a pop. Well, the manager remembered it, because the buyer—a lifeform matching the description of your Jym Ragobar, I might add—cleaned out their stock and paid cash. Based on their records, it looks like TwinklyTechs all over the planet were cleared out of that one particular item."

"What? What item?" Bertram demanded.

"The ImpeneTrouble™ Scalable SafeT Shield," she announced. "Perfect for your home-unit, isolationist cult compound or personal planet!"

A peal of laughter escaped from Xylith. "The GCU's been held hostage by an off-the-shelf burglar alarm?"

"Oh, not one, Xylith. Hundreds of them," Meena's eyes were aglow. "All amplified to their highest capabilities. The system is modular, but I daresay it's never been used at this scale. Which is why they needed so many of them. And there is no alarm."

"Unless, of course, you count the shriek of some poor schmuck as he gets disintegrated," input Bertram.

"I'd call that more of an add-on feature, Mr. Ludlow," said Meena.

"The tricky part," continued Rollie, "is it has to be implemented by someone on the inside. Someone who's competent enough to carry off the plan, hungry enough for advancement to willingly trap himself somewhere at length and dispensable enough so things won't fall to blasted pieces in his absence."

"Middle management," everyone agreed.

Bertram stroked the stubble on his chin. "But if these middle managers are on the inside, and nothing and no one can get through, how would they know when to shut the fields off?"

"Er, yeah," Rollie sighed, closing his eyes and resting his head against the sofa back. "That's the bit I haven't quite pinned down yet."

"Well, what about Proximetra?" asked Xylith. "Did you finally get to talk to her?"

"Oh, we talked." His tone was black.

"You appealed to your years of friendship?"

"Possibly the only thing that kept her from fragging me on the spot. Then again, she may prefer to pace out her friends' murders. All depends on her schedule."

"She didn't say anything about hiring Gibbis, did she?" Bertram asked.

An orange eye popped open. "No. Would she?"

"Xylith, tell Rollie about our Gibbis theory," said Bertram.

"*Bertram's* Gibbis theory," she told them. "Why, the more I get to know this man, the more I realize you cannot beat the Tryfling mind for its sheer—"

"Beat!" Rollie shouted. He sat up suddenly, eyes wide. "Of course, rhythm! What else would it be? It's so fraggin' Gropkor, I almost can't stand it." He turned to the Epsilonian woman. "Meena, when we were in Rentar's offices, what planet was on her screen? The one in the satellite footage?"

"Oh stars, Rollie, that feels like ages ago. Diwaal-3, I think," said Meena.

"Diwaal-3." He leapt to his feet and gave an eager clap. "Right. No time for lolling about. Tell me your Gibbis theory on the way, eh?"

"To Diwaal-3?" asked Bertram. He liked the idea of a little more piloting time, but...

"More local," said Rollie. "Rentar Proximetra's ship. She'll be at the party a few hours more; I only need fifteen minutes. Oh, and Xylith?" He curled a finger at her. "Do I ever have a job for you!"

4X8

It took longer for the ramp to reach the ground than it did for Rollie to crack Proximetra's ship.

A special transmitter (illegal in thirty-two systems) and a little inside knowledge (an educated guess that her security code was the solar new year coordinates for Gropkor) and breaking and entering was a breeze.

Given her military background, Bertram had expected the place to be spare. Instead, the walls were layered in pasted clippings and snippets, doodles and graffiti, like a living scrapbook belonging to a frustrated mental patient with a journaling fixation. Most of it was hard to read—probably in Gropkor—so Translachew kept making alternate suggestions, few of them helpful.

"I don't get it," said Bertram. "You were just in here this morning, weren't you? You said you didn't find anything."

"I didn't find anything then," Rollie responded, pulling down blinds on the portal windows. "But that Anything, which turned out to be Nothing, is different from the Anything now, which might well be Something." He moved to a cabinet filled with rows of encased data cards the size of postage stamps and then he crouched down. "Unless it, too, is Nothing. 'Cept it'd be a different Nothing than the first Nothing, because, see, everything's changed now, hasn't it? Might as well be a whole other ship, for how Completely Not the Same it is."

Bertram turned to Meena. "Life-merged to him twice, huh?"

"I scarcely believe it myself sometimes." Meena peered over the Hyphiz Deltan's shoulder. "Rollie, what are we looking for? Tech related to that satellite footage?"

"Stellar guess! Cosmic thinking! Smart and perceptive as always, *na tseenee*." He opened the cabinet and slid the glass door. "No."

One dark blue eyebrow shot skyward. "No?"

"Xylith's on top of that." He ruffled through the tiny media.

"I thought Xylith went back to the party."

He selected a stamp, withdrew a multitool containing a magnifying glass, examined the stamp's plastic outer casing and then put it back. "Right. She's there, Rentar's there and I suspect Rentar'll have it on her. That It being different from our It, of course." He rose. "And these music cards are definitely not Our It. They're organized. They're dusty. If you was It, where'd you be?"

"Here?" Meena grabbed a stack of cards on a counter and fanned them out like it was the GCU's tiniest game of gin rummy. She frowned at the covers. "Gropkor folk music, on a format I haven't seen in years. In fact, the last time, it was at the Museum for the Laughably Quaint on Zagnut-9."

"Rentar believes in keeping her heritage alive, all right."

"Are we looking for something specific?"

"A song. One she'd find meaningful. Course, that could be anything. It's not like we sat round listening to tunes during the fraggin' Feegar Rebellion."

"So this is the player?" Bertram noticed a device about the size of a yoonie card. He drew closer. He picked it up. He peered through its minute window, like Godzilla into a Tokyo high rise. "Guys, something's still in here."

He set it down and pushed a button no bigger than the head of a pin.

The room blasted with a layered orchestra of alien instruments. The blinds rattled. The floor shook. The Uninet system, which had been on screensaver, jarred awake to show a satellite shot of a small planet covered in the swirling viral field.

Bertram, Rollie and Meena rushed for a volume control the size of a dollhouse doorknob. Fortunately, Meena's fingers were small enough to grip it.

All the movement had knocked over a tiny empty case next to the sound system. Bertram picked it up and strained to read it. "Hey, give me that magnifier?" Given the spotty nature of Translachew, he wasn't even sure why he bothered. But as he scanned halfway down the tracklist, he found himself rewarded with a jolt of recognition. "Rollie? I think you're going to like track fifty-seven."

And before Rollie could respond, Bertram entered "57" into a miniature keypad on the sound system. "Yep, coming up next on *WGCU: Tunes to Burgle By*, I'm sending this dedication to a special lady whose head shines as brightly as the knife she'll stab in your back. The tune is called *Fuumere Solif Snuvvid*, and this one goes out to you, Rentar." Bertram hit play.

BOOM.

BOOM-BOOM.

The song thumped the audience to attention, using all the percussion the Gropkors had at their disposal, which included everything from tom-toms to TNT.

BOOM.

BOOM-BOOM.

It reverberated through the ship in hollow despair until...

Silence. It was just about the time Bertram assumed the band had blown themselves to bits, the orchestration and vocals stepped in. These revealed a complex storyline where the pounding symbollized a lifeform trapped in the core of a planet made of poor choices, mental illness and cooled-off stardom. That was the gist, anyway; they didn't listen to the whole thing because, according to the liner notes, this song was seven Gropkor days long with the members playing forty-two different characters. The guy on the tintinabulum, whatever that was, died of old age a third of the way through the recording session, but they didn't find that out until after it was done. One member was quoted as saying, "I recalled thinking the smell was suspicious, but then, we also ate a lot of cheap delivery food in those days."

Clearly, the album required more time for analysis. Bertram was searching for the Eject button and wondering whether Proximetra might have stashed some rubber gloves somewhere, when Rollie flipped off the lights.

"Hey!" said Bertram. "I'm evidence-gathering here."

"Leave it," Rollie told him, raising the blinds and moving to the door. "It's time to go."

But…" Bertram stood rooted in the half-light, "this is what we came for."

"Oh, we got what we came for, Ludlow." His voice sounded smooth, calm and pleased; that rarely meant anything good.

Meena recognized the tone herself and shot him dubious look. But Rollie just guided her to the hatch. "Aw, don't you worry. All we need now is for Xylith to work her magic. And tomorrow will be a day the Underworld won't soon forget."

It couldn't be done.

Xylith Duonogganon watched Rentar Proximetra from a safe spot behind a decorative plant, and she sighed. Because it was an Empathy Fern, it sighed, too. It didn't even ask what the trouble was.

Yep, stealing a handheld satellite control off of any savvy member of the Underworld without them knowing … it would be challenging enough. But finding and extracting the thing from Proximetra in her current state of couture? Well, that was absolute folly.

To call the woman's traditional Gropkor mourning garb "somewhat elaborate" would have been like calling Jym's rocket send-off "a quiet, understated event." First there were the buttoned leggings and boots and the over knickers, and the abbreviated skirt, and the undertunic, and the tunic, and the hypercorset, and demijacket and supreme overvest, and then, if it were a chilly night, which this was, possibly a supracoat just to cut back on the nip. This ensemble was how the woman once managed to smuggle three hundred thousand handlasers through Belglastnast customs, the major score that secured her post as Quad Two Manager.

Snatching one gadget from that maze of fabric would be enough to stump the best in pocket-pickery. Xylith Duonogganon, it so happened, held the current Underworld record for the most perfect grab-and-goes this year, and she did not plan to relinquish that honor tonight to poor judgment.

"It can't be done," she murmured. "It simply cannot be done."

The fern curled a few fronds around her.

"Thanks," she said, drawing a little hope from the gesture. "You're right. I'll figure it out. I just need to keep a clear head and be patient."

The frond patted her shoulder.

So Xylith watched. And Xylith waited. Until a shadow fell over her that changed everything.

11(152-149)

"Where the frag is she?" asked Rollie from his seat, scanning the auditorium entrance. After the previous evening's hovering media frenzy on the roof of Loova's, the Underworld had chosen a less-elevated location for their nominations. And you couldn't get lower than the Crater Club.

"Are you sure she didn't come back at all last night?" Meena asked for the third time, concern creasing her brow. This time she addressed it mainly to Bertram, like he had some insider knowledge of the lady's whereabouts and was holding out on them.

Bertram shook his head, finding this new responsibility for Xylith's presence—or absence—surprising and awkward. One interspecies interlude, no matter how supernova, did not great insight make. "Maybe she went back to her rental-unit."

"And not buzzed?" asked Rollie. He'd vis-ued her several times over the past few hours to no response. His worry was worrying.

"Well, she is kind of... free-spirited," suggested Bertram.

"Yeah. So was Jym-blasted-Ragobar. That went well." He had a point.

"And well, well, well!" echoed a voice. "Greetings and morning salutations, my fine Underworld mates!" This was

"Backspace" Bungee, funneling into the row ahead of them, followed by Wilbree. They'd all met months ago, when Bertram Ludlow was still an unevolved lifeform. "Isn't it a beautiful day for nominating a new Quad Three Manager?"

His downy yellow hair had been combed with extra care, in that he'd bothered at all. The buckles on his frayed coat were polished, and his grin was as bright as the morning he hailed.

Rollie was having none of it. "Either of you seen Xylith?"

Wilbree peered palely over the seat back. "Since last night, you mean?"

"And how about last night, eh?" chuckled Backs. "Did you see that red contraption she had on? Did she buy it at a shop or an injection molder's? Not to say I don't approve of the effect, but—"

"Fess has gone, too," Wilbree interrupted. "He was going to meet us here, but he's run late." Wilbree wiped his sunglasses nervously with a silk handkerchief and tucked it back in his pocket. "That's not like Fess at all, is it? He wears at least six tentacle watches at a go. It's sort of his thing."

It was true. Bertram supposed when you and everyone on your planet were largely eyes and arms, you did what you could to make a personal statement.

Bertram was about to ask whether Wilbree had given Fess a buzz yet, when his attention was caught by a running figure out of the corner of his eye.

It was Prinny, and she was in such a hurry she hadn't had time to shift forms completely. Now she was all running legs and Jell-O mold body.

"Flamin' Altair, people, this is big! Big!" she shrieked. "Put on the news! Put on the news!" Arms appeared, and she waved them for emphasis. A hand grew from the end of one arm, and she pointed at Twerk Xanthwoggle, a mole-like being near the front of the room. "Does that screen connect to the Uninet?"

Twerk scrambled to the AV console and flipped on the giant holoscreen hanging over the auditorium. With a few adjustments, a fifty-foot Qwerty Zaqwer from the *Heavy Meddler* newsroom extended dimensionally above their heads.

Underworld members socializing in the hall rushed in to see what all the noise was about.

"For those of you just tuning in now," said Zaqwer, perched on the edge of her seat, "moments ago we received official word from the Coalition of Planets' Anti-Viral Task Force that the number three has been found. I repeat: the number three has been found!"

A cheer shook the room. Lasers shot the ceiling. Members hugged. Interpretive dance broke out. Bertram brushed stalactite dust from his hair and thought how he hadn't seen this kind of spontaneous mass levity since Pittsburgh Penguins' captain Mario Lemieux scored his fortieth career hat trick.

Zaqwer continued, "Due to its ongoing investigation, the Coalition of Planets would not reveal specific details about the number three's return. Our Coalition source did say it may take several Universal days for three to populate throughout all Uninet systems, but many locations are already seeing improvement. Let's go to Pate Maesyn in the Qweb system."

The screen split to show the head in the jar, perched in a hoverchair, in the middle of a factory. "Thanks, Qwerty. I'm here now at the RocketRoll Ball Bearing Company on Qweb-2. The company had been trying to adjust their automated operations ever since the Number Three Virus swept the GCU. Yet moments ago, this manufacturing line came to life, as Pi calculations were suddenly recognized by company systems. Finally, after weeks of silence, RocketRoll has balls once more, and the managers just couldn't be happier."

"I understand neighboring Qweb-3 is still surrounded by a viral field. Is that right, Pate?" Qwerty asked.

"That's right, Qwerty," said Maesyn. "The anti-virus corrects Uninetworked systems only. The viral fields remain in place. The Coalition of Planets would like to reemphasize that the fields are a separate issue and they're doing all they can to address them as soon as possible."

Qwerty nodded. "Thanks, Pate. Stay tuned to the *Heavy Meddler* for more virus news the moment it breaks. Or possibly before, if we can think of anything even remotely related, to use up air time." It was a relieved buzz in the auditorium as Twerk Xanthwoggle turned down the volume and members continued to filter in.

"So the Coalition of Planets finally got the anti-virus running," said Bertram, feeling all warm and fuzzy about his role in the process. "That should force Proximetra's hand with the viral fields, shouldn't it? There's no point having them run now."

"There is, if Rentar still thinks she can pin the scheme on Skytreg," said Rollie.

Bertram frowned. "I don't understand."

"Oh, I do," said Meena, waving her hands excitedly. She leaned around Rollie to see Bertram better. "If Mr. Skytreg's supposedly responsible for this whole thing, well, he's in confinement and being monitored constantly. So he can't very well undo the fields, or direct someone else to do it, without the officials finding out. Which means Proximetra can't do it without casting doubt on Skytreg's guilt. Or, at the very least, making it look like someone else is in on it with him, reducing his culpability."

"And it can't be blamed on Jym Ragobar since he's dead," Rollie said, nodding.

"Exactly! She missed her opportunity, and now she's stuck between the proverbial tarpit and a scorchy place."

Bertram massaged his temples. "But with that thinking, if Skytreg is convicted, then Tryfe and Treyfab-3 and the rest of them will never be free. Not until he serves his sentence or gets parole, anyway. That could be years."

Rollie gave a bitter laugh. "Yeah, that's the trouble with these big, flashy crimes, innit? So much to go wrong, no matter how hard you plan." He craned his neck around the mostly-filled room. "Now where is Proximetra? And why do I feel this doesn't bode well for Xylith?"

Twerk Xanthwoggle's voice droned over the PA system. "Will all registered Underworld members please take a seat? In five minutes, we'll be starting the nominations for Quad Three Underworld Manager. Five minutes, everyone."

"So sorry I'm late," said Xylith, noticeably out of breath and wearing clothes from the night before. She slipped into the chair next to Bertram. A moment later, Fess had joined them, wriggling into a seat next to Backs.

"We miss anything?" asked Fess, pushing up his faceted bottle lenses with a tentacle.

"Where on flamin' Altair were you?" Rollie directed the bulk of this to Xylith but shot a look at Fess for inclusiveness.

"You would not believe the evening I had." Xylith patted her hair, noticed something in it and pulled out a leafy twig. She reached around Bertram with a smirk and tucked it into Rollie's breast pocket like an awkward boutonnière. She patted the pocket with satisfaction. "You know that little job you asked me to do?"

"I think I can recall it."

"Well, the mission was totally off-orbit from the start."

Rollie looked surprised. "Why?"

"I should have known you'd be completely blind to the complexities associated with my career niche and fashion." The lips on one face were pursed with irritation, while the other received a fresh coat of lipgloss. "Anyway, I followed said target back to her ship and waited in the bushes all night. Do you know what's in the bushes of a Vos Laegos City ICV lot at night? I'll tell you. Bodily fluids, Smorg wrappers and other lifeforms waiting in the bushes, most of whom do not share my pure intentions."

"Yes, yes, very disturbing, you endured horrors. Did you get it or not?" asked Rollie.

"Finally," she continued, "after hours of waiting, our target emerged, having changed into something more appropriate to our needs. So I trailed said target to breakfast at Klinko Buffet Nice—"

"Aw, I wanted to go there," said Bertram, before he could stop himself. "Was it any good?"

"—There," continued Xylith, giving him a look, "I met with some skilled decoy hands I'd bumped into at the party last night and arranged to have on-call. You know, just to ensure the bump-and-grab was a true success." She smiled in duo at Fess.

Fess shrugged. "Hey, what's friendship, if ya can't lend a flipper now and then?"

"And it was a good thing I did, because our target was so busy dealing with Fess' rude reach and tenacious tentacles that I was able to swiftly extract the object in question over the pureed paargraath, incident-free." And with this, she pressed a small gray gadget into Rollie's palm.

"Ah." Rollie gave it a quick glance and pocketed it. "I knew you'd come through for us. If you weren't slightly caught and murdered first, o' course."

"Such faith," she sighed. "And, um, what exactly do you plan to do with the item?"

"One minute," came Twerk Xanthwoggle's voice over the sound system. "One minute before the nominations."

Rollie smiled. "I think you'll just have to wait and see."

"That means he doesn't know," Xylith told Bertram and Meena, rolling her eyes. "He always says 'wait and see' when he doesn't know. You ever notice that?"

It was here Bertram noticed Meep-Meep and Flutterbitt enter, followed by Proximetra, looking strangely rumpled for a person with no hair. To call the expression on her face "dark," instantly made dark stars and the Dark Ages five shades lighter, just for the comparison.

"I think someone's having a bad morning," sang Meena softly.

"Good. It'll match the bad afternoon she's about to have," said Rollie.

Twerk Xanthwoggle had taken the podium. "Greetings, members of the Underworld," came his mild monotone. He blinked small eyes in the bright light. "Thank you for taking the time to be here this morning. As you just heard, the number three is returning to our Uninet systems. It is my belief that soon the Third Quadrant will follow, which makes these nominations for a new Quad Three Manager all the more timely. While we will miss Jym Ragobar, Jym would want the

Underworld Society to continue climbing to new heights of low dealings. And strong leadership is an important part of that. So I ask you, Underworld members. Is anyone willing to stand up and cast a nomination for Quad Three Manager?"

Five rows up, Prinny turned to look at Rollie, and Rollie's orange glare could have boiled her gelatin. She looked away quickly and settled into un-nominating silence.

Fess, Backs and Wilbree, however, seemed to be having some kind of quiet argument, that ended with Backs poking Wilbree, until the poor man stood up.

Wilbree raised his hand. "I'd like to nominate Oogon 'Backspace' Bungee for the position of the Quad Three thingy. Because he's a cosmic guy and also, because he told me t— Ow!" He rubbed his arm and gave Backs an injured look. "Er, because he's done loads of zonky-clever crimes this past year. Like, he's the inventor of the DriftGoods Party."

Xanthwoggle squinted into the crowd. "And what is that exactly?"

"It's a new kind of scheme where Backs gets non-Underworld people to sign up to fence pirated shipments for him. They sell 'em to their friends and get their friends to sign up. It's like a special deals club."

"That sounds very innovative, Wilbree," agreed Xanthwoggle, taking notes.

"Oh yes, and he's really good at it. We only got Klinkoed for it the once and—Ow!" He rubbed his arm again. "Er, Backs for Quad Three Manager, pleasesirthankyou." Wilbree sat down.

"Is there anyone to second this nomination?" Xanthwoggle asked.

There was more muttering and an elbow to the gills before Fess rose—"I'll second it."—and sat.

"And Oogon Bungee, do you accept this nomination?"

Backs practically bounced from his seat. "Aw, gee, mates, this is such a surprise, awful nice of you, and hardly deserve it and whatnot and—yes! Yes! Absolutely! I accept the nomination!"

"Then Oogon Bungee, you are a contender for Quad Three Manager," said Xanthwoggle. Bungee's name appeared on the holoscreen above them in happy flashing lights. "Do we have any other nominees?"

Bertram watched the nominations process as Nefled Borzo, Nuu Sh'Akk and Melore Funbolt were all suggested, seconded and added to the screen above.

"Stellar," said Xanthwoggle. "All right now, before we close, are there any other last nominations for Manager of Quad Three?"

Rentar Proximetra stood up. "One more sun rises," she announced.

Xanthwoggle's whiskers splayed out in surprise. "Rentar Proximetra, do you have a nomination you'd like to put forth?"

She nodded. A murmur rippled across the audience.

"What is she doing?" hissed Xylith. "Isn't there some rule that the other Quad leaders are supposed to remain impartial about this?"

"Not formalized," whispered Rollie. "Just unspoken."

Proximetra said, "In light, there is hope. And a lost sun of Hyphiz shines brightly this morning."

Rollie's jaw clenched. "She wouldn't."

Meep-Meep stepped forward. "I believe what my esteemed colleague Rentar is saying is that she would like to nominate…"

"She won't," Rollie muttered. "Bleedin' Karnax on a comet, she *can't*."

She pointed into the crowd.

"…Captain Rolliam Tsmorlood for the position," announced Meep-Meep.

"Aw, frag," said Rollie.

"And what are your reasons for this nomination?" asked Xanthwoggle.

"For cold embers that have flared to life," Proximetra explained.

"Because of his remarkable survival from Altair-5," translated Meep-Meep.

"For a quest that shone well and wide upon dark planets," Proximetra said.

"For his showmanship in a popular Uninet program, which helped us hit Underworld PR goals this quarter," Meep-Meep said.

"And for the forces unseen that draw our worlds together," she told the crowd.

"And last, but not least," translated Meep-Meep, "because of his unyielding loyalty to our Underworld cause and wanting only the best for the Society, while understanding that sometimes we have to take extreme measures to achieve goals and perhaps it's good to overlook the occasional oopsy moment when differences of opinion happen between old friends."

"Wow," said Wilbree, "I should really brush up on my Gropkor."

"Interesting," murmured Rollie, "Proximetra's trying to make up."

"Will anyone second the nomination?" Twerk Xanthwoggle asked.

Even with last night's party a misty memory, there was still some enthusiastic support. "I will!" said Prinny, emboldened.

"Me, too!" said someone else.

"Me, too, too!" said Wilbree, standing up.

"What're ya doing?" whispered Fess, " Sit down, man. You can't double-nominate."

"Oh." Wilbree returned to his chair. "Caught up in the moment, wasn't I?"

"Captain Tsmorlood," asked Xanthwoggle, "do you accept the nomination?"

Expectant silence fell over the room.

"Do I accept the nomination?" Rollie muttered, scratching his chin and sizing up Proximetra, then Meep-Meep. He rose from his seat. "Well, thing is, Twerk: anyone who knows me at all, knows ordinarily I don't go in for this political muck. I've always said anyone who needs a title tacked to their name's got a gaping black hole for an ego, and there's no filling it."

He turned to Bungee. "No offense, Backs."

"None taken, son. Long as you're dropping out." Backs grinned.

"But I also know that the Underworld's in a fraggin' mess," Rollie continued. "I like a good cause, me. And I care deeply about the work we do. Proximetra knows that better than anyone. And this is the ultimate cause." Proximetra was nodding, that secretive little smile on her lips. "I can see clear as a Blumdec sky that what we desperately need is a return to the Principles, a return to the days of honor among members. And the Underworld deserves the kind of leader who can take you there."

Members in the crowd cheered. Proximetra surveyed the scene with warm satisfaction and folded arms.

"You are still talking about me, right?" asked Backs, looking concerned.

"There's just one problem ..." Rollie pulled the satellite remote from his coat pocket. Bertram's gaze flew to Proximetra's face, which turned as gray as the remote, her lips becoming a thin line. "...I can't give you that honor. See, I come to realize, I'm every bit as duplicitous as the worst o' you. Like this thing." He held up the remote for everyone to see. "This was my good friend Rentar Proximetra's. Yet I plotted to get it off her without her knowing. Broke into her ship a couple of times, too." He smiled at Rentar. "You'll want to change your keycode for your hatch system, by the way. Location of Gropkor in its new year coordinates?" He shook his head. "Beneath you, really."

"Candor is as fresh water to parched lips," she said. "Wisdom is sensing *when they have drunk their fill.*" Bertram didn't need a translator to know she was just barely controlling her anger. She moved from the stage into the audience practically steaming from the ears. "But now the day is done. Play is over. The ergowohm must return to its nest." She extended her hand for the satellite control.

"Ah, but I've just begun to play, Rentar," Rollie told her, and he turned to his fellow members. "This isn't the remote to her ship, by the way. It's to a DMB-20 satellite she's got orbiting Diwaal-3. Had it there for a while now. No one's paid it much attention. Why would they? Just like a million others we see every day. In fact ..." He pulled Bertram's portable Uninet from his coat, and Bertram wondered when he'd taken it. "You can see the planet right now on the Diwaal Uninet site. Well, I can. See, there's poor Diwaal-3, snug in the viral field. And there's Rentar's satellite bobbing round it."

Twerk Xanthwoggle might not have known exactly what was going on, but he didn't hesitate to pop the channel up on the auditorium holovision, in place of the nominations list.

The room saw Diwaal-3 in all its viral-wrapped splendor, its satellite like a diamond in the sky. Or a hunk of metal. Either one.

Proximetra drew closer now. "The ergowohm must return to its nest," she said again. She pulled an XJ-42 on Rollie with one hand and reached for the satellite device with the other.

It was like dominoes. Xylith leapt to her feet. She whipped a handlaser from her boot and held it on Proximetra.

Meep-Meep directed a gun on Xylith.

Fess drew three different guns and some kind of grenade and brandished them all at Meep-Meep.

One second later, everybody in the entire audience was aiming something at someone. Bertram had his vending machine handlaser aimed at a lifeform he didn't even know, and he wasn't sure whose side the guy was on. Even Meena had some weapon she drew from somewhere.

Twerk Xanthwoggle remained the only one unarmed. "It appears we have reached a jeff," Twerk observed, referring to the GCU version of a Mexican standoff. Bertram had heard about these and thought jeffs were species-specific, but apparently the term was general purpose. "In the interest of Underworld unity and also time, because I only have this room rented until lunch and they really stick it to you on the overage charges, what I'd like to suggest is that we all take a few deep breaths—all non-breathing lifeforms count to five or something—and if Captain Tsmorlood could get to the point?

Why do we care if Captain Proximetra owns satellite property? This is no concern of the Society."

"You care," said Rollie, "because this satellite of Proximetra's serves one purpose and one purpose only. It shoots an offensive beam."

"At Diwaal-3?" someone asked. "But that's in her own home system!"

"Right you are, random person in the crowd who I didn't quite see and whose voice I don't recognize," said Rollie. "But you may have noticed, everything that physically breaks the field gets obliterated before it goes through. It also makes this pretty blue blip."

Rollie pressed a button on the remote. A beam shot from the satellite onto the world of Diwaal-3. The viral field blipped blue.

"So if you wanted to, say, signal some people on the other side of the viral field, saying it was okay to turn off the shield barrier now, you might pre-arrange a little patterned code of blips, which they could see on their end of things. And if you're Rentar Proximetra, you'd be likely to arrange that pattern to the opening rhythm of your favorite Gropkor music piece, *Fuumere Solif Snuvvid*."

He pressed the button once, then twice in succession.

BLIP.

BLIP-BLIP.

The Crater Club auditorium was still and silent, as the crowd fixated on the shield before them. Rollie repeated the sequence.

BLIP.

BLIP-BLIP.

Nothing happened, and Bertram's heart was pounding its own frantic rhythm now. Was it the wrong song? Was it the wrong concept? Was it the wrong person altogether, and were they going to have some very tricky apologizing to do, possibly with the begging and the pleading and the fragging?

All-in-all, was it just another blip on Diwaal?

It was at the very moment Old Bertram was ready to make a break for it and even New Bertram had the ship remote readied in his hand, that ... One! ... Two! ... Three! ... Four! The viral shield fell away from the planet in chunks.

The crowd gasped and Diwaal-3 stood free and shiny, like a freshly-peeled hard-boiled egg. Only bigger and more uniformly round.

The audience clapped and shouted. And they were still applauding as, before their eyes, four small dots on the screen gradually transformed into four small ships pulling away from the planet.

"And that's who, Ludlow?" Rollie asked as the Underworld settled into silence.

"Oh, um ..." Bertram tucked his handlaser under his arm and rummaged in his pants pocket for his list. He unfolded it and cleared his throat. "Glorble Jonsin, Shrooty Shendopple, Wibni Jinner-Froo'sha'ow and ... Kurt?"

Rollie nodded. "Right. Now they're off to signal four other shielded locations. Then those freed Underworld members will do the same for others. Eventually, it'll filter through all the sectors. In a few Universal weeks—and that includes travel time—the entire GCU should be back to normal."

"But ... but this means Rentar Proximetra set the viral fields?" someone shouted from the crowd. "My auntie is caught in one of those fields!"

"And my Paternal Archetype!" someone else shouted.

"And my clones! They get ideas when they don't have regular oversight!"

Members of the crowd turned to Proximetra for answers.

That's when Lyuna Flutterbitt, in a move that not only defied physics but broke any remaining sense of jeff, pressed a button on her belt and simply evaporated from her place at Proximetra's side. Members scanned the auditorium, looking for sight of the little pink figure.

"Where'd she go?"

"Did you see that?"

"Was that *beaming tech*?"

A buzzing sound overhead triggered a chill down Bertram's spine, and a high-pitched voice trilled out over the crowd.

"Soft!" it squeaked, and Bertram looked up to see Lyuna Flutterbitt covering the room with two large, high-powered selections from her personal arsenal. "You've gone soft! 'My family's trapped in a field.' 'I miss my infopill-of-the-day.' 'My friend Jym is dead.' Listen to yourselves! Zenith Skytreg has created an Underworld of wimps and whiners. I can't take it anymore. It's time for change, people!"

"Ah," a smile returned to Proximetra's lips, "the world turns three-sixty. The moon shifts the tides."

"And right on time." Meep-Meep may have been smiling, too, but Bertram couldn't see the back of the manager's head. "Everyone, I suggest you put down your weapons."

"Not so fast, my colleagues," Lyuna said, turning her sights on Management. "You two don't really think you're exempt from this, do you? First we had Jym: 'Oh, I didn't know we were framing Skytreg, I thought we were splitting the ransom four ways! Boo-hoo!' And then here's Meep-Meep: 'Oh no, my fake designer leviboots are popular for being fakes! How can I possibly live down the humiliation?' And you: 'I can't just plan the biggest crime in the history of the Underworld; I have to use some stupid obscure symbolism no one other than me can possibly understand because I like to pretend I'm so artistic and deep.' Uninet flash: you want to know why your people died out, Rentar? You bored yourselves to death."

The metal of Proximetra's handlaser flashed, but Flutterbitt hit a button and disappeared into the ether, the blast striking the ceiling. Rock crashed to the floor, flattening a refuse robot. Xanthwoggle would not be getting back their rental deposit.

They heard the giggling before Bertram actually saw where she'd reappeared. "Ah! See?" Flutterbitt hovered by the holovision screen now. "That's more like it. At the heart of things, that's what we're about. We like to pretend we're all so elite and clever, but at the core, life is cold, hard battle. You can smear a coat of WarpWax on it and polish it up, but that's all it will ever be. So I ask you, the members of the Underworld, who do you want to follow? An old Underworld, built by actors, afraid to be who they really are … Today's Underworld, that's completely sold out to topside business … Or do we embrace our darkness, gather our true, vicious strength together and cut out some of this dead weight once and for—"

Handlasers blasted at Flutterbitt in what would become the first unanimous decision on any matter in Underworld history. Energy hummed through the air. The holovision screen exploded from stray beams, showering the audience in broken glass and technology. Wires burnt and smoke blackened the ceiling, as the Quad One Manager crashed to the ground in a pile of steaming pink glitter and taffeta. She skidded down the auditorium aisle with a screech before her structural integrity released and dust danced on the air.

Xylith glanced at the smoking laser in Bertram's hand and raised an eyebrow.

"What? I set mine to Level Eight stun," Bertram said, checking the controls. "I think."

Fess eyed the space where Flutterbitt had been and wasn't. "Not everyone did."

Rollie, Bertram noticed, had slipped from the aisle and was approaching the two remaining Quadrant Managers, who looked jumpy and wary now.

Proximetra had her weapon on him in a nanosecond. "Ah," she said, "the event horizon."

"Principle Twelve," observed Meep-Meep. "Never miss an opportunity for a dramatic showdown."

"Wrong," Rollie said. "Principle Hundred and Twenty-Seven."

"Hundred and Twenty Seven?" Meep-Meep muttered, frowning and exchanging glances with Proximetra, who shook her head and shrugged. "I believe we are unfamiliar with Principle One Hundred and Twenty Seven."

"Not surprised," he said. "It's 'Always know your limits.'" And he pulled back his coat to draw…

The petition against Zenith Skytreg. He held it up so they could see it, then flung it to their feet. "Consider this my withdrawal from the Society," he accounced. "If you need an official letter, I'll kidnap a lawyer to write one up. Otherwise, I am done." He turned to leave.

A murmur swept the crowd. A few members shouted protest. A few clapped.

Meep-Meep just stood blinking at the unexpected lack of showdown. It took a moment before the Manager found words. "Well, er... You do that! But before you go, Rollie, tell us one thing." Meep-Meep was clearly trying to make the most of Principle Twelve.

Rollie stopped and turned, looking intrigued.

"Everyone knows how you feel about Zenith Skytreg," Meep-Meep pressed on. "We were on the same side. We even had the same ultimate goals. So why? Why couldn't you just go along with it?"

"Because you don't understand why," Rollie said. "And I learned I'm not a joiner."

"Galaxies will collide," Proximetra vowed.

"Oh, I have no doubt you'll come for me," the Hyphiz Deltan said quietly. He surveyed the scowling, very armed crowd closing in around the managers and added, "*If* you make it out of here today. But I'll be following my own Guiding Principles from here on out." The thought of this made him smile. "Don't know exactly what they'll entail yet, but I'm feeling very creative. If I was you, I'd remember that before coming to see me."

And with a sloppy salute, he swept to the exit.

Bertram and Meena were getting up to follow, when Fess paused at the end of his row and pitched his membership card next to the petition at Proximetra's feet. "Me, too," Fess said. "I quit. And here's a little note for your hit list: most of me grows back."

Hot on his heels, or tentacles, came Wilbree. "Yes, well." Wilbree pushed up his sunglasses. "I'm...um..." He tossed his card. "...You know. Like those ones said." And he ran up the aisle.

"I'm out," chimed Prinny. Her card hit the floor.

"Absolutely!" said Xylith, throwing her card into the growing pile. Then she bent and grabbed it back up. "Okay, I'm sorry," she said, blushing, "I'm of two minds. I'll get back to you."

Backs looked around and realized his whole section had cleared out. "Aw, flamin' fireballs ..." He scratched his head. "Well..." He stood and hitched up his pants. "My constituents is gone, anyways." He tossed in his card and left.

They were moving through the back kitchens of the Crater Club on the route out, when Bertram noticed how hard it was to be stealthy with a small crowd trailing you.

"So where are we going?" asked Prinny, skipping to catch up. "What's the plan?" She was back to her saucer-eyed toddler form.

Rollie scowled down at her. "Why are you asking me? I'm an independent operator now."

"Oh, I know," she said. "We just thought we'd operate independently with you."

He turned, as the group nodded hopefully.

"Typically, independence," he explained to them, "is not so fraggin' congested."

"I tell you what..." This was Backs. "Everyone: come back to my ship, and we'll discuss it more there. DriftGoods just got in a few crates of *tchutsaree* steaks, only expired yesterday. I'll donate a few to the cause, and we'll celebrate our new opportunities with a hearty meal and a few restoratives."

Few could resist the temptation of free probably-not-quite-perilous meat.

"Sounds stellar. Just stellar," Rollie told them warmly, in a way that Bertram found instantly suspicious. "So you all do that and ..." He got to the service elevator first, yanking Meena, Bertram and Xylith along with him. "...We'll catch up with you all later, eh?" And with a punch of the button, the elevator doors clanged shut.

34

A happier, more hopeful Vos Laegos City stretched out before them, as they made the journey to Meena's ship. Bums picked through public refuse disposal robots with a merry whistle on their lips. Hovercar services hesitated whole seconds before attempting to mow down pedestrians in the crosswalks. And Non-Organic Simulants of the night offered late morning discounts just "because." Yes, with the number three slowly making its way back into the Greater Communicating Universe, optimism was in the air.

Bertram's little band of travelers, however, moved outside of this sentiment, caught in some metaphoric viral field of their own that even the jubies could not permeate. Bertram, Xylith, Meena and Rollie trudged through the streets silently, while less disillusioned lifeforms were only beginning their blind and bedazzled adventures toward ultimate disappointment and insolvency.

The world turns three-sixty, Bertram thought.

They were turning the corner onto G'napps Boulevard when one of the local billboards cut in the middle of a Klinko Buffet Nice ad to reveal Pate Maesyn at the *Heavy Meddler* newsdesk. Or rather, on it.

"We interrupt this advertisement for an Ultra Special Report," said Maesyn from his shiny glass container. "Diwaal-3, located in Quad Two, has just been released from the viral field. Its protective barrier is gone!"

All those optimistic people cheered optimistically. Hovercrafts honked. Strangers embraced, even ones who hadn't paid others to do so.

"But this exciting news prompts many new questions," Maesyn continued. "Why Diwaal-3? Will this be the first of many freed planets? Did Zenith Skytreg shut off the field while in Coalition of Planets custody? Or is Skytreg an innocent victim of an elaborate frame job, as supporters suggest? We join the Coalition of Planets press conference already in progress."

At the podium stood a serious-looking lifeform labeled: "Dr. Makka Fee, Lead Investigator, Coalition of Planets Anti-Viral Task Force."

Fee said, "Surveillance footage proves Zenith Skytreg has been in complete isolation while in Coalition of Planets custody. Our team is looking into alternate reasons for the sudden release of the viral field on Diwaal-3. Recent evidence suggests that the late Quad Three Underworld Manager Jymkrax Ragobar may have been responsible for the Uninet portion of the numeroterrorism attack. We are examining connections between Ragobar, Skytreg, and any possible third parties. In light of these new circumstances, medical analysts are also reexamining Ragobar's death."

Someone called out, "Do you suspect foul play?"

"Evidence suggests those involved were not playing. Our Analyzing Teeny Tiny team has found no residue of mirth, piffle, tomfoolery or fiddle-faddle. We believe the party and/or parties involved were all, in fact, deadly serious."

"In your opinion, has Skytreg been framed?" another reporter pressed.

"In my opinion, I have no opinion on the topic of frames at this time. I leave that sort of thing to my life-merge partner."

"But this morning, wasn't an Oopsy 4-21-Beta filed with the Vos Laegos City Medical Examiner's Office in respect to the Ragobar suicide investigation?" someone asked.

"We cannot affirm the affirmation of that, due to current scenarios and potential detriment to our investigation and also my job that I like. I'm sorry," said Fee, looking considerably relieved, "that's all the questions we have time for right now."

They cut back to the newsroom. "In related stories," began Maesyn, "Skytreg's production company has also released its first single from the Underworld leader's new autobiographic musical *The Unfraggable Zenith Skytreg*. The song is called *The Vos Laegon ZapTrap Flap* and it has already rocketed to the top of the GCU's pop charts. Skytreg developed the number while in Vos Laegos City confinement, and the Anti-Viral Task Force has scoured the catchy dance hit for coded messaging related to numeroterrorism activities. No encrypted information was found beyond causing the irresistible need for lifeforms to boogie. That's the news for now. We'll let the *ZapTrap Flap* play us out to your regularly scheduled billboard advertisement."

A bouncy, throbbing dancebeat took over, layered with some futuristic instrumentation. On the screen, five lifeforms—the central figure a vaguely Skytregesque dude in a silver wig—stood in clear glass tubes with badly-animated lightning bolt special effects around them. They sang:

> Keep your elbows to your sides
> So your body don't get fried
> You can give a little hop
> That the RightGuides just can't stop...

Against his will, the tune was still flapping through Bertram's head several blocks later when they arrived at an ICV park.

"Well," sighed Meena now, "this is me." She pressed a button on her remote, and the ramp jarred to life on her Cosmolux. "It was a pleasure to meet you both." She extended rough, warm hands to Bertram and Xylith. "I do hope our paths will cross again. But for now, I must get back. Technically, I'm not supposed to be off of Hyphiz Epsilon at all."

Both of Xylith's faces grew concerned. "Oh no! You didn't skip bond to come here, did you?"

"Oh, not a skip. Hardly a skip. More of a ..." Meena's fingers wiggled as if struggling to grasp the word in the air. "...A glide. A tiny glide. A glidelet, really. Just a whisper of a glide. I doubt anyone's even noticed I've gone."

"But your trial ..." said Bertram.

"Actually, it's the strangest thing." Her gray eyes looked very bright. "My lawyer vis-ued this morning. Apparently the media we ran into are now claiming the accident was entirely their fault. That, with the massive expanse of space at their disposal, they didn't exercise enough care to dart out of the way when ships came flying at them. So it's all being sorted out now. At this point, it's unlikely there will be a trial at all."

Bertram exchanged glances with Rollie. "Gibbis, making the slate clean again?"

"He likes clean," said Rollie. "Sounds as if he also likes a bit of dirt, long as it's on someone else. Wonder what he's got on the press."

"I did have to give a vis-u statement to some commander of the Vos Laegos law," Meena continued. "Apparently my friend Dax Q. Phlyjollee visited her and went into some detail about the recent chase I was involved in and the violation of my studio. As he appeared to be telling the truth, I confirmed what he said. I hope I won't regret that."

"Phlyjollee's never let me down before," Rollie said.

"She wanted to know where Mr. Phlyjollee was now. But I told her he's a book buyer and moves around so much, I'm afraid I didn't have current contact information for him," she said. "She also asked me about my former life-merge partner, the late Rolliam Tsmorlood. She feels the resemblance to Mr. Phlyjollee is uncanny. I told her some people do feel all Hyphiz Deltans look alike, but that I didn't see it."

Rollie chuckled. "So it sounds as if your career as an

interstellar menace may very well be coming to a close."

"And what of yours?" she asked. "The way you left it with Proximetra and that Meep person … If they make it out of the Crater Club intact, are you sure they'll let you leave the Underworld? I'd rather you didn't go the way of your friend Mr. Ragobar."

Rollie smiled. "I knew you still cared."

"We are not getting together again," she said. "Not even in a post-action-sequence, desperate and fleeting, denouement sort of way."

"That would be cliché," he agreed. "Anyway, we'll always have Vos Laegos."

She blinked. "Did we have Vos Laegos?"

"You pulled a handlaser and tried to rob me. So that's special."

Bertram was starting to understand. Relationships in the GCU were complex.

"Well …" Meena clasped pale hands before her. "Do take care, Rollie. You can keep the rest of the yoonies. I'd say use them to invest in a personal deflective shield but…"

He sniffed or maybe it was a laugh. "I think I've had my fill of deflective shields for a while," he said. "But thanks, Meena."

She nodded solemnly. "Oh, and Rollie?"

She yanked him down to her level by a sudden jerk of the coat lapels. Then she kissed him in a way that probably was cliché in the Hyphiz System but seemed to involve a startling intraoral anatomy about which Bertram could have lived quite happily—and slept more soundly—without ever, ever glimpsing.

Bertram became fascinated with the cool patterns on his knockoff-knockoff hoverboots and only knew that whatever was happening was over when he heard Rollie clear his throat in an awkward way.

"We are not getting together again," Rollie said raspily.

"Oh, I know." Meena's voice was mostly air and held a smile in it. "Disaster. Why would you even think it?"

"*Paar too*, Meena."

"*Tsaargh too vektoree tsoov taal vee.*" Which Translachew translated roughly as, "I hope when we next cross paths you're still existentially operational."

Rollie was still chuckling about this as her ship took off.

"So what now?" Xylith asked. "Tryfe will be free soon, won't it, Bertram? I imagine you'll be ready to return home."

Bertram wasn't sure why he was surprised by this, but then it was just like so many vacations; one minute you think the freedom stretches out before you forever, and the next, you're back to the old grind, feeling responsible for the fate of humankind and stuff.

"Someone has to be the champion of Tryfling rights," he admitted, a little sorry to hear it coming from his mouth. But once it was out there, he felt his resolve strengthen again. "I have to know what's happened. Document the damage from the ownership change and the Number Three Virus. Verify the human race hasn't died of lack of light or been stored in pods or... or... that Mom and Dad aren't riding around on choppers in leather chaps with sawed off shotguns, fighting rival gangs for supplies."

Rollie frowned. "Is that something they'd be likely to do?"

"Mom's an extreme couponer. She gets scrappy when it comes to household resources," Bertram said. "But hey, I could use a good co-pilot. Someone who knows the ship, could more or less pass for human and would benefit from some downtime in a place where nobody'd be inclined to kill him except for, y'know, scientific study."

"Tempting as that sounds, you don't really need my help, Ludlow. In no time, the infopill distributors will be back in production to round out your astronavigational education. One good tutorial capsule on the Penumbra Classic and its maintenance and I'd feel secure sending any of my mates in a ship with you at the helm."

"Aw, really?"

"Least, the ones like Fess where parts grow back."

"Naturally." Bertram turned to Xylith. "How about you? You up for a little backspace adventure?"

She smiled. "Now, Bertram, think about it; does anyone on your planet have two faces?"

"Are you kidding? Mean teenage girls, celebrity reporters and politicians all over our planet," he said. "Anyway, we could get you a holowatch disguise."

"I already have a holowatch disguise." She patted her bag. "A sweet little old lady from Hyphiz Delta."

"See? Then it's done. Let's go."

Four dimples appeared. "Oh, now, I love that you want me to come along, Bertram. I really do, but ..." She shook her head. "I just think someone needs to stay behind in the Underworld right now and see it gets the change of management it deserves. The RightGuides and Coalition of Planets can do all the investigating they like, but it's never going to be a substitution for good old-fashioned Underworld justice. And after what we've seen today, our members are ready. They just need a push in the right direction."

They were passing an electronics store, and Bertram noticed all the holovisions in the front window were playing the video for the "ZapTrap Flap" again. A sizable group of Vos Laegons had stopped for impromptu dancing.

"This is cosmic!" he heard one say. "I can't wait to see Zenith Skytreg's musical!"

"Anyone who could come up with something this catchy and fun can't possibly be guilty of numeroterrorism," observed someone else.

Bertram felt an ironic laugh escape him, even though he narrowly resisted the urge to dance himself. "Okay, well, maybe your keeping an eye on the place isn't such a bad idea after all," he told Xylith.

They had reached the Penumbra, and now Bertram called the ramp.

Rollie leaned on the ship as they waited. "You know, I was thinking, Ludlow ... We'll likely have time for one final tour

before Tryfe's free of the field. So where would you like to go?"
He grinned. "Anywhere at all. Didn't you have your eye on
some fancy nebula? Or was that Ragul-Sfera you was partial
to?"

Bertram accessed all his infopill travel brochures. Visions
swam before his eyes of brilliant natural phenomena, mystical
worlds he hadn't yet encountered and that Klinko Buffet Nice
at affordable prices. He thought of it all in a fleeting second
and in that second, he had his answer. "I did. But you know
what? I've changed my mind. There's one thing we need to do
right here in Vos Laegos City before we go. Oh, and Xylith? I'd
like to borrow that holowatch."

"Not yet," shouted the old Hyphizite woman over the
sound of the hovering ICV. She scrambled across the hoverpad
of Zenith Skytreg's Vos Laegos Underworld Headquarters, and
deposited an armful of parts through the Protostar's open
hatch, like some hasty, reverse Jack the Ripper. CLANK! "Not
yet!"

She thumped down the ramp, seized another armful and ran
up the ramp again. CLANK! "Almost there!"

Xylith came sprinting onto the hoverpad and almost plowed
straight into the woman. She skidded to a stop. "You're not
done yet? What in the seven suns of Sargos is taking you so
long?"

"What? Me? You were supposed to stall them," the elder
shouted with Bertram Ludlow's voice.

"Can I help it if Skytreg has his security people on a
pheromone resistance regimen? I did what I could. And—
Move!" Three security guards burst through the fourth floor
exit onto the hoverpad. Bertram could hear their running feet.

"The hook!" shouted Xylith. "Get the hook! I'll grab these!"
There were a few final parts on the hoverpad floor, which she
scooped up and took with her into Rollie's Protostar.

Bertram jumped up and grabbed the hook dangling from the hovering Penumbra Classic and drew it down to the Protostar's undercarriage. He scanned the ship's belly, eventually wrapping the hook a few times around a large pipe that ran the length of the craft. He gave it a tug.

Bertram was just ducking out from under the base of the ship, when a voice thundered, "Here! Here's another one." Bertram wondered whether security uniforms actually came that big or the guy had to special order. "Where's the Dootett chick?" the guard demanded.

"Pull up the ramp, pull up the ramp!" shouted Bertram.

And the Protostar's ramp began to recede through the hatch.

"She's in there?" The security guard was torn between trying to grab the ramp or cover the old lady. Meanwhile, laser blasts skimmed the Penumbra's surface.

Bertram withdrew a laser and ducked back under the ship, heading toward the landing gear.

"Hey!" the guard shouted, and Bertram felt laser fire fly by, missing him by millimeters. Bertram clung to the landing gear. "Hook's on, pull up, pull up!" came his cry as he pounded a fist against the ship's belly.

The Penumbra's winch line pulled tight and the Protostar began to rear like some spooked tumorous horse. The security guard's eyes grew wide with the realization that, where he had once been underneath the machine, the ship was now scraping along behind him on one end, an end that was barreling down and coming closer. Smaller hovercrafts were being punted aside left and right, one smashing into the side of the compound and another grinding toward the edge of the hoverpad.

By now the Protostar was perpendicular to the ground and the security guard dove frantically out of the way, while his colleagues struggled to corral one hovercraft from pitching off the edge into the gift shop below. The grinding metal stopped at the same moment the Protostar swung off the platform into free air, penduluming itself upside down while Bertram clung to the landing gear for all he was worth. Some parts chipped off the ship like LEGOs, clattering down, down into the city streets.

It was only as the swinging eased and the Penumbra soared more smoothly over Vos Laegos City, Bertram Ludlow released his grip enough to right himself. He surveyed the landscape below as buildings gave way to desert dust. He marveled at how much things had changed for him since that one fateful morning on Tryfe so long ago.

He also wondered when, exactly, he'd started doing his own stunts.

"Didn't think to hook it to the roof at all?" Rollie asked, arms folded, squinting up at the Protostar before him. Its landing gear reached skyward like a dead roach.

"Tell ya what," Bertram said, clapping him on the shoulder, "next time we steal an ICV on a hoverpad in the middle of the city from an intergalactic crime boss, I'll pilot the lead ship, and you secure the winch hook with armed thugs coming at you."

Rollie considered it. "Fair enough."

They were many miles outside of Vos Laegos City, a gray scrubby world far removed from the lights and chaos of the planet's capital.

Bertram finally remembered to push the button on Xylith's holowatch, and the Hyphiz Deltan woman that he wasn't presumably faded away. "Are you okay?" Bertram asked Xylith now.

She was pressing a hand to her leftmost temple where a purpling bruise was already starting to show. "I got harnessed up in time, but the same could not be said for the ICV parts." The left face winced. "It's okay, though. The left part of the Dootett brain only guides the short term memory and ... Something else. Hey, look!" She pointed. "They're coming."

Bertram turned to see a large object vaguely reminiscent of a green metallic seashell creep over the horizon. It grew closer, closer, until it was casting a shadow between them and the sun.

A voice vibrated over the loudspeaker. "HEY, BUDDY: HEAR YA NEED A TOW."

It was Fess and the gang. And it wasn't long before they had hitched the Protostar to Fess's ship.

"I'd have done a double-bluff knot on it," said Backspace Bungee, surveying the work, "but I imagine it probably won't drift off into the eternal void, if you're gentle with her."

"So where we taking it?" Fess asked.

"Ultimately? Little planet of Dax Q. Phlyjollee's in Quad Three, called Ejellan," said Rollie. "Gonna be my home base for a while. But I'm willing to lie low anywhere until Quad Three's available. Shouldn't be too long now before they start chipping away at it."

Bertram frowned. "Hey, how'd you afford a planet, anyway? I hear they run in the billions."

Rollie laughed. "Not this one, mate. I got a sweet deal, what with the infestation." At Bertram's expression, he said, "What? It's character."

I'll have to bring Rollie some books from Earth, Bertram thought three Universal weeks later, as he plugged the coordinates for Tryfe into his Penumbra. Based on its contents, the Hyphiz Deltan's secret hideout on Ejellan was more like ninety percent public library, five percent Underworld base and five percent monastically-sparse living quarters. The tomes were indiscriminate of topic and diverse in age, and Bertram would have kidded the guy about his passion for something so wholly archaic, if Rollie hadn't just plugged half a dozen giant poisonous bug things living in the facilities without so much as batting an eye. You didn't kid a guy with reflexes like that. You just remembered to bring the guy books when you saw him next.

Bertram pretty much figured Rollie would be fascinated with whatever print Earth had to offer. If the Earth still had print, that is.

Bertram considered mentioning the library on Ejellan to Rozz, who sat there now in the passenger seat, but he didn't want to ruin the good gloom she had going. When he'd first vis-ued her asking if she wanted to join him for the journey back to Tryfe (er, Earth) he could tell she wasn't into it. After six months trapped in a spaceship with someone, you get to know the little mannerisms that give away what they're thinking.

Also, she'd said, "I am so not into it, Bertram."

But it was the day Bertram was eating his last supplemental piloting pill, that Rozz buzzed him back and said if he were going to Tryfe, "she might as well kinda go, too," in a tone not unlike she was saying her dog had just died and they might as well bury him under the old chestnut tree where he'd liked to poop. Her programming gig had dried up with the Number Three Virus. And for the first time since the glitch had taken over, Rozz Mercer had finally had downtime to think about her home planet and the people there.

"It's like Thanksgiving, isn't it?" she said now, turning the doe eyes on him.

"Oh," Bertram said and searched for the similarity. "Because we survived near death, and the universe was taken hostage and yet we made it through alive and we have a lot to be grateful for?"

"No." She looked at him like he was two drumsticks short of a full turkey. "Because we're going home, hoping stupidly somewhere in the back of our naïve hearts that it'll be great and everyone will be happy to see us. But there's no way of knowing what mess of dysfunction, misery and madness we're walking into, and we don't want to believe it's probably worse than we could even imagine."

"Um ... So how old were you when your parents divorced again?" He couldn't remember.

"Funny," she said. "You're a funny guy, Bertram. Paargraath jerky?" she offered, holding up one of a number of foil packets she had brought with her.

"No thanks." He pressed on his stomach. "I had laser-fried insect back on Ejellan, and it's still sitting there. Rollie said he'd burnt off all the poisonous tendrils. But I feel like he missed a couple." Bertram decided when he got back from Tryfe—or if—he'd have to go easier on the diet. Cut out a few carbs. Maybe taste-test fewer arachnids. Use more discretion. "You know, you didn't have to come with me, Rozz."

"Oh, but I do," she said.

"You do?" Bertram thought of Xylith, and how he'd promised to vis-u when he got back. "Well, I feel obligated to tell you that I'm kinda seeing someone. Sorta. Well, once, and you couldn't quite call it a 'date,' but she likes me. She thinks I'm exotic. And—"

"We have to go home," she said, raising a bright pink eyebrow, "because it's an unspoken rule. No matter how much you've changed, no matter how much has changed without you—maybe especially if you've changed—you have to go back. Plus, there's the guilt. The guilt if you don't go is even worse than how much it sucks when you do."

"You never really came to terms with the whole nearly dying in space thing, did you?"

"I was busy putting the Universe back together, Bertram."

"Me, too," he said. He could see the Ergowohm Nebula off the port side. It was as beautiful as he had thought it would be, the beak and neck of colored gas and wings of newborn stars. He stared at it a long while. Yet the more he stared, the more he thought it really did look like… "Thanksgiving, huh?"

"All you can digest," she said.

ABOUT THE AUTHOR

Jenn Thorson is a marketing writer by day and an author by night—so sort of like Batgirl, but with less crime fighting and more carpal tunnel. She lives in Bertram Ludlow's hometown of Pittsburgh, PA, but is definitely mostly sure she's never met extra-terrestrials there. Her stories have been published in the *Humor Press*, the journal for the *Lewis Carroll Society of North America*, *The Timber Creek Review* and *Romantic Homes* magazine.

IF YOU ENJOYED THIS BOOK...

The Purloined Number (There Goes the Galaxy, Book Two) is an independently published novel. So if you enjoyed this book, the author would be delighted if you'd tell a friend about it.

One way to help is by reviewing the book on **Amazon.com**. Amazon ranks its books, in part, by the number of customer reviews a book receives. So you can help *The Purloined Number* reach *even more* eyeballs by going to Amazon.com, searching for the book and creating your own review.

Other ways to help share *The Purloined Number* with fellow Earthlings are:

- "Like" *There Goes the Galaxy* on **Facebook**, for news and spacey fun, at: **Facebook.com/ThereGoestheGalaxy**

- Visit **TheReGoesTheGalaxy.com** and snag one of our FREE book badges for your blog or website!

- Follow the author, Jenn Thorson, on **Twitter** at **Twitter.com/Jenn_Thorson**

www.ingramcontent.com/pod-product-compliance
Lightning Source LLC
Chambersburg PA
CBHW031436240626
47154CB00001B/290